RIVER OF THE SUN

Also by Patricia Shaw

Valley of Lagoons
Brother Digger
Pioneers of a Trackless Land

RIVER OF THE SUN

Patricia Shaw

St. Martin's Press
New York

Library of Congress Cataloging-in-Publication Data

Shaw, Patricia.
    River of the sun / Patricia Shaw.
      p.   cm.
    ISBN 0-312-08284-3
    1. Australia—History—1788–1851—Fiction. 2. Australia—Gold
discoveries—Fiction. I. Title.
PR9619.3.S4815R5 1992
823—dc20
                                    92-28500
                                       CIP

First published in Great Britain by Headline Book Publishing PLC.

First U.S. Edition: December 1992
10 9 8 7 6 5 4 3 2

RIVER OF
THE SUN

PROLOGUE

The big river sang and glittered in the sunlight. It toppled from the mysterious jungle heights of Irukandji territory down huge granite bluffs to hurtle life into the parched inland, tracking westward through the lands of the fierce Merkin tribe.

The people were proud of this river. It was known as River of the Sun because, becalmed after summer torrents, it was a delight to watch. In the mountain pools, in deep gorges, in crannies and crevices, and all along the river bed, far across the plains in drying creeks and billabongs, yellow stones reflected the sun. They glittered and sparkled and gleamed in magical array, littering the sandy shores, winking from the crystal clear depths.

High in their mountain fortress, at the headwaters of the river, the superior isolated Irukandji clans could see far to the west over the endless expanse of land but it held no interest for them. They preferred to look east into the morning sun, to admire the dramatic blue of the ocean and the ripples of the coral reef far yonder. Another river fed on the mountain torrents but this one rushed down to the sea. It was known simply as the Green River because it took its colour from crowding foliage before entering the sheltered bay. They did not know that a century before the time of which we speak a white sea captain had named this bay after his ship, *Endeavour*.

Irukandji people came down past the falls to fish in the sea shallows which were safer than the crocodile-infested Green River. Crocodiles were their only enemies these days. The reputation of this savage tribe had been well-established over the centuries. None dared intrude into their territory without permission.

But now danger was looming. From time to time they had seen strange beings come ashore from big ships to take water from their springs. Stealthy watchers had allowed them to depart unmolested, secure in their ability to defend their tribal lands. But couriers and traders from other powerful tribes had brought disturbing news, that these strangers were creeping across tribal lands to the south, and though they didn't look like warriors they were evil and dangerous.

Chief Tajatella conferred with the elders and a decree was issued to the Irukandji people that this menace would not be tolerated by the proud mountain clans. 'No more!' Tajatella ordered and his warriors stamped their approval at a special corroboree as the chant echoed through the hills. 'Kill the evil ones! Drive them back into the sea!'

PART ONE

1

1862

As the schooner *White Rose* sailed quietly south down the Whitsunday Passage, Captain Otto Beckman could see the smoke from native camp fires in the hills but it didn't concern him. There were Aborigines living all along the Queensland coast but ships were safe from them. It amazed this German seaman that Englishmen should choose to live in such wild outposts as Somerset, at the tip of Cape York. It was surrounded by impenetrable jungle and hordes of wild blacks, the settlers' only contact with the world through the occasional visits of supply ships and passing vessels like the *White Rose*.

He shuddered and made the sign of the Cross. To drown at sea was a clean death but to be hacked to pieces by bloodthirsty heathens! *Gott!* They had to be mad to stay there. And yet John Jardine, formerly police magistrate at Rockhampton, now the official Resident in charge of Somerset, didn't mind. He was determined his little settlement would succeed, claiming it would become another Singapore. With the help of grumbling marines, a medical officer and a few intrepid pioneers, he was busy building a township. He had constructed barracks, a hospital, and a fine Residency overlooking the lovely seaway known as Albany Pass. He was presently marking out streets on cleared land and surveying allotments for future citizens.

'You should buy one, Beckman,' Jardine had said. 'You can have have a superb spot with a view for twenty pounds. A bargain, what?'

A bargain? Beckman didn't believe the tiny port could survive, despite the optimism of this tough, resourceful man, but he could not afford to offend Jardine. While it lasted, Somerset was a convenient port of call. The trade route between Batavia and Brisbane was lucrative but dangerous, especially around the Torres Strait. Murdering Asian pirates preyed on slow-moving ships that travelled tenderly to avoid reefs, and shipwrecked sailors on isolated islands were at the mercy of wild blacks, if they didn't die of thirst on white-hot coral atolls. Jardine had saved the lives of many seafarers by putting to sea in his own rig, with his marines, to fight off the attackers. He was an extraordinary fellow. Best of all, Somerset had good, clean, fresh water.

'Thank you, sir, a bargain indeed,' Beckman had replied, 'but I have a house in Brisbane, my home is there.'

'Never mind. Time to think about it. I believe your wife is on board *White*

Rose this time. You must bring her ashore to dine with us this evening.'

'Unfortunately this is not possible. Mrs Beckman got a sickness in Batavia.'

'Batavia? Filthy place. Would you like our doctor to visit her?'

'No, thank you. She is over the worst but left with an indisposition and does not wish to leave the ship.'

Jardine had stared at him and then grinned. 'I see. Got the trots, has she? Yes, embarrassing for a lady. Embarrassing for any of us. Flour and water does the trick, bind her up. But get rid of that bloody Batavia water, tip the lot in the drink. Nothing for them to have dead animals in their wells. You must come to dinner though, Captain. Stay over at the Residency. We don't often have visitors, we'll make a night of it.'

A night of it? Beckman's head still ached when he recalled Jardine's hospitality. Gussie had been disappointed but dared not venture ashore. Poor Gussie, this voyage had been a disaster for her. With her husband at sea so much she had become lonely living in Brisbane. A good woman and an excellent housekeeper, she wasn't much at making friends and the rowdy, raucous neighbours, many of them former convicts, terrified her. She missed their son. Frederick had intended to migrate to Australia with them, but his wife had changed her mind at the last minute. Gussie missed her family and the orderliness of their lives in Hamburg. She had become so listless and despondent, Otto had finally agreed to allow her to accompany him on this voyage. He had reminded her that she was prone to seasickness but she was too excited to care.

But she'd been seasick all the way, and instead of recovering her strength on solid ground in Batavia she had found the sodden air a further trial, her nostrils assailed by the stench of harbourside refuse mixed with the sickly perfume of exotic blooms. Finally she had succumbed to a tropical illness that weakened her so much she had to be carried back on board.

Beckman sighed. That dinner party with the Englishman! After listening to Jardine's tales of countless attacks on the settlement by Aborigines whom Jardine had airily identified as Yardigans and Goomkodeens, Otto had not slept well. They sounded more like fierce goblins to him and the screeches of night creatures in the dark, looming bush were constant reminders of danger. He'd wished himself back on the ship. Rum, wines, port – Otto hadn't drunk so much in years.

When the dawn finally came, and he lay hot and sweating on his bed, he noticed movement in a dim corner of the room. His eyes were pools of pain as he tried to focus, then suddenly he was up and on his feet. Comfortably overweight, like Gussie, he had slowed down over the years but his reflexes were still sharp. As the huge snake uncoiled from its night's rest, Otto grabbed his clothes and fled naked from the house.

That morning he was in a foul temper, railing at the shore crew to get aboard, shouting at his first mate Bart Swallow that they'd sail on the early tide. He took hurried leave of his host, and with relief sent the *White Rose* bucking into the southerlies, fresh winds beating a cool tattoo on his reddened, overheated face.

And now, a week later, as he stood at the wheel, he knew but would never admit that he had been over-hasty in bringing forward the sailing time.

'Say again, Mr Swallow!' he roared.

'We're nearly out of water, sir.'

'And why are we nearly out off wasser?' His tongue was thick with rage.

'There was a mix-up at Somerset, sir. The men emptied the casks of Batavian water and refilled one. They meant to fill the others the next morning but they were overlooked.'

'Overlooked! What sort of blubberhead word is this? Overlooked! Do we overlook to cast off? To set sail? I wager you neffer overlook the rum, you hear me?'

'I'm sorry, sir.'

All around them the men on deck had slowed to listen, eyes flicking from one to another, slow, mean grins spreading to hear the captain bawling out the first mate. Beckman turned on them. 'You listen good to me, you scabby lot. You laugh. You think we get to port easy with one cask of water. You're fools.' He waved an arm angrily at the placid, sapphire-blue waters. 'You think this is a pretty place, a safe passage from the great oceans, but under us are reefs ready to cut the heart out of my ship. God forbid that happen, but if we smash up aground on a reef, we could die of thirst. In this heat it don't take long. So I don't sail no further without plenty water. You hear me?'

'Yes, Captain,' voices hissed.

'A flogging it should be for you, Mr Swallow, but instead you go for water. And you take with you the water men. Who were they? Who else neglected their duties?'

Swallow licked his lips. 'I take full responsibility, sir.'

'And can you row the longboat, and carry the casks all by yourself?'

'No, sir.'

'Then give me the names.'

There was a rustle of curiosity and the men looked around them to see who would have to go ashore.

'Billy Kemp,' Swallow began, 'and George Salter and Dutchy Baar.'

'Good. We'll drop anchor at the mouth of the Endeavour River in the morning. My charts show fresh spring water can be had there, close to shore. You four will get us water.' He sniffed the air, nose wrinkling. 'What's that smell?' And then he shook his head in despair. 'You again, Gaunt!'

The cabin boy was standing gawping with a foul-smelling bucket of slop. No need to guess where it came from; Gussie had been vomiting again.

'Get rid of that,' Beckman shouted, 'or I'll throw you overboard with it! And scour the bucket too.' He turned away in disgust. How he'd let that old rascal Willy Gaunt talk him into signing on his dim-witted son he'd never know. 'Gawping Gaunt' was a damn good name for him, always standing around waiting for someone to tell him, again and again, what to do. Nothing seemed to sink in. Fortunately he had one saving grace: he was kind to Augusta. He didn't seem to mind looking after her, cleaning up after her, running up and down with cups of coffee and biscuits, and he did her washing as well as any Chinee laundryman. Gussie liked him, that was something.

Beckman went back to his charts to study the coastline around the Endeavour River outlet. He couldn't afford to miss it.

2

Willy Gaunt had his son's career all mapped out. Edmund would begin as a cabin boy, spend years before the mast, save money, obey orders, be brave and upstanding, and promotions would attend experience like sure steps up a clear path, until he reached the pinnacle where he would be issued with the precious ticket to master his own ship.

This idea had come to him in a flash of enlightenment. It was the first real idea Willy had ever had and it was such a beauty, even now he could hardly contain his excitement. Until that day, Willy had tumbled with the fates, no more in control of his life than a stone rattling down a cobbled street. In the dark Liverpool slums where he lived, locals had to compete with hordes of starving Irish immigrants for a slice of daily bread. Theft was essential. A competent thief was admired, envied, talked about. Willy was neither a good thief nor a bad one, he simply laboured at the profession, never thinking of himself as battling to survive because he had no conception of the war.

When the prison gates clanged on him, like the closure of winter on the thin, wailing populace, Willy was among his mates. They shuffled, sneering, through the cattle-yards of the courts, while magistrates, like auctioneers, shouted their worth to the only bidders, the colonies.

Willy was indifferent to the fact that he'd become a world traveller, led through Sydney Town and on to Moreton Bay prison, walking past the graves of other convicts to exit with a ticket-of-leave to labour in Brisbane. He lost count of time until a bored clerk advised him that he'd been a free man for more than a year.

His convict wife, Jane Bird, assembled the necessary ten guineas to buy a proper house in which to rear their son. By this time Willy had become accustomed to labouring so he just kept on, prospecting here and there and, from habit too, dealing in stolen goods.

Being free meant a lot to Willy. He'd never been able to appreciate 'free' as a lad because the concept hadn't occurred to him, but now he had a paper to prove it. And he had a son who had a chance to become an important person. A boss even.

A few favours and winks down at the Brisbane wharves had led Willy Gaunt into the presence of the German, Captain Beckman, master of the *White Rose*, a coastal clipper. The eagle-eyed Willy had soon made a

11

judgement: Beckman was a good fellow, a man to be trusted. It took some fast talking but eventually he persuaded the captain to give his boy a chance, and Edmund joined the crew of the *White Rose* as a cabin boy.

Jane had died when the boy was ten, begging her husband to see to the lad, and Willy had kept his promise. He loved his son and was proud of this boy who could read and write as good as any squire. Now Edmund's life as a sailorman had begun.

Three nights a week it was Edmund's turn to mind the watch, to stand by, run messages, check the lanterns, be another set of eyes.

'Young eyes,' Captain Beckman had said. 'Half the time they don't know what they're looking for but at least they're not dulled with stolen rum.'

Edmund sat high on a spar, eagerly surveying the calm, moonlit seas of the Whitsunday Passage. He was feeling better now, safe from the heave and surge of the open ocean. While everyone else on the ship feared the thousand-mile stretch of coral reefs that lay off the Queensland coast, Edmund was grateful for its protection, allowing the *White Rose* smooth sailing and keeping his stomach in balance.

From the minute the ship had sailed out of the Brisbane River into Moreton Bay and headed north into open ocean, Edmund had been violently seasick, made worse by shock and humiliation. It hadn't occurred to him that he would be sick, let alone be reduced to such a cringing mess that he expected to die. He had begged to be allowed to crawl into his canvas hutch under the longboat but Mr Swallow would have none of it. 'Get away with you, lad. If you throw up enough there'll be nowt left to throw. Get on with your work and don't be sick on the deck or I'll have your hide.'

Only the captain's wife, Mrs Beckman, felt sorry for him, because she too had been sick, vomiting into buckets that Edmund had to empty, apologising and commiserating with her fellow sufferer. Once they reached the Whitsundays they had both revived and the voyage north to the little settlement at the tip of Cape York had been uneventful, but now, on the return journey, the captain's wife was sick again. At both ends.

Knowing that Mrs Beckman was a poor sailor, the crew laughed and made dirty remarks. Edmund thought they were cruel but they hoped she would learn her lesson and stay home. They didn't want a woman aboard, let alone a fat German frau. It was bad luck, they said, an ill omen. They were always talking about ill omens, every second thing that happened was an omen of some sort. Not that Edmund was a disbeliever, by no means. Their stories scared him shitless and he was anxious to learn how to keep safe. He bartered his rum ration, gave it to Billy Kemp every day in exchange for a shark's tooth which now hung round his neck. That was a good bargain. If you wear a shark's tooth and you fall overboard or get shipwrecked, no shark will come near you. 'They'll take off faster than a whore's drawers!' Billy had said, and that was a real comfort. Edmund was terrified of sharks.

Movement below startled him from his dozing and he slid down to the deck, feeling the welcome chill of a pre-dawn breeze. The sea was pink right across to the horizon, real pink; it never ceased to amaze him that seas could have such colours. The sky over to sun-up was streaked with rosy grey far off into nothingness. He wondered what was on the other side of the ocean.

'Don't just stand there, you great galah, lend a hand here!' Billy Kemp shoved Edmund towards the longboat. 'Get it free. The lads are bringing up the casks.'

Billy was like that, always giving orders. You'd think he was an officer, not just an ordinary sailor. Edmund fumbled with the ropes but other hands were faster and the longboat was swung overboard. The ship was busy now with helpers and watchers, and the casks were brought up. Edmund prayed they'd find water, he didn't want to die with a swollen tongue too big for his mouth; that's what happened when the thirst got you, so he'd been told.

The captain was standing watching, not a peep out of him and hard to tell what he was thinking with that bearded face. When his mouth was closed, all you could see were those steel-grey eyes of his. One day, Edmund promised himself, he would have a beard like that, neat and clipped. It would be like wearing a mask.

Mr Swallow had a gun, a revolver. Edmund shuddered. He was glad he wasn't going; they were a long way out from the shore but the land looked a creepy place.

Mrs Beckman came puffing on to the deck hitching her hefty skirts out of the way to see the shore party rowing towards a tiny strip of white beach.

'Can't we get any closer?' he heard her ask the captain.

'Too risky. We have to stay out here in the channel. You're looking well this morning, my dear.'

'Yes. It is a good time of day before that brute heat starts.'

'You should stay up here in the fresh air. It's much better for you. Get the lad to make you comfortable and bring your morning tea.'

Too late. They had spotted him. Miserably, Edmund dropped down to the galley. This was supposed to be his bunk time, he'd been on watch half the night, but once the cook grabbed him he'd have to help serve the crew, then do the cabins and every other bloody job that got foisted on him. He'd be lucky to get any sleep before nightfall.

The shore party stared nervously at the forbidding green mountains that loomed behind the coastline, their peaks swathed in mist like a huge grey shawl as the steam rose with the sun from the sweaty jungles below. Hard green mangroves waded into the sea at the mouth of the river but on the southern side a glittering white beach had cut a swathe into the relentless green.

Billy Kemp was first into the boat. He was thirsty. Beckman had refused to allow any of the culprits a drop of water since they'd found the dry casks. So now, surrounded by inviting but undrinkable water, Billy was anxious to get going. He was already shaping up an oar as the others dropped in beside him. 'Get a move on,' he snarled. 'The sooner we're in and back, the better.'

'Take an oar, Dutchy,' Bart Swallow ordered.

Dutchy grinned at Billy. 'Pull hard, lad. We'll be first to the water and drink a bellyful.'

But George Salter was worried. 'What if we can't find any water?'

'Ah, shut your gob, you Limey bastard,' Billy said. 'Mr Swallow knows where the water is, don't you?'

Swallow nodded uncertainly. 'I think so. Captain Cook beached here for three months.'

'Jesus Christ,' George said. 'That was a hundred bloody years ago!'

'I know that,' Swallow snapped. 'He was the one who first found water here, but there've been plenty more since. Reports say there's a trail of marked trees to the springs.'

'Any trail'd be well overgrown now,' Billy commented. 'In this climate the bush grows like wildfire but it don't matter, the wet season's just finished, that great bloody hill'll have creeks and gullies runnin' down it like ribs.'

'How would you know?' George asked.

Billy ignored him, enjoying the challenge of keeping pace with the big Dutchman who was as strong as an ox, his brown sinewy arms making light of deep-dipping strokes that were sending the heavy boat skimming fast for the shore.

How would he know? He knew about water, but he bloody knew more about no water. About droughts and the godforsaken stupid bloody farm the old man had bought. Free settlers, too, with the world at their feet, no taint of crime in the Kemp family, no scars of the whip or the chains. His parents had come smiling ashore with their two little sons and been conned into buying a postage stamp farm on past Bathurst. Madness! Billy could tell them now, too late, that you had to buy big in this country or not buy at all. But his Ma and Pa had had their dream of a farm and of maybe one day getting bigger and turning into squatters. Fat chance.

Their desperate little sheep farm never had a hope. Out here you needed a monster spread and an army of sheep, but they'd battled on. Dingoes grabbed the sheep. Crows picked their eyes out. And Billy had watched his parents disintegrate along with the lonely little farm. When his young brother died of snakebite, his mother became wild-eyed mad, always wandering around searching for the dead boy, calling out for her Harry so often that the crazy mimic parrots had taken up the call. Little budgies hopped about crying 'Harry! WhereareyuhHarry' in their squirrelling pippy voices, and smart-arse cockatoos had latched on too, doing better. Tame as hens, intrigued by humans, they swung in the trees and clomped in the dust by the house with a chorus of 'Harry! Hello, Harry! Come home, Harry!' as clear as a bloody bell! It was enough to send anyone out of their brains. And rain? They never saw rain. They forgot what green looked like, everywhere just dust and more dust. And when the last of the sheep died, the old man went down to the dried-up creek and shot himself.

'Steady now,' Bart Swallow said, 'and keep your eyes peeled. The place looks deserted but you never know. The tide's on the turn, keep well clear of those rocks and make for the beach. Steady, take her quietly in.'

'Do you reckon there'll be blackfellers in there?' George asked.

'We're not staying around long enough to find out,' Swallow told him.

They heaved the boat up the beach, and lumped three casks ashore. 'I'll mind the boat,' Billy said. He didn't fancy a stroll in that jungle; it'd be alive with snakes.

'I'm giving the orders here, Kemp,' Swallow said. 'You come with me, Dutchy, I need you to carry the casks. You two guard the boat.' He picked up two machetes and handed one to Dutchy. 'We'll have to slash a path, by the looks of things.'

'How do we guard the boat without a weapon?' Billy asked. 'If we get attacked are we supposed to throw bloody sand at them? Give me the gun.'

'He's right,' George said. 'We shoulda brought a couple of rifles.'

'No need for that.' Swallow unbuckled his belt and holster. 'I'll leave you the gun. You take it, George, and here's the ammo. If you need us, fire a shot and we'll come running.'

Billy laughed as they disappeared into the bush. 'He's bloody useless, that Swallow. He forgot the rifles, just like he forgot the bloody water. How were we to know he hadn't put someone else on the job? Let's go up in the shade, we'll fry here. This sand reflects heat like a bloody looking-glass.'

They followed the others up the beach and sank down on to a frayed carpet of sparse seagrass. They couldn't see Swallow and Dutchy in the tangled scrub, strung with huge lawyer vines thick as ropes, but they could hear them swishing inland. Billy hoped they wouldn't be long, this was no picnic. He watched George buckle on the holster and examine the gun. 'Is it loaded?'

'Sure is.'

'Then mind you don't shoot your bloody foot off! Give it to me.'

'Get lost. I can shoot. You think you know everything, Kemp. Bet you couldn't even shoot a crow.'

'If you could shoot a crow,' Billy said lazily, 'I'd give you a gold clock. They've got more brains than you have, mate.' He leaned back against a tree, keeping an eye on the boat. Shoot? Anyone could shoot. Except his old man. He hadn't even got that right. When Billy had gone tearing down to the creek and found his father, half his face shot away and the blood pumping out, he'd screamed and cried. Well, he was only ten. He'd knelt in the mess beside his father and grabbed hold of him, and that eye had stared up at him, beseeching! He was still alive. Oh shit! It was an awful thing to keep remembering. Billy had taken the rifle and finished the job. Well, he had to. Like they'd had to shoot dying, suffering, blind sheep.

Jesus, he was thirsty! His mouth was dry as dust. He got up and moved along the beach, keeping in the shade, looking for a coconut tree. A swig of coconut milk'd be just what the doctor ordered, but there wasn't one in sight. 'Wouldn't you know?' he muttered to himself. 'From the ship there looks to be thousands of them trees along these shores and just when you want one, not a jigger around.'

By the time he returned, George was dozing, his head flopped down. Billy spat and kicked him hard in the ribs. 'Some bloody guard!'

'Whatcha do that for?' George yelped, leaping up. 'I was just restin'.'

A flock of lorikeets whirled red and blue from the bush and flew screeching out to sea. Billy whistled in admiration. Boy, they could move! They wheeled in unison and shot back towards land in a long sweeping arc. Billy nodded. There must be a hawk around somewhere. They'd give him the dodge.

He hitched himself up on to the thick ledge of a pandanus branch and sighed, wishing the others would hurry up. Surely they'd located some fresh water by this time. He squinted over the white glare of sand. Someone had come out of the mangroves at the far end of the beach. It was a blackfeller, marching along without a care in the world, and he was all alone, thank God. Not wanting to share this with George just yet, Billy watched, realising the native was fishing, and bloody good at it he was too. Time and again he waded into the sea, standing still like a shining black statue against the blue, and then the spear would flash and up would come the catch to be thrown in the dilly bag. As he came further up the beach, Billy saw it was only a lad. But then when he bent over the bulky dilly bag, small peaks of breasts came into silhouette. It was a girl! Naked as Eve and without the fig leaf!

Billy grinned, licked his dry lips and slid down from his perch. The black girl was standing erect now, body sleek as an eel, staring at the deserted longboat. Enticed by curiosity, the girl dropped the fishing spear by the bag and came slowly forward to investigate.

Billy caught hold of George. 'Sssh! Be quiet. Look what we got out here.' He pulled George back into the scrub. 'Nice bit of tail there, my lad.'

George, eyes glued, managed a nod.

16

'We'll grab her,' Billy told him. 'But we'll have to be quick. We can pull her in here to our spot.'

George nodded again, shivering with excitement.

'Besides,' Billy said, 'she'll be able to lead us to water so we'll have the drop on the lot of them.'

The two men split up, moving stealthily under cover of the bush until they were either side of her and then they barrelled across the beach to converge on their quarry.

Billy saw the terror in her face as he was coming at her before she spun away to collide with George. But she was too quick for him. She twisted and hurled herself into the sea.

'After her!' Billy yelled, leaping across the ripples. They were waist deep before they caught her. She put up a hell of a fight; it was like trying to land a barramundi with your bare hands, and she had teeth to match. She landed a kick on George's chin that sent him reeling backwards into the water but Billy pounced on her, laughing, an arm round her chest, feeling the silky delight of her skin and the brush of nipples.

'Hang on to her, man,' George spluttered as he dived for her feet. Billy tried but she was fighting and pulling him into deeper water. She rolled and twisted, waves breaking over them, and soon Billy could no longer touch bottom. A few feet further out George had started to panic. 'Help! Billy, help me!' He disappeared and came up again screaming, 'I can't swim!' arms thrashing uselessly.

Distracted by George, Billy lost his grip on the girl, and suddenly she was gone. He looked wildly around but there was no sign of her. The sunlight reflecting from the shimmering water was blinding. 'Oh shit!' he said, more amused than annoyed that she'd got away. He swam a few yards to get hold of George and pull him back to the shallows. 'You bloody idiot. You'd drown in your bath.'

'Where'd she get to?' George spluttered.

'Buggered if I know.'

'Serve her right if she drowned,' George whined. 'She bloody near broke me jaw. Got a kick like a mule.'

Billy plodded back to the sand. 'She ain't drowned. She's like a fish in the water. She's out there someplace, stayin' clear.'

George began to run off down the beach.

'Where're you going?' Billy called.

'We got her catch!' he yelled over his shoulder. 'The fish!'

Billy shrugged. He could have the fish. Now where did the mug drop the revolver? Must be back in the shady spot opposite the boat. Just as well he didn't have it on him, it'd be nice trying to explain how they lost the bloody gun.

He was heading for the boat when Dutchy came roaring out of the scrub. 'Heave to!' he screamed as he ran, and Billy needed no second telling. He sprinted down the wet sand and shoved the boat with all his might. Within seconds Dutchy was beside him. 'Get aboard! Fast!'

'George!' Billy shouted. 'Get back here!' He looked around for Swallow, but Dutchy was already dragging at an oar.

Billy had been in enough nasty spots in his life to know that in these situations a man jumped first and asked 'Why?' later, but the Dutchman was heaving the boat to sea. 'Hey, wait for them, you bastard!' Billy shouted, but changed his tune when a mob of Aborigines, cruel-looking, white-painted savages, burst on to the beach. 'Run, for Christ's sake, run!' he yelled at George.

George was running all right, flying through the shallows trying to make it to the boat while Dutchy, single-handed, was taking it further out.

'He can't swim!' Billy yelled at Dutchy but then it no longer mattered. He saw the raised arm, saw it arc gracefully through the air and, hypnotised by the movement, watched the spear as it flew at George and plunged into his back. George screamed, threw his arms wide in despair and fell face down in the sea, the spear upright now like a tiny mast.

They rowed fast, wrenching the boat out to sea as the shrieking blacks came on, spears flying. Billy sweated against the heavy oar, certain they were only moving at a snail's pace, certain the blacks, swimming now, would catch up and tip them out. But the load was lighter, the wooden casks were still ashore and there were only two of them left. Where was Bart Swallow?

They were lengthening the distance from their attackers with every stroke, but the ship was a long way out, round the headland, and Billy was afraid the blacks might come after them in canoes. He shuddered at the thought of Swallow left back there but he was glad that it was Dutchy who'd got out; without the Dutchman's strength they'd never make it.

'What happened to Mr Swallow?' Billy asked at last as they edged over to the ship.

'They got him,' Dutchy said through his teeth.

'Is he dead?'

Dutchy turned on him in a fury. 'You was supposed to be on watch, you two. I come out of there thinking I got some fire cover and there's no one at the boat. You nearly got me killed too, you bloody toad.'

'Jesus! You're not putting the blame on me! I woulda had the gun if Mr Swallow hadn't give it to George. I wasn't far away, you can't go blaming me.'

Heads craned over the rails above them as Dutchy grabbed the ropes. 'You're not worth the trouble,' he sneered.

The captain's rage rose and fell like the ocean. He was shocked at the loss of the two men, horrified at the manner of their deaths, furious that they had gone ashore without sufficient arms, and guiltily relieved that the officer in charge had been one of the victims, otherwise he would have had to compound the violence by ordering the man flogged.

In the presence of the second mate, Henry Tucker, and Augusta, who sat nervously in the corner of the day cabin, he interrogated Dutchy and Kemp at length, 'We found a creek,' Dutchy said, 'by just cutting a track straight ahead. No good looking for marked trees in that bush. And I thought this was easy, good fresh running water, deep enough to roll the casks in. We'd just filled one, and I swear, Captain, I never saw a thing, never heard nothin' and Mr Swallow, he stand up and boom! That bloody spear, it come from nowhere right into his throat. Right through his throat. So me, I ran fast back out that track.'

'You just left him?' Tucker said.

'You would have stayed, would you?' Dutchy snarled. 'Easy to be brave sitting here. And stupid. Sure I ran, I didn't even look for the machete.'

'Why wasn't George at the boat?' the captain asked. Again.

'He just went wandering off down the beach,' Billy replied. 'Not for me to tell him what to do. And he had the gun.'

'Then why didn't he use it?'

'Too busy runnin', Captain.'

There was something wrong with Billy Kemp's story, Beckman was sure; the fellow seemed unable to look him in the eye. But then again he could be in shock, it must have been a frightful experience.

Tucker scratched his red beard and leaned forward. 'If he'd fired one shot at those savages and brought even one down, he could have scared them off.'

'Yeah. Well, you tell George that,' Billy said.

Beckman was worried. It seemed cowardly to sail away and not attempt to find the bodies and give the two men a decent burial, but could he afford to put the lives of other men at risk?

'I will make out a full report,' he said, 'and you two men will sign it before witnesses.'

He held a service for the souls of the two gallant comrades who had been foully murdered at the Endeavour River, asking the Lord to have mercy on them since they were shown no mercy in life. He gave thanks to God for sparing the lives of two crewman, and Augusta led the singing of several hymns. Then Beckman ordered a twenty-four-hour guard on the last of the ship's water. 'God help us now,' he told the crew. 'We've very little water, we'll have a thin time of it from now on. Set sail, Mr Tucker.'

As Tucker shouted orders, the crew sprang into action, not one of them sorry to be leaving this evil place. Sails were unfurled in double-quick time, billowing and flapping their farewells, but as Beckman gripped the wheel he was startled by the shout, 'Man overboard!'

'What in Gott's name now?' he roared and Tucker came running.

19

'No man overboard,' Tucker cried. 'There's someone in the water up ahead. It must be Bart or George, they must've got away.'

'Impossible!' Beckman said, but he had to make sure. 'Don't stand there, man, see to it!'

Once again the longboat was lowered. It picked up not Swallow or George, or even one of their bodies being washed out to sea from the mouth of the river, but an Aborigine girl, just a slip of a girl.

3

Kagari saw the strange canoe and was walking towards it when they pounced on her. They seemed to come from nowhere.

The terror was blinding. It tore the sun from the sky, leaving a gaping hole that threatened to swallow her as she wrestled these evil spirits in the sudden blackness. She was screaming but no girl-sound was heard, only vile mutterings and teeth grindings as devil hands, like coiling snakes, grasped and gripped at her arms and legs, her hair, pulling her this way and that, trying to hold her.

But she too knew the way of snakes, for was she not Kagari, named for the kookaburra, the laughing bird, the killer of snakes, the eater of snakes? It was a powerful totem, far more powerful than these land-locked serpents. She turned herself into a sea-snake and her slim body flicked and twisted and rolled from the shallows, slipping away from them, curling into the warm waters, gathering force as a wave washed by and then shooting forward, elongated now, like a spear, heading for the deep.

The silver-blue waters of the big-river bay hid her as, sightless, heart pounding, she fought for air, skimming over the coral sea bed, coiling and thrusting in the manner of a sea-snake, until her lungs rebelled and forced her to the surface.

Kagari could tell by the sudden heat that the sun must still be in the sky but her eyes would not admit the light. A new terror shook her. The evil spirits had taken the power from her eyes! Would she have to walk for ever in the darkness? To be led and fed like her brother Meebal whose eyes had been attacked by the poison tree when he was a small boy, and who now lived behind the gruesome whiteness of vacant, ever-weeping eyes.

The fear was too strong in her to allow her time to mourn the useless eyes. The movement of the waves told her she was facing the shore and the wind brought her ugly sounds, whispering that the evil ones were still there, splashing and searching for their prey. She dived again, deep into a coral chasm. The sea-snakes of the great depths did not need sight to avoid the sharp ridges that could rip and scar them, and neither did she.

Gentle fish nestled by, and the warm waters of this silent world calmed her. A huge fish nudged her with its lips and, for a second, another charge of fright swept through her that this might be a dreaded shark, but then she realised it was a fat mother fish, bigger than herself, just seeking company.

Kagari slid her hands along its back to make certain the telltale fin of the shark was missing, feeling lightheaded with this silly bravado. For surely if it were a shark, he'd not have wasted time with pleasantries; the cruel arch of teeth would have crunched her in half by now. No. This was a dugong, the tamest fish in the sea next to the long-snouted, squeaking, smiling dolphins that always travelled in families. She clung to the dugong, using her as a guide and protector, making for the surface again.

Where were her people? Surely they would miss her and come looking for her. They would see her fish basket by the shore. They would know she would never leave her catch to rot in the sun or be stolen by sea birds. But what if the evil spirits were still there? Kagari shook water from her face and rubbed and rubbed at her eyes, trying desperately to see. Was this a nightmare? A sleep dream of darkness, where even a cry of fright made no sound? She was treading water, sniffing the air. No, this was not a dream, this was real and she was a long way out from the shore, too afraid to let the waves deliver her to solid ground again. All she needed to do was to settle down, banish this awful fear, and wait. Kagari was strong. Her father, Wogaburra, had many children but she was his favourite because he knew the lords of the Dreaming had endowed her with some of his magic powers. Not all, of course, that would be unthinkable, but enough to set her apart from the rest, as he had been as a boy.

Wogaburra had grown taller than anyone in the tribe and developed into a great warrior and hunter, but the elders had soon recognised that here was a man of wisdom. They allowed him to enter the world of secrets, finally admitting that a new magic man had emerged, who had powers well beyond their understanding, a man who had to be accorded the respect of all Irukandji people. He was now feared far and wide, for his spells could cure or kill, they could bring fortune or misfortune, and foretell disasters to protect his people.

Kagari smiled. Her father's magic was so powerful, those evil spirits had better look out. Even Tajatella, chief of the Irukandji, liked to keep Wogaburra by his side for protection against evil.

Kagari wondered about the evil ones at the shore. They had to be spirits because the Irukandjis had no enemies now. Not any more. Their land was the most beautiful and bountiful in the world. They knew about the cold lands and the dry lands and the hungry lands because in the old days that was where most of their enemies had come from. And sometimes terrible men from the north had fallen on them to steal their women, but the people had fought back and under a succession of great chiefs had taught the invaders lessons they would never forget. Yes. The evil people who tried to capture her had to be spirits. The Irukandjis were proud of their warriors, the most feared in the land; there wasn't a tribe in the world that would wittingly cross their borders without permission. Scouts occasionally brought traders to sit by their camp fires and they were funny to watch, as nervous as little birds.

Her mother Luka, that shy, smiling woman, the best singer in the family, she'd be worried, sick to her heart in fright, with Kagari missing. She'd have raised the alarm by now.

The sun was burning the salt on her face, so Kagari dived again, feeling lost and lonely, slipping through the water, going nowhere in particular. She felt a sudden chill pass over her as if the sun had gone behind a cloud and reappeared again, but clouds didn't move that quickly. As she swam on, almost dismissing the incident, the solution came to her in a flash. It was a canoe! Her father was searching for her! She sped to the surface, arms waving, shouting, calling for him to come back.

As soon as the hands reached down to grab her and pull her into the canoe, Kagari knew she was done for. The smell was enough. The spirit men smelled foul and their grunting voices were deafening. She fought again, kicking and biting, but they were too strong and as they hauled her up she felt a crunching blow across the back of her head. She dropped limply among them, a little girl, surrounded by monsters.

No matter how much the crew might harp and haw about the captain's wife being aboard, they still accorded her respect. It was a contradictory element of the rough male society, especially in the colony where women were in such short supply, that men boasted they knew how to treat a lady, rummaging in maudlin memories for tender tales of their dear old mums or grandmums, who, besides being remarkable cooks, were accorded honour.

Augusta Beckman was a ranking lady, thanks to her husband, so as she came buttressing across the deck, elbows pumping like oars and one loose blonde plait flying, waves of men parted to allow her to view the catch, the black girl wet and polished on the timbers like a long, sleek, black porpoise.

'Gott in heaven!' she screamed, appalled that all these men should be standing over the girl, studying her nakedness, her small peaked breasts and the shadow of pubic hair. 'Get a blanket!' she cried, flopping to the deck, trying to hide the girl's shame with her skirts, feeling the air with a grasping hand behind her until someone obliged.

She put her face to the girl to find she was breathing easily enough and rolled her in the blanket. 'She's half drowned,' she told the watchers.

'No fear, missus,' a voice said. 'She ain't drownded. She fought like a scalded cat, Taffy's got the scratches to prove it. We was only trying to save her, so we had to give her a tap on the head, jes' a bit of a tap, like, to quiet her down.'

'You could have killed her,' Mrs Beckman accused. She made certain the blanket was firmly in place and then turned to her husband. 'Otto, you and I, we'll carry her down to our cabin.'

'Yes, of course,' he said, but he was able to pick the girl up without her help.

When the captain was out of earshot one of the men grumbled. 'Why bother? She's one of them bloody savages as killed our two mates. I say we should chuck her back in the drink. Let the sharks have her.'

Edmund was shocked. 'She's only a girl. You can't do that.'

'Little cats can grow into man-eating tigers. She's spawn o' them murderers. What do you say, Billy? They nearly got you.'

Billy Kemp had been standing well back. This was a day of shocks. He'd recognised her as the girl he and George had tried to catch, he didn't want her on board. She'd survived in the water all this time, let her stay there. 'I say we don't want the bitch! An eye for an eye! Throw her over.' Christ, if she came to and pointed the finger at him he'd be in trouble. Not that she'd be able to speak English. He hoped. Some of those bloody blacks could talk pidgin.

Dutchy seemed to tower over him. 'She ain't done you no harm.' He turned to the others. 'You cold-blood drown her, you're as bad as them savages back there. The captain, he'll know what to do.' He took Billy by the arm and marched him away. 'You look at that little girlie like you seen a ghost, Kemp.'

'I never.' He tried a grin. 'The bint was stark bollicky, mate.'

'Never call me mate,' Dutchy growled. 'What was George carrying when he came up the beach? I saw him throw something away.'

Christ. The bastard had eyes like a hawk. 'How should I know?'

'Why wouldn't you know? Nothin' else to look at. Now me, I look all the time. While we was rowing I saw the scratches on your arms, and that one on your neck. You didn't have them on the way in.' He grasped Billy's arm and twisted it forward. 'Fresh cuts, same as Taffy's got.'

'They're nothin' ' Billy whined. 'Ease up, you're hurtin' me.'

'Then you listen good to me, toad. You do anything to hurt that girlie or say any more—'

'What'll you do?' Billy spat at him. 'Go to the captain and tell him you got a new story?'

'Oh no. Too easy. You back off or one dark night you'll be the one overboard. You understanding me?' He shoved Billy aside and strode away.

'You're mad, Dutchy, you know that?' Billy called after him.

'Hey, Billy.' The cabin boy, Gaunt, had come up to him. 'I was the one saw her first. In the water. I spotted her.'

'Good for you,' Billy said savagely.

The girl's eyes snapped open and she let out an agonised howl that reverberated around the cabin.

Gussie tucked her firmly into the bunk and batted her on the lips with two tapping fingers. 'Shush. Shush.' And just as suddenly the noise stopped.

Otto handed his wife a mug of water and Gussie tried to make the girl drink. 'Come now, little one, water. You must have water.' But she could get no cooperation as her patient twisted and fought, sending the water flying. Unperturbed, Gussie took a small towel, dipped it in water and squeezed it against the girl's dry lips, dripping water into her mouth, pleased to see a tentative response as she began sucking on the cloth.

Cooing to the girl, soothing her, Gussie bathed her face and placed a damp cooling cloth on her forehead. 'Look at her hair,' she said, pushing aside the long tangled mass of black curls. 'It's never seen a comb.'

Beckman laughed. 'What would you expect, mother? She's wild. No more tamed than her hair, so better you watch out. She come to proper, she's likely to fight you.'

Gussie flexed her muscles and grinned. 'I can hold a scrap of a girl.'

'You better, then. If she gets away, she'll jump overboard and we're not stopping again.' The girl was rubbing frantically at her eyes. 'They must be stinging from the salt,' he commented.

'What's she doing swimming out this far?' Gussie asked, almost indignantly as if parental control were lax.

'Probably swimming and got washed out on the tide. That's a big river. I'll have to find a safe place to put her ashore as soon as she's well enough.'

'How will she find her way home?'

'They know their country, I won't put her in the middle of Sydney.'

Gussie stared at the dark face with its even, young features. 'She's only about eleven or twelve. It might be dangerous for her.'

'That's all I can do,' Otto said. 'She's lucky we picked her up. I'll send Gaunt in with some soup for her.'

'Soup, yes. That will be good,' Gussie said. The girl was trembling now, like a frightened puppy, so she patted her and made an attempt to dry her hair but was pushed away again.

All night Augusta sat with the girl, wrestling her back on to the bunk, not minding when, in her fright, the child wet the bed. She replaced the wet blankets with fresh ones and watched over the girl as she turned and twisted in her sleep and called out in a strange guttural tongue.

Augusta was pleased to be a useful person at last in this floating household. It hadn't taken long for her to discover that the crew resented her presence on board, although she hadn't mentioned it to Otto, and her seasickness had made her a hindrance instead of a helper. Gussie had hoped to be able to assist in the galley, she was a very good cook, but even that had been denied her. On the few days when she had felt well, she'd gone to the galley to see what she could do but was met with stern resistance from the cook. And then Otto had told her, kindly, not to interfere. There was no place for her on the *White Rose*, she knew that now, but she dreaded returning to the lonely Brisbane house.

Otto had bought a pretty cottage in Charlotte Street, not far from the river, and Augusta had looked forward to making a home there but everything had gone wrong. Her neighbours were a hard-drinking common lot and that was the best she could say of them. The women were by far the worst, content to live in squalor and shout abuse at the houseproud German woman. She had also hoped to grow her own vegetables and flowers in the scrubby patch at the back of the cottage but that had been cut short.

No stranger to hard work, Augusta had rolled up her sleeves and waded into the yard with a pick and shovel to clear the tangled undergrowth and on the first day had stood back with satisfaction at her progress. A week or so would see the work done, then she would burn off the rubbish and fork the ash into the lazy old soil.

On the second day her screams had brought the neighbours running, if only out of curiosity. Yanking at a hardy nest of ferns, Gussie had disturbed two huge snakes. One had even reared up, almost to waist height, hissing at her, its wicked tongue spitting and its head weaving back and forth to strike. Gussie had fled in terror.

None of the neighbours were enthusiastic about searching for the snakes. 'You never know how many more are in there!' they said, backing away, although one man did retrieve Gussie's garden tools for her.

'You better keep your back door closed,' a woman laughed. 'They get in the house too!'

The woman was only being a torment, Gussie knew that, but she allowed it was a possibility. Snakes terrified her. They gave her nightmares. She could cope with the tarantulas, to a certain extent anyway, since someone told her the huge, hairy spiders fed on mosquitoes; and she could live with the ants, and cockroaches, and the tiny lizards. But snakes? Never.

Gradually she became housebound, a recluse, friendless; no one to cook for, little work to do with the cottage gleaming like a new pin, waiting desperately for Otto to come home.

Now, sitting here all through the night, she had time to think. From this distance, her neighbours didn't seem so bad. Who were they anyway? Poor English trash. Able to observe her former behaviour objectively, she wondered how she could have got into such a state. Back home in Hamburg she had been a jolly, busy person, sharing homemade pickles and cakes and sausages with family and friends. Her sausages had even won a prize at the annual fair. And yet two years in Brisbane had reduced her to a whimpering, shivering jelly. Come to think of it, none of the neighbours had ever hurt her, or entered her property without permission. Proud of her German heritage, she'd been shocked that the English (they were all English to her although some claimed that being Australian-born, they were not) despised Germans, even the wife of a respected sea captain. Yet Otto was never subjected to the jeers she had to suffer. Cowards, all of them! But was she any better, lurking behind her curtains, washing and pressing her good linen almost weekly to fill up the hours, complaining to her husband about her loneliness?

When she got back to her home, Gussie decided, things would be different. She would come and go as she wished, with her head up. She would make more preserves and give some to the neighbours. That would surprise them. She was a fine cook, they'd find out. And she'd make cheeses like she used to do back home, and sell them.

It seemed amazing, looking back, that she had spent so much time stripped of every vestige of her true self, a woman near fifty, turned into a mouse, only able to leave the cottage to scurry to church. Sometimes when she was out of supplies she would go without rather than venture into the street, even under her big floppy hat, afraid . . . afraid of what?

As soon as all this realisation unfolded, Augusta was faced with another problem. How to tell Otto that she had decided, after all, she would be better off at home. He had thought she was stupid with all her silly worries, not being able to cope on her own. Now he'd think she was even more stupid, changing her mind. For hadn't she begged and pleaded until he agreed to let her join him on the *White Rose*?

The girl awoke suddenly again with the same howling and began to fight, so Gussie grappled with her. It was like trying to pacify a babbling lunatic, but Gussie knew she was not mad, just terrified as the sun came up and she found herself in this strange place.

Edmund brought in breakfast, taking every opportunity to stare at the girl, and Gussie found her appetite had returned. The seasickness had left her, and she was really hungry. 'Pass me the sausage pie and the bacon,' she said.

'That's for the captain,' Edmund told her, setting out her usual tea and biscuits.

'Bring some more for the captain, Edmund. Today I eat.'

He grinned and hurried away. Gussie ate some pie, making certain the girl could smell it, then she waved the warm hunks of bacon under her nose, delighted to see a reaction. The girl stirred and chewed hungrily as Gussie pushed the meat into her mouth, then she sat up, feeling around her for more.

Feeling around her! Gussie was stunned as she fed more bacon and pieces of pie into the hungry mouth as if she were feeding a helpless chick. The child was blind!

She began to talk to her. 'That's a good girl. Take this piece in your hand. Here in your hand. You take it. Good. Feed yourself. Now some bread, there you are.' On and on. She kept her occupied until Otto came in.

'You won't be able to put this one ashore,' she said. 'The child is blind.'

'She can't be blind. Let me see.' He waved a hand in front of her face and although her eyes did blink she gave no indication she had seen anything. He took a hand mirror and held it where she couldn't miss it. 'She'll not have seen herself like this before, mother. The mirror will tell.'

And then he shook his head. 'God help us, she is blind. It might be sun-blindness. You should bandage her eyes.'

'I don't think she'll like that, it will frighten her worse and I've just got her quiet. Nothing like a feed,' she grinned. 'I'll keep the room dark, is all we can do. Will her eyes get better?'

'That's for a doctor to say. She'll have to come to Rockhampton and we'll drop her off there.'

'Who with?'

'Lord knows. I can't be worried. We put her ashore there and that's the end of it. More important is the water supply. Whatever you do, don't waste water. We're all down to a cup of water a day. If you're thirsty, drink some wine. Not much of that either.'

Within a few days, Gussie realised the girl's eyesight was improving, and she tried to dissuade her from rubbing at them. She was also stronger and confident enough to take a few teetering steps around the cabin.

Gussie had become quite fond of her and was waiting for an opportunity to inform Otto of the decision she had made.

It would be her Christian duty to care for this heathen waif. They couldn't dump her alone in Rockhampton; she would take her home to live with them, teach her the language and show her how to live as a Christian person in a proper home. She would be company too. Surely Otto would not deny her this, once she admitted that she was not cut out to be a sea wife.

'You have decided to stay home from now on?' he said, with a tease in his voice, when she told him.

'Yes, my dear. And I'll have the little girl to look after.'

'To tame, you mean. Her eyesight's still poor, she can't talk to you, and she's still wild. We can't even let her out of the cabin. You might as well try and tame a snake.'

He wondered why he had thought of a snake. The girl was far from reptilian with high firm breasts and well-rounded hips. Just as well Gussie had been on board. Who in this crew of lechers could he trust to tend a ripening girl? And maybe Gussie was right to offer to look after her. She would be lost in Rockhampton, and Otto could see no way of getting her back to the Endeavour River beach, short of letting her take her chances on another ship which was no guarantee she would make it unmolested.

'I'll think about it,' he said. 'I must think about it.'

4

Kagari lay still. She tested the swaying base of the great spirit boat, recognising the touch of timber, pressing her cheek hard against the uncommon smoothness of this wood. Her flaring nostrils picked up the sour-sweet smell of human feet that gushed from wood that had long since lost its sap. All around her the smells were so strong that she guessed these were not spirits at all but enemy tribesmen. Above her, mutterings grew to hard rattling voices that became shrill with laughter until a woman shouting in a strange language shut them down.

Soft skins were wrapped round her, quelling her shivers, and she was bundled up like a baby and carried away in the darkness.

When she awoke she was still blind, she knew it, and vile hands were touching her. She cried for help as loudly as her voice could manage, a long dingo cry that would carry and carry on the wind so that her father could hear her. Tears splashed down her face and she was shivering again, not so much from the cold as from terror of these beings. And she felt water drops in her mouth, not salt but pure, delicious water so she sucked and sucked, despite the stinging pain of her poor cracked lips.

Days and nights, she couldn't tell how long, she had been on this giant boat that was now being battered and pounded by rain winds that sang of the coming of the big devil wind, strong enough to lift the ocean and hurl it over the lowlands; the same devil wind that tore at the jungle, ripping trees up by their roots and scattering them around like seaweed. Her people would be far away by this time, sheltering in the caves up in the hills. Kagari sobbed, fighting back tears. She must not despair. As soon as these enemies got close enough to shore, she would escape and make her way home.

Her terror had subsided as her eyes cleared and she was able to take in her surroundings, to try to make sense of this strange place. She tried to keep her eyes closed as much as possible, surreptitiously glancing around whenever she thought the peculiar woman wasn't watching, trying to take stock of her situation.

They had fed her. No one had beaten her. No one had tried to attack her. All that had happened so far had confused her more than any beating would have done. Men had come and stared at her and had gone away but the woman stayed, feeding her, making strange little baby noises, mopping her head with cool cloths and talking away as if Kagari should understand. The woman must be a prisoner too, Kagari concluded, and quite mad. Touched. Wearing heaps of cloths from head to toe, the woman sweated all the time in the airless heat of their dim prison and kept covering Kagari with more rugs every time she tried to kick them off. Still, she felt safe in here with the mad woman; outside she could hear the shouts of her captors.

Rain was still driving hard against the boat but not a drop seeped in, not even on the floor, and that was a wonder. The sea was getting rougher as the winds gathered strength. She could feel this big boat swishing along, very fast, and was childish enough to be exhilarated by the pace. Never in her life had she encountered such speed, she could almost see the great waters rushing beneath them. At least with the devil winds imminent, these tribesmen knew enough to run away.

She sighed and wedged herself in the corner of the bunk, studying the articles in her prison, trying to work out what they were made of, what they could be used for. She dared not touch anything; any one of them could be an evil totem.

The woman had undone her hair, amazing sand-coloured hair – Kagari had never seen the like – and was brushing it as she did every day before knotting it back in place. Kagari like to watch this ritual; for some reason she found it comforting.

Her eyes roamed around the clutter of strange goods with silky precision, feeling the dark knots and grooves of the flat table in the centre, and the smooth carved seats that these people used. She marvelled at the sturdy walls that held large boxes that opened and shut with ease, and contained all manner of treasures. Her gaze halted at a painting fixed to the wall. She decided that the artist must be the best in the world. Her people painted on bark and on walls of caves, some of which were too sacred for women to see, but they were known to be beautiful and they told brilliant stories of the ancestors, but this painting was perfect. Anyone could see it was a picture of a giant craft on a tiny sea. It could even be a painting of this very craft. The recognition excited her and she giggled at her cleverness.

The mad woman heard her and bounced over, joy on her face that Kagari could laugh, hugging her, and then she rushed to one of her boxes and came back with a tiny present, urging Kagari to eat it. Since none of the other food had poisoned her yet, Kagari put it in her mouth, her taste buds gushing at the familiar honey and nut flavour. It was good. Budgeri.

She grinned enthusiastically. 'Budgeri' she said, and held out her hand for more.

Captain Beckman was uneasy about taking the girl home. Not that the authories would object, the blacks were irrelevant. And if a kind woman like Gussie were to give a lubra shelter then it was no more than the missionaries were trying to do. But there was more to it. This girl had an

30

arrogance about her that was rare in the blacks, rare even in a white girl that age. They both agreed she was about twelve years old, tall and still growing, and a man couldn't help noticing the body was flowering into a very desirable shape. (He was keeping his thoughts understated.) Her small chin had an imperious tilt and the eyes, now clear, (although Gussie, to prime her case, still insisted her eyesight was poorly), glittered. There was something familiar about that glitter in her huge brown eyes. They had a glint of gold, too moist to be metallic, and were so solemn and steady. Or was it the way she held her head? Yes, that was it. Her head, still encased in that thick, tangled mop that Gussie was gradually unravelling, was poised on the long graceful neck. Poised, always still, never dipping and nodding and twigging like most little girls. She kept her head perfectly still when she looked at you. Otto tried it himself, not an easy thing to do. Muscle power, he decided, bred in them probably for survival in the wild. It gave her an air of serenity that was in fact totally absent; the girl was thoroughly confused.

He frowned. Augusta was standing at the rails watching the activity on the wharves and waiting patiently for him to escort her ashore. He was relieved that she was content to stay home in future. If only she would give up this idea of keeping the girl.

He went out to talk to her. Perhaps now, back in civilisation, she would see things differently.

'I was thinking,' he said quietly, 'we could hand the child over to the blacks here in Brisbane, and they could take her back to the bush where she belongs.'

Gussie turned on him angrily. 'Do you see her as some sort of animal? A squirrel maybe, that someone finds and then lets loose in a forest?'

'No, no. I did not mean that. I just think she would be better off with her own people.'

'They are not her people. You told me this yourself. They are different tribes. You might as well put her in Berlin as Brisbane, with no one responsible for her.'

'Where is she now?' Otto asked. A leading question.

'Locked in the cabin.'

'Exactly. And you'll have to keep her locked in or she'll run off.'

'No, she won't. I will care for her. And she isn't the first black to come to live in the white world.' She pointed at a group of Aborigine boys, dressed in battered European clothes, making their way along the wharf, laughing and skylarking with a lasso. 'Look at them. There are plenty of natives in Brisbane, and they speak English.'

'Yes, poor things, and what becomes of them? Don't pretend you don't know. They're doomed, those poor blacks.'

'This won't happen to my girl. I will see to it. I have christened her and called her after Governor Bowen's lady. Such a beautiful woman.'

'You have called her Diamentina?'

'No. Just Diamond.'

Otto nodded. He liked that. The Countess Diamentina impressed him too. Brisbane was a wild, rough, frontier town, he'd had second thoughts about bringing his own wife to live here. But it hadn't deterred the wife of Queensland's first governor. It was now 1862; she'd stuck it out for three years already. An aristocratic personage in her own right, Lady Bowen tripped around the rowdy town in clothes that would turn heads in Paris. She was renowned for her grace and beauty and attended receptions in satins and laces and such magnificent jewellery that the drab populace was stunned. But they loved her, that was the most astonishing part. They adored her! Bowen himself went on quietly with the business of creating this new state while his lovely wife went out to meet one and all, a hand extended in friendship.

Yes. He approved. Diamond was a nice name; Diamentina would have been inappropriate. And when it was all boiled down, there wasn't much they could do with the girl except keep her. And his Gussie was a wise woman; the girl, Diamond, would be in good hands.

Edmund Gaunt was cock-o'-the-walk for the rest of that miserable voyage, all of them just about dying of thirst, thanks to the pitiful rations, and then pitching south, racing away from hurricane weather. Mrs Beckman was only sick once but he'd been queasy all the time, even wishing he could get proper sick and be rid of it. But apart from these troubles, he was the only one in the crew who got to see the black gin every day and all the men wanted to know about her. Especially Billy Kemp.

'Is she better?'

'Oh yes. Mrs Beckman's got her eating now.'

'What does she say? The gin, I mean.'

'She don't say nothin', Billy. She can't talk English.'

'Not even pidgin?'

And the other men wanted to know if she was wearing any clothes yet, and he'd said Mrs Beckman kept her in the bunk. Then when he'd reported that she was up on her feet, they were at it again. 'Does she walk around in the nuddy?'

'No. Mrs Beckman made her a shift and she wears that.'

'But what about drawers? Has she got anything on underneath?' Even Edmund had to laugh at the thought of the skinny gin in Mrs Beckman's huge drawers. But he thought they were all awful, old men getting randy about a kid just because they'd seen her in the raw and she was black! If they wanted to see good-looking girls, they should see his next-door neighbour, the Middleton girl. She was twelve, three years younger than him, but Edmund had always thought she was pretty, and she was getting better every day, with long fair hair, thick as flax.

He had often seen her, watched her, in the yard washing her hair in an iron bucket and rinsing it in another. Always the same careful operation, wet hair streaming, then the towelling and the fluffing of golden, glinting strands, and the combing, wrestling with knots, grimacing and frowning. He wished she would stop there, hair flowing like a soft mantle, but finally she plaited it, rope by rope, so evenly he thought she was wizard being able to do it so well. And then her mother would call her: 'Perfy!'

Edmund's old man didn't like the Middletons. He didn't like soldiers. Perfy's dad was a sergeant in the army and Willy Gaunt reckoned he'd sold out. Come out here a ringlock passenger, just like the rest, married a convict woman, just as Willy had, and then when he'd been set free he'd joined the army. 'Turned,' Willy called it. 'Joined the bosses.'

Edmund had wondered about that. 'But he ain't no boss, Pa. He's just a soldier.'

'These blokes!' Willy spat. 'They're not real bloody soldiers. Where's the bloody war? They're just puppets of the bosses. What good does the army do us? None. They work for the squatters, guarding their land, riding around the countryside, and the squatters get their services free. If they were honest, they'd join the police.'

'I thought you didn't like coppers?'

'No one likes coppers, son. You're not listenin'. But at least we know what they're there for.'

Edmund was sorry the old man wouldn't talk to the Middletons, and vice versa. And Pa laughed every time he heard their daughter's name. 'Perfection! Fancy giving a kid a handle like that. They bung-on, that pair, I tell you. Got above 'emselves well and truly.'

To his shame, Edmund always laughed too, but secretly he thought it was a lovely name, Perfection Middleton. It was her. She was the most beautiful girl in the world and she lived right next door to him and he'd never spoken to her. She never even looked in his direction.

One night he'd told Billy Kemp about her, and Billy, too, had laughed.

'You wait till you see her,' Edmund had said, but Billy wasn't interested. But of course Billy was old too, he was at least twenty and he'd been at sea for years.

They just walked off the farm. Billy had hitched up the old mare to the dray, piled in their belongings and the few bits of furniture worth flogging, and set fire to the house his father had built. The bastards could have the land but they could build their own house. He'd been fifteen, about the same age as this wet-behind-the-ears cabin boy. Had he ever been that young? And dumb? He doubted it.

His mother hadn't known what was going on; she was away with the pixies. She'd just sat in the dray not even asking where they were going, never once looking back.

So he took her down to Sydney, found a squat in the Rocks district, about the worst in Australia but cheap. He sold the mare and the dray, then he set about making a living for them. It was hard. He scavenged and stole, picked pockets, scrounged around the town but he'd kept her fed. And among his father's papers he found the receipt for two hundred pounds for the purchase of that worthless land. What a bloody con! The world was full of them. Sold to him by a Mr J. A. Ganderton, Agent, of Paddington.

Billy marched across town to get a look at this crook and found the single-storeyed, smart-painted office place, with blackboard signs propped along the wooden verandah offering great cheap properties for sale. He smiled. 'What's good for the goose is good for the gander,' his dad had always said. Well. Why not?

That night he burned down the offices of J. A. Ganderton, Agent.

PART TWO

1

Kagari didn't mind living with the other mother now, but she still missed her family and the evergreen loveliness of their forest. One day she would go from this ugly white-hot village and find her way home, and what tales she would have to tell! She'd be the centre of attention. People would come from near and far to hear of her adventures, and they would listen to her with wonder in their faces. Wogaburra would be proud of her, his daughter, this girl who had seen so much and who had walked bravely through the camps of the white tribes. All her life she had heard stories of the courage and daring of the Irukandji people, she knew the names of all the bold warriors and heroic women who featured in legends and she had always burned to join the ranks of the honoured.

She wouldn't tell them, though, that when they'd first caught her she'd been terrified, and when they brought her to this house she'd been so scared she'd crawled into a corner of the woodshed and refused to come out. The big boss had tried to pull her out after several days but she'd clawed and bit him until the blood ran, and his woman had pulled her off him. She was very strong, the woman, she looked fat and sluggish but she had the strength of a man and Kagari liked that. She had come to admire Missus who could do all sorts of clever things and cooked food fit for the lords of the spirit world.

And they called her Diamond. That was peculiar but she got used to it, the same way she got used to everything else. Eventually.

One day Missus had brought some grinning, giggling, black girls in to see her but they were a different tribe and she couldn't understand their language either. It was much easier to learn new words from Missus who was constantly teaching her, making a good game of it. Later, she had seen the same black girls at the gate and they'd managed to let her know that she was in a safe place and she shouldn't fuss, and so Diamond had come to the conclusion that she'd been captured as a bride for a white man. Back home when there weren't enough young women to go round, rather than marry an old one, Irukandji men would go hunting to catch fresh young gins from another tribe. She'd often seen them come home, pleased and proud, to show off their shy, pretty prizes. The new girls were accepted into the families and usually settled down well. It was rare for them to run away. And dangerous.

So time passed, the lessons continued and Diamond became good at the language, but there was still no sign of the white husband.

Augusta Beckman had no intention of letting any man, black or white, catch Diamond. She kept a gun in the house and waved it madly at any men who came sneaking along their front verandah or creeping into the yard, shouting fiercely at them to be off!

'You beware those men,' she told Diamond. 'They give you babies and beat you. Bad people!'

And yet her husband was kind. Captain was away a lot on his big ship and when he came home he busied himself making and carving furniture, then polishing the wood to colours that astonished and intrigued Diamond. Only once there'd been trouble. Captain and another man were clearing the thorny bushes and high dry grass from the back yard when they saw a fine snake. Captain grabbed a tomahawk to kill him and Diamond flung herself forward, knocking Captain over to stop this terrible thing. They didn't need the food and the pretty snake was harmless, so long and sleek, with glittering black scales and bright intelligent eyes. The men backed off, yelling, while Diamond wound the snake round her neck and down her arm, skin to skin, soothing it because it was frightened. No one stopped her when she walked away into the bush to find the snake a new home and that incident was the real beginning of her new life. She realised they didn't mind if she went for small walks as long as Missus knew where she was. She soon learned to find her way around the big huts.

Every morning Missus made her learn real English, not the pidgin the blacks talked, and she taught her letters, and writing, buying picture books which Diamond loved. She was convinced the old lady enjoyed the lessons more than she did; Missus was so eager to get started each day, she even made the washing wait. Then when Captain came home from his ship, Diamond had to show him what she had learned, and recite pretty-sounding pieces for him. Her favourite was Dickory, dickory, dock. She thought it was very funny but Captain didn't laugh, he clapped, and Missus was pleased.

'See,' she told him. 'They say these blacks can't learn, but Diamond can. My Diamond is smart.'

Captain was happy. 'Ah, but she has a fine teacher, Gussie. You should have been a school teacher.'

Missus was so proud, her chest stuck out like a turkey's.

They were happy together, the little family. Diamond helped with the work in the house and in the garden and she had her own sleepout on the verandah.

The other blacks in Brisbane Town were a lot worse off than her, many of them sick and starving. They had never heard of Irukandji, which was disappointing, and they knew nothing of the far north country. Diamond found them to be kind people despite their sufferings, but their miserable lives spent hanging about dirty lanes upset her. 'Why don't you go back to your own country?' she asked.

'This is our country,' they shrugged. 'White man takem up.'

And one old gin told her exactly the same thing Missus had. 'You good clean gin, Diamond. Now you a woman, you keep allasame way from blackfellers and whitefellers. You tell 'em bugger off.'

The next time Missus issued the same warning, Diamond announced, 'I know. I'll tell them to bugger off.'

At first Missus had been shocked and then she'd laughed, her plump face and rolls of chins wobbling in merriment. And of course next time Captain came home Missus made sure Diamond repeated her answer to him. Everything they did while he was away was recounted to him in detail and he always enjoyed the telling. He, too, was amused. 'We'll find Diamond a good husband one day,' he said, and strangely that didn't please Missus at all.

She planned a special celebration for Captain's next homecoming, with a good rich fruit cake, which she would ice on the day, and candles, and bonbons. She and Diamond were both looking forward to it. Although she hadn't been able to specify which day, Missus had warned several of her friends in the Altar Society that their invitations would have to be at short notice, but they didn't mind. Gussie's 'little teas' were more of a feast than the English teas, and her homemade apple ciders were deliciously strong, they added jollity to these occasions.

Everything was in readiness and she even had time to finish embroidering a fine damask table cloth. And then begin appliquéing Diamond's initial on the two lace-edged pillowcases she had made for her. Time began to drag. It was always like this, Diamond recalled, sometimes the *White Rose* was delayed by storms or by unscheduled port calls with extra cargo, so they were never sure when to expect Captain. At these times they lived in a drifting world like two clouds in an empty sky.

And then Diamond had a dream. The kookaburra came for her, and she flew easily with him far into the mountains and deep into the fragile still-ness of the rainforest and her people were there, somewhere. She called her name, shocking the silence. 'Kagari! Kagari!' She could feel their closeness but they would not respond. A bee came to rest on the gaping maw of a feeding plant, and the mossy green mouth closed swiftly, trapping it. The tiny movement startled Kagari and she turned to see Captain coming towards her, passing right by her, a wraith of grey-white light. She was afraid to reach out and interrupt his majestic progress but not so Missus, who came pounding along behind him, skirts hitched up, puffing noisily, ludicrous in these surrounds, her multi-coloured vestments clashing in this cathedral of green.

Instantly, cicadas burst into shrill chatter, birds flapped and Kagari called to her, 'Missus, I'm here. Missus!'

The woman turned, looked back at her, shook her head, and ran on to disappear in the heat mist. And then the forest disappeared too and Kagari was standing far out in the desert, a stony land, a country bereft of life.

When she awoke, sleep-muddled, depressed, Diamond stole into the bedroom and sat cross-legged in a corner to watch over Missus, to fend off more evil spirits, because she knew Captain was dead.

The men came, heads down, clutching their hats, feet shuffling, mumbling their news and condolences.

'Gone down, ma'am. The *White Rose*.'

'A fine ship. A fine man, Captain Beckman. Yes, lost at sea.'

'Hit a reef, see. A hurricane they say it was.'

'How do we know? Two survivors, ma'am. Two men got to shore.'

'Off Cape Manifold 'twas. A terrible thing. A terrible thing.'

'How do we know? Telegraph, ma'am. From the Port Officer in Rockhampton. A terrible storm.'

Mrs Beckman wouldn't have it. She questioned them and questioned them, sinking lower and lower, cringing, into her big armchair with her hands knotted in front of her, until despair set in, all hope gone.

There seemed to be nothing Diamond could do to console her. Missus lay on her bed weeping, she wandered the house unsteadily, she became hysterical when friends came to offer sympathy and at night she screamed his name, wailing at his fate.

Diamond couldn't imagine change. It hadn't entered her conception of the white man's world, any more than that of her own people. But as the mourning subsided, Missus was forced to take stock of their situation. She went out most days. 'On business,' she told Diamond. 'I'm a widow now, I have to face these things, the banks and the shipping people.' And she wrote long sad letters back to Germany.

In the quiet of her own room Diamond, too, wept for Captain. It was difficult to imagine their lives without him. They would be lonely. And then she noticed a recurrence of the tears. Missus seemed to be crying all the time lately, any little thing would set her off and Diamond supposed it would take a long long time to get over the loss of her dear husband.

'I have to sell the house,' she told Diamond, in such a quavering voice it sounded as if she were almost afraid to say the words.

'Where will we go?'

'That's the trouble, I have no money to live on. Otto was buying the boat and he still owes the bank money.' She sniffed and comforted her nose in a large handkerchief, then she took a deep breath. 'Diamond, this is a sorry day. I never thought this would happen.'

'No, of course not.'

'I'll have to go home to Germany to live with my son and his wife.'

Diamond was astonished. 'You're going to live with that lady you say is the mean one? In her house?'

40

'That's all I can do for now. It's a bitter, hard world.' She took Diamond's hand. 'I have to tell you now, I can't take you with me.'

Was this the dream? Was this Missus running from her into yet another strange world, following Captain?

'Do you understand, Diamond?'

'Yes,' she said to please Missus.

'I've been searching around for somewhere for you to live, and it has been hard. Places are all full up, that's why,' she added too quickly to sound convincing. 'But I've got you a live-in job. And you'll be safe there.' She gave a grim smile. 'You'll be safest there of anywhere.'

'What place is this?' Diamond asked, her heart sinking.

'At Government House. The captain had many important friends in Brisbane, thank the good Lord, so you'll be going to live at Government House. This is a great honour.'

'The job, though. I've never had a job. What can I do?'

'In the laundry. You help them in the laundry and be a good girl and soon they'll see . . .' She stopped and threw her arms round Diamond. 'I'm so sorry. I don't want to leave you here alone but what else can I do?'

Alone! Diamond was frightened. She would be alone. No family. And what if she couldn't do this job? What would become of her? Missus was weeping again and Diamond remembered that she must be brave, she must not cause Missus any more unhappiness.

'It's all right,' she said. 'Don't cry, Missus. I'll be all right.'

2

'I want a drink of water.'

'Shush, Laura Stibbs. You be quiet,' Perfy told her.

'Why? They can't hear us.'

Perfection Middleton sat up straight, head up, shoulders back the way her father had taught her, knees together, feet together. Her mother said only sluts let their knees slack open so people bending down could see their britches. From this Perfy had concluded that Brisbane Town was awash with sluts. You saw britches everywhere, all shapes and sizes, fancy and plain, on women who sat outside shanties fanning themselves in the heat or working in the market gardens, skirts hitched up out of the dust; or even riding astride on big half-wild horses.

Her mother worried about her all the time, stuffing cotton wool in her ears when they walked past taverns and other low places so that she wouldn't hear dirty talk, and made her wear stiff poke bonnets, blinkered like a horse, unable to look sideways. Her mother didn't like Brisbane. Apparently when her father was posted to the town, she hadn't realised that it used to be the infamous Moreton Bay prison colony, the most vicious penal settlement outside of Norfolk Island! And even though those terrible days were long gone – the convict system had been shut down ten years before Jack and Alice Middleton arrived – her mother claimed that she could feel the presence of those poor tortured souls; their ghosts, she said, would never leave. Certainly, everyone had a tale to tell of someone who had heard the clanking of chains and ghastly shrieks at midnight in the streets of Brisbane, but her father said it was all nonsense, and Perfy was inclined to believe him. She had always wondered why ghosts picked midnight to go a-clanking and that had added to her suspicion that it was all codswallop. She hoped.

But then her mother still lived with the emotional stress of having been transported to Sydney as a felon. And her father, too. That was a fact. Perfy had been confronted with the taunt at the Fortitude Valley school by friends of that snivelling Edmund Gaunt from next door. She hadn't believed a word of it and had gone rushing home. 'The kids say you're crims too. You weren't convicts, were you?'

'Exiles, dear,' her mother had said, her only comment, ever, on the subject, but her father had been more specific.

'Nothing for you to worry about, girl. Most of us out here got the shove out of England on those transport ships, so don't go upsetting your mother about it. They were cruel times, best forgot. We earned our keep and we can hold our heads up now.'

Perfy was wide-eyed with shocked interest. 'But what did you do? What was your crime?'

'Necessity, girl, that's all.'

And that was disappointing. Perfy loved stories of adventure. She wished he had been a gallant highwayman, riding the highways and the byways on his trusty steed, his cloak billowing in the night winds. No such luck.

Since her mother hated Brisbane, her dad was saving to buy a little farm, hardly the style of a latter-day Robin Hood. And now it was her turn to help, to get a job. It was her first job, so she was on her best behaviour. She was determined to get it because her mother would be thrilled to have her working at Government House, meeting the beautiful Countess Diamentina, Lady Bowen.

Perfy looked down at her boots. They were not new but were well polished and had new laces. Laura's boots were new, bought specially for the occasion; her father was a blacksmith and could afford them. And as for Amy Campbell, the third member of the trio, all in their best white dresses, sitting on the bench under the mango tree, she had shoes. Real shoes. Perfy looked at them with envy. She had never owned a pair of shoes; most people wore boots because shoes got ruined on the rough dusty roads and were useless in the wet season. It was all very well for the Campbells, old Jock Campbell owned the biggest store in town so he didn't have to pay for them.

'It's not fair making us sit here all this time,' Laura said.

Amy agreed. 'I bet we've been here a full hour, and I'm boiling. I don't want the job anyhow.'

'The woman said we had to sit still and wait,' Perfy told them. 'I thi? she's the housekeeper. She looks very smart.'

'Oh pooh!' Amy sniffed. 'She looks more like a black crow, and wit? beak of hers she's got a face to match!' She lifted her arms. 'I'm sweat? a pig.'

'You won't want them to hear you talk like that if you're ? service,' Perfy whispered.

'Hear us?' Amy said. 'That damn big house is a couple of c? don't know why we're stuck right down here. They could at le? the back verandah. They've probably forgotten us. We oug? tell on them.'

Perfy was shocked. 'We're going to meet the Countess? Amy Campbell. I'm staying if I have to sit here all th? rather hoped Amy would go home, one less candidate?

Laura nudged her. 'Look who's coming!'

All three heads turned to watch the Germ?

43

Beckman, coming through the gate of the tradesmen's entrance, looking like a dark shadow as she moved through a lush tunnel of frangipani, the black veil on her hat completely covering her face. The housekeeper in her black dress had been tall and skinny. Mrs Beckman was just the opposite in a wide, black, old-fashioned crinoline. She looked around her uncertainly and then came tiptoeing across the lawn towards them, followed by a tall black gin.

They studied the black girl. She was dressed better than any gin they'd ever seen, in a crisp white blouse and a long black skirt belted neatly at the waist, and she was wearing shoes and black stockings! Native women always went barefoot.

'Good morning, girls.' Mrs Beckman lifted the veil to talk to them. 'Where can I find the housekeeper, Mrs Porter?'

'Up there, I suppose.' Amy pointed towards the mansion. Mrs Beckman hesitated, not sure what to do next. Her face was red, perspiring under the stifling veil, and Perfy felt sorry for her. 'Would you like to sit down?'

'No thank you, dear.' Mrs Beckman looked up at the sun. It was moving relentlessly on to the bench where the girls had been instructed to sit. 'I'll wait there in the shade.' She moved over to a garden seat under the eaves of a shed and the black girl followed again, to stand beside her like a guard, not like most gins who hung about, heads drooping, toes turned in. This one was their own age, maybe a bit younger, but she stood erect, head high, like a statue, her close-cropped hair, thick as a rug, suiting her sharp profile like a well-formed cap. She looked so strong and so sure of herself, she made Perfy feel uncomfortable.

'Surely she hasn't brought that gin along to apply for the job?' Amy whispered. 'They won't give it to a nigger.'

'She must have,' Laura said, and they sat quietly again. Even the birds were silent now, taking refuge in the trees from the hard noonday sun, but the three girls waited valiantly in their appointed places. Despairing, Perfy felt moisture trickling from her armpits and down her neck, sopping her freshly starched dress. She hoped the same thing was happening to the others.

And then at last the woman, who they guessed must be Mrs Porter, came down the back steps. She beckoned to the German woman who almost ran over to her.

'Are you Mrs Beckman?'

'Yes, that is right.'

'And you're looking for a position for your ward? Is that her over there?'

'Yes, a good girl, and a good worker.'

The housekeeper glared at Diamond. 'I'm not happy about having black on the staff, they're as silly as wheels.'

'this one.' Gussie didn't like the cold hag of a woman but she didn't

44

wish to offend. 'It would be a Christian thing for Lady Bowen to employ her . . .'

'All very well to expect the Countess to be Christian, but is she a Christian?'

'Oh yes. She is baptised and knows her bible.' Gussie smiled. 'In fact we called her Diamond after the Countess, we hold the good lady in such esteem.'

Mrs Porter grunted. 'Well, I won't have that, for a start. Her Excellency would be more embarrassed than pleased.'

Gussie's eyes narrowed. 'Her name is Diamond and you will please remember that.'

'Really? If I take her on.'

Her heart pounding, Gussie resisted the urge to push this woman aside and go searching for Lady Bowen. 'My late husband,' she said, 'was a friend of the Premier, Mr Herbert. Now Mr Herbert has spoken to her ladyship about Diamond and I was assured she would be taken on. If you want to argue with the Premier, you go see him.' She saw the woman flinch.

'She will have to work in the laundry, we don't have blacks in the house.'

'That was my understanding,' Gussie said quietly. And yours too, she thought. This housekeeper person was just showing off her authority. Well, two could play at that game. 'Now will you please show me where she is to sleep.'

'Madam, only two of the staff live in. Myself and the cook. We have our own rooms, and neither of us intends to share with a gin.'

Gussie tossed the veil away from her face angrily. 'I don't like that word gin. It makes Diamond sound like a nothing.' In her anger the word came out 'nuffink'.

'Oh, for heaven's sake, the blacks use that word themselves.'

'Yes, but in English it sounds bad.'

'Well, I can't be worrying about that. The point is, the girl can't live in.'

'She must. I am going back to Germany and she has no one here.'

'No family? Where does she come from?'

'Up north, a long way.'

'I suppose that's a blessing, we won't have the rest of her tribe hanging around looking for handouts. They can be the most dreadful nuisance. I imagine I can find somewhere to put her.'

Gussie knew she had won her point and decided to leave before the woman changed her mind. She had wanted to tell her that Diamond not only spoke good English but she could read and write, but caution warned her that perhaps it wouldn't be wise to mention that right now. It was possible that the woman would resent Diamond even more. 'I'll bring her tomorrow with her things,' she announced, 'and I'll write a letter to Lady

Bowen thanking her for her kindness. She will always be in my prayers.'

As she left with Diamond she nodded to the three girls. Such nice girls. The housekeeper might be a cranky one but Diamond would be in good company here, and protected. Where better for any young girl than under the roof of the Governor himself?

Irritated by the pushy German woman, Mrs Porter made short work of the interviews with the three applying for the position of housemaid. There wasn't much between them. They'd all gone to the same school and had all been sent on the recommendation of the same school mistress. She stood them in a row under the mango tree and questioned them for a few minutes. Time was wasting, she and Cook liked to have a glass of porter before the luncheon rush.

She decided to choose the Middleton girl. His Excellency would appreciate that she had given preference to the daughter of a British military man, even if he was only a sergeant. His Excellency liked to give encouragement to the families of army men and marines posted so far away from home. Yes, far better to employ her than the daughter of a blacksmith or a tradesman.

'That is all,' she said curtly to them. 'Thank you for coming, girls. Miss Middleton, you may commence work in the morning. Be here at six sharp.'

Perfy was cross. Someone had to get the job, there was no need for the other girls to be so nasty about it. They'd flounced off in another direction leaving Perfy to push on home alone.

She tramped down Queen Street, counting her steps. One thousand seven hundred and sixty yards to a mile – she'd work out the quickest way to get to work by counting the steps. It would probably be quicker to go along by the botanical gardens. But she had the job! And to think Mother had been worried, not even sure that she should apply, believing that the nobs wouldn't want a daughter of convicts working there. Poor Mother, she worried about so many silly things, she was always concerned about what people would think, and at times it was really annoying. Who cared what they thought? And who were 'they' anyway?

'Miss! Miss!'

Perfy turned to see Mrs Beckman and the black girl hurrying after her.

'Miss! Do you work at the Governor's House?'

'Yes.' Perfy felt quite proud to say it. 'I start tomorrow.'

'Ah, good. What is your name?'

'Perfy. Perfy Middleton.'

The German widow woman beamed and took her hand. Her hands were hot and clammy but Perfy didn't like to pull away.

'I am Mrs Beckman and this is Diamond. She starts there tomorrow also.'

Since she already knew Mrs Beckman's name, Perfy nodded to the gin. 'How do you do?'

'Very well, thank you, miss,' Diamond said with none of the usual Aboriginal shyness. 'I'll be working in the laundry.'

'That's nice,' Perfy mumbled.

'You girls can be friends,' Mrs Beckman announced, and Diamond smiled at Perfy like an approving elder sister, which confused Perfy who felt it should be the other way round. And besides, no one had black girls for friends.

'Where do you live?' Mrs Beckman asked.

'Fortitude Valley.'

'Ah. We go that way. We can walk together. Come along.'

Perfy had no choice but to walk with them. She wished she had said she lived somewhere else, or had to go visiting or something, but it was too late now. Mrs Beckman hardly stopped talking. She wheeled them down the hill telling Perfy about the death of her sainted husband, the captain, and the tragic loss of the *White Rose*. 'Only two fellows survived.'

'Yes, I know,' Perfy said. 'Edmund Gaunt lives next door to me.'

'Edmund? I remember him. He started on the *White Rose* as cabin boy, years ago. They told me another sailor saved his life.'

'That was Billy Kemp. He kept Edmund afloat on some sort of raft for two days and then some blacks saw them and went out in canoes and brought them in. They were lucky,' Perfy added. She was about to say they'd heard in the street that Edmund and Billy had been just as scared of the natives as they were of drowning, but she remembered Diamond's presence. 'The black people were kind to them,' she said, looking to Diamond for some reaction and perceiving nothing. The girl seemed unconcerned.

Mrs Beckman had tears in her eyes. 'If only they could have saved my dear Otto.'

'It must have been a terrible storm,' Perfy said. 'Edmund's too scared to go back to sea now. He and Billy want to go out to the goldfields but Mr Gaunt, Edmund's dad, is dead against it. He says Edmund has to be a sailor.'

'I thought those two lads might have called on me,' Mrs Beckman said sadly.

'They've only just got home,' Perfy told her. 'We don't have much to do with the Gaunts but Billy Kemp is staying with them, and I find him quite polite.'

That was an understatement. Perfy was impressed with Billy Kemp, the hero, who often said hello to her over the fence. He looked a real rascal and was as bold as brass, calling her 'Perfy' first up as if he'd known her all his life. He was good-looking too, in a reckless sort of way, with sun-bleached straight hair allowed to hang loose over his tanned face. Dark hair would look plain untidy like that, but Billy's, almost white, was attractive, and he had a wicked grin.

Billy Kemp was fast, Laura and Amy had decided when they'd taken a covert look at him from behind the curtains, and rough as bags too, but the girls had agreed he would have appeal for a certain type of woman.

They had stopped at the gate to a well-kept cottage. 'This is where we live,' Mrs Beckman said. 'Would you like to come in for tea?'

'Thank you, but I can't. My mother will be anxious to know how I got on.'

'Of course. I'll give you some roses to take home to your mumma. Diamond, will you cut some roses for Miss Perfy?'

The black girl nodded and hurried inside, and Mrs Beckman turned to Perfy. 'Be kind to Diamond,' she said, 'and God will bless you. In two days' time I have to leave for Germany and it breaks my heart to leave her behind. She is a very clever girl, she can read and write and do her sums same as you girls. A waste putting her in the laundry but all I could find for her.'

They watched as Diamond returned with scissors and cut some full red and pink blooms, wrapping them in coloured paper.

As she handed them over, Perfy thanked her, then for something to say, added, 'Mrs Beckman tells me you've been to school.'

Diamond grinned. 'Not school. Missus taught me. They don't let black girls go to school, do they, Miss Perfy?'

Perfy stared. It was the first time Diamond had addressed her directly and even though she sounded polite, Perfy felt an edge to the remark, which engendered a need to defend herself. 'I don't think so,' she said. 'But then they're not like you, Diamond. They wouldn't fit in. I mean to say, they haven't been brought up in the ways of white people.'

'I don't think they'd let me in anyway,' Diamond countered. 'But it doesn't matter. I wouldn't like school. They hit you, don't they?'

'My word, they do,' Perfy responded eagerly to the familiar theme. 'I don't know how many times I got the cane and it hurts.'

Diamond was intrigued. 'No one has ever hit me. I had a good teacher. Captain always said Missus was the best.'

Mrs Beckman sighed. 'We must get on with our packing. You young girls are so sweet, but life can be hard. You have to be strong, you must stand up for yourselves.'

3

Perfy remembered Mrs Beckman's remark when she went to work at Government House. It was all very well saying you had to stand up for yourself, but if you stood up to Mrs Porter, you'd get the sack.

Perfy wore the black dress her mother had made for her and was issued with a starched white apron and mobcap. Her heavy plaits had to be pinned up inside the small cap and Perfy found it difficult to manage. Mrs Porter soon fixed that. She grabbed hold of Perfy and twisted her plaits so sharply, her hair felt as if it was being pulled out at the roots, and then she dug pins in so hard they scratched her scalp.

The housekeeper was rough with all the girls, pushing them to get moving, thumping their backs, slapping the little scullery maid for not turning out sparkling dishes. And Perfy heard that the black girl in the laundry was getting a lacing.

It was Lady Bowen's fault, Perfy decided. The house was beautiful, a lovely two-storeyed mansion overlooking the river, built in the prettiest sandstone with graceful, covered verandahs on both floors at the front. The Countess liked it to be perfect inside and out. As a result, this terror of a housekeeper was let loose on the staff and, worse, was for ever being praised by the Countess for keeping the household running so smoothly. But Mrs Porter never dared bully the men who worked there, the butler and the silly-looking footmen who had to dress up in gaudy red, white and blue satin livery, with satin kneebreeches and white stockings. The girls and even the cook thought they looked stupid but that was typical of the Countess. She had designed the livery herself. She might be all sweetness and light to people out there, visiting the poor, but she made up for it when at home. This was her palace and at all times formality befitting royalty had to be respected. She never spoke to the staff; all communication was through Mrs Porter.

Perfy's time off was supposed to be Sunday afternoons but the house-keeper usually had other ideas. She would decide the floors needed a polish and Sunday, when the house was quiet, was the best time to do the down-stairs rooms. So Perfy and Anna, the other housemaid, would have to spend their spare time on their knees, scraping off old thick polish with small knives, in readiness for a new layer.

Perfy sometimes glimpsed Diamond outside but did not have a chance to talk to her until it was her turn to take the laundry down to the wash house, bundled into knotted sheets. Diamond, being black, didn't eat in the staff room, her meals were sent out to the laundry. Perfy thought that probably wasn't so bad really; at least she wasn't stuck under the eagle eye of Mrs Porter.

'How are you, Diamond?' she asked as she dumped the linen on the laundry floor.

'All right,' Diamond said, poking clothes into the steaming copper.

She was wearing a long grey calico shift, which looked terrible, but Perfy pretended not to notice. 'Where do you sleep?'

'Out here. They let me have the shed next to the wash house. It's not bad, I cleaned it up and put some curtains on the windows. Mrs Porter pulled them down but I put them up again so she took my books away from me. Have you got any books you can lend me? Any sort of books.'

'Yes, of course. I'll bring you some.'

The washerwoman came striding back into her laundry, sleeves rolled up, perspiration running from her neck to the low-cut bodice. 'Gawd, that bloody sun's a trial. Get that load out of the copper now, Mary, they should be done by now.'

'Her name's not Mary,' Perfy said.

'It is now,' the washerwoman retorted. 'Mrs Porter don't put up with any high-falutin nonsense from blacks, she's lucky to have a job. And it ain't your place down here, you get back up to the house and mind your own business.'

A few days later Anna told her that 'Mary' was outside and wanted to see her. Perfy went down through the kitchen to the back door where Diamond was waiting.

'This is for you,' Diamond said, handing her a neatly wrapped parcel. 'Mrs Beckman left it for you. I haven't had a chance to give it to you before this.'

'Thank you,' Perfy said, surprised. She opened the parcel and gasped in delight. 'Why . . . Diamond, it's beautiful!' Mrs Beckman had made her a superb cream silk blouse with a double lace collar and pearl buttons. 'Isn't it pretty?' she cried. 'I love it.'

Mrs Porter came stamping out of the kitchen. 'What's going on here?'

'Diamond brought me a present from Mrs Beckman,' Perfy said, showing her the blouse. 'Isn't it lovely?'

'Put it away!' Mrs Porter ordered. 'And her name is Mary. I won't tell you a second time.' She turned to Diamond. 'Where were you this afternoon?'

'I had to hand in the keys of Mrs Beckman's house.'

'Who gave you permission to leave the grounds?'

'It was my rest time. I was only away an hour.'

Suddenly Mrs Porter slapped Diamond across the face. 'Don't you cheek me, you wretch. And don't you ever leave the premises without my permission. I know what you black ingrates get up to.'

Perfy was stunned, not knowing what to do, or say, as the housekeeper raved on. Diamond stood straight, head high, her dark eyes burning with such rage Perfy wondered that Mrs Porter couldn't see it. She recalled Diamond saying she'd never been hit. Well, times had changed. She saw the tip of Diamond's tongue flick out and move along her top lip but, apart from that, she withstood the tirade without moving a muscle.

'What are you doing, still standing around?' Mrs Porter yelled at Perfy. 'Get back to work!'

Perfy took a deep breath. 'You've got no right to hit her,' she said.

It was the housekeeper's turn to be stunned. 'What did you say?'

'You heard me.'

'You bold brat! How dare you speak to me like that. I'll have your apology or you're fired. Right this minute!'

Perfy looked to Diamond who gave a slight nod. 'I'm sorry.' It nearly killed her to say it, but she managed to get the words out.

'I should think so. And for punishment you can scrub out the pantry on Sunday afternoon.'

Perfy wondered if she'd ever get any time off. Work, she had discovered, was ten times worse than school.

That same night there was a terrible row next door with old Mr Gaunt shouting his head off. And the language! Alice Middleton rushed to close the windows and then went back to her darning. 'Just as well your father's not home to hear all that.'

'What could he do?' Perfy asked, teasing.

'He could go in there and remind Willy Gaunt that there are ladies in this house.'

Perfy smiled. Old man Gaunt was always fighting with someone, and her father took no notice. This was just her mother's way of emphasising his status in the street.

'A better man never lived than your father,' she added defensively, 'and there's no need to pull a face even if I have said it before.'

Before? Perfy thought. Once a week at least, as if she were compelled to keep reminding everyone, to drown out the echoes of those convict days.

'You'll do well, my girl, if you find a man as good as your father.'

Perfy sighed. She agreed, she loved her father, but her mother overdid these lectures. 'Amy Campbell says she's going to marry a squatter.'

Alice sat up. 'Who?'

'She hasn't found one yet.'

Alice relaxed. 'Humpf! Silly girl. She should stick to her own class. Those gentlemen with all their money, they marry their own.'

Perfy supposed they did. She had seen the older squatters with their wives and daughters coming into town in their buggies, staying at the best hotels, strolling down Queen Street, noses in the air. But the young men! Oh my, they were a handsome lot! They'd come whooping past on their beautiful horses, hell bent on having a good time in the 'city'. And then there were the others, men from outback stations, heavily armed squatters leading their bands of followers down Queen Street, weary men, but still tall in the saddle, seemingly unaware that all eyes were on them, wondering who they were and how far they had travelled.

'Sometimes station people stay at Government House,' Perfy said.

'Well, of course they would. It's what I said, the moneyed class stick together,' Alice replied. 'What are they like?'

'They seem all right, but we're not allowed talk to them. I don't see much of them, we only do their rooms when they've gone out.'

The noise had stopped next door and Perfy went outside to sit on the back step. It was too hot to sit inside. Besides, if she stayed there she'd have to help with the darning which she hated.

Fruit bats were squabbling and screeching high in the old gum tree, wide wings flapping across the night sky like dark swooping sheets. Her mother was frightened of them but they were harmless and Perfy was fascinated by them. Years back they'd been mystified to find mangoes chewed through to the stones lying around their back yard, but eventually they had realised that the bats, or flying foxes, as other people called them, stole the mangoes from neighbouring trees and came back to their own tree to devour them.

There was a rustle in the bushes along the side fence and Perfy peered into the darkness, wondering if it was their cat. But the movement was heavier.

'Who's that?' she called, poised, ready to dash inside.

A man emerged from the shadows. 'It's all right, Perfy. It's only me.'

She recognised the voice before she saw him. 'Billy Kemp! What are you doing?'

He laughed. 'Hang on a minute.' He seemed to be searching for something. 'Ha! Here it is!'

Perfy stood up. 'What?'

'Eddie's swag.' He picked up a bundle and came over to her.

'What's it doing in our yard?'

'I threw it there. Eddie and me, we're off to the goldfields. The old man won't let Eddie go, he wants him to go back to sea, but after that last lot we've had the bloody sea. We mightn't be so lucky next time. There's sharks in that sea as big as horses.'

'It must have been terrible. You saved Eddie's life, they say.'

'Saved my own at the same time.' He hitched up the swag. 'I had to sneak this out of the house so the old man wouldn't twig we're off. Soon as Willy's asleep, Eddie'll nick out the front. Hey, listen, I'm sorry if I gave you a fright.'

tawny snake's head slid out, never dreaming that this time he was being hunted. Diamond grabbed him by the back of the neck and held him tight. He spat and cursed and dribbled his fangs but he was helpless, and as she moved silently towards the back of the house and an open window, she shook and shook him, making him mad enough to bite a log, and then she threw him inside.

When Perfy came to work the household was in uproar. Both the Governor and Lady Bowen had heard the shrieks during the night and they'd come rushing down. From next door Cook, too, had heard the screams and was first into Mrs Porter's room with a lantern. But when she realised that the housekeeper was screaming 'snake', she'd bounded out again in hysterics.

A footman on night watch was sent for the doctor. The Governor couldn't apply a tourniquet since the poor woman had been bitten on the neck, so Lady Bowen ordered shredded soap poultices. A guest raced to rouse the butler from his cot in the coach house and put him to searching, unwillingly, for the snake. Brandy was administered to the patient, the very best brandy, in the hopes it might be strong enough to ease the pain and hush her agonised screams, but all to no avail. Mrs Porter sank into a coma and by the time the doctor came galloping up the drive she had gone to her Maker.

'God rest her soul,' Cook said, relating all this drama to the other servants as they came on duty. 'A sainted woman she was, and don't let me hear none of you speak ill of the dead.'

The new housekeeper considered it a stroke of good fortune. Privately. To escape the embarrassment of being jilted by her fiancé of four years, she'd sailed for the colonies armed with an introduction to the Governor of Queensland, provided by a distant relative, and had come knocking at the door at just the right time. She was amazed at her pleasant, even luxurious, surroundings in this tin-pot town on the edge of nowhere and was charmed by the Countess who had her household running like a top. The staff were a cheerful lot, even the black girl, the first native she had ever met, who spoke well and said her name was Diamond.

'Do you think you'll like it here?' Cook asked her.

'Indeed, yes. Everyone is so kind.' And the Governor's aide-de-camp, a marine captain, was single.

PART THREE

1

The Buchanan brothers and their stockman rode into Sherwood Station, just one hundred miles north of Brisbane, their long journey nearly over. They'd covered nearly a thousand miles on their cattle drive but they'd taken it quietly, allowing the cattle to graze along the stock routes, and had made it to the stockyards with the loss of only a few steers and all the rest in tip-top condition.

All the way south they'd worried about getting their price. With seven hundred head, the yearly drive could make or break the station. Although Caravale was one of the best spreads in the north, the markets were meagre up their way so the cattlemen had to head for Brisbane. They considered themselves lucky. In their father's day, the drives had extended as far as Sydney Town or even Melbourne.

Darcy and Ben were determined to take nothing less than seven pounds a head. They worked out a route that would take them via the Gympie goldfields where they would offload as many head as they could and push the rest on to Brisbane. Seven pounds a head. What a joke! Butchers had fallen over themselves to buy their cattle, to feed all the mad diggers assembled in chaotic diggings that looked like a mess of human anthills. They'd sold the whole herd at ten pounds a head! The drive was over, right there at Gympie.

With their saddlebags stuffed with cash and gold, the stockmen now acting as armed escorts, the five-man team rode hard away from the desperate inhabitants of Gympie. They covered the fifty miles to Sherwood Station swiftly, stopping only to spell their horses at a clear stretch of the river where there was no chance of an ambush. The roads from the goldfields to capital cities were favourite haunts of bushrangers.

Jim Kendall welcomed the visitors. He and the late Teddy Buchanan had been mates for many years, and he was pleased to see the sons, knowing they'd worked hard to expand the station their father had pioneered. 'How are things at Caravale?' he asked.

'Couldn't be better,' Darcy said. 'The weather's behaving.'

'That's good. You're looking fit yourself, Darcy. Got some muscle on that lanky frame of yours now. And this is Ben, eh?' He shook hands with Ben. 'God Almighty, Ben. Last time I saw you, you were just a nipper.

Will you look at him? Solid as a mallee bull! Jesus, time gets away. How old are you now, Ben?'

'Twenty-two, sir.'

'So you would be, and that makes you twenty-five, Darcy. You married yet?'

Darcy laughed. 'No. Too busy. Anyway, who'd have me?'

'Whoa, don't say that to my wife. She'll have you snared in a flash. Especially when you're set to make a fortune.'

Darcy stared. 'What fortune?'

Jim just grinned, making them wait for his news. 'Let's see to your blokes first.'

'What's it to be?' Jim asked when the Caravale stockmen had been introduced and handed over to Sherwood Station hands. 'A rum or a shower?'

'Both,' Ben replied.

'Fair enough,' their host said and marched them round the back to the showers. Sherwood was one of the finest houses in the district and Mrs Kendall didn't take kindly to any of the men coming in from the trail dusty and dirty, even the boss. They dressed for dinner too, and since men like the Buchanans weren't expected to have formal gear in their swags, she kept a supply of dress clothes for their convenience.

'What's this fortune yarn?' Darcy wanted to know.

'Oh yes, that.' Jim seemed unconcerned. 'They've struck gold on the Cape River.'

'What?' Darcy's naked soaped body came crashing out of the shower room.

'It's a true fact. Right there on your doorstep, son. Only about a hundred miles from Caravale.'

'Shit! We've driven the herd all this way for nothing.'

'No fear, you haven't. You got your price. It'll take a while for the main body of prospectors to figure out how to get to the Cape and by that time you'll be home and hosed and ready for them.'

Darcy shook his head. 'I can't believe it.' He went back to his shower. 'We better get right on home,' he said to Ben.

'The hell we will. We can't do anything in the wet and you promised me we'd have a holiday in Brisbane. Everyone goes to town in January, why should we miss out?'

There were nine at dinner and Jim Kendall brought out champagne to celebrate the arrival of the Buchanan lads. Katherine Kendall had been very fond of Teddy. He had been both a fine bushman and an asset in the drawing room, always well-mannered and cheerful, and could hold his liquor. It was sad that he had died so young. Darcy had been only fourteen then, and Ben . . . eleven, she supposed. A shame. But Cornelia Buchanan had hung on and, as everyone said, young Darcy was a tower of strength, he worked like a trojan and, more importantly, seemed to know what he was doing.

Katherine had never met Cornelia, but Jim and his friends who had been up to those northern stations spoke highly of her. A Scottish woman, they said, with plenty of pluck. Katherine had great admiration for women who had the courage to go with their husbands to open up isolated stations, weathering all sorts of setbacks, not the least marauding blacks, and she had often written to invite Mrs Buchanan to visit Sherwood but she had never accepted. Katherine understood. It was a long way and, as far as she could ascertain, Cornelia never even came down to Brisbane these days.

Katherine looked about her table. Besides the Buchanan boys, there was Ginger Butterfield from BliBli Station, and John-Henry Champion, the local Member of Parliament, who seemed to her to be permanently tipsy; and then her own family, daughter Fiona and her husband Jack, and their younger daughter Kitty who was still single. Katherine noticed that Kitty was taking a smiling interest in Darcy. That was a relief; she'd been nursing a crush on Ginger but unfortunately Ginger was still fond of Fiona. He'd been devastated when Fiona had announced her engagement to Jack, the Sherwood station manager.

Katherine sighed. She and Jim hadn't been too impressed either, they'd have preferred Ginger as a son-in-law, an only son and heir to the large Butterfield holdings. Girls these days! They never listened to good advice. But Darcy was an interesting prospect, tall and handsome, and a bit shy. Nothing wrong with that. She thought his brother Ben was rather a swaggerer, a little too self-important for his age.

The maid brought in the saddle of beef and Jim stood up to carve. 'This looks good. Pass the plates, Kitty. And have some wine, you boys. I can recommend the claret.' He whisked the carving knife against the matching ivory-handled steel with a flourish. It didn't improve the cutting edge but made a pleasing impression.

'It's Kitty's birthday soon, Darcy. It would be nice if you and Ben could stay awhile on your return journey and join in the celebrations,' Katherine said.

'Thank you, Mrs Kendall,' Darcy replied, 'but we plan to go home by ship. We'll sail to Bowen and get on home from there.'

'What a pity,' Katherine said.

'And I'm a bit worried about Mother now. Those diggers we saw at Gympie were a fierce-looking lot, we wouldn't want any of them hanging about the station.'

Ben laughed. 'The manager's still there. And I wouldn't worry about Ma. Any of those diggers come snooping around the homestead, Ma's just as likely to put a bullet in them.'

Kitty's eyes sparkled. 'I heard your mother did shoot a man once. Is that right?'

'Kitty!' Katherine said sharply, but Ben didn't seem to mind.

'She sure did,' he said. 'We were only little. Dad was out in the bush and this stockman went berserk, crashed into the house, tried to attack Ma and she shot him dead in his tracks. Right in our front hallway.'

'Oh dear,' Katherine murmured. 'How awful.' These stories were commonplace in the west, the women were always armed, they had to be, but she didn't appreciate hearing about bloodshed at the dinner table.

Darcy and Ben stayed only two days at Sherwood before heading on to Brisbane. Jim Kendall and Ginger and half a dozen Sherwood stockmen went with them. Darcy was glad of the company; he wouldn't relax until the cash was safely deposited in the bank.

'Where are you staying in town?' Ginger asked him.

'At the best pub I can find.'

'That'd be the Victoria,' Ginger said. 'But why don't you come with me? I'm staying at Government House. It's quiet at this time of the year with the festive season behind them. I'm sure Lady Bowen won't mind, she's a wonderful woman.'

'No thanks,' Darcy said. 'I'd rather stop at a pub and please myself what I do.'

'You speak for yourself,' Ben said. 'I'd like an invite to Government House, Ginger. Can you really swing it?'

'Sure I can. The Governor and his team often rest up at BliBli when he's out on his rounds. These things are reciprocal, old chap, remember that. One day he might need your hospitality at Caravale.'

Ben nudged his horse closer to Darcy's mount. 'Don't go knocking back an invitation like that,' he said quietly. 'It's not going to cost us anything and it is Government House, after all . . .'

'You mean all the right people?' Darcy laughed.

'What's wrong with that?'

'Nothing, I suppose, but it'd be too bloody formal.'

'Kitty Kendall often stays there,' Ben said with a sly grin.

'What's that got to do with it?'

'Are you blind, Darc? She's got eyes for you! She'd like to know you're in the Governor's set too.'

'She's a nice girl, Kitty, but too swell. I wouldn't take a girl like that up to Caravale.'

'What's wrong with Caravale? We've got a real nice homestead. Any woman would be proud to live there.'

'But girls like Kitty are society types. They might have been brought up on stations but they're used to other women around.'

'That's bloody rot,' Ben argued. 'Kitty's a real catch, you fool. Ma'd be pleased.'

Darcy turned in the saddle to stare at his young brother as if he'd just seen him for the first time. 'Ma? You're joking! Ma's not going to like it if we bring home a duchess.'

Ben grinned. 'Yeah, well, sooner or later she's going to have to put up with it. And I reckon you're wrong. She'd be impressed by Kitty.'

'Then you marry Kitty. Me, I'll find a nice plain girl one day.'

Ginger dropped back. 'You looking for a wife, Darcy?'

'Yeah,' Ben told him. 'He wants an ugly one.'

'I didn't say that,' Darcy scowled, but Ginger was amused.

'You won't have any trouble there, Darcy. Plenty of ugly ones in Brisbane would jump at the chance to marry a rich young squatter.'

Darcy couldn't be bothered arguing with them. He lit a smoke and rode on alone, cantering comfortably within sight of the lead riders. It was difficult to explain. He knew they had to keep up their standard of living on the outback stations, and that was fine, but he didn't go in for all this stuffed-shirt business, station people dressed to kill every night as if they were all off to the opera. A man should respect his home, fair enough, fresh-washed and clean clothes when he came in of a night made a man feel better anyway, but Darcy could do without the frills. In this climate, and it was even hotter in the north, stiff shirts and tight ties and dinner jackets were a punishment he had no intention of inflicting on himself. Now Ben, he liked that sort of thing. Darcy decided they'd have to build another house on Caravale. There was no shortage of space. He'd build one for himself in the hills overlooking the river, where he could live as he liked and Ben, with his wife eventually, could make Caravale as formal as he liked. Then he laughed, wondering how Ben would go about turning their lanky black housegirls into prissy maids, decked out in frilly aprons and white gloves. The north was another world and always would be, and the sooner Ben woke up to that the better.

As they turned on to the Brisbane road, the rain was teeming down. Good rain. He hoped Caravale was getting its share. The men around him looked like grey ghosts in their oilcloth cloaks and dripping, drooping hats. Most of the men wore what they called American felt hats, good wide hats for the sun but they weren't holding up as well as his home-made leather in this rain. So much for fashion.

Brisbane was a shock. Darcy hadn't been to town for four years – they usually sent drovers down with their herds – and he hardly recognised the place, it had grown so. There were hundreds of people in the muddy streets, even in this weather, spilling out of the pubs and lounging under awnings, grinding carts through the rain. And the noise! Pianos jangled on the night air, struggling to be heard over the shouts and raucous laughter that emanated from well-lit pubs and taverns, and wild-looking women called out to them from high verandahs.

'Jesus!' Darcy said. 'What a racket! What's going on?'

'Gold,' Ginger said as they slowed their horses to a walk to avoid trampling on drunks staggering in their path, waving bottles at them. 'Gympie gold. The town's packed with diggers these days. The smart ones don't hang about. The rest turn up with their gold, blow the lot on women and booze, and then have to get back to the diggings and start again.'

'I've never seen anything like it,' Darcy said, staring around. 'A man would think it was New Year's Eve.'

'It is to them,' Ginger laughed. 'Every night. Brisbane's a boom town now. You'd better come with us, Darcy. You'll never find a bed in town.'

'No, I'll be all right. You take Ben with you. And our cash. I reckon it'd be safer at Government House than anywhere near this lot.'

Now that it had come to the point, Ben was unsure of himself. 'I can't go to Government House in these duds, Ginger.'

'Yes, you can. I'll explain to Lady Bowen. We'll fit you out with some decent clothes in the morning. There's the Victoria Hotel, Darcy. I don't like your chances.'

Neither did Darcy as he stared at the big two-storeyed building and the crowds lining the street outside. 'I'll be all right,' he said again. 'I'll meet you at the bank tomorrow, Ben. Be there at ten.'

He rode down a lane to the stables at the back of the hotel and with the aid of a pound note managed to find shelter for his horse. 'What's the boss's name?' he asked the stable hand.

'Brian Flynn.'

Darcy picked up his swag, hung his rifle over his shoulder and headed for the back door of the hotel. He stuck his head into the kitchen. 'Where can I find Mr Flynn?'

The kitchen was big. And busy. Half a dozen women were working furiously serving meals on to a sea of white plates, while in the background others were up to their elbows in the sinks, clanking plates and pots and pans on to the benches, and waitresses dashed in and out with large trays. Finally one woman looked up and laughed. 'Behind you!'

'I told you girls to keep this back door locked.' A burly, balding man shoved past Darcy and locked the door himself. 'In or out?' he said.

'In,' Darcy replied quickly. 'Are you Mr Flynn?'

'Yeah. And I don't have firearms in my hotel.'

Darcy hitched his rifle again. 'What am I supposed to do with it? Leave it on my bloody horse?'

'I don't care what you do with it. Just don't bring it in here.'

'Can I leave it in your office then?'

'Christ Almighty, it's not a bloody cloakroom.' Then he relented. 'Oh, all right. Give it to me. You can pick it up in the morning. The bar's that way.'

'I'd rather get a room first,' Darcy said.

'You and a hundred others,' Flynn replied, giving Darcy the once-over and guessing his occupation. 'Go on down to the Wattle boarding house.

The woman there, she doesn't like diggers, she takes in cowboys.'

'I can pay,' Darcy said but Flynn shook his head.

'Who can't these days?'

Darcy stood his ground. 'I had my heart set on staying here. They told me this was the best hotel in town. I've come a helluva long way.'

'That's your bad luck, son. Look, I'll buy you a drink, that's the best I can do. How far have you come anyway?'

'Well, I'd say more than a thousand miles as the crow flies, from the north.'

'Holy hell!' Flynn said. 'Rugged country up there. Where in the north?'

'Caravale Station,' Darcy told him. At least he'd got the hotel-keeper interested.

'Caravale? Wasn't that Teddy Buchanan's property?'

'That's right, I'm his son. Darcy.'

Flynn stood back and stared at him. 'Well, blow me down! Teddy's son. I thought there was somethin' familiar about you. I been tryin' to place you, lad. Teddy's son, eh? He was a mate of mine in the old days, God rest his soul. Well, I suppose if I don't find you a room he'll come back and haunt me.'

They met at the bank. Darcy had the fiercest grog headache he'd ever suffered, made worse by the steamy heat.

'Did you get a room in a hotel?' Ben asked.

'Yes. The Victoria.'

'Good Lord,' Ginger said. 'How did you manage that?'

'Maybe they liked my looks,' he said. 'And how was the Countess?'

'I didn't meet her,' Ben told him. 'She's staying with friends by the seaside.'

'Don't blame her,' Darcy said. 'God knows what possessed them to build this town in a valley where you can't get a whiff of a breeze.'

'You're looking a bit pale on it, old chap,' Ginger laughed. 'Heavy night?'

'Yes, as far as I can recall,' Darcy said. 'Let's get this business over.' They banked the money and then made for Campbell's general store which had been extended into several departments since Darcy's last visit.

'First the clothes,' Ben said.

Guided by Ginger, the Buchanans bought their 'city' clothes as well as working duds and boots for home wear.

'Now that we've finished our chores,' Ginger said, 'we'll go up to my club and have a drink. They serve excellent meals there too.'

'You go on,' Darcy said. 'I've got the rest of the stuff to order yet.' He went in search of Jock Campbell who had been handling the Caravale supplies for years.

'Pleased to see you, Darcy,' Jock said. 'Is your mother well?'

'Yes, thank you.' Darcy dug in a pocket. 'Here's her shopping list, a hefty lot this time. She wants bed linen and towels and mosquito nets and God knows what else, and I've made out another list of station requirements. We need tools as well as food. Do you still carry those lines?'

Jock nodded. 'Aye, lad, I'll see to it, but I'm short-handed, most of my staff have gone rushing off to the diggings. Could you come back Monday?'

Darcy shook his head. 'There's a ship leaving for Bowen tomorrow and I wanted to get the whole order sent together. The sooner I get it away, the sooner it'll get out to the station. I've arranged for a carrier with a horse team to watch out for it in Bowen.'

'I see. Well, leave it with me. Come back in the morning and we'll go through it then and see if there's anything else you need. I've got a lot of new goods in stock your mother might like, and I can take the time to show you.'

'But tomorrow's Sunday.'

'All the better. We won't be interrupted, we can take our time. I wouldn't want to let down my far-country customers.'

'That's good of you, Mr Campbell.'

'No trouble. And what about you, Darcy? Not married yet by the sound of things.'

'If I had a wife she'd be doing the shopping, not me,' Darcy laughed. 'I'll see you in the morning then.'

They met old friends and new at Ginger's club, headquarters of the Cattleman's Association, and then went off to the races, making a day of it.

And once again Darcy awoke at the Victoria Hotel feeling as if his head had been tramped on by steers, and then he groaned. Jock Campbell! He had to get down to that store and see to the station orders. If he had any sense he'd get on the ship and go with them; it didn't seem much of a holiday if he was going to wake up crook every morning.

2

Hester Campbell ducked and dived in and out of the kitchen to the dining room where Amy was setting the table, jingling the silver and the crockery in a chorus of excitement. 'Is that silver clean? Make certain the table-cloth's straight. Put the lilies in the centre. I wish we had some decent flowers. Heavens, girl, what are you doing? The soup spoons go on the outside. How many times do I have to tell you? That father of yours inviting a visitor to eat with us at the last minute! And what will he think of us? If I'd known, I'd have had a proper Sunday dinner. Us only just back from kirk, what else can I do? I told him we were only having cold collations, and he said Mr Buchanan won't mind. What would Jock know? Go and get me more tomatoes. No, I'll slice these thin. You slice the onions. And don't take any pork, tell your brother, too. There's just enough for the men, it will have to do with the cold corned beef. Mr Buchanan will think we're a poor lot. Those squatters, they probably have fine Sunday dinners with maids to serve them. Do they drink wine for lunch? Luncheon they call it, I hear. Oh Lordy Lord, the cake's burning . . .'

Her mother made her nervous. Amy, too, was sorry that they didn't have more notice so that they could put on a real meal to impress Darcy Buchanan, but at least he would be here. In the house. Amy had seen him in the store with his brother and Ginger Butterfield, who was a good catch too, all of them eligible bachelors from the bush, but Darcy was the best looking. Taller, more manly somehow than the others. Imagine Dad having the sense to invite Darcy today! A good chance to meet a fine gentleman socially. And a wealthy one at that.

Amy had been helping in the store for as long as she could remember. She'd tried to get outside jobs but there was nothing decent offering. She knew all the customers, especially the station people. Or rather she knew of them, since there were quite a few who rarely came to town, they just sent lists or shopped by catalogue. Caravale Station had been on their books for years, and they were always good payers. Amy knew that a lot of squatters and graziers lived like kings and expected to be treated like kings when it came to paying bills. 'They can't pay in the bad seasons and they won't pay in the good,' her father always said. He'd learned never to fill a second order if the first one hadn't been paid for and laughed when they took their business elsewhere. 'Let someone else carry them.'

Darcy Buchanan! Wait till her friends heard! They'd be positively green! Amy was wearing a new dress, from the shop, a beige taffeta with brown grosgrain piping on the collar and cuffs, and a tight-fitting embroidered bodice in the Basque mode. Amy would have preferred the lighter, blue muslin in this humid weather but her mother said the taffeta was more refined.

'You all dressed up to catch a beau?' Her young brother, Ross, could be relied on to say something stupid like that.

'Mum, make him shut up! Does he have to eat with us? Send him next door.'

Hester, too, had dressed for the occasion in her dark brown Sunday suit and she had a tea towel temporarily tucked round her neck to sop up the perspiration as she leaned over the oven to rescue a tray of scones. 'You behave yourself, Ross, or I'll have your father take the belt to you.'

'I'm not allowed speak in this place. I just wanted to know is she going to marry the bloke from the bush.'

'Go and put on a clean shirt,' Hester told him. 'You're not coming to table like that. And clean your fingernails!'

'Mum,' Amy stood well back while her mother whipped the cream, 'have you ever met Mrs Buchanan?'

'No. Your father met her years ago but she doesn't come to town any more. He says she's a very grand lady, and her husband was a fine man, very popular in Brisbane. Get me the good strawberry jam out of the pantry. And you watch your manners today. If you marry a man like Darcy Buchanan you'll be stepping straight into society. You'll never have to pinch and struggle like your father and I did . . .' She was still talking as Amy wandered away to study herself in the hallstand mirror. Her mother had taken pains to swirl her hair up over a 'mouse', as she called it, which made her hairstyle look full and luxuriant. She would keep it that way; she was seventeen, after all, and suddenly, on this important day, she thought she really did look ladylike.

There was no getting out of it. Jock Campbell had insisted that he stay for lunch and Darcy couldn't think of an excuse. He had no plans for the day and was no good at making up convincing lies. 'The least I can do, after making you come down here on Sunday,' Jock said as the last of the Caravale orders of equipment and supplies were loaded aboard a lorry to be delivered to the *Samson* at the wharves.

Darcy decided to make the best of it. 'If I won't be in the way, thank you.'

'You'll not be in the way, lad. I like to look after my good customers.'

He led Darcy inside and introduced him to Amy, whom he had already met in the shop, and the boy, Ross, and his wife, who fussed around telling them to sit right down.

'I thought Darcy and I might have a cold ale first,' Jock said with an inquiring glance at Darcy who nodded in appreciation. He needed a drink.

'Nothing to stop you drinking it at the table,' Mrs Campbell told them. 'I'm sorry, Mr Buchanan, it's catch as catch can today, that Jock, he caught me off guard, we were only having a cold luncheon.'

'That's fine,' Darcy said. He glanced at the table. It was quite a spread, with platters of cold meat, sliced tomatoes set on beds of shredded lettuce topped with onion rings and radishes and things, plenty of preserves, bread and butter, and hot scones. 'It looks pretty good to me.'

Jock poured the beer in tall glasses. It was ice cold and Darcy felt refreshed. He was going to enjoy this meal. He spotted a sponge cake on the sideboard, oozing with cream, and smiled. He loved cream cake. His favourite.

'I'll get the soup,' Hester Campbell said. 'At least that's hot. A good Scotch broth.'

Amy turned in her chair uncertainly but her mother waved her back. 'You stay there, dear. There's only five of us, I can serve.'

She delivered the soup to the table and was just about to sit down at her end when there was a knock at the door. She went to investigate.

'Why, Perfy,' she said. 'What are you doing here? We haven't seen you for ages.'

'I know,' came the reply. 'I always seem to get caught up on Sunday afternoons, my only time off. Is Amy home?'

'Yes.' Darcy heard Mrs Campbell's tone and wondered why this visitor didn't seem too welcome.

'Can I see her?'

A silence. The room seemed poised, waiting for the reply. Ross filled the gap. 'She's in here, Perfy,' he called.

The girl walked into the dining room and then halted, embarrassed. 'Oh, I'm sorry. I didn't know you had visitors. A visitor, I mean.'

Darcy stood but Jock remained stonily seated at the head of the table while Hester manoeuvred round the newcomer as if to touch her would cause friction, and yet it was obvious the girl was accustomed to calling here informally.

'How're you doing, Perfy?' Ross said with all the cheerfulness of a fourteen-year-old oblivious of tension.

'Good, thanks, Ross,' she replied. 'Look, I won't stay. I'll come back later.'

Ross turned to Amy with a wicked grin on his face. 'Aren't you going to invite her to stay for lunch? She stays other times.'

Amy blushed. 'Of course I am. Come and sit down, Perfy.'

'I'll set another place, here, next to Mr Buchanan,' Hester said through thin, pursed lips.

69

Ross pulled a chair forward for her while Jock made the introductions. 'This is Mr Buchanan, a business associate of mine. Miss Perfy Middleton.'

'I am intruding,' Perfy apologised. 'Maybe I should go . . .'

'Sit down,' Hester instructed. 'Our soup is getting cold.'

Darcy had been gazing at Perfy since she walked in the door. Time, in a rare act of kindness, had held her in his gaze while the Campbells procrastinated; had allowed him to feel the radiance of her as he took in the sweet face, the long honey-coloured hair that hung frothily from a single blue ribbon at the back, and her eyes . . . so deep blue, like sapphires. Incredible!

And now she was sitting beside him and he had forgotten her name. How could he forget her name? He must be going mad. Miserably he sat listening to their small talk as the meal progressed. She was a girlfriend of Amy's. They'd been to school together. Hester questioned him about the station. Jock weighed up the good and evil of gold rushes. Hester served tea with the cake and as he reached for the sugar Darcy tipped over the bowl. Hester leapt up and rushed around with a brush and a small brass shovel, tut-tutting and making such a to-do over it, Darcy murmured, 'I don't think it'll stain,' and heard a giggle beside him.

Jock did most of the talking, moving on to sing the praises of Scotland, which interested Darcy. His mother came from Scotland; she'd never say where, and she rarely mentioned the place. She said it was as cold as a frog's bum and all Scots were mean-minded wowsers. Darcy smiled, thinking about that. From his own observations, Scots changed a lot when they got out here. Most of the Scotsmen he'd met were prodigious whisky drinkers.

Young Ross Campbell had heard about the Highlands and the heather many times before. He wriggled in his chair for a while and then, interrupting his father, abruptly changed the subject. 'How's the Governor, Perfy?' Darcy was relieved. At least he now had her Christian name.

'He's in good health as far as I know,' she replied.

'Perfy works at Government House,' Hester said, emphasising 'works' so that their guest didn't get the wrong impression. 'She's a housemaid.'

'Then you must have met my brother, Ben. He's staying there.' At least he could turn and address her now.

She blinked, recalling. 'Mr Buchanan. Of course! He's sharing a room with Mr Butterfield. Is he your brother?'

'Yes.'

'Oh. Well, I haven't actually met him. We're not allowed to speak to the guests, but I've seen him around.'

Hester pulled the conversation back. 'Where are you staying, Darcy?'

'At the Victoria Hotel, Mrs Campbell.'

'By the way, Mr Campbell,' Perfy said, 'they're running low on linen at

Government House and talking about buying more. You ought to hop in and have a word with the housekeeper.'

'Is that right? Well, I might just happen to drop by tomorrow. I've got a fine supply of the best Manchester. She'll not do better than my prices.'

'And she likes chocolates,' Perfy told him.

Jock laughed. Perfy's intrusion was forgiven as his business interests took precedence.

'More tea, Darcy?' Amy asked.

'No, thank you, Amy. My word, I did enjoy that cake.'

'Amy made it,' Hester crowed, and Darcy squashed a grin as Ross raised his eyebrows in a comic query, giving the lie to that claim. 'Would you like some more?'

'No, thanks. I really must be going now. It was the best lunch I've had in ages.'

Darcy hoped that Perfy (what a strange name) would choose to leave also, so that he could walk her home, but no such luck.

Disappointed, he walked across town to Government House, sat on a nearby fence and watched as a number of coaches pulled away. Then he joined Ginger and Ben on the front porch. 'Looks as if there's been a party here today,' he said.

'The Governor had twenty for luncheon,' Ginger told him. 'Excellent fare. See what you're missing.'

'I had to get our supplies organised,' Darcy said. 'I wanted to get that over and done with. Where's the boss?'

'Taking a siesta,' Ben said. 'There's another luncheon here tomorrow, to introduce country visitors to the Premier. You ought to turn up this time. One should get to know the right people.'

'That's a good idea,' Darcy said.

Ben, expecting an argument, was taken aback. 'You'll come?'

'Wouldn't miss it for the world,' his brother replied.

Darcy cursed his luck at having to sit through the splendid luncheon next to a twirp like Clive Jenkins from Southbend Station which bordered Caravale. He and Ben were great mates and they were always up to some sort of tomfoolery. Many a time Darcy had booted Clive off home after the pair had caused ructions, annoying the station hands and harassing the blacks with their stupid jokes. In addition, he'd been placed with his back to the wide doorway which meant he had to keep craning round to see if he could catch a glimpse of Perfy if she happened to walk by. He studied each waitress, knowing Perfy worked as a housemaid but hoping she might have been roped in to assist in the dining room. Stranger things had happened, he told himself. But obviously not today.

The luncheon was a gentlemen-only affair. The table was scattered with politicians, eagerly vote-snaring and plying their opinions in this rare

71

opportunity to bend the ears of station owners who carried a fair bit of clout in their districts.

'Knew your father,' the worthy on the other side of Darcy said.

'So I believe, sir.' This was the cantankerous Charles Lilley, Member for Fortitude Valley, hence known as Lilley of the Valley.

'I wanted a word with you, Mr Buchanan,' Lilley said. 'Herbert's a fair Premier, for our first, but he can't seem to get things done. Too slow for my liking. I'll be Premier one of these days, you mark my words, and I need younger blood in the House. There'll be a new electorate of Bowen any day now, and you'd be just the man for the job.'

'Not me, Mr Lilley. I've got my hands full at Caravale.'

Clive had been listening to the conversation. 'You'll never get Darcy off the land, Mr Lilley, but I reckon Ben would be interested.'

'Who's Ben?'

'My brother,' Darcy told him. 'He's sitting over there with Ginger Butterfield.'

'I'll have a talk with him,' Lilley said, and Darcy was pleased. Ben was young for that sort of job and knew nothing about politics, but who did? This was the first Parliament in Queensland and they were all new at the game. Ben was beginning to chafe at having to take orders from his elder brother. Politics would give him something else to think about and make him more accountable. He could be bloody irresponsible at times. Besides, Ben would jump at the chance to get to Brisbane more often, mixing in with his precious society mob. Yes, Darcy thought, the Buchanans can afford a politician. I'll get the Kennedys to give him a shove in the right direction.

Darcy had never known lunch to go on so long. Finally, at four fifteen, they adjourned to the cool of the east verandah where sissy-looking footmen proffered port and cigars. Darcy couldn't believe grown men would let themselves be rigged out like that, and said so.

'Shut up, Darcy,' Ben whispered. 'Do you want people to think you're a country bumpkin? And listen, I've got some real news. Lilley's prepared to nominate me for the seat of Bowen. I'm going to be a politician.'

'Or an alcoholic, if you have to turn up at too many of these shows.'

'Ah, give over! These people are important, and we have to make a good impression. It won't kill you to walk around and talk to a few of Lilley's friends on my behalf.'

Darcy did as he was asked, moving along the verandah making small talk with acquaintances, old and new, until he came to the Governor, where he paid his respects, thanked him for the excellent lunch, and slipped away, unnoticed.

He tramped down the lane at the side of Government House, found the tradesmen's entrance and marched across the yard. There was a black girl taking washing off the line so he strode over to her. 'Excuse me, I'm looking for a lass called Perfy. Do you know her?'

72

The black girl turned and smiled. 'Yes, she works here.'

'What's her name,' he asked. 'I only know her as Perfy.'

'Middleton. Miss Perfy Middleton. But you can't see her now, she's working and they don't allow callers.'

'What time does she get off?'

'Six, usually.'

'Six? That's not long. I'll wait. Can you tell her Darcy Buchanan is waiting for her?'

'Sure. Where will you wait?'

'In the lane.'

He settled himself under a tree near the gate and lit a smoke, thinking of that black girl. He supposed if they had fancy footmen then he shouldn't be surprised at coming across a black gin who calmly addressed him as an equal and who spoke English without a trace of pidgin. If anything, he ruminated, she had a slight German accent. He could do with a long, long drink of cold water after all that wine, but didn't want to leave his post in case Perfy Middleton slipped away on him. Miss Middleton. He hoped she wouldn't mind his turning up like this, but he had to see her again, to talk to her. Then he began to worry. What would he talk about?

She didn't mind his being there; she seemed more dismayed at being found in her work clothes, a black skirt and white blouse. For the street, she'd added a wide straw hat with a red ribbon.

'You look wonderful,' he assured her, 'so nice and cool, while I've been sweating away in these dress-up clothes, waistcoat and all.'

'Then take your coat off.'

He was tempted but decided against it. 'I can't very well escort a lady in my shirtsleeves.'

She laughed. 'Where do you think you're escorting me?'

'Where would you like to go?'

'Home. I'm tired.'

'Righto, home it is. You lead the way.'

'It's cooler to go through the gardens,' she said, 'if you don't mind, Mr Buchanan.'

'Call me Darcy. And why are you called Perfy?'

'It's short for Perfection. My doting parents saw the name in a newspaper and pinned it on their baby.'

'I like it. The name suits you.'

'Everyone says that.' They turned into the street and she looked up at him with a tiny wink. 'They can hardly say it doesn't, now can they?' She took his arm as they picked their way across the muddy, churned roadway, making for the gardens. 'I knew you were in there,' she said. 'I heard them saying in the kitchen that Mr Buchanan's brother was there. I tried to swap jobs with one of the waitresses but she wouldn't be in it.'

'Why would you want to do that?' There was a light challenge in his voice.

'Oh, I don't know. So I could poke you in the back perhaps. Or watch you spill the sugar.'

Darcy burst out laughing. 'You knew I would come looking for you?'

'I hoped you would.'

He loved her. He loved this guileless person who looked him straight in the eye when she spoke. No simpering pretence about her. And she made him laugh. And God she was beautiful, even with that lovely hair hidden, plaited under the hat. 'How long have you been working at Government House?' he asked.

'A couple of years.'

'And do you like working there?'

'Not particularly.'

'Why not?'

'Would you like to work as a housemaid seven days a week?'

He grinned. 'I don't think they'd have me. But I thought . . . with girls . . . I mean it's a nice place to work.'

'It's boring,' she said. 'And housemaids in hotels get paid more than us. They're so lousy at Government House. They think it's a privilege to work for them.'

'I thought people like that would be free with their money.'

'Our money,' she corrected.

'What?'

Perfy stopped. 'Darcy Buchanan! Surely you don't think Their Excellencies are using their own money to run a place like that and entertain in grand style.'

'No, I suppose not. But then again, Perfy, the Governor of the state has to keep up a good front.' She was standing so close to him, he wished he had the courage to kiss her, but the moment passed.

'Well, it sickens me,' she said. 'The poverty in this town is frightful, immigrants and gold diggers flat broke, stranded here, families penniless. The gold rush has made everything in the town so expensive, too, and yet they live like kings, serving great banquets to the wealthy.'

'They're only doing what's expected of them. They wouldn't get far if they used "our" money to turn Government House into a free-for-all soup kitchen.'

'You're laughing at me!' She strode away from him but he caught up.

'No, I'm not.'

'Oh, what's the use,' she said. 'What would you know? You squatters, you've no idea what people really have to put up with.'

Darcy thought about the agony of riding through a parched landscape of dead and dying cattle, of having to shoot the poor beasts to put them out of their misery, of having to dig huge trenches to bury hundreds of cattle, burying years of work in soil you could sharpen an axe on. 'No one's free of troubles, Perfy,' he said. 'You give the impression of being such a cheerful person and yet now you seem so unhappy. What's wrong?'

She walked over to a park bench. 'I don't know. I think that place just gets on my nerves! I don't want to go home yet, can we sit here awhile?'

'Sure.' He joined her, his long legs stretched out, but made no attempt to talk. Her acceptance of his presence was important. This quiet time with her in the lush green of the gardens was significant. It reminded him of that time when a wild horse is finally quiet and will allow an approach. When you can reach out and stroke without getting your head kicked in.

Eventually, he took her hand, gently. 'Tell you what,' he said. 'One day I'll get you a fine white horse and you can ride like the wind. That'll make you feel better.'

She giggled. 'Yes, a white charger with a mask on and all the trimmings, like the knights used to have. Except for the armour, it's too hot for that.'

'Done,' he said.

'You promise?'

'Promise.'

'Oh damn.' Perfy said. 'It's starting to rain again. I'm sick of the rain.'

He took his coat off and put it over her shoulders. 'My dear girl, if we're going to be friends, you can complain about the Governor but never about the rain. Let's go.'

Brisbane Town now seemed alive with good humour. The drumming of rain on tin and shingle beat a happy note; men and women ran, laughing, for shelter, horses shook and whinnied their pleasure, and sounds of merriment came from behind steamed-up windows.

Darcy bathed and dressed with care. He'd spent most of the day at the stockyards talking to other cattlemen and listening around, and had examined the sale stock with care. As a result he'd bought a prize bull and a good strain of horses for stud, strong-looking animals with intelligent eyes. He was exceptionally pleased to have found them, and had handed them over to the Caravale stockmen to take home, warning his men to guard them carefully all the way. Not that the warning was necessary, they were reliable men, and would have the sense to join up with other parties travelling north.

It was time to meet Perfy again, so he went down the street and hired a small carriage and driver. He could hardly walk her across town in the teeming rain.

When she came out of the gate he was waiting for her with an umbrella and rushed her down the lane to the carriage.

'Darcy, this is so thoughtful of you,' she said as they climbed in. 'I thought we'd get drenched. But tell me. If your brother is staying at Government House, why aren't you?'

He tapped the window for the driver to set off. 'Well now, let me see. Maybe I thought the place would get on my nerves.'

Perfy sat back and laughed. 'You're a tease.'

75

'Since we've got the carriage I thought we might go for a drive. I haven't seen Brisbane for years. Do you mind?'

'Not at all, it's fun.' She settled back and Darcy wished it was a cold day instead of this clammy heat, so that he could sit closer, even put an arm round her. Romancing a girl was one thing, but when you really meant it there was an element of terror in the proceedings. He pretended to be viewing the town as the horses trotted up George Street, but in fact he was trying to summon his courage for a serious conversation here. Maybe he should put it off for another day. But this was an ideally private place to propose. Just thinking the word made him nervous. What if he offended her? Oh what the hell, he decided, he had something to say and he might as well get it over with. 'Perfy, can I ask you something?'

'Yes. What?'

'Well, I'll only be in town a few weeks and then I have to go back to the station. To Caravale. And God knows when I'll get back here again. So . . . I'd like us to be friends.' Coward, he'd pulled up in the straight!

'I thought we were already friends.'

'Good. That's settled. But I'm thinking further ahead. I'd be honoured if you'd consider marrying me.'

That surprised her. The blue eyes stared at him. 'It's a bit sudden. You hardly know me.'

'That's true. I'm sorry. I hope I haven't embarrassed you.' And then he shook his head. 'No. I'm saying one thing and meaning another. The truth is I'm in love with you and I don't want to leave here without you.'

She smoothed her skirt and studied her hands. 'You are making it awkward, Darcy. A young lady should say "I'll consider it" and eventually give you a reply, but by that time you'll be on your way home.'

'That's right. This is a special case.'

'Yes, it is.' She moved closer to him. 'You wouldn't really go without me, would you?'

For a second that didn't sink in but then he laughed. 'Not a chance,' and he kissed her.

The world was a marvellous place that Tuesday evening as the lovers made their plans and the carriage trotted through the valley and out along Breakfast Creek until the road came to an end.

The air was misty, a legacy of the rain that had finally allowed some respite. An irreverent patch of pearly green peeped from a break in the clouds over the mountains, like a child's face, at once naughty and innocent, popping out, having no place in the serious drama of troubled skies. Dark ominous storm clouds soon trundled forward like a sluggish curtain to obliterate the gaffe.

3

To say her parents were surprised was an understatement. When Perfy told them she had decided to marry a man she had only known a day or so, a fellow they had never even heard of, let alone met, they reacted with a complexity of emotions: anger, disbelief, bewilderment, worry, resentment, which developed into the inevitable family argument. Perfy decided she might as well tell them the rest: the wedding would take place in a few weeks, as soon as Darcy could arrange it.

'What will people say?' Alice demanded of her. 'They'll think it's a shotgun wedding!'

'How can it be a shotgun wedding?' she said. 'I've only just met him.'

'God Almighty!' Jack yelled. 'Do you listen to what you're saying? You don't know this bloke.'

'Yes I do. He's tall and handsome and a really lovely man.'

'He must be,' her mother cried, 'to be sneaking around back streets with you.'

'We weren't sneaking. He just called for me after work.'

'He's a squatter, you say. Where from?' her father wanted to know.

'Caravale Station. It's up near Bowen, I think. And anyway he says he's not a squatter, he's a grazier.'

'What the hell's the difference? He's pullin' the wool over your eyes. Have you got any idea what some of those bloody stations up there are like? They're primitive, isolated huts stuck jam in the middle of tribes of wild blacks!'

Alice became thoughtful. 'Not all of them, Jack. I mean, they say some places, on those big properties, are very refined.'

'Yeah, that's right, the big ones with plenty of dough. They're a toffee-nosed lot, I tell you. And they stick to their own class. This is what comes of letting her work up there with the nobs, it's gone to her head. You're riding for a fall, girl, if ever I saw one.'

The argument raged and in the end Perfy was shouting at them. 'I don't care. I'm going to marry him. And he's coming to see you, Daddy, to ask your permission.'

'My permission? Fat lot you care about me. You've already said what's on.'

'I know, I'm sorry. But you have to meet him. You'll like him.'

'Did you tell him how your mother and me happened to lob out here? Did you tell him that?'

'No, I didn't, not yet. I don't see it matters.'

'Perhaps his parents were exiled too,' Alice murmured. 'Perfy's right, Jack. There's no need to mention the past.'

'I don't know why you make such a fuss,' Perfy said. 'I have every intention of telling him.'

'I don't believe that would be wise, Perfy. And what about his parents? Are they in town? Have you met them yet?'

'His father's dead, and his mother lives on the station.'

'How big is this station?' Jack asked. 'And what do they sell up there? Kangaroos?'

'It's a cattle station, but I don't know how big it is.'

'Ha, right! A little matter he forgot to mention.'

Perfy had had enough. 'I'm going to bed. You can ask him all these things yourself tomorrow night.'

'I won't be home,' Sergeant Middleton growled.

'Yes, you will,' his wife instructed.

Ben Buchanan was furious. He couldn't believe that Darcy had asked a housemaid to marry him! And one from Government House at that. 'Are you mad? Or are you doing this to embarrass me? You're jealous because Lilley wants to nominate me for Parliament.'

'Oh, yes, Lilley. I've heard a bit of talk about him. He's not too popular with the lads. Lilley's got radical ideas about forcing big landholders to relinquish leases on large hunks of their properties to accommodate immigrant farmers.'

'Where'd you hear this rot?'

'At the sale yards. Lilley might be a smart fellow, a barrister, but he's not overburdened with horse-sense.'

'You can talk. You're behaving like a donkey, talking about marrying this person. Where'd you meet her? In the bar?'

Darcy scowled. 'You be careful what you say or you'll end up with a busted ear. I met her people last night, he's a sergeant in the army. A nice man, too.' He grinned, remembering. 'As a matter of fact, he didn't take too kindly to the idea either, but he's got better manners than you. He listened, he thinks it's a bit sudden too but when I explained that I have to get back to Caravale, he finally gave his blessing.'

' 'Course he would. Did you tell him about Caravale? What did you say? "It's just a little old cattle station. Only about a thousand square miles!" It's a wonder he didn't handcuff you to the seat and call a preacher right off. You're a sitting duck for women like this, Darcy, and their bloody families.'

'Are you finished?'

'No, I'm not. You have to think about this. For a start off, she couldn't be received at Government House.' Ben grinned. 'Which entrance would she use?'

'I don't give a shit about Government House. And I don't give a shit what you think. If you don't want to be best man I'll ask Ginger.' Darcy was relieved to see Ginger come in. He had invited the two of them to lunch with him at the Victoria so that he could tell them his good news but he hadn't reckoned on Ben making such a song and dance about it. Ginger wouldn't dare be as offensive as Ben.

His brother sulked while Darcy explained the situation.

'I gather Ben's not too enthusiastic,' Ginger said.

'He can mind his own business,' Darcy replied.

'Then might I make a suggestion, Darcy?' Ginger asked. 'Since you have proposed to Miss Middleton and she has accepted, you are therefore engaged, so why don't you leave it at that for the time being? It's quite normal for people to be engaged for a year or so, a sensible practice. You really shouldn't rush the girl. Why not set the wedding date for some time next year.'

Darcy listened patiently, he knew Ginger meant well. 'We've already discussed that option, but we don't want to be separated for such a long time. In fact we don't want to be separated at all. Perfy has agreed to marry me here in Brisbane and come home with me, and that's what I want. She's a warm, lovely girl, and we're very much in love.'

'Will you listen to it?' Ben mocked. 'It's the soppiest tale I ever heard. Wait till Ma hears you're marrying a bloody housemaid, she'll throw a fit.'

Darcy leapt up and whacked Ben across the head with the back of his hand, sending him crashing to the floor, his chair upturned on top of him. 'That's the last time you ever speak of Perfy with disrespect,' he said, standing over Ben. 'You bloody learn to behave yourself or you'll get a decent hiding next time.' He turned to their friend. 'Sorry, Ginger. You two have lunch here. The food's good. Put it on my bill. I need a walk to cool off. See if you can talk some sense into his stupid head. I don't need to defend Perfy, you'll see how fortunate I am when you meet her.'

He strode away, ignoring the interested stares of the other customers in the saloon bar, but when he walked outside he remembered what Ginger had said. Engaged! Good Lord! So he was! And the correct thing to do was to buy his fiancée an engagement ring. He probably should have had it ready last night, when Jack Middleton had eventually relented and shaken hands with him. He liked Perfy's father, the mother was rather shy, but they were nice people. What the hell must they think of him? He marched along Queen Street until he found a jeweller's shop and then nervously studied all the rings they could display.

'I'll take this one,' he said finally. 'If it doesn't fit, can you fix it?'

'Oh yes, sir,' the jeweller said.

'And if she doesn't like it, can she exchange it?'

'Certainly, sir, but I think any young lady would be delighted to receive such a beautiful ring.'

Darcy examined it again just to make sure. 'The stones in it, they're real, aren't they?'

'My word, sir, the very best quality.' He held it up to the light, and the large sapphire gleamed in its setting of glittering diamonds.

'It is pretty,' Darcy said. 'I'll take it.'

Perfy was incredibly happy. And nervous. She'd given a week's notice at work, showing off her glorious engagement ring. Even the Countess had come down to have a look at it, raising her dark eyebrows. 'Good heavens!' she'd said, and then: 'Be careful you don't lose it.' As if Perfy was silly enough to let it out of her sight.

Her mother, aided by lady friends, made the wedding dress, as well as other dresses, underwear and night gowns for Perfy's trousseau. Since the shops were all closed by the time she left work, the bride didn't have much say in these matters. Giving notice at work was a mistake. She should have quit right then, but the housekeeper had convinced her to stay on so as not to upset the smooth running of the house. Every evening Perfy had to stand interminably while the ladies draped and pinned clothes on her as if she were a shop dummy. They were even more excited than Perfy. The ring had set them off and then they'd discovered that the Buchanan boys were wealthy cattlemen and Caravale was one of the biggest stations in the north.

'She's done well for herself, Alice,' they said, over and over again, until Perfy found their remarks embarrassing, and her mother's enthusiasm numbing.

'We've always wanted a farm,' Alice said. 'And now Perfy's going to live on a fine station. And her fiancé, Darcy, he's such a dear boy, says we can visit any time we like, and stay as long as we like!'

Jack Middleton weathered all this with a grin. 'You caused it, Perfy. Let the ladies enjoy themselves.'

Darcy decided they should have the wedding breakfast at the Victoria Hotel but Jack Middleton took him aside. 'I'm sorry, son, I couldn't stretch to that. I was thinking we'd have the reception here at home. Alice will do the catering.'

'No, Jack, it's my treat. I'm taking away your daughter, the least I can do is shout a good party. Anyway, with time so short, Mrs Middleton has enough to do.'

'If you're sure it's all right,' Jack said.

'Of course it is. Now, the lads are giving me a buck's party at Carmody's pub down by the wharves on the Saturday night before the wedding. You're invited.'

Jack shook his head. 'If you don't mind, Darcy, I don't think I'll come. I'm a bit old for those shows. You lads have a good time.'

Looking back, after what happened at that buck's party, Jack regretted bitterly that he had not accepted. But he thought the world of Darcy, this was the son he'd never had, a fine young fellow, honest, easy-going and a real gentleman. He didn't want to intrude.

That week of work dragged, but at last Perfy had time to look around, to think about what was happening, even to stroll down by the wide river and sit by the streaming beauty of her favourite tree, a weeping willow, dreaming, in the luxury of freedom. She felt as if these days were just on loan, that any morning now she would once more have to be up at five, hurrying across town to begin again those endless chores.

Darcy called for her. 'I've got everything sorted out on my side, now we have to deck you out.'

'What do you mean? Mother's packing up my clothes.'

'I know, the sewing beehive is in full swing, but even Alice can't make riding boots and hats and I thought you might like some tailored riding habits. Once we leave Bowen we'll be riding out to Caravale. Buggies are too slow and awkward. You can ride?'

'Of course I can.'

'Side-saddle?'

Perfy hesitated. She hated riding side-saddle but she knew it was correct for ladies.

'You'd rather ride astride?'

'If I can.'

'Of course you can. The reason I'm asking, a lot of women ride astride these days and they buy these very smart divided skirts. That solves the problem. They sell them at Harvey's store, he caters for all sorts of riding outfits. Would you like to have a look at them?'

'Darcy, I can't afford these things.'

'Not I, my darling. We. You can't buy this stuff up north, and you're going to need them, so we have to buy them now. All right?'

She was uncertain, but Darcy was in charge. He took her off to Harvey's where she had enormous fun, guided by him, buying her 'country rig', as he called it. She noticed that instead of paying cash he simply signed the invoice and gave Mr Harvey his instructions, and instead of carrying off their purchases, Darcy had the lot sent to Perfy's home.

Next stop was at his lawyer's office. They went into the cool chambers of Messrs Jauncy and Bascombe, where Perfy was introduced to Henry Jauncy, an elderly man with a balding head and a thick, fair moustache who smiled and took her hand. 'I am very pleased to meet you, Miss Middleton. And I congratulate you, Darcy. You're a very lucky fellow to have found such a beautiful girl to keep you in order.'

Darcy beamed his delight. 'She'll do that, don't worry.' Then he turned to Perfy. 'Would you mind waiting here just a few minutes? I have some papers to sign. I won't be long.'

She sat on a polished bench, more like a church pew than a normal seat, and watched the clerks hard at work under a large ornate clock, wondering what they were writing about. Were they penning information about criminals or bushrangers? Or were they just toiling over the long, involved land leases Darcy had told her about.

As promised, Darcy returned in what seemed no time at all and Mr Jauncy came out to see them off. 'I'm looking forward to the wedding,' he said, 'and my wife is too, she loves weddings.'

'Now, my girl,' Darcy said, 'we've done the chores so let's go to lunch. I've invited Ginger Butterfield and Ben to join us. I want you to meet them. Ginger will be my best man. I know you've seen them in your travels but you have to meet them properly, get to know them.'

Perfy wondered, mildly, why Ben wasn't the best man, but she supposed it was Darcy's choice. She had asked Amy Campbell to be her bridesmaid but Amy had rather curtly told her she'd be away that weekend, with her family. And so she turned to Laura Stibbs, now Mrs Gooding, who was thrilled to be asked, and would serve as matron-of-honour.

Perfy had never been inside any of the big hotels and she found the Victoria weirdly ornate, with its red velvet drapes trimmed in gold and wide red carpets criss-crossing through the foyer and on into the dining room. She giggled nervously; following the carpeted paths was like being led to a royal audience. She wasn't looking forward to meeting Ben and Ginger; she felt inadequate now as if she really were getting above herself.

The room was crowded but at a far table Ginger stood to welcome them. Even though he had quite a toffy accent, Perfy liked him immediately, and why not? she thought. He was charming, and free with his compliments, making her feel so much at ease. He had ordered chilled champagne to toast the happy couple.

'I've never tasted champagne before,' Perfy said.

'Better still,' Ginger said. 'I love people to try out new things. Now, tell me how you like it.'

She sipped the champagne from the fine crystal glass. 'Oh, it's delicious.'

'Great!' Ginger enthused. 'We're in business, Darcy old chap. I'd have hated to send it back.'

They had finished the bottle and Ben still hadn't arrived so they went ahead and ordered their meals. 'That Ben, he's always late,' Darcy said.

'Oh, you know Ben,' Ginger offered, 'he's off and running with this politicking business, probably lost count of time.'

The soup came and went, and then oysters and roast chicken, and more champagne, but Ben still did not appear. Although they were having a merry time, Ginger and Darcy teasing each other mercilessly, telling Perfy

82

wonderfully funny stories about their younger days, she could feel tension building up. 'Is anything wrong?' she asked.

Darcy shook his head, but he looked cross.

'Of course not,' Ginger assured her. 'I think Ben must have forgotten us, but I'm blowed if I'm going looking for him. They serve jolly good puddings here.'

Perfy was not sure that she believed him. She and Darcy had been engaged for ten days now and Ben had not come forward. She wondered if he were avoiding her, if he wouldn't accept her. And what about their mother, the grand lady who lived on the station? If Ben disapproved of her, how would the mother react?

But the lunch was fun, with Ginger at his entertaining best, and friends from other tables coming over to congratulate Darcy and comment on his lovely fiancée, making a fuss of her, inviting them to visit. It was all splendid. Darcy was sure that Perfy had no idea how beautiful she looked, how those dark blue eyes sparkled when she laughed. He'd noticed the way people looked at her, the women genuinely approving, the men nudging him: 'You're a lucky devil, Darc!' As old Mrs Partridge had said: 'My, you do make a handsome couple. You'll have beautiful children, so don't go wasting time!'

In a way he was pleased Ben hadn't turned up to put a damper on the show. The bastard. He hadn't even come up with an engagement present, some expression of good will towards Perfy. Darcy vowed that if Ben did anything to upset Perfy he'd break his bloody neck.

'You're quiet,' Perfy said as he walked her home.

'The wine's wearing off,' he laughed.

'Oh, I see. Darcy, there's something I want to tell you.'

'You've changed your mind?' he teased.

'No. Don't be silly. Did you know my parents were convicts? They were transported to Sydney years back.'

'No, I didn't know that,' he lied. Ben had dug out that information; it had caused another row. 'Does it bother you?'

'Me? No. I just thought I ought to tell you.'

'Well, you've told me, but I like them, so we won't swap them. They say my great grand-daddy was a pirate, a bloodthirsty old brute who plundered ships off the coast of Tasmania.'

'How exciting!'

'Yes, but don't mention it to my mother. She's not impressed.'

'Where does she come from?'

'Scotland. But she won't talk about Scotland either. Apparently she sailed out here as a young woman to stay with a dear old aunt and met Teddy, my late father, and they got married. It seems her family were a high-falutin lot because my father used to say that when he met her she was beautiful, and dressed in the finest clothes, very smart for Sydney in those days. But whatever her family did to upset Cornelia, she's never forgiven them. Scotland, for her, just does not exist.'

'Cornelia? Is that her name? It's very pretty.'

'Yes, it is, I suppose. I've never thought of it before.' He shuddered. Ma could be a tartar, and with Ben offside, undermining Perfy, his wife could run into problems with the pair of them. He couldn't be home all the time to see they didn't gang up on her. With a station as big as Caravale, he or Ben were frequently away for up to a week at a time, checking the cattle and the boundaries, burning off. There was always work to do. Often they stayed over at their manager's outstation, forty miles from the homestead. He decided he'd build a house for himself and Perfy right away, and while he was in Brisbane he'd take the opportunity to pick up some plans.

'What are you thinking of?' she asked. 'A penny . . .'

'I'm building our house in my head,' he told her. 'We have to have our own place. To be private. I've got the site picked out and we'll have the fun of Cork building it just how we want it. I'll have them start as soon as we get home.' He saw the relief on her face and put an arm round her. 'We'll be right, love. There's nothing to worry about.'

Ben Buchanan and four of his mates had been playing cards in the back room of Carmody's Hotel earlier in the night, but now as the whisky bottles emptied they lost interest in the cards and became enthusiastic about Ben's idea: the bachelor party practical joke. It would be a whopper! The best yet!

But David Cran wasn't so sure. 'Are you really going through with it, Ben?'

'Yes, this joke will top them all.'

'You don't think it's a bit over the fence?'

'Listen to who's talking,' Clive Jenkins said. 'You're the one who dumped whitewash on Craig Bottomley the night before his wedding.'

'I was drunk. But to kidnap Darcy! Jesus, he'll kill us. No, count me out.' David picked up his coat and lurched unsteadily towards the door. 'I'm off.'

'Just keep your mouth shut then,' Clive called to him. 'And don't tell Ginger Butterfield, he's gone all starchy these days.'

'On my honour,' David said. 'Nary a word!'

Clive burped loudly. 'Beg pardon, gentleman. But let us not forget it was Ginger and his mates who grabbed Fiona Kendall's husband, whatsisname, after his buck's party and tied him starkers to a tree in the bush. If some Abos hadn't come along he'd still be there.'

Neville Roberts laughed. 'Yeah, I remember. Ginger was pissed off, he wanted to marry Fiona himself.' He reached for another bottle. 'And he should have, too. She was a fool marrying their manager, the Kendalls have never really accepted him.'

'So how do you think my mother's going to feel when Darcy lobs home with his housemaid,' Ben said, 'and then trots out her convict parents? He's bloody mad.'

The fifth member of the gathering was Les Stohr of Tambaroora Station, via Rockhampton. He was having the time of his life in Brisbane and counted himself lucky that Ben Buchanan was in town. Ben had introduced him to all the right people, had taken him to parties at the Russell mansion and even carted him over to Government House. There was no doubt that his mate was headed for the big time here in Brisbane, he seemed to know everyone. Les shook his head. 'I can't understand Darcy. I heard that Kitty Kendall's got a mighty crush on him.'

Clive whistled. 'Kitty Kendall, eh? There's a catch.'

'Don't rub it in,' Ben moaned. 'So what does Darcy do? He gets himself into a real spot proposing to this harpie the first time he meets her.'

Neville blinked, trying to focus. 'The first time?'

'That's right,' Ben said. 'Now he can't get out of it. This wedding's going to be hell. He's stuck with the housemaid, and the matron-of-honour is Stibbs's daughter – you know, the blacksmith. God knows what sort of a motley crew will be invited. I'm glad Mother's not in town.'

'You ought to wish she was,' Les said. 'She'd put a stop to it pretty damn fast.'

'Yeah, you're right,' Ben agreed. 'That's why we have to make a move, just a joke to give him time to slide out of it.'

'An excuse, that's what we're giving him,' Clive said.

Neville couldn't grasp the problem. 'Why doesn't he just back off, explain things are going a bit too fast? Or pay her off? I mean, she hasn't got a bun in the oven has she?'

'No, nothing like that,' Ben said. 'He's just got himself cornered and now he feels he has to do the right thing.' He ran his hands through his damp hair. 'Christ, it's hot in here.'

'Have some wine,' Neville told him. 'That whisky's crook. It's giving me a headache. So what's the plan, Ben? Give it to us again.'

'It's simple. You grab Darcy after the booze-up, tie him up and take him across the wharf to the *Louisa*. She's a coastal ship, leaves early Sunday morning. I've spoken to the captain, it's all lined up. They'll drop him off at Rockhampton—'

'Hang on,' Neville said. 'It won't be easy grabbing Darcy.'

'Christ, Nev, there'll be three of you, and Les is as strong as an ox.'

Les grinned. 'No problem. But where'll you be, Ben?'

'I'll be on the ship waiting for you and we'll simply pop the lad in the cabin I've booked for him.'

'He'll miss his wedding,' Neville laughed.

'That's the general idea,' Ben explained. 'It's just a joke. If he's that keen he can come right back and marry her and there's nothing more we can do. But he'll have a chance to think about it without her around pressuring him, and if he wakes up that this marriage isn't the best idea in the world, he's got the perfect out. He can just keep on going.'

'I think it's a ripper idea,' Clive said. 'a bloody beauty! And no harm done. In fact I reckon we're doing him a bloody favour.'

The more they talked about the plan, the more they laughed.

4

The bachelor party at Carmody's Hotel didn't start out too well even though Tom Carmody went to a lot of trouble to please the thirty young gentlemen assembled in his Commercial Room. He'd put on a splendid buffet and, as instructed, had provided a plentiful supply of his best liquors as well as a couple of kegs of beer. And he had made certain of his money by insisting that Ben Buchanan paid him in advance. Carmody had seen enough of these parties to know they'd all end up drunk and wander off leaving him to chase after the cash.

As soon as Ben arrived, Darcy confronted him. 'Where have you been hiding?'

'I haven't been hiding. I've been busy. I've had to meet a lot of important people in Brisbane while you've been mooning around. I notice you haven't given me any support.'

'Don't try and squirm out of it. You've been snubbing Perfy. I ought to belt you one, you little snot.'

Ginger intervened. 'Miss Middleton is charming, Ben. Absolutely the nicest girl, you'll like her. It's a pity you haven't had the time to meet her.'

'I have met her,' Ben said. 'She used to do our room at Government House, remember?'

'God, you're a pain in the arse,' Darcy growled.

'What am I supposed to say? Pretend I never saw her there. You're too touchy, Darcy! You're the one looking for trouble. You spring this marriage on us out of nowhere and expect everyone to drop everything and pay attention to you. And you're as prickly as a bloody porcupine! The only thing I have to say about this marriage is that you should have given it a bit more time, and if that's being beastly, well, stiff luck!'

Other guests were arriving with jovial handshakes and congratulations for Darcy. He wondered if he was being too touchy. Maybe Ben was right on that, but for the rest, no. He loved Perfy, time wouldn't make any difference. As it was, even now he begrudged the time away from her, but he had to go along with the party. Ben, he admitted, had made this gesture to celebrate his wedding, rounding up their friends. He sighed. Better get on with it. 'Who's for champagne?' he called.

A piano player led the revellers in a sing-song after dinner, and three girls in skimpy Eastern costumes arrived from the Theatre Royale to entertain them with their exotic dances and then stayed on to join in the fun. The party became noisier, hilarious. Darcy was enjoying himself. It was a great send-off. The best buck's night he'd ever attended. He was getting drunk and he didn't care but in among the endless toasts he began to notice a few extra nudges and giggles and he wondered what rag they were up to. They always did something stupid to the poor fool guest-of-honour at these shows, like debagging, or dumping the victim in a bath of Condy's crystals, turning his skin purple, crazy things, but this time they'd miss out. He was awake to those tricks! He slowed up on the booze to keep his wits about him.

By the early hours the guests had begun to stagger off. Someone vomited and was thrown bodily out of the room. Ginger and another fellow had passed out under the table and the pianist was slumped drunk across his piano. The girls had disappeared, and as he looked around at the remnants of the room, Darcy noticed that Ben had gone too.

'That's it then,' he said to the last three stayers, Clive, Neville, and the burly Les Stohr. 'What say we call it a night?'

He drifted into the back yard with this trio to relieve himself and then agreed to help Clive saddle his horse.

It was then that they jumped him, laughing like maniacs, and Darcy realised that a rag was on.

'Oh no, you don't,' he said shoving them away, and at the same time noticing Clive had a rope. 'Whatever you've got in mind,' he yelled, struggling with them, 'it won't work this time. Now let me go.'

They were getting rough in their determination to overpower him and, wrestling with them, Darcy became angry. 'Give over,' he said, gritting his teeth and grabbing Clive by the hair. Clive punched him to make him let go.

Big Les grabbed him from behind but Darcy kicked loose, pleased to hear Neville let out a yell of pain. Then one of them struck him on the side of the head. It was a hard-knuckle punch, past a joke now, so Darcy swung round to attack Les. Somehow this fool of an episode had turned into a full-scale brawl; there were shouts and curses in the darkness as Darcy took them on.

He flattened Clive and kicked Neville in the groin but they kept coming at him, and punching Les was like whacking a water tank. The fight was mean now, there was blood on his hands, someone had a bloody nose. Darcy felt he was getting the better of them, that he could just about cut loose and run for it when something heavy clouted him on the back of his neck and he crashed to the ground near the hotel wall, smashing his head against the raised stone gully trap. He lay there, panting, for a second, feeling the blood running on his face. When he got his wind back, he'd get up again and really give it to these bastards. He sucked in some precious air, then breathed it out in a long final sigh.

Jack Middleton, on the night shift at the army barracks, heard about the fight at Carmody's Hotel. That was nothing new in this town, there were brawls every night, but since Darcy's party had been at Carmody's, he decided to go down to the police lockup. Darcy might be among the lads the coppers had pulled in. 'Can't have my son-in-law in the nick,' he told himself. 'If he's among them I'll have a word in the right ear and get him out before the magistrate gets out of bed.'

Kookaburras cackled and hooted from tall gums as he passed. The bushmen's clock, he mused, that's what they were called, and a man on night shift was always glad to hear them. They were the first to wake, their calls echoing around the neighbourhood a good half-hour before the dawn, regular as clockwork. Forget the roosters, they were outclassed here. Next came the crows and then the honey-eaters with their own brand of clatter. The big tuneful birds like the magpies and the butcher-birds waited for the day. Jack reckoned they liked an audience. He grinned. One saving grace about this rough-house of a town was the birds. He loved birds. Out there on that station of Darcy's, there'd probably be more breeds of birds than a man could count. He was looking forward to going right out into the real bush, more so than he let on at home.

Queer the way things turned out. A nice fellow, that Darcy; he hoped Perfy appreciated how lucky she was, he'd told her often enough. And harking back, with everything turning out so well, God bless that magistrate who'd sent them to this country. He didn't know what a good turn he was doing the Middletons.

The constable on duty was Gunner Haig.

'You picked up some blokes at Carmody's,' Jack said. 'A brawl, they say.'

'Yeah. Squatters' sons this time. But not so smart now, a snivelling bunch.'

'Names?'

Haig turned the book round and Jack read the three names above Gunner's stubby finger.

Jack grinned, relieved. 'My daughter's fiancé was there last night, they were giving him a bit of a celebration, like. Thought I'd better check.'

Gunner glanced at him. 'What's his name?'

'Buchanan,' Jack said proudly. 'Darcy Buchanan.'

Gunner swallowed. 'Is that right? Ay now, Jack, what about a cuppa tea? Come on through.' With the deftness of practice, Gunner eased Jack quickly into a back mess room where a tea kettle waited on top of a still-warm stove. 'Nothin' like a cuppa tea, I always say,' he continued. 'Seems those blokes in there got into the booze and ended in a punch-up. You know the way these things go.' He poured a mug of black tea and handed it to Jack. 'But it got out of hand. The chief's out there now rounding up the rest of them, and Carmody's been here himself, threatening to shoot these blokes we've got locked up. It's been a real schemozzle . . .'

'Someone got hurt?' Jack said, putting down the tea without touching it, apprehension building inside him. Gunner's face had turned a pulpy yellow.

'Yes, Jack, an accident, they say. They say he fell and hit his head.'

'Killed?'

Gunner nodded.

'And it was Darcy? Darcy Buchanan?'

The constable sighed. 'I'm sorry, mate. Yes, that was the name. I'm real bloody sorry, Jack.'

Sergeant Middleton stood stiffly at attention, as if sentence were being passed on him. He said nothing, he just stood there. A stone. Not moving. Waiting for the shock waves to pass as he knew they would. A convict and an army man was no stranger to sudden death. It was a matter of timing, a bulwark for a man against the onslaught of grief. In a little while he would trust his voice.

5

The two men, Jack, and the Irishman, Carmody, sat grim-faced at the back of the courtroom, witnesses and partisans in the parade of British justice which they despised and relied upon.

Carmody's evidence had been heard, with interjections from the coroner that the innkeeper should couch his replies in less emotional terms, that his opinions were not required, nor were certain unseemly adjectives. And eventually it was ascertained that Carmody had heard the scuffle commence and had locked the hotel to keep the brawlers, once out, staying out. He had gone to bed but as the noise increased and the brawlers were resorting to 'unseemly' language, his wife had sent him down to chase them off. By the time he found the keys, one of the men was hammering on the back door, yelling for help. He stepped out into his yard to see two men staggering around and one down, and on examining the man on the ground he had found him to be dead. And yes, it was the deceased, Mr Darcy Buchanan.

The innkeeper had then taken his shotgun and bailed up the three other men, locked them in his cellar and sent for the police. And yes, in the course of making a citizen's arrest he may have inflicted several injuries on his prisoners, but this was unavoidable.

The three men involved in the fight were questioned at length despite their sorry state and occasional tears, and a succession of other gentlemen who were present at the celebratory function came forward. None could add any further evidence regarding the fight but all, including Mr Ben Buchanan, insisted the three prisoners were highly regarded in the community, were of good character with no prior convictions, and there was no malicious intent in the altercation with Mr Darcy Buchanan.

When the latter subject was raised yet again by a witness, it was too much for Carmody. 'What would ye call that now if it's not a bloody opinion?' and was promptly ordered from the courtroom.

Jack waited outside with him until Gunner Haig came over to tell them that the coroner had returned a verdict of accidental death. He watched Darcy's friends spill out sombrely into the street and melt away among the crowds. 'Will they be charged, those three blokes? They still killed a man, accident or not.'

'No,' Gunner told him. 'Too many of the gentry involved.'

'What about Darcy's brother? Why doesn't he insist?'

'They say he's too cut up to know what's going on. And anyway those three young blokes are high-steppers and word has it the Governor's not going to take on the squatters, they'd gang up on him. And it *was* an accident.'

'Bloody accident!' Carmody said. 'So what? If that'd be you or me, Jack, or even you, Gunner, we'd be for the high jump. They'd be measurin' us by this.'

Jack nodded. He was still shocked by Darcy's death and being back in a courtroom made him squeamish. You never got over the fear that for some reason or another they'd grab you again. This was why he'd joined the army. If you can't beat them, join them, and he'd felt the safety of numbers. Jack could never have shouted out like Carmody did, even though he knew Carmody was right. But the Irish were different, they liked to stir. Carmody had been transported too, and he'd done his time hard, on the chain gangs. Jack had been relatively fortunate. He'd been assigned as a labourer for a stonemason who couldn't have his workmen chained.

'You're looking crook,' Carmody said. 'Come on back with me, Jack, and we'll find a bottle of my best Irish whisky.'

'It's right good of you,' Jack said. 'I'll come over another time. I have to get home. My girl, she's taking this hard.'

'Ah, the poor darlin', I'll have a Mass said for her too.'

The women were so distraught, Jack didn't know what to do or how to console them. Despite his wife's protests, he had insisted that Perfy attend Darcy's funeral. All the weeping in the world wouldn't bring Darcy back and somehow he felt being present at the service might make his death final, help with the cure, because every so often, when she did talk, Perfy spoke as if he were still alive.

As it turned out, Perfy didn't see Darcy buried. She collapsed at the beginning of the service, passed out cold. They had to carry her to the buggy Jack had hired and take her home.

Only one of Darcy's friends called, a Mr Ginger Butterfield, and he brought a bunch of beautiful white roses, but Perfy said she couldn't face him.

'Yes, you will,' her father said. 'I don't care if you howl your eyes out, it's only natural. He won't mind. He'll understand. If he's good enough to call, you be good enough to see him.'

She had received a letter of condolence from the Governor, but nothing from Ben Buchanan.

'I suppose the poor man is in as bad a state as Perfy,' Alice said. 'But can you imagine the poor mother? It must be terrible for her, so far away, and not even able to say a prayer over his grave.' Alice wept again.

Weeks passed, people came to commiserate, but Perfy seemed to get worse. She wouldn't eat, she wouldn't tidy herself up, she stayed in her room staring, gaping, unable to sleep.

Diamond arrived at the door one day asking to see Perfy but by this time Alice was discouraging visitors, they only set Perfy off again, into such fits of tears that she ended up dry-retching.

'I'm sorry, she's not well enough to see anyone,' Alice explained.

'Yes, I heard that,' Diamond said. 'I thought I might be able to help. Miss Perfy was always very good to me.'

'I don't know how you can help,' Alice replied but Jack drew her aside.

'For God's sake, if she thinks she can, let her. Perfy'll end up a half-wit if we don't do something. She looks like one already.'

They heard the black girl singing weird monotonous songs in a low humming voice, and they heard her talking on and on, but her voice was so soft the words were indistinguishable, as monotonous as the singing. And there wasn't a murmur from Perfy.

'Sounds like some sort of heathen rite,' Alice objected.

'I don't care if it's Hindu,' Jack said. 'It sounds to me as if she's telling her stories. The blacks are good on stories, fairy tales, like.'

'Why would she do that?'

'For God's sake, I don't know. To get her interested, I suppose. To get her interested in something. At least she's not bawling.'

Diamond came round every night after work and managed to get Perfy out of the house, taking her for walks in the quiet of the evening. Jack had no idea what they talked about but Perfy was improving. Diamond even had her eating, a little at a time, sitting outside under the trees, peeling mangoes for her, making little apple sandwiches that Perfy used to love as a small child. It seemed to Jack that Diamond was bringing her out in a strange process of having her grow up all over again. Whatever it was, he was grateful to the Aborigine girl.

A letter came for Perfy from the firm of Jauncy and Bascombe, requesting her to call at the office, and Jack decided to go too. Lately he had been worried about all the expensive country clothes Darcy had bought for her, boots, riding habits, hats and so forth, all still neatly in their boxes. Jack recalled Perfy saying that Darcy had just signed for them – she had been impressed. Seeing them stacked there in the corner of Perfy's room caused him nagging concern. What if Darcy hadn't got round to paying for them? Or for that ring? A man had to look at these things realistically. If Darcy had died before the bills were paid, then someone would have to cough up and it wasn't going to be Jack Middleton. He would just have to tell them, and Perfy too, that everything would be returned forthwith and make an end to it. It was bad luck about the ring, but as for the country clothes, well, she'd never need them now anyway.

On the tick of two o'clock he ushered his daughter into Mr Jauncy's office.

The solicitor immediately offered his heartfelt condolences to Perfy which, predictably, reduced her to tears. After they managed to calm her, the two men talked in vague terms, Jauncy explaining that Darcy had been not only a client, but a good friend. And he had also handled the late Teddy Buchanan's affairs. They spoke of the weather which was cooling a little now after the rains and of the pleasant autumns experienced in this climate. The collar of Jack's best uniform jacket was tight, cutting into his neck, but he sat stoically, waiting for the axe to fall.

When they left the office his head was spinning, and Perfy was shaky. She took her father's arm as they crossed Queen Street. 'What he said . . . would that be right?'

'No doubt about it,' he replied. 'Let's get home. I could do with a pot of tea.'

'No doubt about it,' he told his wife. 'Darcy wrote a new will recently, all signed and sealed by that solicitor feller. Perfy's rich. He left her everything. Money in the bank and a half-share of Caravale Station. It was just like Darcy to make certain to take care of her.'

'Who owns the other half of the station?' Alice asked.

'The brother. Ben Buchanan.'

'What about their mother? Where does she fit in?'

'Ah yes,' Jack said. 'Mr Jauncy told us, in confidence, that the father didn't get along too well with his missus for the last few years so he left the station, lock, stock and barrel, to his sons, allowing Mrs Buchanan to stay on there as long as she lives, or wants to, I suppose.'

'Well, for goodness sake!' Alice Middleton put the kettle on again. 'So what's to do?'

'I'd like to see the station,' Perfy said sadly.

'It's a thousand miles away.' Alice frowned a message to Jack. 'You couldn't make a journey like that on your own. And it would only upset you.'

'Your mother's right, Perfy,' Jack said gently. 'It's hard enough for you now. Going to where he lived would be like self-inflicted wounds, you're not up to it.'

'I'd still like to go,' she said stubbornly.

Jack ignored her. 'The best thing Perfy can do is to sell her share of the station. Probably the Buchanans would want to buy it, the solicitor said, and then she'll have cash money in the bank. She can take her time then deciding what to do with the money.'

'You could afford to buy a farm,' Alice said to Perfy, who wouldn't reply. She was staring at the ring on her finger, the ring Jack had thought might have to be handed over. There'd been no mention of those bills at all. Not that it mattered now, Perfy was a very rich woman.

'I think I'll have a brandy instead of that tea, Alice,' Jack said. 'I'm feeling a bit queer over all this.'

* * *

When everything seemed to have quietened down, old Will Gaunt, their cranky neighbour, came in to pay his respects to Perfy, and he even brought her a watermelon.

'Wonders will never cease,' Alice breathed, and Jack felt he should at least offer the man a drink.

'Wouldn't mind,' Will said, 'I thought I might get a bit of a yarn with you.'

The two men retired to the back yard with a pint of rum and a couple of pony glasses; Jack didn't feel inclined to share too much of the pint with this old codger.

'Well, the rain's gone,' Jack said, for openers.

'Yeah. But I don't mind the rain out here. Back home it'd freeze you to the marrer.'

'You can say that again. Have you heard from your lad, Eddie?'

'Oh, yeah,' Will said. 'He can write real good, you know.'

'How's he doing?'

'Bloody useless, like I said he would. He and that mad Billy Kemp didn't do no good at Gympie so they've packed their swags and gone hoofin' it up to the Cape River diggin's. I had me heart set on Eddie bein' a sailor. Bloody kids!' He stopped and tapped Jack on the knee. 'Didn't mean your girl, of course. Good as gold, your little girl. They say she took that lad's death hard.'

Jack nodded.

'And so she should,' Will said. 'Feller like that, cut down in the prime of life, so to say.' He cocked a squinty eye at Jack. 'You liked him?'

'Yes.'

'I mean to say, he wasn't just another of them posh squatter blokes?'

'No fear, not Darcy,' Jack told him. 'He took us as he found us. He was a bloody good bloke, no side about him at all.'

Will lit a grimy old clay pipe. 'I hang about the wharves a bit,' he commented and Jack nodded again. It was not a subject to encourage, everyone knew Willy Gaunt would lift anything that wasn't nailed down.

'I hear things,' Will went on, a hint in his voice, and then he seemed to take a different tack. 'That inquest is all finished now, quick smart, they say. And them louts as accidental-like killed the lad have all gone scuttlin' off home to their mums.'

'That's right,' Jack said.

'And there's no gettin' away from the fact it was an accident,' Will continued. 'A fight gone wrong. But did you ever find out what the fight was all about?' His face was screwed into a hard quizzical stare.

Jack shook his head. 'None of them could remember much, they were all too pissed. Something about saddling up the horse was all I could find out.'

95

'That's all the coppers could find out,' Will said, 'but I heard different. The Buchanan lad had a cabin booked on the *Louisa*, to sail for Rockhampton that morning.'

Jack grabbed hold of Will's shirt. 'I won't have that talk! Darcy wouldn't have run out on Perfy!'

'Hey! Whoa!' Will pushed him away. 'Not Darcy, mate, the brother. The way I get it, he lined up his mates to press-gang Darcy on to the ship so he'd miss his weddin'.'

'That doesn't make sense. Why would they do that?'

'Use your head, man! The brother's a toff. He arranged to ship Darcy out of harm's way. They say he was on board the *Louisa* waiting for them to deliver his brother. He was on the bloody ship waiting!'

Will held out his glass for a refill and Jack poured automatically. He was confused. 'No,' he said finally. 'That's the trouble with these tales, they don't fit the facts.'

'It fits all right,' Will said, 'and I don't want you to go taking this to heart like, I'm only passing on what I heard.' He hesitated, not sure of the reaction he would get, but Jack nodded for him to go on. He had just figured it out for himself but he wanted to hear it said.

'That Ben Buchanan told the captain the marriage was what they call unsuitable.'

'Unsuitable,' Jack echoed dully.

'That's it. So it's what I told you. They were getting Darcy out of harm's way, away from this girl. 'Course I pricked up me ears when I heard they was talking about the bloke who got killed, not knowing your lad's name but knowing as how Perfy's boy friend had bought it. Didn't take much to put two and two together. But listen, mate, you never got it from me, remember?'

'Yeah, I'll remember,' Jack told him. 'And I'll remember Ben Buchanan too.'

Will Gaunt licked his lips and grinned. 'That's the spirit. Doesn't hurt to know the facts.'

When they sat down to supper that night, Jack looked at Perfy. Her wide-eyed baby-look had gone, and the set of her chin gave her a strained expression. 'Do you still want to see that station?' he asked her.

'Yes, I do,' she said firmly.

'Oh dear, let's not start this again,' Alice said.

'Well, I've been thinking,' Jack told them. 'Maybe Perfy ought not to rush in and sell up her share. I mean, with gold strikes in the vicinity, that station is going to double in price, and remember what Darcy said. It'll be boom time for cattlemen up there, with thousands rushing to the diggings. The cattle themselves'll be worth gold to feed the multitudes. There aren't any towns up that way.'

'That's right,' Perfy said. 'That's exactly what Darcy told us.'

'Would you rather hang on to your share of the station, love?' her father asked.

'I ought to. Darcy wanted me to have it.'

'No reason why we shouldn't take our time with this,' he murmured.

'Are you mad, Jack?' Alice cried. 'She can't go up there on her own.'

He sat back from the table. 'She's not going on her own. What if I quit the army and we all go up to Bowen for a start, and see how the land lies?'

'Bowen?' his wife said. 'Where would we stay there?'

He turned to Perfy. 'You can afford to buy a house in Bowen, it'd be a base for us. What do you say to that? They tell me it's a pretty little seaside town, and your mother has always wanted to leave Brisbane.'

Perfy smiled for the first time in weeks. 'I'd like to get away too, and it would be wonderful to have our own house.

Alice disagreed. 'It's one thing to buy a house, quite another to think you can keep half that cattle station. You're getting above yourself, Perfy. You're not dealing with Darcy now. How do you think those people are going to feel when they find out half their property belongs to someone they don't even know? They'll chew you up and spit you out, and I'll tell you what, I wouldn't blame them. You ought to have more sense, Jack, encouraging her.'

'We'll sleep on it,' he said, to avoid further argument.

He walked out into the gathering dusk and watched a formation of big white pelicans making for their island nests, a grand sight against the pink-purple sky. Alice was right in her way, under normal circumstances, but if Perfy backed off, then Ben Buchanan had succeeded at the cost of his brother's life. He had got rid of the 'unsuitable' connection. Perfy must never know about this, she was still grieving, and at times, Jack thought, not quite the full pint. They'd find her standing in the hallway or halfway down the yard, seeming to be lost, not hearing them when they spoke to her, not seeming to be able to remember what she was supposed to be doing. The healing process was taking time; she was young though, she'd get over it, as long as she didn't hear the tail end of the story. Why, even he got upset thinking about it. Darcy's sorry, futile death was directly related to his love for Perfy, and if she started thinking along those lines, she'd be blaming herself and the shock could easily cause her a real and proper breakdown.

The assault on Darcy, Jack decided, was also an assault on his family, the Middletons. Not good enough for the Buchanans eh? He'd see about that. 'You didn't get rid of us, you bastard,' he whispered. 'You've got us for partners.'

At first, in his rage, he'd wanted to kill Ben Buchanan, but that had simmered down. No revenge was worth going back to prison. It was time for the velvet glove. A handshake if necessary, but this time the Middletons would be making the rules; whether he liked it or not, Mr Buchanan would have to defer – yes, that was the word – defer to the wishes of Miss Middleton. He laughed. And until it suited Perfy to sell, fifty per cent of the income from that fine station was earmarked for her already healthy bank account.

6

The laundry had become Diamond's home, her little white linen world. She had been in charge for a year now, since the washerwoman had gone off to marry a farmer. And she too had an assistant, or rather a series of them, Aborigine girls, most of them only about two or three years younger than herself but timeless years behind in understanding what was expected of them.

Diamond despaired for these poor girls. She did most of the work herself, covering for their ineptitude, and desperately trying to teach them, not only their duties, but to take an interest, and have pride in themselves. And while they worked, she tried to improve their speech and their understanding of English, disturbed to find they resented her.

She was freer now, taken for granted. After work she could come and go as she pleased, but she was still careful walking abroad at night. Brisbane was a dangerous place for black women, they were at risk from the black as well as the white men. After wrestling free from some whiteys as she passed a hotel, she had taken to wearing a strong sharp knife strapped to her leg, well hidden under her long skirts. She grinned, sitting now in the safety of her room behind the laundry, with moths flitting at the oil lamp. The next time some men had grabbed her in the dark, unlit streets, she'd flashed the knife, slashing viciously at them, and they'd gone for their lives.

She visited the blacks' camps, foul, squalid collections of gunyahs and rotting tents and rusting sheets of corrugated iron. Every time she went there she ran the gauntlet of hoots and whistles from the men and the heavy-lidded gaze of the women, but she persisted, seeking out the mothers or relatives of her laundry maids to beg their cooperation. She had to impress on them that the girls must come to work clean, and they could not stay home whenever it suited them. But these poor mixed-up relics of tribal discipline could not grasp the system of employment. The laundry maids were paid in 'staples' – flour, tea and sugar – which they dutifully took back to the camp to share, but they rarely came back until they needed more.

Diamond refused to give up on them. Sooner or later she knew this generation or their children would grasp the intricacies of living with white people, given a chance. They had to, to survive. But was she much of an example? She might dress neatly and speak well but she still wasn't paid, she still worked for her bed and board and, she was well aware, for the safety of her surroundings. No one in the colony would dare loiter in the grounds of Government House. She had no money, nowhere else to live; she was a voluntary prisoner who could find no means of escape, and had nowhere to run to anyway.

Lately, though, she had been thinking more about her own people. At least the blacks here had each other, families, and in all their misery they could still laugh and joke, and they cared deeply for each other. She, Diamond, had no one. And none of these people had ever heard of her tribe, Irukandji. It was a shock to find that a lot of them felt sorry for her, unsettling her, because she was alone.

She was nearly eighteen now, she figured, and she could see herself stuck here for the rest of her life, so she began to think more and more about her own family and wonder if they had forgotten her. She fantasised about going home and being welcomed by her mother and father and her brother Meebal and all the others. They would have a great corroboree to celebrate and such stories she would tell them, until going home became an obsession with her. One day she would go north, somewhere in the north, she knew that much, and she would find them. Captain Beckman had always avoided mention of where they'd found her and Missus had said she didn't know. Not that Diamond had ever really asked; at that age, she'd just drifted along, accepting that she was their girl, kept interested and intrigued by Missus and everything around her. But she never forgot her real name. Kagari.

When she heard the talk in the kitchen about Miss Perfy, Diamond had been very upset. They said she'd gone off her head with grief at the death of her fiancé. They said that happened to a lot of people, and they never recovered, they turned into the mad loonies that you saw wandering alley-ways, or they got put in the lunatic asylum, the most fearsome place in the world.

So she had plucked up the courage to find Perfy's house, and knock on the door. She saw for herself that the girl was truly slipping into the mist world; Perfy hadn't even recognised her. Diamond could feel the emptiness, the coldness in the room; the warmth of love had been snatched so suddenly, Perfy was left in a void, staring into a looking-glass, denied a reflection.

Diamond sat cross-legged on the floor under the window, smelling the sweetness of jasmine and the last of the summer honeysuckles, so she spoke of them, and how the flowers came to be, festoons left by the spirits to gladden sad hearts, and her voice took on a hum, like the distant thrum of a didgeridoo. She talked on of other mists, deep green forest mists, mantles sparkling with magic, that were only seen by special people who, once they walked through the mists, were for ever blessed.

She didn't mention Darcy by name when she went back to Perfy's house the next night and the next, but she told of his everlasting place in nature, that Mother Earth needed him now to replenish her world. 'He might be a great eagle now, or a tall tree, or even a lightning spirit.'

'No, not that,' Perfy said softly and Diamond was tremendously relieved; she had been listening after all. 'He'd be a rock. No, better still, a headland, protecting a lovely bay. He has to be. I'm so frightened, Diamond. Every time I think of him now I see him in that grave with worms eating at him and it's frightful.'

'Hush now,' Diamond said.

But Perfy screamed. 'They say their hair keeps on growing!'

Diamond held her tight to quieten her. 'He is not there. He has been reborn, gone with the spirits to stand proudly in the place they have set aside for him, that headland – they will know it is his place.'

'Tell me again,' Perfy said, 'about the Oonji sisters who made the well.'

'In the time of many dry seasons they locked arms and collected dew into a well. The spirits looked kindly on them, and in time the well overflowed and became a waterfall and the waterfall became a stream that became a great river and their people never again suffered from thirst. The sisters are still there, two beautiful polished rocks, and every year the people take them flowers in thanksgiving.'

Diamond told her many stories, dredged up from the past, exciting stories of the Dreamtime, of heroes who became spirits and joined forces with Mother Earth, challenging lightning and thunder and other enemies from beyond; and were rewarded by her, turned into beings who would never again have to leave their beloved people. 'There's Burrumgillie,' she said, 'the great canyon, with feet of green. He was a fine warrior.' As Diamond gave names to rocks and rivers and mountain peaks, and overhanging teetering spurs, and ancient trees and serpent vines, she had no idea she was describing landmarks in Irukandji country above the mouth of the Endeavour River and the headwaters of a river later known as the Palmer.

She took Perfy for walks and together they watched busy insects, marvelling at the organisation of ant colonies, wondering who told them which scout to follow and how many thousands should go with them. And she pointed out the birds and what they were up to: swallows dipping over water, collecting moisture on their wings to add to earth to make mud for their nests, and she called to homecoming kookaburras who answered her, delighting Perfy, who laughed and clapped her hands, because she was stronger now.

There was a knock at Diamond's door. It was one of the footmen. 'A message for you,' he growled. 'Not my job to be bringing you messages, but it's from Perfy. She's going away and wants to see you before she goes.'

It had been months since she had seen Perfy. Diamond's visits had

101

dwindled off. She thought she might have helped a little bit, and when Mrs Middleton had told her that Perfy was gradually accepting Darcy's death, Diamond knew that time would do the rest. Like Mrs Beckman, Perfy had to get on with her life. She was not surprised Perfy was going away, it seemed to her that was what white people did. Even the Governor and Lady Bowen were going back over the seas. Not right away, but it was being talked about. 'Going home', they said, and all the time Diamond had thought this was their home. A new governor would be coming and a new lady but no one knew who this would be, and the staff were worried. Change frightened them, especially the housekeeper, who was afraid the new ones might bring their own house-keeper. They all seemed to have homes somewhere else. The Governor's home they said was England, like most people here, and Mrs Beckman's home was Germany. Diamond wondered again where her home was.

'We're going to live in Bowen,' Perfy told Diamond.

'Where's that?'

Perfy searched around in the household muddle. There were boxes every-where, packing cases, piled-up furniture, but eventually she found a map in the small tin trunk that contained family papers. 'Here,' she told Diamond. 'It's a small town up north, on the coast.'

'North.' The word stung Diamond. 'North.' It was singing to her. She was barely listening as Perfy explained that Darcy had left her a lot of money and the Middletons had bought a house in Bowen already.

'How did you do that?' Diamond made an effort to converse.

'Father wrote to an agent, a Mr Watlington, asking if there were any decent houses for sale, and Mr Watlington wrote back saying we were very lucky because Bowen was overrun with prospectors in and out to the Cape River goldfields and there wasn't a spare cot in the town, but this house had just been vacated, a really nice house. He urged us to buy it right away, otherwise not to consider coming to Bowen for a while because there's absolutely no accommodation for a decent family anywhere.'

'Oh, that's nice,' Diamond said vaguely. Bowen was north.

'Daddy went to the bank and arranged with them to send the money, so now we own our own house. Mother is so excited, she can't think straight.'

'I always thought you owned this house.'

'No. We only rent it. Mother and Daddy, they've always been so good to me, and they've had really hard lives, it feels good for me to be able to do something for them at last.'

'Yes, of course,' Diamond said dully.

Diamond helped. Mrs Middleton insisted they scrub every corner of the house so that the new tenants would not be able to talk about them. Diamond took a wire brush to the stove, inside and out, and when she'd finished, Perfy polished it with blacking.

'I'll be going out to visit the station,' Perfy told her.

'What station?'

'I now own part of Darcy's cattle station. He left it to me.'

Mrs Middleton was listening. 'You needn't think I'm going right out there, it's hundreds and hundreds of miles and no proper roads yet. I'll stay and mind our house.'

'Can I come with you?' Diamond said quickly.

'Where to?' Perfy was surprised.

'To wherever you're going. Well-off ladies have maids. You know that. When they come to Government House they often bring their own maids.'

Perfy turned to her mother. 'What do you think?'

Alice Middleton stopped and looked at Diamond. 'We're not used to maids, not people like us.'

'Oh please,' Diamond said. 'I don't mind what I do. I don't want to stay in that laundry for the rest of my life.'

Alice was trying to pack cumbersome pots and pans into a box. She studied Diamond again. 'Maybe it's not such a bad idea. If you go out to that Caravale place with your father, Perfy, there may not be any women to travel with. I'd feel better if you had another girl with you. Besides,' she added, 'they say it's pretty grand. Maybe they'd expect a young lady to have a maid with her. Yes, maybe they would.' She smiled. 'If Jack approves, I suppose you could come with us.'

As Diamond was leaving, Perfy whispered to her, 'Daddy won't mind, but listen, Diamond, can you ride a horse?'

'No.'

'Then you'll have to learn, but we'll do that when we get to Bowen.'

PART FOUR

1

Herbert Watlington was a happy man as he made his way along the main street of Bowen. It was nothing more than corrugated ridges of dried mud, caught like Pompeii in the aftermath of the wet season. One minute it was a sea of knee-deep squelch caused by struggling wagon wheels and the steady pumping of horses' hooves, the next minute baked dry, mud petrified by the swift onslaught of fierce sunlight freed from monsoonal clouds. It amused him that this was called Herbert Street. A good omen.

And the rains had gone at last. Sent packing. He smiled at that thought and a passer-by responded, tipping his hat, but Herbert's amusement was associated with the picture of his father sending his son packing, ordering him off to the colony to mitigate his disgrace. The Colonel had envisaged this country as an outsized poor-house where convicts and their more genteel contemporaries suffered humiliations, heads bowed, waiting for the glad day when they could return to the bosom of Mother England, scandals forgotten and therefore sins forgiven. He was way off the mark. Herbert had indeed suffered setbacks but he regarded his progress in Queensland as being more hilarious than miserable. The place and the populace were, in his eyes, absolutely outrageous. There were rascals and ruffians galore and their escapades made his fall from grace seem small beer.

The main street was like a ploughed paddock. Herbert trod carefully, not wishing to wrench his ankle again or fall down and spoil the neat tropical suit which marked him as a gentleman, a businessman, in this chaotic hamlet.

Three bearded horsemen trotted by and one of them called to him. 'How're you goin' there, Herbie?'

He lifted his wide planter's hat in an exaggerated acknowledgement to amuse them. 'Exceedingly well, gentlemen,' and they grinned their approval.

'Bring me back a sample,' he yelled after them, a standard joke in Bowen, and they waved, laughing.

No need to ask where they were going, horses rigged for the trail, ropes, rifles and pistols carefully in place, swags rolled behind their saddles and a packhorse keeping pace with them. Bowen was crowded with prospectors headed for the Cape River diggings and, better still, with men returning from the goldfields with money to burn. Herbert liked Bowen, a free and easy seaside village with a main street as wide as a playing field. He wondered what it must have been like before the diggers came pouring in like a plague of locusts.

He tried to imagine what would happen to his home village on Lyme Bay if they suddenly discovered rich reefs of gold twenty miles inland – twenty miles there being equivalent to a couple of hundred in this impossible landscape. Lyme Bay locals did not appreciate strangers, and they were all so terribly refined and sombre. What a hoot that would be, to watch hordes of diggers and desperadoes clambering all over the place and opening up grotty pubs, not to mention rows of wide-open raucous whorehouses where the girls hung over the balconies to entice customers! And that reminded him, he had to call on Glory Molloy.

'Ah, 'tis the boyo himself!' she cried, hugging him to her familiar breasts, that no bodice could ever seem to contain. 'Come on in, me darlin'.' Glory winked as she led him into her private parlour. 'Come and meet Barney O'Day. Barney, this is Mr Watlington.'

A blunt-headed Irishman with the unmistakable silly grin of a man with pockets full of new-found gold heaved himself up from the sofa and proffered a grimy hand. 'Pleased to meet you, sir.'

Herbert took the hand as lightly as he dared and then removed himself to an armchair by the window. The fellow smelled.

'Will you join us for some coffee and cognac?' she asked. 'Barney here has just ridden into town, terrible tired he is, the poor feller, and all the hotels booked to the ears.'

Glory was laying on the brogue with a trowel so Herbert matched her with his best British upper-class accent. 'Coffee and cognac would be delightful, my dear. But Mr O'Day, surely you must be able to find a room somewhere?'

'Not a cot,' Barney groaned. 'And here I am looking forward to a proper bed and a bath after months on them diggings.'

Glory served the coffee and poured three glasses of her best cognac. Herbert took the hint; they'd performed this routine many times. He shuddered. 'The diggings! You don't have to tell me about them.'

'Ah yes,' Glory said. 'Mr Watlington tried the gold digging but was no hand at it at all.'

'Damn near starved to death,' Herbert told Barney. 'Couldn't find a speck of gold, couldn't stomach the rations and got too ill to swing a pick.'

'Ah, 'tis no place for a gentleman,' Barney said. 'Hard going, that I won't deny. And I never met so many spivs and shysters outside of a county jail.'

'Are you just visiting our little village?' Herbert asked.

'Oh sure, for a few days. I've only come in for a bit of celebratin' and then I'll be headin' back. I'm doin' right well enough now and I'll be a rich man before I'm through.'

'You're more fortunate than I was,' Herbert said. 'I came stumbling into

Bowen without a bean, quite down and out, but I met Glory, and in her kindness she took me in.'

That was almost true. His weeks on the diggings had been disastrous, but then he'd met a fellow called Flash Jack who had struck it rich and paid Herbert to accompany him as a bodyguard into Bowen. It was a typically mad choice, Herbert thought, since he'd be more likely to bolt than stand and deliver, but fortunately the bushwhackers must have been busy elsewhere.

It was during those riotous weeks helping Jack spend his money that Herbert had met Glory Molloy, or rather she had collared him. She had a piano but no pianist, and this Englishman on the tear with Flash Jack could play up a storm. Glory offered him the job as her piano player and since he'd run out of cash and had no intention of prospecting again, he'd stayed. He often slept in her large downy bed. For a woman of forty, or thereabouts, fifteen years his senior, Glory was still an attractive woman. Herbert watched her now, chatting to Barney, hanging on his every word, flattering him; competition between the brothels was hot, and Glory wouldn't let new customers out of her sight. It was time for Herbert to speak up.

'Surely you could find a bed for Barney?' he asked innocently. 'There must be somewhere he can rest.'

She shook her head. 'Ah now, Mr Watlington, I have my rules, you know that. I can't afford the room, you understand, Barney me love. These days we're busy all the time, my house is known as the best.'

'Come on now, Glory,' Herbert persuaded. 'I'm sure Barney here could match your price. I mean what's the point of money if you can't buy what you need?'

'He's right,' Barney said eagerly, dragging a small pouch from inside his battered waistcoat and dropping it on the table. 'How's that for starters now? You keep it, Miss Molloy, and let me know when it runs out.'

Glory confiscated the gold. 'Well, I suppose I could make an exception . . .'

Barney was on his feet. 'And you'll not be sorry. I'll dance at your weddin', me lovely.'

'Charlene!' Glory called and the beaming Barney was led away by a buxom lass with a mop of blonde hair and a wobbly behind.

'I wanted to see you,' Glory said to Herbert. 'The Giesler house is for sale.' She had sported Herbert his new clothes and paid the rent for a small office next door to the Palace Hotel. 'I've decided with your pretty looks and fine English voice, you should go into commerce,' she'd told him.

'And what exactly is commerce?'

'I don't rightly know but it sounds very respectable. I want you to be a stock and station agent.'

'A what? I don't know a fig about stations and I hate cows.'

Glory considered this. 'Commerce is making people spend their money, Herbie, and there's wagonloads of it coming into Bowen. What about being a house and land agent then?'

'How do I go about it?'

When Glory Molloy made up her mind to do something, she was off and running before anyone else drew breath, and Herbert had been 'in commerce' for some months now. Glory knew everything that went on in the town and made an excellent silent partner.

Now the Giesler house. It was the best house in town. Giesler had built it himself in the style of residentials popular with the British in India. Herbert had seen sketches and photographs of identical buildings handed around among family and friends back home, cool-looking places with wide verandahs and french windows which opened out to catch a breeze.

'Why is Giesler selling?'

'Because, me darling, he made a killing on the goldfields. He's so rich now he's taking his family home to Germany to live happily ever after.'

Herbert was surprised. 'I didn't hear about this.'

'Of course you didn't, because Giesler's the smart one, not a word to a soul,' she grinned, 'except my friend Mr Tolley, my favourite bank manager. Now listen here, Herbie, you go down there and give him your groans about how hard it is to sell a house these days with everyone coming and going, and you buy it for me. One hundred pounds I'm offering. Buy it in your name because he'll expect more out of me.'

'I'll try, but it's worth a lot more than that.'

'So it is, but Giesler is anxious to be off.'

'Very well. I'll give it a shot. Have you decided to live there?'

'Me, good God in heaven no. When he leaves we'll triple the price and sell it. You'll get your cut both ways, so be a good lad and push off.'

The purchase was easy, Giesler threw in the furniture for an extra ten pounds. Glory was right, the German was too excited at going home to care about his sale price, he just needed to dispose of it. Herbert inspected the house, careful not to let the German know that he was impressed by the aura of this lovingly constructed building, with its high ceilings and large airy rooms, ideal for the climate. And the furniture, imported, was quality. There was even a piano. Herbert ran a short chromatic scale over the keys, and sighed. It was in tune, not like Glory's jangling piano.

'You play?' Giesler said, delighted. 'A shame we find out now.'

Herbert wandered through the rooms. He'd love to own the house himself, but he couldn't stretch to a hundred pounds yet, not with gambling debts hanging over his head. Besides, Glory Molloy was his partner and protector in this brawling town, he wouldn't dare try to cross her. She liked to have him around, she said he gave the place class.

No sooner had the Giesler family departed than Tolley put Glory on to buyers from Brisbane looking for a house in Bowen, a family by the name of Middleton. Herbert negotiated the sale through a firm of lawyers, Jauncy and Bascombe, at a price of two hundred and eighty-nine pounds, plus sixty pounds for the furnishings.

Glory had to know everything. 'Why are these people coming here? These Middletons.'

'There's a gold rush on, old dear, didn't you know?' Herbert drawled.

'If they're after the gold they don't bring money with them, and they don't buy expensive houses before they go prospecting.'

'Maybe he's a government official, a new customs agent, or land surveyor.'

'That won't do at all,' Glory mused. 'Them fellers don't have that sort of money.'

Weeks later she came bowling into his little office, decked out in a startling rose taffeta dress with a huge flowered hat atop her thick black hair. 'You ought to put signs out there on the porch,' she admonished him.

'What sort of signs?'

'Lord, Herbert, you can't be sitting here a-dreaming. Get some blackboards and write messages on them. "Land for sale", "Cheap house for sale".'

'I haven't got any houses for sale, there aren't enough to go round now.'

'There will be if you flutter hard cash under their noses. These people will sell anything with the gold spilling out on their laps. But this isn't what I came for. The Middletons. I found out. Do you know Caravale Station?'

'I've heard of it.'

'Right then. Owned by two brothers, rich squatters, but one of the brothers got himself killed in Brisbane, and what does he do? He leaves all his worldly goods to his girlfriend, including half a station bigger than Ireland.'

Herbert grinned. Glory had never set foot in Ireland.

'And guess who the lucky girl is?' Glory continued. 'Miss Middleton. That's why they've come to Bowen!' she concluded triumphantly.

'So?'

Deflated, she shrugged. 'I just thought you'd like to know. And get those bloody signs out there!'

He watched her leave, envying that common woman. Heads turned as she sashayed past, wielding a furled crimson umbrella like a strutter's stage prop. She skipped over the uneven ground as sprightly as a mountain goat. But let a well-heeled gentleman appear, and poor Glory would tip and scramble, requiring his manly assistance. She never missed a mark. Glory Molloy knew who she was and what she was, and she was content. That irritated Herbert. He knew who he was, an English gentleman, fallen, temporarily, on hard times, but the trouble was, in this place, no one cared. He was accepted as a friend of Glory's by the sort of people he would not normally have addressed, and that hurt. It stung. He yearned for respectability, to seek his rightful status in society, such as it was in this country. But that took money. And the awful part was, Glory understood, she felt sorry for him, which was another reason for shoving him into this shady agent business. So that they could both make more money. He just wished she'd stop telling people he was 'in commerce', such an ignorant expression.

Feeling sorry for himself, he took out a pack of cards and shuffled expertly, flipping them on his desk, wondering vaguely where one might purchase such a thing as a blackboard.

2

Cornelia Buchanan ran along the verandah, shouting and waving her walking stick. 'The horses are in the orchard!' she yelled. 'Get them out, you hounds!' She watched as the two black gardeners, Jumbo and Lazarus, leapt the fence and took off after the horses.

'Who left the damned gate open?' she shrieked. 'I'll have your hides for this!'

Hearing the commotion and knowing full well they were out of bounds, the three horses took off in all directions, swerving in among the trees, snapping branches and trampling younger trees.

'Don't chase them!' Cornelia yelled from her overview of the rows of fruit trees. 'Haven't you got any bloody sense? Go quiet, Jumbo, walk them out before they wreck the whole place.'

Disgusted, she turned to Mae, her housekeeper. 'They'll never change, these damn blacks, not in a million years. I've told them never to leave that gate open.'

'Don't worry, Mrs Buchanan,' Mae said. 'They'll get the horses out.'

'But how long have they been in there? That's Darcy's horse, Clipper. It'll get the gripe if it eats too many apples.'

'He's a villain of a horse,' Mae laughed. 'He can open gates himself.'

'That's no excuse, they should chain the gate. You tell Jumbo if he lets them in again he'll be punished. Severely punished.'

'Very well,' Mae said, pursing her lips in the way that always irritated Cornelia. Mae was too soft on the blacks. All very well for her, she'd only been at Caravale for a couple of years, she didn't know what it was like in the old days, trying to turn a wilderness into a viable property. The blacks hadn't just been a nuisance then, they'd been dangerous. Many a night she'd had to stand guard with a shotgun while Teddy was out on the range, cursing the blacks for hanging around outside the house, and cursing Teddy for bring her to this Godforsaken place. The station, as Teddy had predicted, had prospered and she now had a fine house, but she would never forget those first few years, living in the old hut, cooking outside in a bush oven, never seeing anything but black faces for months on end.

She lowered herself carefully into a comfortable cane armchair. Her back was playing up, legacy of a fall from a horse a long time ago. 'Put a crick in your back,' the doctor had told her. 'It will give you a pinch or two when you get older.' A lot he knew, it hurt like hell lately.

She could see Tom Mansfield riding up the drive.

Some women claimed their backaches predicted rain. Cornelia's aches, she was certain, warned of trouble.

What did Mansfield want? He was manager of the outstation but, in the absence of Darcy and Ben, had taken charge of the whole of Caravale. Not that there was much to do, with the wet season lingering, except chase the latest pests off the property, the gold diggers. She noticed he'd finally learned to scrape his boots properly before stepping on to her verandah.

'Good afternoon, ma'am,' he said. 'Brought in the mail. Met up with a bullocky and his team out on the trail. He was headed for Charters Towers and real pleased to see us, saved him the trouble of turning off.' He handed Cornelia a bulky canvas bag.

'It's about time they had a proper mail service out this way instead of us having to take pot luck with whoever is coming out.'

'They're talking about it,' Tom said.

'They're always talking about it.'

'Hot and steamy still,' he remarked, his eyes on the bag, but she had no intention of opening it until he left. She still had some authority around here.

'We found the carcass of a steer out near the west boundary. Some of those mongrel miners must have butchered it. Didn't even bother to bury the carcass. Wouldn't be surprised if they've grabbed some of our cattle too. The bullocky says it'll get worse. He said miners are tramping to the Cape like grasshoppers on the land, bringing their families and all, and they don't know nothing about the bush. Lot of them ain't even got supplies.'

Cornelia tapped her cane impatiently. 'No use complaining to me. You know what to do. If they're rustling our cattle, shoot them.'

'It's not so easy. I hear butchers at the Cape don't give a tap for brands, and I don't have enough men to keep our perimeters properly patrolled.'

'Then use blacks. They'd sell their mothers to get on a horse.'

'But I can't arm them, it's against the law.'

Cornelia laughed. 'So give them spears. They've probably forgotten what they're for, the lazy lot, living here on our charity. Anyway, the gold will run out soon and all those fools will have to trek back home again.'

'Doesn't sound like it. They say they're finding more and more gold in the Cape tributaries. Some reckon these goldfields will match Ballarat.'

'We'll see,' Cornelia said, dismissing him. Mansfield always had something to complain about.

The real misfortune was Teddy's choice of land. He'd marked off a thousand square miles; Caravale extended for thirty-five miles east to west. If he had gone further out, the Buchanans would have owned the goldfields – they were only a hundred miles or so to the west. They'd have been millionaires a dozen times over. That was one more thing she'd never forgive Teddy for.

She opened the mailbag, tossing aside newspapers, catalogues, mail for the station hands, bills. She didn't care about the bills, not since the day she was told that Teddy had cut her out of his will and left everything to the boys. Everything, the station, the house, her home! After all those years, there was nothing here she could call her own. The bastard! Fortunately she had good sons, they loved their mother and they denied her nothing; she was still the mistress of Caravale, she could still entertain in style when it suited her. But for how long? What would happen when they brought wives home? Those women needn't think they could shunt her out. Just let them try.

A letter from Ben! And about time, written on fine embossed paper too. As she read, Cornelia gaped in amazement. Ben's words were tumbling over themselves with excitement. They'd sold the whole herd at top price, they'd stayed at Sherwood Station, very grand, and he had been invited to stay in Brisbane at Government House! Oh my! She almost called out to Mae to share this news but wanted to savour it herself a little longer. She read on. Ben was being nominated for the Queensland Parliament. He was to be a Member of Parliament. Her son! She sat back. Delighted. He would be one of the most important men in the state. He might even bring the Governor to visit, Governor Bowen and the Countess, for heaven's sake. She'd have to see about having the homestead renovated. Completely renovated.

She rang the little hand bell to summon Mae. 'You can take this lot away, but leave me the catalogues. I think there's a letter in there for you too. And I won't have tea this afternoon, bring me the gin, and cold water, and sliced lemon.'

'You heard from Ben,' Mae said, noticing her letter. 'They got to Brisbane safely then?'

'Oh yes.' She'd announce her news in her own good time, it would be wasted on Mae and all over the district before she had a chance to see their faces. 'My back is so bad today, the gin will ease the pain.'

She waited until Mae came back with the tray, a silver tray with a crystal decanter and crystal glass. Then she poured herself a straight gin, to celebrate.

Ben went on to say that Darcy had cottoned on to some girl, but he doubted it would come to anything. Cornelia frowned, she wished Ben hadn't spoiled his letter with that ominous remark. Still, the boys were bound to find women in Brisbane, she didn't expect them to be saints.

Cornelia picked up her glass. The gin was the very best you could buy and she swallowed it with relish, remembering the days when at a penny a glass the stuff tore at your throat.

'You've come a long way, Nellie,' she exulted. She was glad Teddy was not around to enjoy this. Serve him right. There was no one left to point a finger at Cornelia Buchanan . . .

Winter at Caravale was her favourite time, warm days and chilly nights, free of that thundering summer heat and rain, and this time of the day was special to her. The men were out mustering, the tutor had taken the boys for a walk to the falls, and, wonder of wonders, the black housegirls had managed to get through their work with a minimum of confusion, so Cornelia had the place all to herself. Finished at last, this lovely house was hers, the Caravale homestead, and she was so proud of it, proud of herself.

She strolled through the rooms touching everything with a sensuous tingling joy, stroking the polished furniture, the glittering lamps, the gilt-edged mirrors, the sturdy sofas. As she passed the mirror again, she laughed, seeing that silly farm girl who had run away at fourteen to seek the bright lights, chasing over the border down through England, all the way to London where she had met Clem Bunn.

Cornelia frowned. Why had she thought of him? She still had night-mares about those years in London, grim brutal dreams of scavenging in murky lanes, stomach knotted with hunger, thieving, mugging; and that cellar where they'd lived, the scampering of rats. She shook her head and went to the bookshelves, searching out a light novel to wash away all that misery. It was over now. She was the wife of Teddy Buchanan, of the well-known New South Wales squattocracy, and the mother of two fine boys. They'd been married fourteen years now . . . My, how time flew!

She and Teddy ordered their books from catalogues, dozens at a time, and it was fun sorting through them when they arrived. Quite a few she hadn't read yet. She selected a slim book, *Pearls of the Heart*, and sank into Teddy's big armchair, with the footstool, but she still couldn't settle. Nostalgia. She hated these clouds of memory that drifted over her every so often; she didn't know why people had to think about the past at all. Teddy and his mates were always reminiscing about the old days, boring stuff, although at one stage they had mentioned Walter McKenzie and that had given her a start. Walter, fortunately, had died about four years ago of a bad heart. Not surprising, they said, the old billy goat. It had been Walter who'd rescued her from steerage class on board ship and moved her into his cabin on the long voyage from London to Sydney, and she'd done well by him, up to a point. He bought her a fabulous wardrobe of fashionable clothes in Capetown and since he was married, set her up as his mistress in a house he owned at Potts Point. She couldn't have had a better introduction to Sydney Town, with no money worries and time to behave like a lady as he had taught her over the four months at sea. But then Walter's mates started turning up, old fogies, encouraged by Walter himself to share his mistress. Cornelia had tossed the lot of them out on their ears.

116

She, Cornelia Crabtree (she had reverted to her maiden name), wouldn't have them on for all their cash. Any fool knew that once a man permitted his mates access to his mistress, she was on the skids.

Fortunately it was about that time she'd met Teddy Buchanan at the races. She told him she was living with her old aunt. Teddy was truly smitten with this well-dressed, red-haired Scottish girl, begging her to marry him, to come to Brisbane with him where he was negotiating to buy land in the north. And Teddy wasn't hard to take, tall, easy-going, always cheerful. They had married in Brisbane and eventually moved out to this property of his which was hell for a start, but now . . . Unbelievable what these men could do, turning all that wild country into a big cattle station running about twenty thousand head of cattle. She smiled. She adored her house and she was happy with Teddy. You couldn't help liking him, he made people laugh with his dry humour, nothing ever seemed to bother him.

Sometimes she wondered how Walter had felt when he'd gone to the house at Potts Point. She had simply disappeared, leaving the place spic and span, scrubbed clean from top to bottom, and not a stick of furniture. She'd sold the lot on him. That was his payout for trying to inflict his boozy friends on her.

Poor Walter, dead and buried, what a shame! And here she was living happily ever after, mistress of Caravale.

Cornelia opened the book: the heroine, Gwendoline, was a poor orphan, her parents had just died in the poorhouse, and she was all alone . . . Cornelia peeked at the last few pages. Good, she liked happy endings. She read on, relaxed now, peaceful.

Someone sounded the knocker on the front door. Irritated, Cornelia put the book down and walked out into the hall, noting that Teddy's loaded rifle was hanging on the hook by the hallstand. On these isolated stations a person always had to be on their guard; strangers, white or black, could be dangerous.

The visitor was a bearded stockman standing like a dark shadow against the outside glare.

'Didn't you see the sign on the gate?' she asked angrily. 'It says keep out. The stockmen's quarters are round the back.'

The insolent character made no effort to obey her instructions. 'Steady now, missus, I just wanted to have a talk with you.'

'You'll get talk if my husband finds out you're hanging around the house.' Which he would, she'd make sure of that.

'No need to get cranky. A civil word don't hurt no one.'

She went to close the door but he put a firm hand against it. 'Come on now, Nellie, you wouldn't be shovin' off an old friend.'

'I don't know you,' she gasped. No one had called her Nellie in this country. Ever.

'You mean to say you don't remember your old man, Nellie Bunn? I'm Clem. Don't you recognise me?'

'I've never heard of you,' she bluffed, her heart pounding.

'Now, now, don't get smart. It's taken me a long time to track you down, I'm not going off that easily. You better ask me in.'

'No.'

'Then I'll have to go and see Teddy after all. Not so's he can talk to me, mind you. I'll be doing the talking.'

She stepped back a few paces and allowed him into the hall, unable to stop him closing the front door. 'What do you want?'

'Well now,' he said, leaning against the door as if to prevent interruptions. 'We got a score to settle. You put me into the law, Nellie, and took off with our money.'

'I did not. I left because you were a drunken pig. Now get out of here.'

'Not so fast. I know it was you had me nabbed. I did five years in Newgate. Gave you plenty of time to run, didn't it? But I'm ready to let bygones be bygones. I'm a fair man. Do you know, Nellie, I been here two weeks now and you didn't even notice me.'

'Why should I?'

'Fair enough. But you'll start noticing me from now on unless you want your old man to know you've got two husbands living on the station.'

Cornelia stood firm but her stomach was churning. 'I asked you what you want.'

'Right. What do I want? I'll tell you. You're a rich woman now, Nellie. I want five hundred pounds and I'll be on my way.'

She shook with fear. 'I can't just get five hundred pounds, I'd have to ask my husband.'

'Nellie, you're as tricky as a tin of worms. You'll figure out a way.'

'And after that, if I do get it, you promise not to come back?'

'On my honour as a gent.'

She glared at him, still seeing a stranger except for his pale watery eyes. 'You're a liar, you'll be back in a month.'

Clem laughed. 'No flies on you, Nellie. I'd say that's possible. 'Course I might go to the Cape and pick up a bucket of gold, then I won't be so needy, like. But see, you owe me. I'm doin' you a favour, believe me, keeping my mouth shut. There ain't a soul out in the bunkhouse as knows I'm married to the missus. Now we can be friends. This is a real nice place you got here, the least you can do is bring me in for a drink. It's not manners to keep a man standing in the hallway.'

Cornelia stepped back a few more paces, and a few more, appearing bewildered, stunned, her palms outstretched in front of her, watching his grinning, triumphant face. What had he said? That he hadn't told anyone about them. Good. He'd never get another opportunity.

She snatched the rifle and levelled at him, pleased to see the shock on his face.

'Hey wait, Nellie. Now don't be stupid, girl. I'll go.' He reached for the doorknob.

'No, you won't,' she snapped. 'Come away from that door,' and she backed further down the hall. 'You come in, walk very slowly.'

He began to step forward warily, one step at a time in his dirty boots, and Cornelia shot him right between the eyes. As he dropped, blood and bone shattering, she let the rifle fall, messed her hair and ripped at her blouse and skirt. She smashed a vase of lilies from a pedestal, knocked photos from the hallstand, breaking the glass, skidded the hall runner out of shape and went screaming out the back of the house towards the blacks' camp, knowing they would create more hysteria at the Missus being attacked than a herd of wild horses let loose in the house.

Now, another ten years down the line, reading Ben's letter, she felt justified. None of it had been in vain, there was no scandal. Mrs Buchanan had been attacked by an intruder who had chosen a time when the men were out mustering and so she'd had to defend herself.

But Teddy, with his blasted conscience, had made inquiries about the identity of Clem Bunn and almost a year later, had confronted her. 'That fellow was your husband. You never divorced him. We have no marriage.'

The Teddys of this world knew all about protecting the family name for the sake of their sons. He moved into another bedroom, was polite but distant to her, and never said another word about the matter. Cornelia didn't really care, it wasn't much of a penalty, and Teddy had kept her safe.

She poured another gin, a larger one, remembering his will with rage. That had been her punishment. Teddy had left her nothing. She owned nothing. In reality she was simply tolerated by her good-natured sons. She was pleased it was Ben who was being nominated for Parliament, he could be hard to handle. She would urge him to buy a house in Brisbane, find a wife and settle down there. Darcy was more like his father. She would find some nice, quiet, country girl for him, someone who would do as she was told.

Good! Gin always made her feel a mighty sight better. There was always an answer to problems.

3

A dust-storm held the station under siege, choking red dust that came sweeping from the inland and then hung like a pall, blotting out the sun, turning the light of day into an eerie orange haze. Birds were silent, native animals tucked themselves away, cattle huddled together, heads down, sheltering each other, and the homestead was battened down like a fort.

Cornelia hated these storms. Sometimes they lasted for days, making the house unbearably close and, despite their precautions, infiltrating the building, covering everything with layers of dust. She leaned on her cane as she walked restlessly through the rooms. Her back was killing her, and she could taste the dust; it was in her hair, in her mouth, in her nose. These storms had a smell about them, an ancient smell, like old bones, musty and nauseating. Nowadays there were other stations, way out west, much bigger than Caravale, ten times bigger they said, and they were welcome. She ran a finger through matted dust on the sideboard. 'I'd hate to see the far western stations,' she said to Mae, 'if we're getting their topsoil dumped on us like this.'

'It's so gritty, it feels more like sand,' Mae said.

'Rot, it's plain old useless dust. It'll take a week to clean this up.'

Mae pulled a curtain aside and peered outside. 'I think it's lifting a bit.' She stood, staring out. Visibility was poor but she thought she could see four horsemen approaching. In a trick of light they seemed to shimmer and fade in the distance, like a mirage. It was a long, straight track from the main road to the homestead. She shuddered. The men looked unreal, dark shapes, wraiths, moving steadily, rhythmically, outlines blurred. 'There are men coming,' she whispered to Cornelia, as if afraid they might hear.

'What men? Who'd be abroad on a day like this?' She yanked back the curtain and stared through the haze of dust. 'I don't like the look of them. Fetch my gun.'

'Which one?'

Cornelia had a new Colt revolver but she always felt more comfortable with her rifle. Darcy had bought her this one, the very latest. The boys were proud of their mother, she was an excellent shot and liked to compete with the men at target shooting. She loaded the rifle, watching the strangers approach the house; their horses were bagged to keep the dust out of their eyes and the men were rugged up, hats down over their eyes and neckerchief masks across their faces. Impossible to tell who they were.

'They could be bushrangers,' she said to Mae. 'Run out the back and rouse the men! Don't stand there, move!'

Cornelia dropped the curtain and watched through the lace as the men dismounted at the homestead gate. Heads down, hands covering their eyes, they came in the gate, slowly, she thought, too slowly, and trudged up the path towards the front door. Quietly, as they mounted the steps to the verandah making for the front door, she unlatched a french window and stepped out, rifle levelled: 'Don't move!' she snapped.

Startled, they turned their heads to look at her. She stood ten feet away along the verandah. They were still, very still. She couldn't recognise any of them.

'Mrs Buchanan,' one of them began, but Cornelia wasn't going to let conversation throw her off guard.

'Shut up!' she said, the rifle very steady. 'Just stand right there or I'll shoot, and don't go thinking I won't.'

And then the station hands came running, round the verandah, over the fences, all armed, to take over and identify the strangers.

One of the men was the sergeant of police from Bowen. With him were two of the Connor lads, friends of Ben's from the South Bowen Station, and, of all people, the Reverend Charlie Croft, but there was no laughter.

As the station men melted away and Mae rushed off to organise refreshments, Cornelia led the visitors inside, apologising.

'No need to, dear lady,' the Reverend Charlie mumbled. 'Perfectly understandable. Very wise of you.'

'Sensible, I'd say,' the sergeant added, 'the way things are out here these days.'

They were shuffling, crushing their hats, not inclined to sit and she saw what she thought was fear on the dust-grimed faces. 'Where have you come from today?' she asked. 'A bad day to be on the road.'

'We've come right on from Bowen,' Dicky Connor blurted. 'We came as fast as we could.'

'Bowen?' Cornelia was amazed; it was a three-day ride at best. 'What for? Why, what's wrong?'

The Reverend took her arm gently. 'I think you should sit down, Mrs Buchanan.'

Cornelia shook him loose. 'No. Leave me alone. What's wrong?'

It was the sergeant's turn. 'We have bad news for you, ma'am. Bad news. There's been an accident. Down in Brisbane.'

The perspiration on her body turned to ice and she shivered in the sudden clammy cold. 'Who? Who was in an accident?'

'Darcy,' he said. 'It was Darcy. In a fight.'

There was a small respite. A fight. Darcy had been in fights before, the men out here . . . She looked at the silence. 'How bad?' Charlie Croft had tears in his eyes.

The sergeant heaved a sigh. 'I'm sorry, ma'am, real bad. Darcy is dead.'

Darcy? This was not true. He was only twenty-five. 'Who says so?' she demanded, fighting this wild story. 'How do you know?'

'Telegraph, ma'am. Telegraph to let you know as soon as possible.'

'Where's Ben?' She was still defiant.

'In Brisbane, ma'am. He's all right. He stayed on to make all the arrangements. The funeral like, and the Reverend, he's come with us to conduct a service here—'

'If you wish,' the Reverend interrupted. 'Only if you want me to.'

Cornelia stared at him. The others seemed to have retreated, heads bowed, out of focus, chains away from her. 'Darcy's dead?' she asked him, her voice plaintive, pleading. 'My Darcy?'

Hands held her, Mae was there, weeping, men whispering, the ceiling whirling, a noise in her head like a roar of pain as she tried to keep control. 'Will you excuse me?' she said, making for the door, desperately playing the part expected of her, that they would talk about for years. Her eyes were clouded by a welling tumult of tears. 'Mae, see that they are quartered.' She turned back, head high. 'I'm extremely grateful to you gentlemen for your kindness.'

Mae came running after her. 'Mrs Buchanan, I'm so sorry. Are you all right? Is there anything I can do?'

'Yes, give them drinks. Anything they want. And serve them a decent meal.'

'But what about you?'

'Brandy,' Cornelia grated. 'Then just leave me alone.'

It was the first time in her life Cornelia had experienced such agony, and she felt a dull awe that she was unable to control it. She took handkerchiefs and walked around her room, stared out of the window, sat on the bed, went back to the window, but the wrenching sobs would not stop. Darcy gone! He and Ben were the only people in the world she had any time for, even cared about. What had happened? She wanted to know every detail but the shock was too much, she couldn't bear to hear any more just yet.

She heard a wailing in the distance and then a steady thump on hollow logs followed by the demanding drone of a didgeridoo. The blacks had begun their 'crying' for Darcy. The wailing became louder, more urgent. Other times their mourning habits had irritated her but now she was comforted. She wanted to scream and scream, and yet somehow she couldn't. The black women would do it for her, they'd scream and shriek and lash at themselves, because they had loved Darcy too. Cornelia let the hypnotic far-reaching notes of the didgeridoo wash over her, listening to the monotonous repetition, the low drone echo-less in the darkening dun-coloured landscape. A numbness stole over her.

4

Ben had known his homecoming would be difficult but he had never antici-
pated anything like this. Wildly, illogically, he wished Darcy were there.
Darcy could cope with her tempers, he'd had a way of treating their mother
as if he were her big brother, he could quieten her down with his gentle
teasing. Ben felt defenceless against her terrifying rage.

God knows he would have to live with this guilt, on top of losing his
brother. If only . . . Oh hell, it was no use going over and over all that for the
thousandth time. The others had been so overwhelmed with grief they'd
avoided mentioning the awful joke that had gone wrong. That would just
have made things worse. It wasn't only a matter of the law, it had been an accident, after all. It was everyone else. How would they be able to face people
again? And Cornelia. Jesus! If she ever found out! This was bad enough.

He had been delayed in Brisbane after the funeral, a nervous wreck,
desperately seeking legal advice. His whole world had fallen apart. He
wished, he'd prayed, that time could turn back and he could repair his
mistakes. He still wept for Darcy, and the guilt was terrible, but he was paying now. He was being punished. All thoughts of a political career forgotten,
his first priority now was Caravale. He'd been home a week and he still hadn't
been able to tell her the situation. It was all one big mess and he was trying to
think his way through it and at the same time settle his mother down.

She'd had time to grieve. They'd held a service at Caravale and friends
had come from hundreds of miles away, as well as mobs of blacks, to pay
their respects. Mae had told him all about it.

'Everyone loved Darcy,' she'd wept and Ben had felt a hurt, as if they were
all comparing him to Darcy and seeing him as a lesser person.

Cornelia had welcomed him home to share her grief but within a few
hours it had started.

'Who did it? Who killed my son?'

'Mother, you know what happened. I brought you home the coroner's
report.'

'And what did you do?'

'What could I do?'

'You should have shot the bastards!'

'Right! And got myself hanged.'

'So you just let them get away with it.'

'They didn't mean to. It was an accident. Don't you think they feel badly about it too?'

'Of course. They wrote to me. How dare they? They killed my son and they have the gall to write to me. And their bloody parents! If any of them sets foot on this station, ever, I'll kill them myself. You haven't got the guts to do it.'

'Oh, for Christ's sake.'

'No, you wouldn't do it, but you could have paid someone. You still could.'

On and on, night after night, she stormed her hatred, her dreams of revenge. Ginger Butterfield had kindly offered to accompany Ben back to Caravale. He was glad he'd declined, it would have been the last straw to inflict this on Ginger. At the time, he had preferred to travel alone. Needing a friend, Ben was afraid that he might break on the long ride from Bowen to Caravale and tell the real truth. Campfire talks, nights spent in the quiet of the bush . . . The stillness of the land shapes the man, takes over, encourages secrets to emerge as if only God were listening.

Ben was a good bushmen, able to overland in a sure straight line as the blacks did, avoiding the twists and turns of wagon tracks and the plodding mobs of diggers and their families headed for the Cape River. So he journeyed through the bush alone, grateful for the company of the nuzzling, playful thoroughbred he'd bought in Bowen and the sharp little speckled cattle dog he'd found scavenging behind the pub, her paws torn and bleeding. But she'd come good now and he let her ride behind him, sitting proudly on the horse's rump. He called her Blue.

'Anyway, get that dog out of the house,' she'd started on him another night. 'Dogs belong outside.'

'Not Blue, she's mine. I don't want her with the other dogs until she knows the place.'

'There's a dingo strain in her, you can see it in her eyes.'

'Yes, she's clever.'

'Darcy never brought dogs in the house.'

'No, because they were born on the station.'

'He had more sense.'

Ben ignored the remark. 'There's a herd coming through from Merri Creek Station. They'll be sticking to the stock route but I'll go out in the morning and ride with the drovers to see that our cattle don't go walkabout with them. That new stock route to the Cape River is right on our boundary, the north boundary.'

She had dressed for dinner, her dark red hair, flecked with grey, carefully brushed into wide thick rolls, framing her face. Ben thought she looked well in black but dared not say so, a reminder again. She had been drinking and was in her genteel waspish mood, an advance at least on her near-hysterical rantings.

'If you hadn't been so mad to get to Brisbane with all your fine friends, you could have sold those cattle at the Cape and Darcy would be still alive.'

'Will you stop this rot? You know they didn't find gold there until long after we'd left.'

She picked at her meal. 'Why were you staying at Government House and your brother having to put up at a pub?'

Ben ignored her. He'd told her why a dozen times.

'I've been thinking,' she said silkily. 'What would have happened if you'd been the one killed?'

'Sorry I can't oblige you.'

'No. You misunderstand me, Ben. What I meant was, Darcy would never have let those bastards get away with it. Darcy, you see, was very loyal. Loyal to his family.'

Ben shoved back from the table angrily. 'That does it,' he said. 'Let me tell you how loyal Darcy was. I've never mentioned that girlfriend of his—'

'Yes, you did, you mentioned her in your letter. I still have it.'

'Good, you can remember what suits you. But what you don't know is he intended to marry her. They'd set a date. The wedding was all arranged.'

'What? I don't believe you.'

The tables were turned now and Ben felt some pleasure to be able to fire some barbs of his own. 'That party was his buck's night.'

'Darcy would not have married anyone without letting me know.'

'You'd have known soon enough, he was bringing her home with him.'

'Who is this person? Do I know her?'

'Of course not, he'd only known her a week or so himself. She's a housemaid.'

Cornelia stared at him. Then she shook her head, as if to brush aside the matter. 'Oh well, Darcy would have known what he was doing, he was no fool. It's immaterial now.'

'You think so? Well, try again. I've been waiting for a better time to tell you this, but since you are determined to nag me for the rest of my life you'd better consider just how loyal Darcy was. He left all his worldly goods, real and personal, to her.'

She went white. No matter how hard she tried, never venturing outside without a hat, Cornelia's fair freckled skin had tanned over the years in the bush. Now it was pasty white. 'What are you saying?' she demanded.

'I'm telling you the bloody woman now owns half of Caravale.'

5

Jack Middleton was pleasantly surprised when he stepped ashore in Bowen, formerly Port Denison, with Alice and Perfy and their maid, Diamond.

At first view, from the ship, the place had seemed chaotic. The harbour was cluttered with the untidiest collection of craft he had ever seen. There were luggers and schooners, small sailing boats, trawlers, barges, even battered Asian vessels, and standing loftily out to sea several clipper ships and the passenger liner, *Duke of Roxburgh*.

They'd been fortunate, they thought, to obtain passage on the *Duke* but it had been overrun with steerage passengers, gold prospectors by the hundreds. The rest of the voyage, the captain had assured his first-class passengers, would be normal, but since the Middletons were disembarking with the mob, they'd never know.

An extremely long jetty stretched out into the bay from the township, but there was such a crowd of boats that their longboat had had to deliver them to the beach. Sailors assured them their luggage would be delivered later so Jack led his family trudging up the beach along a cleared path lined with palm trees and rich green foliage. They emerged on to the wide main street, sleepily quiet on this hot afternoon. The clean-cut country town seemed to have swallowed up all the gold-diggers reported to have invaded the place.

A young man, nattily dressed in a white tropical suit and wearing a sun helmet, stepped forward. 'Excuse me, sir, are you Mr Middleton?'

'That's right.'

'Oh, thank heavens, I've been watching for you. Might I introduce myself, I'm Herbert Watlington. The house and land agent.'

'How d'you do,' Jack said. 'Good of you to meet us, I must say. You might show us where the house is.'

'Certainly, sir. Perhaps I should find a carriage for you. It's a fair walk.'

Jack turned to his wife. 'What do you say, Mother? Do you want to wait for a carriage or will we step it out?'

'I'd prefer to walk,' she said. 'We need to stretch our legs. I'm still rocking from that boat.'

Jack introduced his family and they set off along the street. 'I've never seen a street as wide as this,' he commented. 'A man can hardly see the other side.'

'Yes, it's rather odd, isn't it?' Watlington said. 'But jolly handy in the mornings when the diggers and their horses and contraptions line up to travel to the diggings. A convoy of sorts leaves every morning, travelling together so they won't get lost.'

'How far are the goldfields?'

'About three hundred miles as the crow flies, but there's many a river and cliff betwixt.'

Jack nodded and looked back at the women who were following, but taking more time to peer into the shops crammed between pubs and banks. He guessed this young fellow hadn't been in the colony long, the accent was still too polished, and he had a real plummy way about him. But credit where credit's due, the money had been paid over, his job was done, he didn't have to go to the trouble of meeting them.

'I've been out here a long time,' he said, 'and I still can't get into my head the size of this state. The captain said we passed more than fifteen hundred miles of coastline to reach Bowen from Brisbane.'

'That is so,' Herbert replied with enthusiasm. 'I had to examine maps to make myself believe it. This town is still only halfway. It's just as far again to the top of the state at Cape York. Queensland.' He laughed. 'I wonder if the dear lady has any conception of the immensity of her namesake state. I rather think she'd not grasp it either. Probably send them back to get their sums right.'

'Where's the nearest town from here then?' Jack asked.

'Nearest town?' Herbert looked at him in surprise. 'Well, I suppose one would have to say Townsville. Two hundred miles north up the coast, I should say, on Cleveland Bay.'

'No. I meant inland.'

'My dear Mr Middleton, there aren't any towns inland. There's a village way out to the Cape goldfields called Charters Towers, but I don't think it's much more than a central supply depot for the big cattle stations out there.'

'Is that right?' Jack was stunned. No bloody towns? How could he take Perfy out into nowhere?

'Oh yes,' Herbert replied. 'One could say we're sitting right on the edge of civilisation. I mean one can't count the goldfields. I've been out there and they're about as uncivilised as possible. Now, your house is up here, this is Carter Street.' They turned the corner and their guide waited until the women caught up. 'Come along, ladies, I know it's hot, but just a little further.' He took them along the street and with a theatrical wave of his hand said, 'Voila!'

'Where?' Alice asked.

'Directly in front of us, across the road,' Herbert told her. 'I wanted you to have your first view of it from over here.'

127

'Good heavens!' Alice said, and Perfy grabbed her mother's arm. 'Why, it's beautiful. What a lovely house.'

Jack could only stand and stare. The house, their house, was wide, high-gabled, with verandahs all round. It was huge, and set in at least half an acre of rich green lawn, shady trees and flowering bushes. There was no fence at the front, just a long, well-trimmed hedge of colourful hibiscus with a flagged path dead centre, from the street to the front porch.

'The chappie who built it was a Prussian,' Herbert said, 'and he was most particular.'

As they made a tour of the house, Jack wondered what his old dad, dead now, would have thought of this. His eyes misted; the stubborn old coot, trying to feed a family on a miner's pay and keep his sons in order with a boot and a bullying. All scattered to the winds now. He probably would have refused to live in a place like this, he was always down on anyone who tried to get above themselves.

Jack sighed and took off his coat. He didn't have much in the way of civilian clothes, not that you needed more than shirts and trousers in this climate. Jesus, it was hot! A strange feeling overcame him, a yearning for the bracing chill of England, to see again the change of seasons, to feel the crunch of autumn leaves underfoot, to see fog and snow and wintery trees. But here it was only hot or hotter, the seasons wet or dry, a world of green, glazed or dripping. He shuddered, as if someone had just walked over his grave. Alice always said that. And then he shook off the depression, turning to the business at hand.

'I like to get my bearings,' he said to Herbert. 'Where can I get a map of this part of the world?'

'Scarce as hens' teeth,' he replied, 'with the diggers clamouring for them. But leave it to me, Mr Middleton. I shall find one for you myself.'

'I'd need one that shows the back country as well, not just Bowen here.'

'Quite. Are you interested in buying land up this way?'

'We might,' Jack said, giving nothing away.

'I'll be off then,' Herbert said. 'I'm delighted you like your house, sir.'

'Not my house,' Jack said. 'My daughter owns it.' There were three women coming up the path, carrying baskets. 'Who's this now?'

'Local ladies, sir. We're a very small residential community really, caught in among all the prospectors and their families, so the ladies like to welcome their new neighbours.'

'Well I never!' Jack said, astonished. He stood back, watching his wife, as she and Perfy received their guests. Alice was clearly delighted. This was really something, to be welcomed to a town as respected members of the community. Her face was a picture. He'd rib her about it later. But right now, he could see, this was the happiest day of her life.

Diamond moved quietly around, helping where she could. She liked the house too. She could feel the presence of the family that had lived here, hear the daughters singing, hear the father, a good man, speaking to them, reminding her of Captain Beckman; and she could hear the German lady, happy in her scrubbed white kitchen. The visiting ladies were explaining all about the previous owners to Miss Perfy and her parents, but Diamond didn't need to be told about them, their loving hands were everywhere. She thought it was a pity that money had seduced them from their tranquil home and felt troubled for them, sensing that they had gone too fast from the present into an ominous future.

But then maybe she was just thinking of Missus, who had written to her a few times, sad letters, feeling the cold of Germany in her bones and still bereft at no longer being mistress of her own home. Missus lived with her family, but was resented by her son's wife. Diamond found this very strange and answered the letters as cheerfully as she could manage. There had been little to relate about her days as a laundress, but now she'd have something interesting to say.

Miss Perfy had bought her blouses and skirts, so she was at last free of the ugly laundry shifts, but there'd been a problem about a hat. Mrs Middleton insisted to Diamond that no woman travelled without a hat but every one they tried looked ridiculous on Diamond's mop of thick frizzy hair. In the end Mrs Middleton had wrapped a scarf round her head in the style of a turban and that worked. In fact it looked so neat, Diamond had several cotton scarves now. They flattened her hair close to her head and were quite elegant. As she passed a mirror she checked again. Yes, turbans really suited her; they accentuated her coppery skin and high cheekbones and, without any hair showing at all, gave her a sleek appearance. What's more, even though she was already tall for a woman, wearing these pretty turbans made her stand taller still, hold her head up. Funny that. But the main thing, everyone was satisfied.

They were all too excited to notice Diamond's disappointment when the luggage arrived and the bedrooms were allotted. There were four big bedrooms, and a sleepout which was in the yard, attached to the laundry. 'The maid's quarters,' the agent had pointed out, guessing her status, and so the sleepout became her room. Diamond shrugged. Why should she think this family would be any different? Blacks did not sleep inside white people's houses. Except that Diamond could never think of herself as being black, of being any particular colour.

Still, she had managed to move herself north and the room with its canvas blinds instead of glass in the windows was big and would be cool at night. She had been thinking a lot lately about her own people, and she knew the word now. She had been kidnapped. She could never hold a grudge against the Beckmans who considered they'd rescued her, fair enough, but little whips of outrage stung her now and then. She felt deprived of her place on the earth; she was certain that her people knew so much more in their own way, things she should know that drifted close to her sometimes but never—

'Diamond!' Alice called. 'Come along now, no time to be mooning about, we've got work to do.'

6

The station was busy. There were always strangers about these days. Cattle buyers couldn't wait for herds to be driven to the goldfields, they came to the stations themselves, yarning at the stockyards, haggling over prices – not that they'd get far with Ben, he'd drive a hard bargain. Cornelia had never seen him work so hard, but she supposed, with Darcy gone, he didn't have much choice. And instead of slackening off, the gold strikes were increasing, spreading thirty miles along the Cape River. And there'd been more strikes, this time near Charters Towers.

There was gold everywhere, and just when Caravale was set to cash in, they'd lost half the station. Cornelia still couldn't believe Darcy would do such a thing to them, but Mr Jauncy, acting as Darcy's executor, had sent confirmation that the title deeds had been lodged at the Lands Department to certify the joint ownership: Perfection Middleton and Ben Buchanan.

How Cornelia hated the conniving hussy. It had taken days for her to get over the shock. Coming right on top of Darcy's death, it was too much for a woman to bear. Just when you think you've got everything sorted out, something always goes wrong. Well, she'd faced trouble before and she'd face it again. Ben had engaged a new lawyer to fight Darcy's will but found there was no chance of overturning it and the best advice the desk-bound fool could give was for Ben to buy her out. All very well for him. Of course the station was prospering, now more than ever, but that meant its value had risen, and so Jauncy was sending out an assessor to estimate the worth of the property, and the stock as well. The hussy even owned half the stock, and Ben had been instructed to keep careful accounts now, to satisfy scrutiny by that turncoat of a Jauncy. She'd never liked the man, he was the one who had informed her that Teddy had cut her out of his will, and he refused to enter into any further correspondence with her about it. History was repeating itself. She wouldn't be surprised if Jauncy had put the idea in Darcy's head.

How could they buy half the station and the stock? They had money in the bank but it was there for bad seasons, which were as inevitable as death in this country. And besides, capital was always needed to keep a station running. Night after night, she and Ben wrestled with this worry. He simply didn't have enough ready money to buy her out unless they borrowed from the banks, and Ben was dead scared of that. 'Once you get into the clutches of the banks,' Teddy had always said, 'you're gone. They'll end up owning your property.' And he was right on that. As Ben had said, only last night, despairing, 'If we take out a mortgage to buy her share, add the interest and we'll be paying out for years – for what is rightfully ours. Then if we strike a couple of bad seasons, or cattle fevers, we won't be able to pay, and they've got us.' Country people, Cornelia knew, had an inborn fear of the banks and not without good reason. No. They had to think of a better answer.

She didn't find a chance to talk to Ben for the next few days. There was trouble in the south-west pastures with trespassers. They'd hacked a trail through the softwood bush, heading in the general direction of the Cape diggings, to make way for their carts and wagons, and horsemen and tramps had followed like shadows, resulting in a confrontation with Tom Mansfield and Caravale stockmen. Shots had been fired, a prospector wounded, and Tom's horse was killed. In retaliation, the Caravale blacks, who probably wouldn't have interfered had a white man been killed instead of a horse, had overturned the lead wagons. Cornelia heard all this from the black house-girls who knew everything that went on, she would swear, for a hundred miles around. Apparently Ben, with reinforcements, had raced to sort it out.

'Those crazy diggers,' Mae said. 'They don't know where they're going half the time. Demanding their right of thoroughfare, the blacks say, chopping through that bush. The way they were going would have taken them to the widest part of the river, and they'd never have got across there.'

'What's Ben doing about it?'

'The gins say he's hauling the downed trees to the boundary and blocking the trail.'

'Fat lot of good that'll do. They should shoot a few more of them.'

'There's too many, Mrs Buchanan,' Mae said. 'All the stations are having the same trouble. They're coming by their thousands. People say Charters Towers will be a big town one day at this rate.'

Cornelia laughed. Charters Towers. It wasn't a one-horse town, it was a half-horse town. Last time she was there, it had been to attend the three-day picnic races with Darcy and Ben . . . Darcy again. She was so confused about him now. She still mourned him, she missed his company, his niceness. So like his father, such a nice fellow, but, like his father, he'd turned on her. Ben was harder than them, meaner, and she had come to realise that her younger son possessed her capacity to fight back. He even looked more like her with his dark reddish hair and stocky build. Darcy had been his father all over again, tall, fair, lanky, and too generous, too much the gentleman. Ben, she knew, despite his airs, was no gentleman.

He was tired. It was late. Mae pulled off his boots.

'Don't bother changing,' his mother said. 'We've kept a steak and kidney pie hot for you, we'll sit in the kitchen. You can go to bed, Mae.'

Cornelia served him pie with crisp-topped mashed potatoes, a large portion of cauliflower in white sauce, and fresh green peas. As she cut fresh-baked bread for him she refrained from the motherly remark about this being his all-time favourite food. She listened to his troubles with the diggers, more beasts slaughtered by the bastards, cattle straying, disturbed by the intruders, and quietly poured them both the excellent claret which she had previously decanted. She was feeling better herself now, watching his tiredness slip from him. He told her that since Tom Mansfield's horse had been killed, he had sold him Clipper, Darcy's horse.

'The only thing to do, really,' Ben said. 'Solved the problem. Clipper was fretting, and he was too much of a reminder of Darcy.'

'Of course it was,' she said. Darcy would have given the horse to Tom, but this was Ben, the one she needed now. Meaner.

'How old is this Miss Middleton?' she asked.

'I don't know, about nineteen or twenty, I'd say.'

'I thought as much. The papers Jauncy sent us state that the father is trustee until she comes of age.'

'That's right.'

'Who is he?'

'He was a sergeant in the army. Quit when his daughter suddenly became rich. Prior to that he was a convict, sent out here for seven years on charges of theft.'

'What did he steal?'

'He broke into a bakery, stole bread and money or something. What does it matter? The man's a bloody thief, with a record.'

Cornelia resisted a wild urge to laugh. An amateur. Nellie Bunn would never have wasted her time on such poor pickings, and Nellie Bunn was never fool enough to get caught.

'Darcy knew this?' she asked solemnly.

'Oh yes. He didn't give a damn.' Ben's expression changed, he looked upset. 'Mother, I don't want to talk about this any more. I've had enough today.'

'I understand, we won't discuss Darcy. But tell me, this Jack Middleton, what are his circumstances?'

'What do you mean? His circumstances.'

'I mean is he married, a widower perhaps?'

Ben lounged back in the chair and laughed. 'Sorry to disappoint you. The man's married and his missus is alive and well.'

Cornelia grinned and tucked a lock of hair behind her ear. 'Oh well, that rules out that possibility.'

Ben stared. 'You'd really consider marrying him if he were single?'

'It was just a thought. We'd have more chance of controlling Caravale.' It was more than a thought, it was a way of bringing Ben around to the real crux of this conversation.

133

Ben was still laughing, pouring himself another claret. 'Ma, you are the absolute end!'

'I've told you not to call me Ma.'

'Very well then, Mother. So you'd marry that clod, just to hang on to Caravale?'

'Why not?'

'It's outrageous!'

'Not necessarily, but if he's married, I can forget that idea.'

'I should think so.'

'What about the daughter? Did you meet her?'

'Not really. I saw her several times. I told you, she was a housemaid at Government House.'

'What does she look like? I have to know, Ben. Sooner or later we're going to have to deal with these people.'

'To be honest, she's quite good-looking.'

'Dark or fair?'

'Fair-haired, good shape, too, come to think of it.'

Cornelia nodded. 'So here we have a young girl, quite nice looking, who is obviously ready and eager for marriage. Who within a year or so will own half of our station outright, without her father's restrictions.'

'So?'

'So, Ben Buchanan, I think it is time you swallowed your pride and gave some thought to marrying her yourself.'

'You're mad!'

'Just you think on it. If you don't marry her, someone else will, she's very eligible now, and then you'll have her husband to deal with as well. If you marry her you've got Caravale back, and it won't cost a penny.'

'No. It's out of the question.'

She brought him a bowl of bread and butter custard and passed over the jug of cream. 'Please yourself. It's nothing to do with me. You make up your own mind. At least by the sound of things she's not ugly, and, my dear, what better dowry could any girl bring?'

'It's ridiculous. What do you want me to do? Write and propose to a perfect stranger?'

'No. Don't do anything. That Jauncy fellow said Mr Middleton will be contacting us in due time. It's my guess they'll be breaking their necks to have a look at their newly acquired property. We'll hear from them soon enough. You're her partner, you simply wait for her to make the first move.'

PART FIVE

1

Chin Ying left his family quarters and moved silently across the compound, head bowed, wrists clenched inside his wide sleeves, knowing all eyes were upon him. A summons to present himself to the Most High Lord Cheong was an honour and the news would already be known to all who dwelled in the master's mansions, from the high-ranking family members, down through the courtiers and ranks of gossiping concubines and eunuchs to the most menial servants.

He wore his most appropriate coat of royal blue padded satin, richly embroidered with gold and red dragons, and a wide orange sash. The coat had long peaked sleeves lined with cream silk and was a respectful ankle length. His best sky-blue skirt with the rich orange border swished along the ground, hiding his unworthy feet in their soft silk slippers. His round black hat, placed neatly on his head, was encrusted with gold and silver beading. Ying thought it rather spoiled his appearance; a plain black satin would have been in better taste, but his mother disagreed. The Most High Lord Cheong and his Lady preferred bright adornments.

Ying travelled through the Happy Red Court to the Fragrant Garden and on to the Scented Lotus Pavilion, ignoring the young ladies who were watching the fish in the pools and who turned to stare and whisper, rudely he thought, as he passed by. He went down the Lane of Singing Bamboos to the Vermilion Pearl Gate, the entrance reserved for high-ranking officials. It was not as ornate, of course, as the entrance to Lord Cheong's court, used by his family members, but it was still imposing. Ying bowed his head in reverence at the very thought of the great family.

Many times he had stood outside on the road watching processions file through the main gates of Lord Cheong's walled domain, impressed by the pomp and ceremony which attended important visitors, and proud that he lived, belonged, inside that gate, a young gentleman of high social standing. The gateway itself was a work of art with beautiful carvings, and the ornate gatehouse was decorated in red and gold. The corners of the roof tilted upwards in concert with all the other buildings inside, distracting the eye from the fact that the gates were made of solid metal, and overhead, behind discreet shutters, armed guards were on constant alert against attacks by bandits or the greed of neighbouring warlords.

Chin Ying had lived within the confines of this gracious household all of his twenty-six years, the happiest of existences. As the son, grandson and great-grandson of a succession of Chief Grain Commissioners, it would shortly be his turn to shoulder this most honourable duty. It was a weighty responsibility for a young gentleman but he was sure he could attend to the obligations of business with distinction. It was not usual for one so young to be appointed to this important position but Ying was confident, he was next in line, following his father's sudden death from heart failure, and he was well educated. Not only had he studied philosophy, literature, the visual arts, and music, as befitted a cultured gentleman, his tutors had schooled him as well in mathematics and the more exotic English language. There were many Englishmen in China these days although Ying had never actually met one, and he was sure that knowing the language would be an advantage when he went out into the province. Several times his father had taken him to witness the harvesting and explain the intricate details of grain collecting and storage, and the taxes and tithes expected from peasants for the common good, and he was grateful now for his father's foresight. Chin Ying would be an efficient Chief Grain Commissioner and, because of his youth, in time to come he might even receive a higher appointment.

His father's death had been a great shock but Li-wen, Ying's wife, was excited by their new status. They had moved into the main room of their villa, since his mother, as befits a widow, had made way for her eldest son and retired with Nanny Tan to the rear wing. Chin Ying was now lord of his own household.

Two servants escorted him across the arched bridge over the Tranquil Lake, with its small weeping willows, to the Purple Isle Pavilion. He had never been here before. They went through a moon gate, good fortune to lovers, and entered Lord Cheong's court. He trembled as he waited, feet sinking into the thick carpet. From the corner of his eye he could see the magnificent silks that adorned the walls. His master was truly a most cultured gentleman.

Wind chimes tinkled as the doors slid back to reveal the State Room. At the far end was Lord Cheong, his glorious canopied throne set high, overshadowing everyone else in the room. As he kneeled in obeisance, Ying took in the rows of courtiers and officials, their state robes a wonderful blend of primary colours.

The Treasurer was seated at a small table, floor level, with his brushes and scrolls, beneath the gaze of the Lord. Ying's father had said he was an ancient, quite in his dotage, but his mother had disagreed; she claimed he was a wily fellow, with eyes and ears everywhere in the land.

Beckoned by a courtier, Chin Ying advanced to within reach of the little gilt rail which enclosed the Treasurer and behind him the Lord's sacred space. He kneeled low, head to the floor.

'Rise, Chin Ying,' the Treasurer said in his old, cracked voice and a servant ran forward with a tiny padded stool whereon the soon-to-be-appointed Chief Grain Commissioner was permitted to sit. He lowered himself gracefully without a trace of awkwardness, although his heart was bursting with pride at the courtliness of this investiture. Soon he would receive his gold chain of office.

Ying was now able to see the Lord himself for the first time. He'd never been this close before, and he thought Lord Cheong's face was uncommonly white, powdered or pasted possibly, the eyebrows blackened to match the thin black moustache that hung down splendidly either side of the carmined mouth. His headgear was high, half-moon in shape, covered (he had to remember to tell Li-wen) in orange silk which was embroidered in gold and dappled with precious gems. He wore white quilted satin trimmed with dark gleaming fur and a wide purple sash, and his fine hands with their elongated fingernails glittered with large rings.

'This is Chin Ying, sire,' the Treasurer intoned, 'first son of the deceased Chief Grain Commissioner.'

His Lordship waved his fan lazily and the Treasurer continued, 'It has been established, sire, occasioned by the sudden death of the Chief Grain Commissioner, that the entries and accounts are not in order.'

Chin Ying jerked up in his seat. It was possible that the last entries had not been made, and that was understandable. Was that what the Treasurer was referring to? Unfortunately Ying was not permitted to speak unless directly addressed. He wrung his hands nervously within his sleeves.

The Treasurer spoke again. 'A careful examination of entries over the years of the late official's employ has shown serious discrepancies. As a result, during this last week, inspectors have interrogated grain growers and their families and we are now of the opinion that the late official had been stealing from My Lord by means of accepting bribes, selling grain privately, and withholding funds due My Lord, by means of written deception.'

It was too much for Ying. 'That's not true, My Lord,' he cried. 'My father was an honourable man.'

The Treasurer sighed. 'Would it were not true. Your father married my niece and I gave my personal blessing to the union. Now she is a member of a family in grave disrepute.'

Ying was shocked, and acutely embarrassed before all these highly placed people. He could feel the heat of redness on his face and neck and he wanted to run from there but it was not possible. Once again ignoring protocol, he spoke to the Treasurer, whispering: 'Are you sure this is true, sir?'

'Your family lived exceptionally well,' he replied, 'and it was attributed by all who noticed to good management by your father. Your elder sister married above her station. Her father-in-law has been interrogated and we discovered that he accepted two dowries to permit your sister to enter his household. The first was to satisfy the Public Administrator. The second, an illicit arrangement, was a much larger amount. This associate-in-crime admitted the illegal dealings to My Lord, this very morning, and he was executed forthwith.'

Executed. His sister's father-in-law! Ying thought he would faint.

'Did you know about this thievery and deception?'

'No, sir, no,' Ying stammered. 'I had no idea. And I am deeply apologetic.' He went down on his knees. 'On behalf of my family, I beg forgiveness.'

The Lord himself spoke, in a high-pitched, trilling voice. 'Forgiveness does not come into it. Restitution is the question.'

'Your Worship, I will gladly repay whatever is required,' Ying replied, face into the carpet.

'Yes, you will repay. We have discussed your case.'

Ying allowed himself to peer up. The white face looked hard and grim. Lord Cheong's hair hung down from the head-dress in long twisted ropes, thin as the moustache, and the aura now was calculating and dangerous. Ying was terrified. Was he to be beheaded too? He felt like flinging himself prostrate to the floor to beg for mercy but thought it better not to put ideas into the Lord's head. His knees were aching now and his back felt as if it could give way any minute.

'From his great goodness,' the Treasurer announced, 'My Lord has made a decision.'

Ying heard a rush of muttering interest around the court as the Treasurer continued, 'Your villa and its contents have been confiscated. Your mother, your wife and their servants are at this time being removed to the Brown Wing compound.'

There was a shudder in the court and Ying steadied himself, trying not to sway with the shock. The Brown Wing compound was a foul place, between the sewerage walls and the prison. It was the home of the lowliest subjects, only one step up from servant class.

'Your sisters will enter concubinage, and your brothers will live and work as peasants in the grain stores.'

Lord Cheong's thin lips spread. 'Grain stores. Appropriate,' he snickered and the audience tittered with him. He nodded to his Chancellor who stepped forward.

'Court is dismissed.'

Ying began to rise, but the Treasurer shook his head. 'Be seated.'

The State Room audience left swiftly and Chin Ying, now quaking in terror, was left to face his master, with only the Chancellor and the Treasurer to hear his fate. Everyone had heard whispers of the torture chambers, of exquisite deaths arranged there instead of the public axings for certain crimes. Was his fate to be so terrible, so awful, that the delicate ears of the courtiers would be offended by the hearing?

The Lord Cheong spoke. 'How will you repay the monies and make restitution for the heinous crimes of your thieving parent?'

Ying's voice was weak and shaky. 'Sire, as yet I do not know. This is a great shock to me, but I will find a way.'

'We consider you are grasping at air, you useless waste-end of a pig. There is no possible way, without guidance, you can make amends.'

'I will accept guidance, sire, please believe me.'

'With our guidance you might be able to restore your mother and your wife to an amenable social level and enable your brothers to become common soldiers.'

'Thank you, sire. And myself?'

'The status of your restoration will be commensurate with the degree of your exertions,' Lord Cheong replied.

Whatever that meant, Ying thought, but at least it sounded as if he would keep his head on his shoulders. He hated this man. 'Your Worship, you are infinitely wise,' he said.

'And you are young and strong,' Cheong said. 'You are to go out into the world and bring me back gold. Not just a handful but coffers of gold. A contract will be drawn up relating to each member of your family and time limits will be set.'

Ying looked wildly around him. Was Cheong mad or was this just another form of torture? 'Sire, I would gladly obey your orders but where are such riches to be found?'

'You see,' Cheong said loftily, 'you are already in need of our guidance. The gold exists and you will bring it back to us.'

Yes, Ying thought bitterly. It was rumoured that over the borders, far away, the savage Mongols had gold. But what was he supposed to do? Enter the land of the barbarians and steal it from their tents? That would mean certain and frightful death at their hands.

'Take him away,' Cheong said abruptly and Ying, with the Treasurer, backed from the State Room, bowing low.

With no chance to rush home, to view the full extent of the disaster for himself, to refer to friends (did he have any friends now?), Ying was whisked away to the library of Wang-tse, a teacher so distinguished he no longer took pupils. He had been engaged to teach members of Lord Cheong's family, but since none had the intelligence or the interest to pursue his sphere of scholarship, mainly the sciences, Wang-tse was able to proceed with his own studies in uninterrupted seclusion.

They took tea with the scholar and, at last, the Treasurer explained the mystery. 'You are to stay here with Wang-tse until he can certify that you are familiar with three important subjects – geography, geology, and what was the other one?'

'Metallurgy,' Wang-tse sighed, obviously unimpressed by the pupil assigned to him.

'Your honourable teacher will show you the whereabouts of gold,' the Treasurer continued, 'and he will tell you all you need to know about it, including the means of obtaining it from the earth. Is this not so?'

'It is so,' Wang-tse intoned.

'There is no time to waste,' the Treasurer warned. 'You will remain in the custody of Wang-tse until I send for you.'

Two days later, and he had not seen another soul, Ying was escorted to the Treasurer's suite, to await an audience. His head was swimming with information about this unalterable, inert, indestructible substance, gold; about ores, carats, and alloys, lodes, veins and reefs, alluvials and nuggets. The only thing he was really sure of was that pure gold was 24 carats. But Wang-tse had warmed to his subject and had provided Ying with a chest of scrolls relating to gold which he could study in the course of his travels. The journey would be long; Wang-tse had shown him his destination, the place where the gold was to be located, on a map.

Waiting for the Treasurer, Ying tried to put on a brave face, but he was desolated. They were sending him to a place as barbarous as any Mongol country, to the far continent of Terra Australis, a sea voyage down past the equator through hurricane-riddled seas. It was insane. Ludicrous. Ying had no doubt that Wang-tse was laughing in his long white beard at the whole idea. He'd seen the amusement in his eyes as he searched through scrolls, examined the globe and handed Ying more detailed maps of a province known as Queensland. A tiny gold star indicated the goldfields which followed the course of a river with the plain name of Cape.

'I'll never find this place,' he wailed.

'Yes, you will. Lord Cheong will see to it,' Wang-tse replied.

'But that land is wild, barely explored, as you have told me, and inhabited by black savages.'

'For a person like you, I should say it is far safer than remaining here.'

'I suppose so. I should be grateful that My Lord has honoured me with this great task.'

'Honoured you?' the old man said. 'He has plenty of men he could have sent on this expedition. Hundreds, maybe thousands of our countrymen are already on their way to those goldfields, many of them bound and beholden as you are, to bring gold back to their masters. The only thing that has saved you from the same disgrace as your brothers is that you learned the English language. This place is an English colony.'

Ying found it all quite bewildering, he had never been outside the province of Hunan, but he remembered Wang-tse had used the word expedition, which was interesting. Maybe he wouldn't have to go alone. He studied his well-manicured nails.

The Treasurer admitted him and gave him further instructions. 'Three days from today, on a fortuitous astrological date, you will leave the household of Lord Cheong and proceed to the goldfields. Two servants have been assigned to you, Yuang Pan and his brother Yuang Lu. You will be travelling on horseback, as befits a representative of the Lord Cheong, and will take with you fifty coolies who will work digging for gold at the assigned place.'

'But how do I get to this place, sir?'

'Do not interrupt me. You will go to Macao, where you will board a ship which is the property of Lord Cheong, and the captain of the ship will sail you to the land wherein is the gold.'

'It is in Terra Australis, in the province of Queensland and the nearest seaport is named Bowen,' said Ying, airing his new-found knowledge. 'I presume the ship will deliver me to this port.'

'Presume nothing. The captain has been given his orders. You will see that he carries them out and then you will proceed to the goldfields, collect the gold, bring it back to the ship and return home.'

Ying's spirits soared. This was not only an opportunity to bring great wealth and distinction to his family again, it would be an adventure of heroic proportions. He would keep a journal that would be handed down through his family for generations.

'You may go now,' he was told, 'and you may see your family. But you may not speak of this expedition to anyone. Simply state that you are going away for a while. Gold fever addles the brain. Other men might be tempted to follow. Greed is a vice, as your late father has demonstrated clearly enough.'

His mother and Li-wen were waiting for him in the deserted Long Pavilion and he wept when he saw them dressed in the cheap coloured jackets and black trousers of the lower classes.

'My dears,' he cried, arms round both of them. 'Trust me, I will rescue you from this humiliation.'

But his mother was suspicious. 'We have been stripped of our home, of our belongings, but look at you, still dressed as a gentleman.'

Li-wen joined in. 'We hear you have been assigned two manservants. Why is this? It is said the Yuang brothers entered our villa and took into their possession, on your behalf, all of your beautiful clothes and artworks and books, everything a gentleman might need, even your toiletries.'

'I do not know about this,' Ying told them.

'You are lying,' his mother wept. 'Tell me this is not true.'

'It is difficult for me to speak.'

'Have the Yuang brothers been assigned to you?' Li-wen demanded. 'I want to know.'

'Yes,' he said.

'Do you know who they are?' his mother accused. 'They were the personal servants of Hsueh Ko, who has been beheaded, and now they are yours. What treachery is this?'

Ying shook his head miserably. 'I can only tell you I must go away but I will be back to clear our name.'

'Clear it now,' Li-wen screamed. 'Your father was the thief, not mine, yet I am punished. I hate you.'

His mother took his arm. 'It is said that you are in great favour with the honourable Treasurer, a powerful man. Why won't you speak for us, your family? Why do you allow this calamity?'

'Believe me, I'm trying.'

'He has sold us out. He's looking after his own hide,' Li-wen said. 'He will not help us, it is useless to beg.' She spat on the hem of his skirt. 'Your mother is right. You are treacherous, you have betrayed us.'

The women walked from him, despising him.

2

The Bishop's house seemed to have shrunk. The ceiling was low, the rooms small, and the staircase! Lew couldn't take his eyes from the staircase where once he'd leapt with vigour and grace, like an Olympian, to reach the landing in three and a half running jumps. Now it seemed to cringe before him. The boy had become a towering man.

'They said he didn't suffer, Lewis,' the Bishop said. 'He died a martyr to the Church.'

'Thank you.'

'Let us kneel and pray for him, and for your dear mother. They both gave their lives for God.'

Lew kneeled. Why was he so tongue-tied with this man? This old man. Respect for age, in the Chinese tradition? No. He couldn't hide behind that excuse, he'd always been scared of the Bishop. As a child he'd constantly been told to be quiet in his presence, not to interrupt, to sit still. Occasionally this old man had heard his prayers like an examining officer. A son of missionary parents was expected to be able to recite all the prayers, to know all the hymns, to be able to recite the bible backwards. Or so it had seemed to him.

The Bishop droned on. Lewis had always supposed the longer the prayers, the more points you built up in heaven. He smiled to himself. Once, long ago, he had deliberately messed up his recital of prayers, got them all wrong, upset the Bishop, shamed his parents, and was severely punished. His father had beaten him and his mother had sent him to bed hungry, but it had been worth it, more fun than fire-crackers.

'We pray for the soul of Elizabeth Cavour,' the Bishop continued in his sing-song voice, 'who gladly gave her life bringing heathen souls to God.'

Who died of typhoid in a filthy Chinese village, Lew corrected silently, leaving her ten-year-old son with a man who served his master, the Bishop, and their church, like a coolie.

'And for the soul of Joseph Cavour, who lived in poverty like Our Lord, who came across the water from Mother England to join our Mission.' His voice rose. 'Joseph Cavour deserves high office in your mansions, Lord. Look kindly on a man who was struck down by the enemies of Christ.'

Who was killed in one of the bloody Chinese uprisings on the outskirts of Xiangtan just because he was there. And if you consider being hacked to death by swords as simply being 'struck down', you're madder than they were to have been there in the first place. Lew said to himself.

Servants brought them tea, served on a small lacquered table. Lew used to think the Bishop's house was a palace; it was so grand compared to the stone farmhouse from where the Cavours ministered to their small congregation of converted Chinese. But now he saw it as it was, just an ordinary two-storeyed house with the usual Oriental wing-tipped roof and functional furniture. It was a disappointment. He disliked the Bishop and all that he stood for, and in his mind, for years, he had sneered at him living in luxury while his parents slogged it out among the peasants, prospecting for souls. They wasted their lives swimming against a tide of millions who already had their own gods. While some, in curiosity or good humour, embraced Christianity, after Joseph's death the waters had closed, he was forgotten, his ministry washed away.

'You went back to Xiangtan, Lewis?'

'Yes, sir. I found his grave. Friends buried him where the church used to be.'

'Used to be?'

Lew took a malicious delight in the Bishop's startled reaction. 'Oh yes, they burned the church to the ground. And the farmhouse too.' It was nothing personal, he knew; the attackers had burned down the village as well, but the burning of the church would concern the Bishop.

'Blasphemous! God will punish them. After all your dear father's hard work!'

Lew nodded.

'We thought you would join the Mission, Lewis,' the Bishop said. 'Your father always hoped you would follow in his footsteps, pick up the standard and carry on, so to speak. After all, you have grown up in China, you're fluent in the language, and several dialects, I believe. You have an enormous advantage over the new people coming from Home. I myself was quite disappointed to hear you had gone to sea.'

Run away to sea, you mean. 'I have my master's ticket now,' Lew said. 'And I have a ship waiting for me in Macao.' He did not add that it was not a fine clipper ship but a Chinese junk; it had taken him too many years to get this far.

'Very commendable, Lewis. Captain of your own ship, indeed. And will you be sailing to England?'

England. Lew had never seen England. He knew every port in the Far East, as the English called this part of the world, but he had never seen his homeland. He had been a foreigner all his life, thanks to these people, and it rankled. They had deprived him of a sane English upbringing, of his birthright, and in their occasional bursts of homesickness they had instilled in him a yearning for that green and verdant land, a lawful, gentle country.

'No,' he said. He had not yet been told where the junk would be headed, but he was damn sure it wouldn't be England. The thought of sailing up the Thames in a junk struck him as funny.

'We want you to have this,' the Bishop said. 'It's the address I read at the memorial service for your dear father, giving an account of the lives of your parents and their great contribution to the Church in China.'

'Thank you,' Lew said taking the Chinese-style scroll and glancing at it. At least it was written in English.

'Well, you've grown into a fine stamp of a man,' the Bishop said, shaking his hand. 'But don't forget the Mother Church, dear boy, the gates are always open. I will pray for you.'

As Lew crossed the bridge down the road from the Bishop's residence, he tossed the scroll into the sluggish river.

He reached the harbour and pushed his way through the screeching chaos of the Macao waterfront, looking for the junk owned by Lord Cheong, a wealthy feudal character from the backblocks of Hunan. A man had to be very careful dealing with these faceless villains. In the Chinese manner, one dealt only with their representatives, bland, smiling Macao merchants who would have your throat slit if it pleased them.

He had promised he would consider their proposal but on his own terms. First he had to see the junk. Their assurances that Cheong's ship was a jewel didn't mean a thing; it would be too late once he'd signed the contract to find he was captain of some old hulk or an overgrown sampan. Secondly, he refused to carry contraband, or women destined for brothels, or prisoners of any sort. His master's ticket was too important to be put in jeopardy.

The go-between, the man who had contacted him in the first place, was Mr Lien, as he called himself now, proud of the English that he had learned in Joseph Cavour's classes.

'Do not be so suspicious, Lew. I myself have given you this great recommendation, and my superiors are immensely pleased that you will accept. You must not let me down. The Lord Cheong is a very powerful man and he will pay you well.'

'Your thoughtfulness will be rewarded, Mr Lien. I appreciate your faith in my ability, but I need more information.'

'Be assured that all is honourable and legal.'

'Then why can't you tell me where they want me to go?'

'Because even I am not permitted this knowledge.'

'And you wonder why I am suspicious.'

He saw Mr Lien, standing exactly where he had said he would be, ignoring a stinking fish barrow lodged beside him and seemingly unaware of the bustle around him.

'I can't find Cheong's boat,' Lew said, 'No one seems to have heard of it.'

'Follow me,' Mr Lien replied and moved easily through the crowds, his pigtail swinging under a mandarin hat, while Lew with his bulk had to dodge and push to keep up with him.

They stepped into a sampan and were taken out into the harbour. 'There,' Mr Lien pointed, and Lew gaped.

'That one?'

'Of a certainty.'

'Good God!' She was huge, a three-master. Lew thumped the timbers as they came alongside. In good condition, too. These junks were built on a solid frame and were practically unsinkable with their below-decks watertight compartments. In his studies Lew had learned that many a modern shipbuilder had tried to use the same safety measure as in the ancient junks but without much success.

Armed crew members were guarding the ship, and with good reason. A vessel like this would be a great prize. The men stood back and bowed as Mr Lien and Lew boarded.

'This is Captain Cavour,' Mr Lien announced and the crew clapped their pleasure.

'That one,' Mr Lien pointed to a burly Chinese seaman with the dark battered face of a man who had gone too many rounds in waterfront taverns, 'he is your first mate, Hong.'

The man stared, his slit eyes cold and hard, and Lew realised an English captain was a shock to them. He bowed to Hong and said in Chinese, 'What's an old salt like you doing on this pretty ship?'

Hong's square face gradually broke into a grin, an evil-looking result, since he had several teeth missing and one of the remainder was gold. Seeing his reaction, the crew clapped again.

'This junk's new!' Lew exclaimed, looking around him at the polished timbers and gleaming brass.

Hong nodded excitedly. 'Surely, sir, never a more beautiful ship.'

Lew noticed that Mr Lien frowned, offended that a crewman should address the captain, but Lew was pleased. Wherever he was going he would need resourceful men to man this beauty, not servile creatures waiting for orders. Right now, he didn't care about the destination. As long as there were no tricks, he would sail this junk. He was in love with her. He motioned to the rest of the crew and addressed Hong again. 'These fellows. Good sailors?'

The crew held their breath waiting for Hong's reply. He turned and studied them slowly. 'Maybe,' he admitted, and Lew's Chinese crew gave a sigh of relief.

Mr Lien proudly escorted him below to view the stateroom, his day cabin, and two sleeping compartments which were furnished in a bizarre mix of east and west. Ornate Chinese lanterns hung over a long sturdy table – man-sized, Lew was pleased to see, instead of the squat tables preferred by the Chinese. Bolted to the floor at each end were high-backed lacquered chairs. Portholes were draped in gaudy red velvet, the bunks were neat and clean with fresh linen but were built like kangs on the third level of wide steps, and the entrances to the cabins and washroom sported colourful beaded curtains. Lew made a note that they would go when he put to sea; it would drive him mad trying to scramble through them every day. Lacquered cupboards and benches lined the bulkheads. But these were minor matters. He toured the rest of the ship checking, especially, the whipstaff ropes to the tiller. There was no wheelhouse, which would make it tough for him in stormy seas but more fun; he had faith in this ship. He ran up the steps to the high, railed poop deck and looked around him, feeling very high and mighty; his former shipmates would laugh like crazy when they heard he was master of a junk, but what the hell?

'You like?' Mr Lien asked.

'She is a truly honourable ship,' he replied in Chinese.

'Then we must hurry. My employers have your instructions, and they expect your humble acceptance.'

'We'll see,' Lew said, sounding, he knew, like his father. He felt a sudden rush of sadness. That last visit to Xiangtan had been his triumphant return, to show his father that he had his master's ticket, that he was not just another seaman knocking around Asian ports. He had wanted his father to be proud of him. Too late. Why that hurt so much, he didn't know. And what did it matter? The road to salvation had been Pastor Cavour's obsession, not worldly achievements. Lew smiled bitterly. Well, his father had reached his goal. If the Lord kept his side of the bargain, Pastor Cavour's soul had been truly salvaged from this sinful world.

3

Lew watched as the sampan approached his junk. He was still laughing. Gold! And he'd been worried that he'd have to refuse their offer if the crafty gentlemen were up to no good. It was a simple expedition. The contracts were signed and the junk fully insured; the voyage through the South Seas could be dangerous. Natural hazards were bad enough but the real peril was pirates. He'd insisted that he be given enough modern arms to defend the ship and they'd complied. Cases of rifles, ammunition and revolvers were already stowed away, more even than he'd ordered. The loss of the ship on the voyage south would be unfortunate, but it would be a catastrophe to lose the expected shipment of gold on the way home.

He should have guessed the destination, hundreds of ships from these ports were heading for the goldfields in Australia, but the junk had deceived him. Most of the prospectors required faster transport. Cheong's advisers were a wily lot; a junk leisurely plying southern waters wouldn't attract so much attention, even a junk this size, there were too many wandering the South China Sea. It was only when they passed by Sumatra and entered English waters along the coast of Queensland that they'd be more obvious.

Their destination was exciting him more than anything about this voyage. He was off to an English-speaking land for the first time in his life. Many people spoke English around the Asian ports but in Australia he'd no longer be a hulking foreigner, he'd be just like everyone else, moving among his own countrymen. All these years he'd been so set on making for England when he became a master mariner he'd forgotten about the English colonies south of the equator. Understandable though. Until the gold rushes no one had known or cared much about them; they were far-off penal colonies to be avoided. But his recent inquiries had revealed that transportation of convicts had ceased, the penal system had been shut down and several colonies on that island continent were now self-supporting and doing a damn good job of it. The big gold finds, of course, would put wind in their sails; they'd really put the colonies on the map. The main colony, he knew, was New South Wales but his instructions were to head for Queensland, a new state in the north and therefore much closer to the Asian mainland. A windfall for all concerned.

'Mr Chin, welcome aboard,' Lew said, bowing to his passenger without batting an eye at this overdressed young peacock accompanied by two servants. It was a cold day but this fellow was dressed for the Arctic in a fur-trimmed padded coat of blue satin, from which emerged a deep purple skirt heavily embroidered in red and gold. His round hat was also trimmed with fur.

Chin bowed slightly, graciously, and spoke in English. 'Good morning, Captain. You will show me to my quarters.'

His servants hurried after them and stood back while Mr Chin examined his cabin. 'Yes, this will do. I want to rest now.'

'As you wish,' Lew said and went back to await the rest of the entourage, the fifty coolies that this gent commanded.

Eventually a convoy of sampans hove to by the junk and Lew watched, amazed, as the coolies heaved boxes and chests and crates on to the deck. They were all carefully marked. Some cases contained equipment for the goldfields and Lew sent them to the hold but one of the servants informed him that the last twenty-two chests were Mr Chin's personal belongings, so they had to go to his cabin.

'They won't fit in his cabin,' Lew said. 'Shove them below.'

Mr Chin was standing at the entrance to their private quarters. 'Bring them here,' he ordered.

'I have just explained, there's no room in your cabin,' Lew told him.

'That is obvious, but there is plenty of room in the central compartment.'

'That section acts as a living room, a dining room, Mr Chin. We can't clutter it up with boxes.'

Chin looked at him coldly. 'That is for me to decide.'

Lew straightened up and squared his shoulders. 'I am captain of this ship, and I make the decisions, not you.'

'I don't think you understand, sir. I am the personal representative of the Lord Cheong, who is the owner of this ship. You are simply employed to sail her to the port of Bowen.'

'Bullshit!' Lew said in English, not caring whether his passenger understood the word or not, he'd get the message. 'What's in the boxes?'

'The contents are personal,' Chin said, but Lew ignored him. He yanked the nearest carved chest open and rummaged inside.

'What the hell is all this?' There were satin and silk robes and jackets, quilted cloaks, beautifully embroidered shirts, brocade slippers. 'What have you got here, costumes for an opera?'

Affronted, Mr Chin sprang forward. He had taken off his coat and was now elegantly attired in a bulky padded jacket with large winged shoulders gorgeously piped in gold, and black satin trousers. His tooled leather belt held a fancy tasselled sword.

Lew stared as Chin's hand went to his sword and his servants lined up menacingly behind him. He kicked the chest of clothes out of the way and confronted Chin. 'A man who would put his life at risk for the sake of a few fancy clothes must be a born fool. You draw that sword on me and I'll chuck you overboard.'

'Not easily, Captain,' Chin said and Lew shook his head in disbelief. They hadn't left port and he had a mutiny on his hands.

'Come below,' he said. Once out of earshot of the others, he turned to Chin. 'What is in those boxes apart from clothes?'

'Personal effects, my own bowls and dishes, of the best porcelain, my books, my night attire and linen . . .'

'Very well,' Lew said. 'Now, we can't have them down here, I'll not be tripping over them every time I move, and besides, they'll be a danger in a storm. You tell your servants they can unpack whatever you need for the voyage, and the rest goes below.' The Chinaman was beginning to realise he was right, so Lew pressed on. 'And listen to me. Where we're going you won't need all that fancy dress. You'll stand out like a shark in a lily pond.'

'A gentleman of my rank must be dressed tastefully,' Chin said, looking pointedly at Lew's battered dungarees and faded black jerkin.

'There's no one to impress where we're going,' Lew said. 'You just have to survive. Anyway, we're headed for the tropics, not the North Pole. I would appreciate it, Mr Chin, if you would sort this matter out right away. I don't have time for such trivialities.' He made for the steps. 'If you leave any boxes lying around this area, they're for the deep, believe me.'

Chin Ying ordered wine and cakes and sat at the table with his books and maps, attempting to study but his nerves were in a flutter. How dare that barbarian humiliate him! That arrogant overgrown Englishman who spoke Chinese with the accent of peasants! Had he considered the move politic, he would certainly have drawn his sword against the captain. His servants, the Yuang brothers, carried daggers in their sleeves and were adept in the martial arts. One move against him and Cavour would have had a dagger in his throat. Very swiftly. And then they'd see who was in charge of the ship. But logic told him that Lord Cheong's agents in Macao must have chosen this fellow for a reason, however obscure, and to kill him would create more problems and jeopardise his own fragile position.

He was depressed and lonely. He wished he could send for a woman and retire, allow her to attend him and assuage his sufferings. It had been a bad start and the thought of months in the sole company of the bullying Englishman added to his misery and reminded him that at the end of this so-called rainbow he might not succeed in finding the pot of gold, let alone the treasure chests expected by Cheong. What then? He dared not think that far ahead.

His servants had unpacked his immediate requirements and removed the boxes, on his orders. Ying was worried. Was Cavour right? Had they indeed packed unsuitable attire? If so, his servants would be punished and sent ashore at the next port to purchase whatever was required. But it was none of the captain's business.

Ying sighed with relief as he heard the creak and wrench of timbers and felt the soft swell of the sea as the junk got underway. The hated captain stuck his head in the door, looking pleased with himself. He seemed to have forgotten their altercation. 'We're off, Mr Chin, pray for fair winds and a pox on pirates.'

Ying's heart took two or three unscheduled leaps. Pirates! No one had mentioned pirates to him! He'd heard of the fearsome exploits of pirates; they were as real to him as the past horrors of Kublai Khan. A hundred thousand Chinese had drowned themselves rather than yield to the Mongol. Maybe he ought to leap overboard now and be done with it. Ah, but his family . . .

Cavour was only about thirty, not that much older than himself. Could this young man take them safely to another hemisphere on this great lumbering junk? Ying had seen beautiful ships in Macao harbour – sleek ships with sails like the wings of birds, huge impregnable liners, and English and Portuguese warships – yet here he was stuck on an ancient craft with sails that resembled unfurled butterfly cocoons. Then a memory stirred and he was comforted. As a child he had often tried to tear open cocoons and found the skin as tough as leather. Maybe Cheong knew what he was doing after all.

He called for more wine. He would remain aloof during this voyage; he would be silent, keep his distance, addressing the captain only when necessary. The fellow would come to understand his status as an inferior, even if he could sail a ship.

Unfortunately it took time for his stomach to become accustomed to the rhythms of the ocean. For the first week he was confined to his cabin in a solitary and humiliating state, attended by Yuang Lu and Yuang Pan who tried a succession of herbal draughts to cure their master, none of which had any effect on his convulsed intestines.

The captain came to see him. 'Mr Chin, forgive my intrusion, but I recommend the air on deck. It is a fine, lively day.'

'I doubt that is possible, sir,' Ying groaned. 'I am distinctly unwell.'

'Sea air is the only cure,' Cavour replied. 'Here, let me help you.' Before Ying could protest, the captain hoisted him out of bed and took him, tottering like a drunkard, to the lower deck where he was grateful to be allowed to sink into a sunny corner, out of the wind, on a makeshift bed of sails.

'You must keep your head up,' the captain said as Ying's servants delivered plump cushions and a rug.

Soon the nausea that had assailed him receded and he felt steadier, able to control the bile that threatened to erupt, and he began to believe that he might yet survive. Each day he took his place on deck, astonished to find he was looking forward to these outings. His strength was returning, he was able to walk about the deck, even sit and read under a canvas awning, and eventually take an interest in the manning of the ship and the awesome beauty of their ocean surrounds.

He had also taken to observing the captain. The man lacked gentility, he dressed in faded clothes and even wore coolies' flip-flops on his feet. His black hair had never been dressed, possibly rarely even combed, Ying thought disdainfully, noting that the unruly mop curled unevenly at the nape of Cavour's neck. However, he had to admit that the big Englishman was unusual. He had an air of authority which one would expect in a captain but also a look of raw integrity. His cold blue eyes glinted with challenge as if daring the world to doubt his word.

Cavour has the sort of power, Ying mused, that springs from self-assurance and native intelligence. What rank would a man like that be accorded in the mansions of the Lord Cheong? He was no peasant, nor was he gentry. As a courtier he would be an abject failure since those eyes would not countenance the necessary sycophantic scheming and back-biting of that class. He'd have no place, in the ranks of scholars and poets, nor could he see Cavour *k'o t'ou* to the Treasurer and his scribes as a ranking official like his father.

Ying still squirmed at the shame cast on him by his father's dishonesty but then he considered the true measure of a grain commissioner's life: always beholden to the Treasurer, having to account for every seed of grain and every tithe collected from the villages, poring over figures that had to be presented weekly, and suffering the complaints, the abuse, the demands for more returns, the fear of punishment. Honest or dishonest, Ying wondered now if that job was worth the worry and the boredom.

These thoughts were almost heretical, but he followed the line of reasoning with increased interest. There was prestige in the appointment, and a comfortable life style but no release from the iron grip of the Treasurer or the all-powerful Lord Cheong. Ying was aware that already a little of his naiveté about the perfect life in the Cheong mansions was slipping away. He was like a bird now, hovering over the enclave, observing the behaviour of the humans below. But what sort of a bird was he? He could not claim to be an eagle or even a hawk, yet he must have a wider view than the little sparrows and larks that nipped and twittered about the gardens. The answer would require meditation. And he would write a philosophical thesis on his new view of the career of an official. The matter of his father's dishonesty was not one for amusement, but he allowed himself a thin smile. What a nerve! To diddle the Treasurer and therefore the Lord himself! He would never dare do such a thing.

Ying returned to his contemplation of Captain Cavour. There was a place for him in the mansions after all. He would have been an army commander. Ying had forgotten the military, they lived separate lives, in barracks dotted over Cheong's territory. The generals held regular meetings with Lord Cheong and his military advisers, but they were not accepted in society. They were considered no better than brigands, a necessary appendage to the community, that was all.

Ying watched Cavour at the ropes, controlling the surge of the junk through the rolling seas, feeling an almost sexual pleasure at the sight of the captain's hard-muscled back. And this he understood. His sexual education had been wide and varied in the accepted manner, from pre-puberty, so that his preferences were well established by this time. Cavour, he assessed, was strongly sexual but unrefined, inexperienced in the delicate nuances of pleasure. He admired the man's body simply as a symmetrically excellent human form, but personally he had no taste for the bulging biceps and trunk-like bodies so much loved and proudly portrayed by European painters and sculptors.

He smiled softly. Yes. The captain could be equated with a general in Lord Cheong's army.

The first gleanings of ambition stole into his soul like a robber in the night, cautious, wary, summoning courage, and Ying, always interested in observing self, entertained the robber with equal caution, heeding his insidious temptations, mulling over his own reactions, measuring his own courage against emerging possibilities. No one at home commented on the notorious dishonesty of Cheong's generals, it was dangerous to express such views, for they reflected on the Cheong family, but Ying was free to think about them now.

He walked deliberately to the bow of the ship, looking back at the horizon that hid Macao. 'So, my Lord Cheong,' he said with a smile of satisfaction. 'I too have a general now, but this one is honest. A small beginning,' he murmured, 'but for an intelligent man, who knows?'

As the big junk moved effortlessly through the sapphire-blue waters of the Whitsunday Passage, hugging the coast of Queensland, Ying marvelled again at the friendship that had built up, so easily, so comfortably, between himself and Lew Cavour. It had been impossible to ignore the man's good humour and enthusiasm which had commenced with their nightly study of the charts and the routes they would follow.

Lew was pleased that Ying knew the geography of the area, and from the second night had invited him to observe as he plotted their course. 'It would be in your own interest, Mr Chin, to learn something about navigation, if you care to do so. The first mate is an experienced sailor but there has to be a boss. Say something happens to me, the lives of all these men would be in your hands then.'

'I don't care for that sort of responsibility,' Ying had said uncertainly, worrying more about his own safety than the coolies'.

'You're an educated man, and you've plenty of time to learn,' Lew replied. 'I don't plan on getting killed, but I am prone to bouts of fever from a sickness I had in Singapore, and while I'm sweating it out I don't want the ship getting off course.'

Ying made a note to examine his medicine chest which contained a large supply of herbs and potions. He would see to it that the captain stayed healthy. However, they'd pored over the maps spread on the long table. They would sail south from the Empire of China past Indo China through the South China Sea, on through the straits of Sumatra, past Borneo and Java, south of the Celebes continuing east, south of New Guinea through the narrow Torres Strait into Australian waters.

With this impossible journey spread out in front of him, Ying had felt quite faint. 'Where might we encounter pirates?'

'All the way. We'll have to be on our guard until we reach the safety of the Whitsundays.'

'That's some relief,' Ying said and Lew laughed.

'Yes, those reefs in there are too dangerous. The pirates won't chance being piled up on what they call the Barrier Reef.'

'I doubt if I'll sleep a wink for the rest of the voyage,' Ying said.

'It's not that bad. Have some wine.' Lew produced a small cask but Ying shook his head.

'I have brought excellent wines with me. However, you have consigned them to the hold. If you will permit, I shall send for some.'

'Lead on,' Lew laughed.

It was a heavenly night out there on the high seas, and Ying got happily drunk, replacing his worries with a reckless exhilaration at the adventures ahead.

'Do you really think you'll find gold?' Lew asked him.

'Who cares?' he replied gaily, a new man emerging.

Now, lazing bare-chested on the deck of the junk, Ying marvelled at the sphere of blue they had entered, the sky a cloudless expanse of azure, and the sea, remarkably, a deeper blue. Only the tropic green of the coastline broke the reign of blue, the two primary colours complementing each other. Ying had recorded various scenes on their travels in water colours but this landscape defied him. Back home his paintings were considered to be of a high standard but he could not capture this world. A man needed courage to attack a parchment with colours as rich as gems; the result could be hard and brittle. He looked around him, trying to resolve the problem. Despite its high colour, this scenery was not harsh, it was placid.

These musings reminded him of the captain, whom he now called Lew. An interesting comparison. The man was not as harsh as he'd first believed him to be. He had a personality not unlike this staggering blueness. His aura was immense. Snarling or smiling, active or passive, he had a presence that could not be ignored. And an essence of danger, like that green and pleasant coastline, behind which, Ying knew, lurked dangerous tribes of Aboriginal savages.

They had been attacked three times, twice at sea, by pirates. Lew had kept guards constantly on watch, and when harmless-looking fishing boats had come too close, his crew had opened fire so suddenly the pirates had been routed both times. The attack on land had been more alarming. It took place at a Javanese fishing village where they had been royally welcomed by the inhabitants as they came ashore to purchase supplies and fresh water. No sooner had Lew, and Ying with his two servants, stepped into the compound than they'd been surrounded by menacing armed villagers. Fortunately Lew had taken the precaution of armed back-up drawn from coolies and crew, and the bandits soon retreated.

Lew had shot the headman and burned the village to the ground, to punish the Javenese for luring unsuspecting seafarers into their seemingly benign company. Inside the huts they'd found grisly rows of human heads. Afterwards Lew had explained that the punishment, though harsh, was necessary and Ying had smiled. Lord Cheong would have executed every single one of them, men, women and children.

Oddly, neither man spoke of their parents. Lew never mentioned his father which gave Ying a polite excuse not to inquire and therefore precipitate discussion of his late unlamented parent.

Lew strolled down the deck. 'Not far to go now,' he said. 'You'll soon have your marching boots on.'

'The day is perfect and you have to spoil it,' Ying scowled. He was not looking forward to the next stage. 'But I have been wondering. Where are the deserts? My tutors informed me that this country was a huge, flat expanse of arid desert.'

'Behind the mountains, I suppose.'

'And I have to cross those mountains to get to the goldfields,' Ying said bleakly.

'Don't worry. You'll have plenty of company. Every ship we've seen has been making for this coast, packed with diggers. They say it's a bigger gold rush than California. We'll reach Bowen tomorrow, and I'm beginning to wish I could come with you. Gold prospecting could be a lot of fun.'

'No! You cannot!' Ying was startled. 'Never! You must stay and guard the ship. You have to stay in Bowen and be ready to take me back to China with the gold. Those are your orders!'

'Don't panic,' Lew said. 'I'll be here. I'll get you home again.'

4

Glory Molloy had been right. As usual. 'Get in first,' she had said, 'and since they don't know anyone else up here, as far as I can make out, you'll get your feet under the table.'

And so he had. This was the fourth time in a month Herbert had been invited to the Middleton household for supper. It had become a weekly event. He was their link with the town and the locals, and had made himself useful accompanying Jack on his search to buy three horses for the family and rent a nearby stable. Then he had volunteered to teach Perfy and her black maid to ride, which had been an experience. Herbert prided himself on his equestrian prowess and had said so, only to find his boast fall flat.

'What's equestrian?' Perfy had asked.

The lessons had begun with Perfy convinced she could manage, while he had pointed out that managing was not good enough, she had no idea how to sit a horse correctly. The maid, on the other hand, was convinced she couldn't ride, when in fact, after she overcame her fear of horses, Diamond wasn't too bad at all.

Herbert was amused that Mrs Middleton's new lady friends treated him with respect, the well-known land and house agent. They had no idea that he was Glory Molloy's former piano player. Why would they? Their husbands were regular visitors to Glory's house but they could hardly admit to their wives that they'd met Herbert inside a whorehouse. The conspiracy of silence among men worked just as well in this frontier town as it did in England. But, thank God, Jack Middleton wasn't interested in the seamier side of the town, he was content with his family.

In their study of local maps, Jack had finally mentioned Caravale Station, that his daughter owned a share in the property and they were waiting for the title deed to be issued. Herbert commiserated with him on the time it took for these matters to be cleared, since all such documents had to be drawn up in Brisbane, but he was also mightily interested. He had no doubt they would sell the Caravale property and he hoped to be able to arrange the sale for them; there would be a huge commission on such a transaction. It also proved that Perfy was indeed a wealthy and eligible young lady.

She was a very pretty girl in a countrified sort of way, but she was also rather intense, sometimes ready to converse, at other times lapsing into long moody silences. And when she did talk, she could be startlingly outspoken. Herbert had decided to court Miss Middleton when he became better acquainted with her but that first step was extremely difficult.

'Just be her friend, Herbert love,' Glory had advised him. 'Every girl needs a friend, especially if he's a handsome gentleman who is kind to her parents.'

'Easy enough for you to say, she's two different people. I don't know which one to expect.'

'Ah, it's just a game ladies play, think nought of it.'

Herbert wasn't so sure. And he wouldn't dream of telling Glory that Perfy Middleton, with her common family, could hardly be classified in his book as a lady. Jack Middleton was pleasant enough as these fellows went, ex-army, a sergeant. Herbert's father was a Colonel, retired, of the Coldstream Guards, and his two brothers were officers in the Colonel's old regiment. That would impress Jack and assist his case when the time came.

He left his office and made off down the street, wondering if he should purchase a pistol. Bowen was changing. It was to be expected that an influx of prospectors of all nationalities would lead to plenty of push and shove, there were any amount of drunks and roughheads in the town, but the two local policemen had so far been able to contain the brawls. Recently, though, hundreds of Chinese had come swarming in. Pig-tailed yellow-bellies with their high-pitched sing-song voices were everywhere, and nasty fights had developed. Bruisers were having a fine time beating up the Celestials, as they were called, and the Chinese retaliated with knives, generally considered unsporting weapons. With all the thieving that was now going on and mobs roaming abroad, a man was hardly safe in the streets at night.

The station men who rode into town were always armed and until now no one had taken much notice of them, they had to bear arms to protect themselves against attack in the bush. But now quite a few local residents were wearing guns strapped to their belts to protect themselves from attack right here in town. The danger was real, a man could be mugged for his purse and, right or wrong, the blame was always placed on the Chinese. It was a nasty situation and the police had requested assistance from troopers based in Townsville to the north, who responded that they had their own troubles. A new and faster route had just been discovered from Townsville to the Cape diggings and that village was growing rapidly. Successful diggers were bringing their gold out through Townsville instead of Bowen, making it a better target for ambush and robbery.

'Ah Herbert, just the man I want to see.' It was Sam Tolley.

'What can I do for you?' Herbert asked grandly. More land had been surveyed on the outskirts of Bowen and Herbert was selling allotments as easily as legs of lamb. He still had his blasted gambling debts but he'd managed to deposit several hundred pounds in Tolley's bank.

'The Middletons,' Sam said. 'Word has it that when they get the title to their share of Caravale Station they intend to sell.'

'First I've heard of it,' Herbert said. 'They've never mentioned any such thing to me.'

'Come on now, Herbert. They'll sell and you know it. You and Glory have already been nosing around to find a buyer with that sort of money.'

'News to me,' Herbert insisted.

Tolley stuck his thumbs in his waistcoat and grinned meanly. 'I hope it is, Herbert. Do you know Ben Buchanan?'

'I haven't had the pleasure.'

'No. But Ben Buchanan knows who you are. And I have a word of warning for you. Mr Buchanan does not want you flogging half of his property.'

'That's up to the Middletons.'

'No, it's not, laddie. You're a new chum here so it's best you learn how the land lies. The squatters are a powerful breed. When you get a message to back off from one of them, I'd advise you to do just that.'

'Why pick on me? They could find their own buyer.'

'They might try,' Tolley laughed. 'You just be a sensible lad and keep out of Ben Buchanan's sights.'

Herbert went on his way. The last thing he wanted to do was to tangle with any of those big station owners, they had their own laws. The sale wasn't as important as his courtship of Perfy Middleton, but he wasn't about to let go that easily.

He approached the house. Perfy and her mother were outside working in the garden. Most of their front hedge had been trampled into the ground.

'Will you look at this mess?' Alice Middleton said. 'We had a terrible night last night, men fighting in the street, and a mob of them shoved right in here. They've ruined our hedge. Jack has cleared away all the broken branches, but what a shame.'

'Yes, it is a shame. You should have sent for me. I could have helped Jack to clean up.'

'It's mostly done now,' Perfy said. 'We'll just have to replant. But Daddy is furious. He's gone down to the gunsmiths to get some ammunition. He says it won't happen a second time.'

'It's so hot,' Alice said, untying her bonnet. 'Leave this now, Perfy, I'll get some lemonade.'

Herbert took the wheelbarrow from Perfy. 'Let me do that.'

She came with him as he dumped the raked-up remains of leaves and ragged roots at the back of the house and he watched as she washed her hands at the tank. 'You're looking lovely today, Perfy.'

'I'm a mess,' she said. 'I hate gardening.'

'It's not the best of occupations in hot weather,' he agreed. 'Not that I've ever really tried it in the cold either,' he added with a laugh.

'What did you do back there in England?' she asked.

'Much the same as I do here,' he lied. 'Arranging sales of houses.'

'Oh.' She seemed satisfied with that and then she turned back to him. 'Mother thinks you're a remittance man. What's that?'

Herbert was stunned. And angry. But he pretended to be amused. 'My dear girl, would that I were. A remittance man is sent to the colonies by his family and paid to stay there out of sight, so to speak. My father would never be so generous.' Then he couldn't help adding, in a hurt tone, 'I'm sorry to disappoint your mother.'

'She didn't mean it to be critical,' Perfy said, walking him back round the side of the house of the front verandah where the family liked to sit in the evening. 'No, not at all. I mean, she wouldn't mind if you were. Who are we to criticise? Why did you come to Queensland?'

He swallowed, remembering the forged notes that his father had to repay to keep him out of prison. 'Gold, my dear. I thought gold prospecting would be a simpler matter.' In fact he'd never heard of such a thing as a gold rush until he reached Brisbane. 'But I was absolutely no dashed good at it at all. So I had to revert to the business I know, hence back to organising sales.' That came out very aptly, he thought, but he was still smarting from the remittance comment. Too close for comfort. 'For that matter, why did you come to Bowen?' His voice had a rare edge to it. He had so accustomed himself to playing the amiable gent, the joker, the rasp surprised even him.

'I'm sorry, Herbert,' she said. 'I've hurt your feelings.'

'Not at all. It's just that, at times, one becomes irritated. Folk are inclined to mistake one's good humour and good manners for weakness. And I am not a weak person.' Once again, not quite correct, but he did long to be a strong decisive person, he'd always preferred the black knight to the simpering Lancelot.

'Of course you're not,' she said, cheering him no end. 'I think you're very nice. And we came to Bowen because I own property west of here.' She sounded as offhand as if she were referring to a corner store. 'A place called Caravale. Do you know it?'

'Your father did mention it but I don't know the area.'

'It's a long way out. Towards the goldfields.'

'So I believe. Absolutely the back of beyond. I can't imagine how people can live out there.'

'Why not?'

There was that intensity again. For a gentle girl, those blue eyes could turn glacial. 'Well, the isolation, for a start.'

'I'd like that,' she said. 'When the papers are all fixed up, we're going out there.'

'Where?' he asked stupidly.

'Caravale, silly. Mother can't go, the travelling would be too difficult, she's happy to stay here, but Daddy and I will be going. I'm looking forward to seeing the station. You should come with us.'

Alice Middleton appeared on the verandah with the lemonade and rescued him from having to reply. Caravale! Sam Tolley's warning echoed like a mournful bell and he felt a sense of dread. Ben Buchanan, that vague person out there in the backblocks, was suddenly very real. An enemy. Damn! Perfy liked him enough to invite him to go along with them, but to march boldly on to Buchanan's territory? No way. He would have to think of an excuse to pass on that hand. 'Why go to all that bother?' he asked. 'You can sell the place just as easily without dragging out there.'

'Who said I'm selling?'

'Oh! I don't know. I just took it for granted.'

'Well, I'm not. Half of that station belongs to me and I intend to keep it.'

Herbert wondered why that statement made him feel even more nervous.

Jack Middleton felt it his civic duty to attend a meeting of townsmen to discuss the growing lawlessness in Bowen. It was such a beautiful place with a glorious shoreline and huge shady trees alive with colour, a great pity that over-population, even temporary, was causing so many problems.

The local magistrate, Arnold Fletcher, welcomed him into his office with the news that the meeting had been cancelled because the police sergeant and his deputy had been called to a shooting outside town. A gold shipment had been ambushed by bushrangers and a posse was combing the hills for the outlaws and the gold. 'Have a drink,' Fletcher said, pouring two rums without waiting for a reply. 'The meeting would have been a bloody waste of time anyway.'

'I don't think so,' Jack replied.

'We have to be careful though, meetings like that and talk of vigilante patrols can give a town a bad name.'

Jack laughed. 'A bad name? The town's packed to billy-o, supplies are short, there's trouble in the streets day and night. The lock-up's full and the hospital is crammed with victims of knife and shot. Not to mention the graveyard.'

'These things are to be expected. It's a hundred times worse out on the diggings.'

'Mr Fletcher, this isn't the diggings. This is, or should be, a law-abiding town. Decent women are not safe on the streets without an escort.'

Fletcher downed his rum and poured another. 'What can we do? Put a sign up on the harbour saying "No Admittance"? The merchants in the town would hang us from the nearest tree.'

Jack stared out of the open door at the confusion of the now busy street. 'It's not just the mobs piling in here. There's racial trouble. Constant strife between the whites and the Chinese.'

162

Fletcher stroked his moustache. 'Ah yes, that happens, but I rarely see the Celestials before my court. They disappear into the shadows and suddenly no speakee English. Difficult to deal with them.'

'I've been through their camps and they seem orderly people, and clean.'

'Best thing to do is ignore them, Jack. Before they came, it was the Abos that got the bashings. Now it's the Chinks' turn. You know what these mobs are like when they get full of booze. Anything can get them riled up – arguments, missing horses, thievings. They have to take it out on someone. So they go on down and belt around a few Chinese, burn a few tents, call themselves good fellers and go back to the pubs.'

'And what if the Chinese decide to fight back?'

'Never.' Fletcher smiled benignly. 'They won't fight white men. They're too slippery for an honest to God punch-up. Come nightfall they're all too doped up with opium. China must be a right weird country, Jack, everyone lying around in poppy dreams. Wouldn't do for the British.'

'No,' Jack said. 'We just sold it to them. The Chinese tried desperately to keep opium out of their country.'

'Rot. I don't know where you got that story from. Someone's been wigging you. China's one big poppy field.'

'It comes from India,' Jack said wearily. He looked out into the street. 'What the hell's this?'

The two men walked outside to see a gaudily dressed Chinaman trotting down the main street, flanked by two more pig-tailed Chinese in black pyjama suits. Behind them came a lone line of coolie bearers with cone-shaped rush hats tied under their chins.

In a few strides Fletcher was on to the road to halt the procession. 'What's this then?'

The Chinese leader stopped and like birds in formation his followers obeyed his instructions without any signal, coming to an abrupt standstill, baskets swaying gently on their bamboo poles. 'Good afternoon, sir,' he said, bowing.

'Did you ever see the like?' Fletcher called back to Jack.

'Some matter is wrong, sir?' the Chinaman asked.

Fletcher was forced to stop gaping and reply. 'Who are you?'

'Mr Chin, sir.' He bowed again, hands hidden in the deep folds of a startling red and gold silk coat with huge padded shoulders. 'From Hunan. I am proceeding to the goldfields and these are my diggers.'

Jack came over to join them. He nodded to the Chinaman and laughed. 'Nothing like doing it the easy way.'

'The easy way be damned,' Fletcher cried. 'They're not fair-dinkum diggers, they're coolies. Must be bloody fifty of them. If they all start this caper, fifty coolies for every Chink boss, we'll be overrun.'

'There's no law against it,' Jack said. 'Let him go on.' The streets were now crowded with curious onlookers. Fletcher had made a mistake stopping the Chinese, Jack could feel resentment all around him.

'Send 'em back where they come from,' a voice shouted.

'Keep going,' Jack said to the Chinese leader, urgency in his voice now, but a man stepped forward, picked up a soggy pat of manure and hurled it at the Chinaman, splotching it all over the front of the fine silk coat.

In a swift reaction, a tall seaman grabbed hold of the thrower and punched him hard, sending him sprawling.

'That way, quickly,' Jack said, pointing to a nearby lane as more missiles began to fly, more manure, clods of dirt and even drinking glasses, which left him no choice but to run with them.

Once in the lane he yelled at the Chinese to keep going but he himself stopped as a mob of men turned in after them. 'You've had your fun,' he shouted. 'Now get back about your business.'

'It's a free country, we can go where we like,' a voice yelled back at him.

'Get out of the way, you mug,' another voice shouted and they surged forward. Angry men jostled and thumped him in the confined space of the narrow lane and he was afraid he would fall, but strong hands steadied him and a stranger thrust and punched a path for them until they were clear of the press.

Panting, Jack leaned against a stone wall. The mob had run on to the end of the lane, to shout and jeer at the fleeing Chinese, none of them prepared to venture too close, in daylight, to the boundary of the Orientals' camps.

'Nice town you've got here,' the stranger said and Jack realised it was the seaman who'd punched the miner in the street.

'Next time, tell your Chinese mate not to march through the place like he was the emperor.'

Lew Cavour laughed. 'I did, and he hates me saying "I told you so!" I'd better go and see if he's still in one piece. The rumpus seems to have died down.'

'I'll come with you,' Jack said, stuffing his torn shirt back into his pants. 'And thanks for pulling me out of that stampede. Bloody idiots, the lot of them. I'm Jack Middleton.' He extended his hand. 'You are a prospector too?'

'Me? Christ, no. I'm a sailor. Lew Cavour.' They shook hands. 'I've got a ship in the bay.'

'Is that right? Which one?'

'She hasn't got a name, I call her the Junk. We came in this morning.'

'The big junk? I saw her, what a whopper! And you're the captain?'

'Yes.'

Jack was intrigued. 'I never knew Englishmen sailed junks.'

'We get around, us Limeys,' Lew grinned. 'And that Chinese gentleman and his entourage were my passengers.'

'You don't seem too worried about them. Don't you like the Chinese?'

They walked out of the lane and headed for an open paddock scattered with all manner of tents, ignoring the sullen glares of the miners.

'I love the Chinese,' Cavour said, 'but I don't have to worry about them. They can look after themselves. I wouldn't like to be in the shoes of the fool who threw the muck at Chin Ying. They'll find him, you know. Loss of face, very nasty.'

They found Ying sitting stiffly on a low fence attached to a stone moon gate which the Chinese had erected to bring good fortune to their camp. The coat was on the ground beside him and he was now wearing a long tunic buttoned up to his neck.

'Disgusting people,' he snorted angrily. 'I will have to burn that coat.'

'Of course,' Lew said.

'I'm sorry that happened,' Jack said. 'I'm a resident of Bowen and we don't like ruffians.'

Ying stood and bowed as Lew introduced Jack. 'Your apology is graciously accepted, sir,' he said solemnly.

'What now?' Lew asked him.

'My servants are preparing my tent accommodation. I will only stay in this town to collect provisions and hire a guide and then I will proceed inland.'

'Do you want help with anything now?' Lew asked him.

'No. Tonight I will resume my studies of metallurgy. Most imperative.'

Lew accompanied Jack back into the town. 'It was good of you to apologise,' Lew said. 'He knows you're not responsible but it helps to cool him down.'

'He seemed calm enough.'

'Like hell he was!'

'Do you have to go back to your ship now?'

'No. I came ashore early to explore the town but there's not much of it, is there?'

'No, she's just a little village, overcrowded now but—'

'Overcrowded? This place? It feels empty to me, coming from the throngs of China.'

'What's the population of China?'

'Oh, they reckon about three hundred and thirty million.'

'God Almighty, and I just found out the white population of this great big state is only about twelve thousand!'

Lew stared at him. 'That can't be right.'

'I think you'll find it is, mate. Listen, I've got to get home. Why don't you come and have supper with us?'

Lew's tanned face lit up. 'I'd be honoured,' he replied, which Jack thought was an odd, old-fashioned sort of reply, but he liked this young fellow and, being a seafarer, he'd have some tales to tell. Jack liked nothing better than a good yarn.

Alice Middleton apologised for their plain fare, but Lew enjoyed every morsel. He'd had many an English meal in his day, at the homes of friends (his parents had only Chinese food in their determination to live as did their parishioners) or at European hotels, but they were always prepared by Chinese cooks. Not that Lew could tell the difference but people complained that it was 'never the same'. Now he understood. Jack's wife served roast beef in large thick slices, with Yorkshire pudding and thick gravy, whole carrots and potatoes and onions, baked with the meat, and boiled cabbage. Plain fare it was indeed, not a spice or a herb in it, but it tasted good, and she heaped the plates as if this were to be their last meal for the week.

'Have you ever tasted Chinese food?' he asked her.

'No, definitely not,' she replied. 'I hear they eat all sorts of awful things.'

'Sharks' fins and nightingales' eyes,' her daughter said, the girl Perfy who was the most attractive English girl he'd ever met.

'Don't be so horrible,' Alice snapped. 'You'll put us off our supper.'

'Would you like to see the junk?' Lew asked them.

'I would,' Jack Middleton replied. 'Never been on one of them.'

'Then what about bringing the family on board for a dinner party, as my guest? I'll borrow Chin Ying's servants, they are marvellous cooks. They won't be able to match your cooking, Mrs Middleton, this is the best dinner I've had in ages, but you might just enjoy their dishes.'

'Oh, I don't know about that,' she replied nervously.

'Come along now, Mother,' Jack said. 'Don't be a stick-in-the mud. We ought to try it.'

'No sharks' fins?' Perfy asked.

Lew smiled at her. 'I promise.'

He managed to persuade Chin Ying to come too. 'They're very nice people. You'll meet enough of the other type, it will be a good experience for you.'

The junk and its fittings surprised them. Lew guessed that Mrs Middleton had expected a grubby old tub with evil Chinks peering at her; she was quite taken with the spit and polish. It was a lovely calm night so the banquet had been set up on deck. Lew showed Jack and Perfy around, leaving Chin Ying to make polite conversation with Alice. A first for both of them.

On his tour Lew explained that the hull was divided by thick timbers into a series of watertight compartments, showed them the tanks for live fish which they carried with them, the salt room, special water tanks, the two galleys and the very comfortable stateroom. His guests were impressed.

The banquet was more fun than he could have imagined. Ying

explained each dish, variations on beef, duck and pork with tiny dumplings and spicy vegetables, and the family enjoyed eating from the little bowls and tasting small portions.

'Goodness me,' Alice exclaimed. 'How many courses do you serve at home?'

'This is not so many,' Ying smiled.

'You do yourselves proud,' Jack said. 'I never thought to see myself liking rice except in a pudding.'

'I thought Chinese people only really ate rice,' Perfy said.

Ying shook his head. 'Oh no, miss. Good food is important.'

It wouldn't occur to Ying, and Lew didn't bother to make the point that Chinese peasants and coolies lived on meagre rations of rice and fish.

After a very pleasant evening, a boatman took the family back to shore but Chin Ying decided to stay on board.

'So you have found yourself a lady already,' he said. 'We shall have some more wine to celebrate.'

'You never miss a thing, do you?' Lew said. 'Was I that obvious? What do you think of her?'

'A virgin. Very handsome, I think, for English.'

'Ying! She's beautiful! Stay as long as you like out there on the gold-fields. I'll be just fine, right here.'

Lew took Perfy and her maid, Diamond, to see Chin Ying off on his trek to the goldfields. He and the guide, a local man, would both travel on horse-back. Yuang Lu and Yuang Pan, Ying's two servants, were on foot. They had large canvas bags strapped to their backs and carried bamboo sticks to keep the coolies moving. Ying graciously presented Perfy with a tiny jade cat, for good luck, which delighted her. She was less impressed by his treatment of the coolies.

'Those poor fellows,' she said to Lew. 'They're loaded up like mules.'

'They're used to it,' he said lightly. Ying, he noticed, was beginning to adapt to his surroundings. Instead of his usual gaudy and impractical clothing he was wearing a sombre tunic and trousers, and looked very businesslike.

'Goodbye and good luck,' Lew called as the column moved off down the dusty track. 'It'll be interesting to see how he gets on,' he said to Perfy.

'Doesn't he know they have to go right into the hills?'

'Yes. Why?'

'Because those men of his will have a terrible time, dragging all that way.'

'No, they won't. They're tough. Coolies can carry up to a hundred and sixty pounds.'

'Just like animals.'

He took her arm. 'Perfy, everyone knows supplies are short out there.

They have to take equipment and supplies. Coolies can travel much faster than the wagons that are constantly getting bogged.'

'Yes, but horses pull them out.'

'And manpower. Europeans need muscle on those trails too, from what I hear.'

'What do they get paid?' It was Diamond who asked this question and Lew was taken aback, not so much by the question as by the person asking it. The maid. He was not accustomed to the laxity afforded servants in this country and this black girl carried herself like the Queen of Sheba. It was all very odd. Not that he disliked her, she was smart and intelligent. 'Their keep,' he replied, 'the same as you, I suppose.' He saw her dark eyes flash in anger.'

From high in the long line of gum trees that formed a wall at the edge of the cleared land he could hear birds warbling, magnificent full-throated clear notes that would do a soprano proud. 'Those birds, they sing so brilliantly. What are they?' he asked to change the subject.

'Magpies,' Perfy replied.

'And butcher-birds, too,' Diamond said.

'They copy each other,' Perfy added.

'And sometimes they compete,' Diamond said.

'What do they look like?' he asked, pleased they were off the subject of coolies.

It was Diamond who replied. 'Magpies are big flash birds, black and white, very sure of themselves. Butcher-birds are smaller, they keep out of sight, you don't see them much but they are very powerful.' The remark sounded innocent enough but Lew felt that something more lay behind what Diamond had said, though he wasn't sure what.

Perfy was studying the little jade cat. 'It's so beautiful. How nice of Mr Chin.'

'He must like you,' Lew was pleased to tell her. 'Jade is most precious to the Chinese.'

'Is it expensive?' she asked.

'Very expensive, that piece.'

'Oh dear, I should have thanked him properly. Was it rude of me just to say it was pretty?'

'Ying wouldn't expect thanks. His gift is his joy.'

There wasn't much to do in a rough town like Bowen so any outing he could think of seemed to please Perfy. It was a holiday for him, a blissful holiday. He would hate to leave. He swam every morning in the crystal clear waters of the bay, went fishing, called on the Middleton family as often as he dared, and drank in the pubs, listening to nothing but gold, gold, and more gold. The country was still strange to him and Perfy was intrigued to meet an Englishman who had never lived on English territory. She wanted to know everything about him, which was encouraging, and he expressly appointed her his guide, to show him kangaroos and wallabies and emus, all the gentle animals that inhabited the land. They had so much to talk about, it was wonderful.

The Middletons invited him on a family picnic under shady trees along the beach, the sort of picnic he imagined the English had back home.

'Dear me, no,' Alice said. 'We never went on picnics back home, we were too poor. That's only for the upper classes. And I don't think they cook beef and chops out in the open like everyone does here. No, I don't think so.'

Another gentleman accompanied them, Mr Herbert Watlington, a smooth-talking proper Englishman who hung on to Perfy like a limpet. When Lew finally got Perfy to himself he said: 'I didn't know you had another beau.'

She just looked at him calmly and said, 'I don't have any beau.'

'Oh yes you do,' he laughed. 'You've got one you can be sure of.' He meant himself but she didn't react at all. It was as if he hadn't spoken.

Later, he went over that conversation dozens of times. At night he paced the junk thinking of her and that was frustrating. He was tempted to try out one of the many brothels in Bowen but was too careful to take risks. He missed the Yuang brothers. On their journey south they'd called at many Asian ports and Ying had sent his servants ashore to bring him 'clean' girls. How the brothers selected the 'clean' girls of varying nationality that they brought back on board, Lew had no idea, but he did know that it would have cost them their lives to fail their master. Ying had graciously 'allowed' Lew to share these tender beauties.

Bowen was beginning to irk him, it was too small, too restricted. He had bought a horse to ride with Perfy but they couldn't go too far. A mile out of town and the bush loomed ahead of them, thousands of grey, leafless tree trunks that gave the impression of a streaked granite wall topped with foliage. It was too dangerous to take Perfy any further so he had ridden out another day on his own. He followed the untidy track into the strange open forest, passing tall anthills and dead trees lying in the coarse grass like whitened bones. A big red kangaroo, grazing in the speckled light, stopped to stare at him, unperturbed by his presence. The meeting pleased him. He dismounted to get a better look at her and from her pouch a little joey peeped out curiously at him. Their acceptance of him reminded him that he wasn't a foreigner in this country; he had been accepted so readily he had forgotten his original enthusiasm. He rode further into the bush but after a while the sameness began to pall and he realised he'd been riding for hours and hadn't seen a soul, not one human being. He turned back to Bowen, depressed, unaccustomed to this lonely environment.

And Bowen was beginning to make him feel hemmed in. He went in search of Jack Middleton. 'I have to take the junk out to give her sails a stretch and keep the crew on their toes. Would you mind if I invited

Perfy? We'll be back by nightfall and I promise to be a gentleman.'

Jack grinned. 'Yes, sure. If she wants to go. You're a bit keen on her, aren't you?'

'That's an understatement. I think she's lovely.'

'So do we, son, so you take care of her. And take her quietly, she's had a few ups and downs, our girl, we wouldn't want her upset.'

'What ups and downs?'

'It's her business. I figure she'll talk about it when she's ready and it'll be a mile better for her to do the talking.'

Perfy sat facing Lew as he rowed them out to the junk. She was looking forward to the day on board, it was such a glorious morning, but she was also feeling apprehensive. Lew made her nervous, he was so . . . what? Masculine. This wasn't a gentle, shy Darcy. When Lew touched her she had the feeling that given a chance he'd whisk her off to the nearest bedroom. And she knew, without being told, that he was experienced in a lot more things than sailing ships.

'If you'd rather not to go on your own,' her father had said, 'Lew won't mind if you ask someone else. Like Herbert.'

Perfy laughed. 'He hates Herbert.'

'Then take Diamond.'

'No, I'll be all right.' She hadn't brought Diamond, on principle. Lew would see through that. When they'd first met, he'd been surprised that young ladies could move about without chaperones in the colony, except when drunks spilled on to the streets of Bowen. To bring Diamond along would be to admit she was nervous of him. Perfy had her pride. She had no doubt Lew would be a gentleman, it was his closeness that bothered her. She still missed Darcy, she doubted she would ever get over his death. Besides, she didn't want to forget him. Why should she?

The crew were lined up on the junk watching them approach, broad grins on their faces as if something enormously important was happening.

'They look pleased with themselves,' she said.

'Yes,' he told her. 'They're very excited.'

'Why?'

'Because we've named the junk. Look here.' Towards the prow of the ship, large Chinese characters were freshly painted on the hull.

'What do they mean?'

'Perfection. The crew think it's a terrific name.'

'Oh!' she said, flabbergasted. 'What a nice thought.'

'I've promised them we'll have a special naming ceremony when you come on board. What do you think?'

'It's a grand idea,' she laughed. 'You must tell them I'm honoured.'

They sailed south in the incredible blueness of the Whitsundays, the huge sails fanned out above them. Perfy strolled the decks enjoying the scenery, the ship itself and the sense of freedom it gave her to be the lone passenger. She felt released from the everyday world, glad now to be alone with her thoughts while Lew put the crew through their paces. Since Darcy's death she'd been under scrutiny all the time. Her parents worried about her and went to a lot of trouble to keep her happy and busy, hence their encouragement of possible suitors like Herbert and Lew, and other young people in the town.

It was amazing the way her mother had settled in. She was more confident now, she'd made friends in Bowen and joined not one, but two groups of ladies, a sewing circle and the Workers for Charity who tried to help the many down-and-outers drifting back from the goldfields with their families. And Perfy was reminded that it was Darcy who had made this possible. Having her own home had given Alice a new outlook. She was no longer timid, insecure, nervous with strangers; in fact she was having the time of her life.

'What about some lunch?'

'Is it that time already?'

'Sure is. I hired a cook for today. Since Ying left I've had to rely on the ship's cook who produces mainly rice dishes.'

'How can a man your size get by on rice?'

'Easily,' he laughed, 'when I have to.'

'What's that island over there?' Perfy asked. 'It looks so pretty.'

'Gloucester Island.'

'Can we go ashore and explore?'

'Definitely not, madam. I promised your father I'd get you home safely. There could be savage blacks on any of these islands and I'm not about to take a chance.'

Lunch was served to the captain and his lady under a canvas awning on the deck and Perfy was so totally relaxed, it was easy to talk to Lew, and to listen. His parents, she was surprised to hear, had been missionaries who had sailed out from England and died in China, but when she asked about them, he became tense and changed the subject quickly. So she told him about Brisbane, how her parents had ended up in Australia. Jack's years in the army, her work at Government House. That intrigued him. And then she found herself talking about Darcy, telling him about Darcy until, to her horror, she was in tears, weeping on his shoulder, his arms round her, feeling she was making an awful fool of herself, spoiling their day. But he didn't seem to mind. 'Crying's good for the soul,' he told her. 'It won't be over until you've cried it all out.'

Later they sailed round the eastern side of Gloucester Island where they anchored so that they could peer into the still, crystal waters at the beautiful fish darting about, and catch a glimpse of the forest of coral far below. And as the sun was setting, dropping fast like a huge golden coin into the darkening hills, they sailed back into Edgecumbe Bay and the rush and scramble of the little port.

171

She was cheerful again by the time he rowed her back to the beach, her lapse forgotten, laughing again. 'It has been a wonderful day, Lew. Thank you so much. Will you ask me again?'

'Anytime you wish,' he said.

As they walked across the sand and under the pandanus trees, he put an arm round her. 'I couldn't very well take advantage of you on the junk,' he said. 'But now on shore you can run if you want to.'

Perfy twisted away from him. 'Oh Lew, don't. Don't spoil things.'

'I'm sorry, I didn't mean to offend you. I'm very fond of you and I thought we'd had such a good day . . .'

'Don't apologise, it's my fault, crying on your shoulder like that. Can't we just be friends?'

'Of course we can, but I have to warn you that Lewis Cavour, captain of the good ship yonder, hopes to court you. He just has to learn the rules of this new land.'

'Don't waste your time on me,' she shrugged. 'I'm not interested in being courted. There are plenty of other girls around.'

'Ah, but there's only one Perfy. She might relent one of these days, you never know.'

'Oh, come on, Lew,' she said impatiently, marching up through the scrub. 'The mosquitoes here are shocking. They come out in swarms at dusk.'

Alice and Jack were in the verandah, waiting for them.

'There you are,' Jack cried. 'Come and join me in an ale, Lew.'

'Be glad to,' he said.

'Perfy, you're sunburned,' Alice said. 'Come inside and I'll put some salve on your face.'

'We're also mosquito-bitten,' Perfy laughed, following her mother inside.

'He didn't touch you?' Alice whispered urgently.

'Oh, Mother, don't be so embarrassing. No, he didn't.'

Alice smiled. 'Your father's a good judge. He said it would be all right. Now put on this salve and do your hair, it's blown about like hay. Jack has some news for you.'

Perfy hurried back outside. 'What's the news?'

'The title deeds arrived today. You're now officially half-owner of Caravale.'

Perfy was thrilled. 'That's marvellous. I thought they'd never get round to it.'

'What's Caravale?' Lew asked.

It's a cattle station out west of here,' Jack replied.

'Darcy left it to me,' Perfy explained, her face reddening even with the salve and the sunburn. She saw her parents exchange glances, and that irritated her. 'They say it's a fine big station,' she added.

'Like a ranch?' Lew asked.

'Yes.'

'I see,' he said, noncommittal, as if the explanation that a station was a ranch was all that interested him.

They chatted amiably for a while and then Lew rose to leave. He was, as usual, genial, pleased that Perfy had enjoyed herself, and went on his way with a grin. But she wished he had stayed longer; she wanted to explain about Caravale, to tell him about it.

An occasional flash of lightning, far out to sea, silvered the night, creating an ominous, brooding silence, for no thunder followed.

In the ensuing months Perfy was to look back on that day as her last truly peaceful time before the real trouble started, and remembering, she clung to it, holding to it like a talisman, like her little jade cat of good fortune.

5

The people of Bowen were of the Bindal tribe and Diamond sought them out as soon as she could. There were quite a few Aborigines wandering around dressed in the usual weird assortment of whitefeller clothes, because they were not permitted within the perimeters of the town 'undressed'. They were healthier, less inclined to cringe than the totally overwhelmed Brisbane natives, but some of them, Diamond noticed sadly, had already succumbed to the grog-induced madness. The passing parade of gold-chasers had no interest in the place at all. Perhaps, she thought, when the gold rush was over, the resident Aborigines might be given a better go in the town, but it was a faint hope.

Dressed sedately, Diamond had explored the area; she still wore her knife but she wasn't so jumpy here. The town was more open than Brisbane and she could outrun anyone who bothered her but, like the white women, she never went out at night alone. For that matter she never went anywhere at night except to stroll with the family or go with them to church concerts. Mrs Middleton was quite proud to tell her new friends that Diamond could read, and read well. It seemed to astonish them, but they were quick to give her books. Prayer books. Every single book they produced was a religious text of some sort! These days, Diamond preferred newspapers, and she studied them with care; there was much to learn from newspapers, although articles about the 'necessary killing of wild blacks' put her in a towering rage. The newspapers often referred to 'tame' blacks, or niggers, and it was a shock to realise that the term applied to her, too. It was something else to face head on, so that it couldn't hurt her any more. Away from the dulling numbness of that laundry, she was becoming stronger in her mind now.

She sought out the Bindal camps and sat down with them, listening to their stories. All through time, Bindal people had rejoiced at their good fortune. They were not warriors, they were gentle, generous people. And why not? The earth they shared provided them with abundant food and wells with plentiful fresh water. Hill people came to visit the Bindal tribes, as did in-country people, they told her, and Diamond concluded that this region must be a 'get-well' place. The Countess and her friends used to leave Brisbane for weeks on end to go to the coast, to the seaside. 'For their health,' Cook had said. Tribal people must do the same thing. That made sense.

Diamond asked them about the Irukandjis but they couldn't help. With much giggling, she was referred to a woman called Barrungulla.

'Where can I find her?'

They pointed round the bay, so Diamond set off along the sand, carrying her shoes, paddling in the shallows, reminded of another beach somewhere, just like this. Instead of getting closer to her goal she was even more confused now. They voyage from Brisbane to Bowen had taken more than a week, following the coastline. For all she knew, she might have come too far north. And to hear that tribal people from other areas visited the coast was depressing. Maybe her family had been on a walkabout, or trading. It was so hard to remember. Her head ached when she tried to force the memories into focus. Words drifted back to her now and then, and she'd try to grasp them but, like feathery clock-weeds, they'd slip apart in her fingers.

She walked a long way; her skirt was sopping but cool around her ankles but the turban was causing her head to sweat so she pulled it off and stuffed it in her belt. Someone was ahead of her and she hurried on until she saw that it was a woman, planted aggressively on the beach to bar her way, hands on hips, a coal-black statue mounted against the shimmering seascape. She was wearing a loincloth and a necklace of mother-of-pearl shells, and she was huge, a mountain of muscle with wild grey hair and a bitterly lined face.

'What you want?' she yelled, and Diamond stopped.

'Talk,' she replied.

A black arm shot out like a spear, finger pointing. Diamond flinched, the action had been so fast she thought the woman had hurled something at her.

'You back-back!' the woman ordered.

Diamond was nervous. This patch of beach was suddenly a scary place, and she could hear ancient voices muttering and mumbling in her head. It was possible she had stumbled too close to a sacred place, but usually all women were off limits. 'No,' she cried. 'I've come to talk.'

'You whitefeller bitch!' the woman screamed, advancing on her, ugly menace in the dark eyes.

Diamond was terrified. Too afraid to run. She could feel watchers in the massive greenery bordering the sand, and for one mad minute she looked at the sea. Hadn't she done that before? Somewhere? But in these clothes, in the thick skirt and all the whitefeller paraphernalia, it was out of the question.

'No,' she shouted as the woman strode at her. She threw out her arms and shouted again. 'Kagari!'

Instantly a kookaburra took up the call, hooting its panic signal, and others joined in, hooting and cackling, shattering the air with a barrage of cadences, warning the enemy that the whole family was now on alert.

The woman stopped and jerked towards the trees as a lone kookaburra sped from the bush and swooped low around them.

175

Diamond knew, as this woman would know, that the cobbled hooting was a prelude to attack, and there could be a force of up to twenty adult birds in the territory. Diamond had seen them plunging headlong at goannas that were trying to rob their nests, risking broken necks to force the lizards to lose their grip and fall out of the trees. Kookaburras were her totem, Diamond had always known that. The birds were everywhere, and were the most loyal of creatures. They'd even attack the red seahawks and the great wedge-tail eagles. They had no fear of humans.

Abruptly the woman sat down, cross-legged, in the sand. In deference, Diamond did too. The kookaburras snapped off to silence in mid-call.

'What feller you?' the woman asked.

'Irukandji,' Diamond said, repeating the name very slowly, but the woman shook her head.

'Are you Barrungulla?' Diamond asked.

The woman glanced up at the trees, obviously concerned not to to set the birds off again, and Diamond saw a partly healed scar round her neck, above the lovely necklace. 'Why you want speak allasame me?'

'I need your help. I'm looking for my family.'

'Fambly,' the woman echoed and Diamond saw a softening. She knew that to all natives of this land, family, in whatever language, meant caring. She began to explain her situation but Barrungulla became agitated. She took Diamond's hands and turned them over. 'You blackfeller all right. But blackfeller all gone from you now. Better you stop walkabout, you lost.'

'No,' Diamond said. 'I must not. Your people here are Bindal, good people.'

Barrungulla grimaced. 'Good people finish. Allatime die now.'

Diamond placed a finger in the sand. 'Here we are. Here's where your people live. What tribes live on past here?'

'Boorgaman tribe sit down that way.'

'And down here?'

She shrugged. 'Cogoon. Me'be Cullinaringo. Here,' she pointed west, 'comin' Ilba.'

'Any more?'

Barrungulla brushed her hand over a coastal area further north. 'Bad feller country there.'

'Who?'

'No good you go there, allasame chop up.'

'Who are they?'

'Newegi,' the woman whispered, and Diamond sighed. She hadn't realised there were so many tribes, each with their own territory. The way the white people talked, this country was uninhabited. Diamond's inquiries had only covered a minor section of the land.

'Thank you,' she said. And then gently: 'What happened to your neck, Barrungulla?'

The woman looked up defiantly. 'You know hang?'

'Yes.' Diamond shivered.

'White man hang this woman.'

'Oh my God. How did you get away?'

'Totem too strong.' she laughed. 'Wihra tree angry. Go bang!' She snapped her large hands to illustrate the cracking of a branch. 'All fall down not dead.'

As Barrungulla talked of the killings and the paybacks that were enacted in Bindal territory behind the pleasant little bay, Diamond began to understand the extent of the silent war that was raging between the whites and the blacks; that not all the people had become 'tame'; that the majority of the Aborigines refused to surrender and were prepared to die to defend their homelands.

'You go now,' Barrungulla said. 'Go home.'

'Where's home?' Diamond said, distressed at what she had heard and despondent that she had no family. At least these people knew who they were, and were united by family bonds.

Barrungulla shook her head impatiently. She had her own problems. The audience was over.

6

Lew was in love with Perfy, he'd told her so a dozen times, and he hoped she could love him if she would only let go of the memory of Darcy Buchanan. It was an impossible job to compete with a dead man who was now a saint according to Perfy. And it wasn't as if he was trying to step into a dead man's shoes; she was, with this crackpot idea of keeping that cattle station. He'd tried to talk to Jack about it but got short shrift from that direction; he had the same attitude as his daughter.

'I have written to Mrs Buchanan,' Perfy told him, 'as a courtesy to let her know we wish to visit Caravale.'

'Why didn't you write to your partner, Ben Buchanan?'

'Because Daddy said since she's the lady of the house it would be better to write to her.'

'And did you tell the lady of the house you're thinking of moving in?' Lew asked angrily.

'You won't try to understand, Lew. They know I'm financially involved with them now, there's no need to explain.'

'It's madness. How would you like strangers to move into this house? Even if they did own half of it.'

She smiled at him. 'Stations are different. This place is huge. We think eventually the answer would be to cut the station in half and build another homestead. Then it would be our own station. We just want to discuss the options with the Buchanans.'

He tried again. 'I can't talk to you any more, Perfy. All you can think about is this blasted station.'

'No,' she argued. 'You're not interested in what I do. You can be very selfish. Don't you understand what a marvellous gift Darcy has given me? It's not just a place, it's a way of life. Darcy said growing up on a station was a great experience. They had enormous fun with their own horses and dogs and all sorts of lovely pets and at the same time they were learning how to run the family business.'

'Sounds just like the King of England. That's how he grew up too.'

'Don't be sarcastic. I do believe you're jealous.'

'Oh, for God's sake, I'm not jealous. Can't you see it's not that simple. You wouldn't have the faintest idea how to run a cattle station.'

'I don't have to. A lot of stations are run by managers and foremen.

Their lives are for more interesting than working in townships. For that matter you could do worse. There's any amount of land going begging in this state. If you had any real ambition, you'd take up a cattle run yourself. People are making fortunes in the cattle business.'

Lew confronted her angrily. 'I hope you're joking!'

'I'm not joking. You should think about it.'

'I have no intentions of thinking about it, Perfy. I'm a seaman, not a farmer.' He was losing her and he knew it but he couldn't retreat from the battle even though his arguments served only to annoy her. 'Did your precious Darcy tell you about the dangers of that marvellous outback life style?' he countered.

'No, he didn't,' she flared, 'any more than you have mentioned the dangers sailors face at sea, which I think would be ten times worse.' And with a swish of skirts she swept inside the house.

Only Alice Middleton seemed to agree with Lew but she was loyal to her husband, and he was adamant that Perfy should take control of her own property.

'What is it about this place?' Lew asked Perfy. 'Why is it that you must be station owners? Do you need the status? To be able to join the ranks of the gentry here? Is that what you're after?'

'Of course not. I just happen to believe that station life would be a happy and healthy environment to bring up children, and think what an inheritance they'd have.'

Frustrated, Lew stood away from her. 'I don't believe you. If you had married Darcy and gone to his home, it would make sense, but the man's dead. You can't re-create the picture he painted, it won't work.'

'It will if I want it to.'

'No, it won't. I think you're pushing for the respectability of being squatters to paper over the fact that your parents were convicts!'

Perfy gasped, furious with him. 'Let me tell you something, Lew Cavour. Your parents might have been the good, proper, holy missionaries, while my parents were forcibly transported out here as convicts, but I'm not ashamed of mine!'

He couldn't believe that anyone would dare charge him with being ashamed of his parents. He left her standing in the garden and strode back through the town to return to the junk. There was no reply he could make to her accusation, he knew it was true. It was just that he'd never faced the truth before. He'd always been ashamed of them, of the poverty, of their mindless obedience to whatever the Bishop instructed; and, most of all, of the ridicule that they had been subjected to among contemporary Chinese. They'd been figures of fun in the village, blundering around trying to inflict their views on a sceptical population unaccustomed to clerical domination. The Chinese revered their ancestors and made daily offerings to the gods, but they were more interested in the here-now than the here-after.

179

Lew poured himself a rum. The crew were settled aft, concentrating on their interminable gambling. On a lugger nearby, some Finns were celebrating. Lew thought of joining them but his mood was all wrong. The Finns were hearty backslappers, good sailors and big drinkers, but he couldn't cope with them tonight. A great sadness overwhelmed him: for his mother, who never saw her son full-grown; and for his father, who had battled on in the service of God.

From what Lew had seen of this colony, Elizabeth and Joseph Cavour would have been better advised to follow their less fortunate countrymen out here. Convict transportation had been stopped thirty years ago but the bitterness was still evident. The convicts had endured dreadful suffering and degradation, Lew had discovered from talking to diggers; surely the missionaries could have made some sort of contribution to the welfare of prisoners. But then he supposed the heathen Chinese sounded much more exotic and adventurous than pitiful, unwanted Englishmen.

A man in search of his own identity, Lew had sought out the colonial diggers, who now called themselves Australians, rather than the American and European prospectors. He felt he had more in common with them, being also of British stock, but they were a contentious lot, though, cynical, with an inbuilt hatred of police, troopers and informers, no doubt as a result of their prison-settlement background. And they were contrary, fighting off attacks by bushrangers like any trooper, yet at the same time respectful of them. None of this made a lot of sense to Lew, any more than did Perfy's determination, aided and abetted by her father, to claim and hold that huge spread of land out west. They were taking on a business they knew nothing about for the sake, he was sure, of becoming one of the hated squatters.

She'd pinned him like a cut-out figure, making him look at his attitude, and it had worked. He was sorry now, remorseful that he'd been so critical of his parents, but perhaps his father had understood. He had never reproached his son for disappearing without a word, and his letters thereafter had encouraged him to continue with his seafaring career.

Lew poured another rum and picked up one of Ying's books. He missed Ying now, that fastidious, irritating, philosophising Chinese gentleman, and wondered how he was faring in the wild west. The very thought of Ying out there made him laugh, and as he glanced over the pages of the book, he saw the written characters representing woman: a broom and a storm.

'That's my girl,' he grinned. 'That's Perfy.'

He leafed through the book of poetry and came across a few lines by Fu Hsuan: 'How sad it is to be a woman!/Nothing on earth is held so cheap.'

Lew stared at his reflection in the mirror Ying had installed. 'That's all very well for the Chinese,' he said to himself. 'But it sure doesn't work down here. They're a law unto themselves.'

Tomorrow, he decided, he would see Perfy again. He would take her a gift. Ying had a box of lovely silks in the hold; a length of silk would make a fine present. And he'd talk to her, quietly and sensibly, without getting into an argument. He would formally ask for her hand in marriage. They could sail to China when Ying returned, and then they'd board one of those big liners and voyage together to see England. Neither of them had been there. What a time they would have sightseeing! After that, if she wished, they could come home to Bowen . . . home. Yes, this would be his home port.

Lew went to bed a happy man, and for some strange reason dreamed of fire.

7

Dear Miss Middleton,

I did receive your kind Letter of Condolence upon the loss of my dear son Darcy and am Sorry not to have Replied but His Passing was a terrible Shock which I will never get over. In reply to your recent Letter I extend an Invitation to you and your Father to visit Caravale, you will be most welcome. These days the roads are None Too Safe with unsavoury characters and miners roaming the countryside, so my son Ben will come to Bowen to escort you out to the Station.

At present he is engaged in the Mustering from the river flats but will attend you in Bowen on completion.

My son knows The Routes exceeding well and therefore can avoid the discomfiture of overburdened trails.

I remain
   Yours most faithfully,
    Mrs Cornelia Buchanan

'See!' Perfy said. 'She has invited us, Lew! She wants us to come out there.'

'I'll bet she does,' Lew replied. 'So she can talk you into letting go of their property.'

'You forget,' she said. 'Mrs Buchanan and I share the loss of Darcy.'

'How could I forget?' he murmured.

Perfy had been thrilled by his gift, yards of the finest blue silk, but the letter from Mrs Buchanan had stolen his thunder. It was all they could talk about.

He appealed to Jack Middleton. 'I might be imagining things, Jack, but I feel something is all wrong here. Do you really believe you'll be welcome out there?'

'No,' Jack replied and Lew stared at him, surprised.

'Then why do this?'

'It's our right. And I don't like to be shoved around.'

'Who's shoving you around, for Christ's sake?'

'No one,' Jack said evasively. 'This is something we have to do. We'll go out there. Stake our claim. Let them know that we're not just names on a bit of paper. And after that it will be up to Perfy to decide what to do about her inheritance.'

'She can't run a cattle station.'

'She can put a manager in,' Jack said. 'A lot of them do. Why don't you just drop it, Lew?'

'Because I want to marry Perfy.'

Jack smiled. 'I thought as much. But let's get this sorted out first.'

After that Lew saw no point in discussing Caravale. He spent as much time as he could with Perfy, but their relationship deteriorated and he became miserably aware she was avoiding him.

Chin Ying wrote, guardedly, from the Cape diggings to inform him that he was doing mildly well, which Lew guessed meant that the expedition was really successful. He wished he could go out and see this wonder, but Ying also said that he should expect visitors shortly. That meant that Ying was either sending back gold for safe-keeping in a local bank, or he was coming himself. Even in Chinese, they both knew it was dangerous to give advance warning of any transport of gold. Mailmen were robbed too.

And then, a month after the letter had arrived from Mrs Buchanan, her son, Ben Buchanan, came to town.

PART SIX

1

Perfy sat easily on her horse and looked back at the sea beyond Bowen. There was a marvellous view from up here, and it was much cooler, the hills capturing sea breezes that overflew the low-lying town. And the town itself looked much prettier from above. She had taken the trees for granted; the assortment of palms, gums, leafy mangoes, huge figs and all the rest had seemed scattered individuals but now their green mantles dominated the bayside scene, dwarfing the white buildings and turning Herbert Street into a shorn streak of mottled yellow, a mix of sand and red dust.

'Come on, Perfy,' her father called. 'We have to keep up.'

She kneed her horse and took one last look out to sea before turning the bend that led deeper into the hills. Lew was still in Bowen, still angry with her. He had so many old-fashioned ideas! Perfy laughed, she was happy setting out on this adventure, she wouldn't allow anything to worry her today. She knew her attitudes shocked him at times, but if he wanted to stay here he'd have to accept that women in this country were entitled to their opinions and entitled to act on them. At least he had promised to call on her mother. And Herbert was there too, he often visited and played the piano for Alice and her friends, so she wouldn't be lonely.

The journey so far had been a pleasure, even though the men treated her like a three-year-old, expecting her to fall off over rough patches and insisting on leading her horse across sluggish, rocky creeks. But Herbert had taught them well; Perfy and Diamond were handling the ride without any trouble. At the last minute Herbert had decided not to come with them and Perfy supposed that was fair enough, he had his own business to attend to. Ben Buchanan had insisted on inspecting their horses and saddles and such things, refusing to take Herbert's word that all was in order. When Ben gave a grunt of approval, Herbert had grinned and whispered to Perfy, 'These bush wallahs, think they know everything about horses, but I could teach him a thing or two.'

Ben Buchanan. Perfy watched him riding in the lead. He was a sturdily built man, not as tall as Darcy but in his facial features he was so much like his brother that her heart had ached at the first sight of him. But there the likeness ended. Where Darcy had been genial and talkative, Ben was moody and his eyes lacked the generous enthusiasm that had made Darcy so special. Darcy had been interested in everything around him, in people, in nature, in the sights of Brisbane Town. For that matter, she realised with a start, so was Lew. Everything in the colony was so new to him, she'd never known a man ask so many questions. He was almost childlike in his eagerness to explore and in his interest in everyone.

Her father hadn't made any comment but it was evident, right from the start, that he didn't like Ben Buchanan. Perfy thought that was rather unfair, just because he didn't measure up to Darcy. Ben hadn't been invited to their home, the meetings had been held at the Great Northern Hotel where he was staying.

The first introductions had been stilted, uncomfortable, and it had been left to Perfy to keep the conversation going while her mother and father sat quietly, as if none of this were their business. But Ben had been pleasant. He'd come right out and spoken of Darcy, of the great loss to his family and friends, which surely included them. And he'd also acknowledged straight away, without rancour, that Perfy was now their partner at Caravale.

'I'm sure you'll find Caravale interesting,' he'd said. 'It's a bit dry at present, not a lot of feed around, so we have to keep an eye on the cattle.'

'What do they do when the pastures dry up?' Perfy asked, trying to make conversation.

'They wander. Or they eat anything in sight. Trees, thistles, bark, anything that's left lying around, stuff that'll kill them. Native animals have got more sense, but not cattle.'

'How many cattle have you got on the station?'

'Hard to tell at any given time,' Ben replied. 'Maybe about thirty thousand.'

On their way home, Jack Middleton growled, 'Hard to say how many cattle they've got! He must think we're dills. Didn't his mother say he was out mustering recently. I'll bet that bastard knows to a calf how many cattle are on that station. I'd take his figure and double it.'

'Don't be so sour,' Perfy said, afraid he might change his mind about visiting the station. 'And why didn't you invite him home?'

'Because we have to keep our distance.'

'I don't call going to visit them keeping your distance, Jack,' Alice said.

'It's necessary,' he replied. 'We're not visiting, we're inspecting Perfy's property. They know that. They have to be polite until they find out what we have in mind.'

'And what do you have in mind?' Alice asked. 'I'm not too sure myself.'

'We'll see when we get there,' he replied. 'I've told you that a dozen times. It'll be up to Perfy then.'

They rode on through the scrubby hills, with Ben up front and Jack riding with Perfy and Diamond. Following behind were two stockmen from Caravale leading two packhorses.

The night before, they'd camped in the foothills and the stockmen had cooked them some chops and potatoes which they served with billy tea, just like a regular picnic, after which they'd thrown up a tent within minutes for Perfy and Diamond. The men had slept outside on their blankets.

Perfy had dreaded bedtime, afraid that she would be thinking too much of Darcy. This was the journey they'd planned to make together. But after a day in the saddle she was so tired she'd fallen asleep instantly and Diamond had had to shake her awake in the morning. Perfy was glad Diamond was with her, it would have been awkward to be the only woman in the party when it came to personal matters.

'My rear end feels like a block of wood, it's so numb,' Diamond whispered to her.

Perfy nodded. 'So does mine, but we mustn't let on, although Ben did say we could get a buggy at one of the stations if the ride was too hard for us.'

'Let's get a buggy,' Diamond was quick to say but Perfy disagreed.

'All the young women out this way ride, only older women use the buggies. We don't want to look like weakies. Anyway, he said we'd make camp as soon as we get out of these hills.'

'The sooner the better,' Diamond said, but then Ben reined his horse and came back to them.

'We've got a bit of a climb ahead of us now. The horses will make it easily enough but once we get to the peak you'd better dismount and let the boys take your horses down. It's a steep landfall and we don't want any accidents.'

When they reached the top of the hill, the horses scrambling the last few strides, Perfy was glad they hadn't argued, it was a steep slope. Far ahead of them she could see a big river winding through a ribbon of green but apart from that they were overlooking plains dotted with lonely trees.

'Does anyone own this land?' she asked one of the stockmen as she handed over her horse.

'They sure do, ma'am,' he replied. 'Down there's Glendale Station and Strathaird's the other side of the river.'

'What river is it?'

'The Bogie, ma'am. We cross over and make for the Burdekin and follow the valley south. If you look north-west there across the plains, you'll see wagons. See them?'

'Yes. Are they miners on their way to the Cape diggings?'

'That's them all right, miners and bullockys, horse teams, and them on shanks's pony. We're travelling parallel, you could say, but in a day or so we strike south and they head on.'

Perfy and Diamond picked their way down the side of the hill, while the men crashed down with the horses. Perfy was glad Darcy had introduced her to divided skirts, she was sure she'd have been in a right tangle trying to cope with long skirts. She'd given one to Diamond, since Alice didn't think it was correct for any woman to be on horseback with her skirts hitched up, not even a black woman. Perfy had noticed Ben and the two stockmen look at each other in surprise when they'd seen Diamond on horseback, and it amused her.

'Miss Perfy,' Diamond had said gleefully. 'I don't think they've ever seen an Aborigine woman on a horse before.'

'Well, they have now,' Perfy had laughed. Men were so set in their ways. They weren't as amenable to change as women, even with their clothes. They all wore the same things and women loved new fashions. And her father! Well! He'd been so cross when she'd thrown out his old ratty slippers and he hated his new ones. She pondered all this while she slipped and slid downhill, clutching at bushes and grazing her palms, a little irritated that Diamond wasn't having any trouble at all.

Their safari took them across open grasslands where cattle grazed peacefully, ignoring them, while kangaroos, taking no chances, bounced away. Skittish emus bolted, skidded to a stop and followed curiously, and a flock of black cockatoos wheeled overhead, screeching their irritation. Perfy watched her father; he was enjoying every minute of the journey, entranced with the wildlife, especially the birds. He had always loved birds and now he and Diamond were having great fun identifying the many species they encountered. They rested a little while at a waterhole that was alive with parrots and cockatoos and little budgerigars, every tree branch a perch for hundreds of them, while pretty pink brolgas remained aloof, standing daintily in the muddy shallows. And then they were off again, cantering on through the brittle dry grass, back into scrublands, glad of the sparse shade of the tall gums, old trees with large knobs on their trunks.

Her horse, a chestnut called Goldie, behaved beautifully. Perfy loved her and thought she was the best of their mounts, but she noticed the stockmen took especial care of the horse Ben was riding. It was a big black steed called Smoke, but the stockmen had said that was only a nickname, the horse had a fine pedigree. It was an arrogant animal and Perfy had been warned to keep clear. Smoke seemed interested only in Ben and the cattle dog that was devoted to both of them. She guessed Ben could make this journey in half the time on that horse without the encumbrance of company, and would probably have preferred to be alone.

She often watched him in his checkered shirt, tight dungarees and wide leather hat riding relentlessly ahead, and wondered what he was thinking about. He must have ridden these trails with Darcy many a time. Did he miss him? And what did he think of her? Of Darcy's fiancée? He had never come forward in Brisbane, which had annoyed Darcy, she knew, but she remembered that he was interested in politics. And, she thought, he'd probably be successful in that field. It was hard to associate the well-dressed young gentleman who'd been staying at Government House, part of that sophisticated world, with this lone-riding bushman, guiding them through strange country.

On the third afternoon Ben called a halt around four o'clock. 'We'll camp here,' he told Jack, 'and ride on to Caravale tomorrow. The lads are leaving us here.'

'Sure you'll be all right, boss?' George, the younger stockman, asked.

'If I say no, you'll weep tears of blood,' Ben laughed. 'They're going to a barn dance over at Merri Creek Station,' he explained to Perfy. 'But the homestead's thirty miles out of our way.'

'Is this the big river?' Perfy asked. They'd pulled up on the outskirts of very thick bush and she guessed a river was nearby.

'No, this is only a tributary,' Ben replied. 'They call it Odd Creek.'

'Why?'

'Take a look at the foliage. Down there's a dead-end gulch. It traps the warm air and retains the moisture so the trees are different, more tropical than anywhere else around—'

George interrupted him. 'Do you want us to take one of the packhorses, boss?'

'No, we can manage. It'll slow you up. But don't forget the Merri Creek mail.'

Diamond didn't like this place. She watched uneasily as the stockmen took off with a whoop, waving their hats in farewell and giving the horses their heads, galloping away, dust flying. She was glad Ben Buchanan had chosen to camp on the outskirts of the miniature jungle; it had a musty air about it. The sweating trees were aged and streaming with vines; trunks glistened with moss and the undergrowth was spongy.

Ben lit a camp fire and erected a framework of stout sticks from which to hang the billy for tea. Diamond felt she should offer to help him but didn't like to intrude. She was uncertain of him, he was a very attractive man with strong shoulders and fine, tanned features, but he rarely spoke to her. She had seen him looking at her occasionally, as if she were some sort of curiosity, and had not missed the winks the stockmen had exchanged as she passed them. Diamond knew that look, she was a black gin to them, fair game, but with their boss and Mr Middleton along, there was nothing for her to worry about. Or was there? She felt anxious, butterflies in her stomach for no reason at all.

Perfy was resting in the shade, busy replacing the net on her hat; there were a lot of flies around.

Ben filled the billy from a waterbag and hung it over the fire, then he took the tin of tea from a pack. He squatted on the ground, waiting for the water to boil, and lit his pipe, resting steadily on one heel with the other leg extended. Diamond smiled. He reminded her of lagoon birds, the storks and the brolgas that stood on one leg, and of the legend the Bindal people had told her: that one day, long ago, a stork lost his leg to a river monster,

191

and all the others felt so sorry for him they brought him food. Then others began to see this was an easy way to live without hunting, so they too stood in the water with one leg hidden, and before long . . .

'Where's your father?' Ben asked Perfy.

'He's gone for a walk,' she said, brushing at flies as she tied the net under her chin.

Ben didn't reply. It was a rather delicate matter, her father could have gone into the bush to relieve himself, but Diamond saw Ben tense up and start looking around. Possibly he was nervous that Jack Middleton would meet some snakes; it began to worry her too, that dense greenery was good snake country.

'And he's – going to take a dip if he can find a good spot in that creek,' Perfy added.

'What?' Ben yelled. 'He's gone for a swim?' He was on his feet in an instant, grabbing his rifle and loading it as he ran, crashing into the bush.

Diamond was running too, she didn't know why, she just went after him as he stormed through the scrub, skidding on greasy ferns, dropping down the gully, heading for the creek.

And then she heard the scream. The most terrible, agonising sound she had ever heard!

Ben changed course immediately and dived off to the right. 'This way,' he shouted to Diamond as the awful screams increased.

Jack Middleton was in the creek, threshing about in water red with blood. Diamond rushed ahead of Ben, reaching out. She was waist-deep before Ben caught her and threw her aside. Then he stood and fired.

In that second she saw the huge reptile. Its tail thrashed wildly and then it reared, lifting Jack with it, his body clenched in the long snout. Ben hurled the rifle aside and plunged in to grab Jack, and Diamond threw herself at the exposed underbelly of the crocodile. Shot through the head, it was rolling back, losing its prey as the huge jaws fell open, but the claws, like great gnarled hands, were still grasping. She lunged at it with her knife and ripped the white belly apart.

Ben was pulling Jack from the bloodied water. There seemed to be a tornado of noise around her. Jack was screaming. Ben shouting. She took hold of Jack under his knees and between them they lifted him out of the creek and staggered up the bank.

'Oh Christ!' Ben was wailing. 'Oh Christ.' He ripped off his shirt and put it gently under Jack's head and then pulled off his singlet to use it to staunch the blood.

Silently, Diamond was screaming too. Jack's arm was almost severed at the shoulder and his torso was pulpy with blood. She clamped her mouth tight to stop the scream and tore off her own sodden shirt, handing it to Ben.

'Your skirt too,' he said urgently. 'Rip it up. I need bandages.'

192

She did as she was told, tearing frantically at the strong wet cloth that now seemed determined to resist, until finally she put her foot on the skirt and tore at it with all her strength, passing each strip to Ben as quickly as she could.

Jack sagged back, unconscious, as Ben knotted the strips of skirt together for more length and bound the arm tight to his body. He was weeping, shaking his head, winding the makeshift bandages round Jack's chest. He put his hand out to Diamond, needing more bandages, but she shook her head. 'No more.'

Ben wiped Jack's face with his hands and Diamond took off her soaked cotton chemise, which Ben accepted without a word, using it to try to clean and cool Jack's face. 'Hang on, mate,' he was saying. 'You'll be right. Hang on now.

'Get the rifle,' he grated at Diamond who ran back to collect it from the water's edge, glancing fearfully at the racking turbulence in the creek where other crocodiles were feeding ferociously on the carcass of Jack's attacker.

In the distance she could hear Perfy calling to them, 'Where are you?' but she was too terrified to reply.

She brought back the gun. 'How is he?'

'I don't know,' Ben said. 'He's taken a shocking hiding. We have to get him out of here. If only I'd kept those blokes with us.' He felt the pulse in Jack's neck, and wiped the hair back from his forehead. 'My life seems to be made up of "if only's",' he muttered, and it seemed such a strange thing to say, Diamond worried that he, as well as Jack, could be in shock.

Jack's eyes opened and he eased his head round to look at Ben. 'You . . . Darcy . . .' he began, coughing on the words and grimacing in pain, unable to go on.

'Does he think you're Darcy?'

'No,' Ben said abruptly. 'You'll have to stand guard. I'm going up for some blankets and things. I won't be long. We can't hump him through the bush in his state, I'll have to make a stretcher.'

He saw her look at the gun. 'It's still loaded,' he said. 'If any of the bastards show a nose, just point it and pull the bloody trigger. Oh Christ,' he added. 'Here she comes.'

Perfy had at last found her way, stumbling out of the bush. 'What's happened?' she cried. 'What's happened to Daddy?' Distraught, she rushed down to him and then stared in horror at the bloodsoaked bandages.

She looked up at Diamond, who had forgotten she was standing bare-breasted now, clad only in muddy bloomers.

'Where are your clothes?' Perfy screamed, totally unable to grasp this scene. Then she leaned over her father. 'Daddy, what did they do to you?'

'He's had an accident, Perfy,' Ben said quietly. 'You keep him warm until I come back. It's important you do that, do you hear me?'

She nodded vacantly, her face as grey as her father's. He was shivering now so she nestled close to him, talking to him, and then she asked again, 'What happened?'

Diamond was frightened. Somewhere back in time she recalled another river, full of these archaic monsters. She had looked down on them, lying smugly on banks like long grinning logs, awful creatures, but she had never confronted them before. She began to shake, but continued to stand watch, finger on the trigger of the gun, alert for those yellow eyes or for any sudden movement from below. She was afraid to reply to Perfy's question, it was too horrible to speak of yet. Instead, she adopted Ben's attitude. 'Keep him warm, that's good. Ben's gone for some blankets.'

'It's a bit cold, love,' Jack said suddenly and Perfy gave a gasp of relief.

'He won't be long, Daddy. Can we light a fire, Diamond?'

'Yes,' she lied, 'but we have to wait for Mr Buchanan to get back.'

'But he's so cold. And he's still bleeding on his side here. Did he fall down?' Fortunately she didn't wait for Diamond to reply. 'Are you in much pain?' she asked her father and he lifted his good arm to touch her face.

'No,' he said. 'It's stopped now.' He sighed, seemed surprised, and his voice was clearer. 'Look after my girl, Diamond.'

Perfy's eyes were wild with tears. 'For heaven's sake, Daddy, I'm fine. What can I do for you? Diamond! Get him some water!'

'Ben's bringing fresh water,' Diamond said, hoping, and Perfy glared angrily at her for not moving.

'Alice . . .' Jack said, and tried to speak again, but Perfy put her hand on his face.

'Just rest, Daddy, you rest.'

He closed his eyes again and she nursed him until at last Ben came back. With blankets. Water. Lamps. An axe. A clutter of things.

As the two women looked after Jack, he began to chop saplings from the bush to make a stretcher. 'Here,' he called to Diamond. 'Strip these branches for me.'

He had brought ropes and canvas, and between them the frame for a stretcher took shape quickly. He thrust the canvas across to Diamond, who suddenly stopped work. It wasn't a silence she felt, but a sudden gulf, an aching wistfulness, as if the sunset, now glowing red and purple over the skies, wished to hold this minute of grandeur. She reached over and touched Ben and he looked up at her, irritated that she should waste a second.

'What is it?' he said. 'Loop the canvas under there. Hurry!'

She shook her head, and he turned quickly to look at Jack.

Silently, he stood up and walked over to Perfy and her father. 'He's

194

asleep, thank God,' Perfy said, and Ben knelt beside her. He felt Jack's face, and neck, examined him carefully and then sat back, defeated. Jack Middleton was dead.

They approached Caravale late at night, chilled by bleak westerlies that swept across the land once the sun withdrew. Trees swished high above them, sounding more like the constant hiss of the sea than dry prairie stands, and ghost-gums, true to their name, flickered eerily as the procession wound slowly by.

Diamond's misery increased at her first sight of the homestead, a shadowy outline on the hillside, marked by orange points of light like evil eyes waiting to pounce. She shuddered as dingoes howled mournfully from their lookouts.

She and Perfy were travelling in a buggy borrowed from Merri Creek Station and driven by George, the Caravale stockman. Behind them a wagon, acting as a hearse, carried the body of Jack Middleton. Huddled beside her, wrapped in a blanket, Perfy was silent, too shocked to take in the present, numbly accepting the bumpy buggy ride. The vehicles had an escort of six outriders, dark-cloaked mourners, heads down, pushing into the wind, their horses straining at the slow pace, and Diamond was glad of their company. Most of the previous night, back at that terrible campsite, she had spent alone with Perfy while Ben rode to Merri Creek Station for help.

Terrified of being left alone in the darkness with Perfy and the dead body, Diamond had pleaded with him. 'Can't you wait until the morning?'

'I have to go now,' he said. 'I'll only be a few hours. Just stay by the camp fire. You women can't ride at night in this country, and anyway we can't bury him here.' He indicated Jack's body which he had wrapped and roped in a strong canvas shroud. 'Merri Creek is the closest homestead, I might as well go now. We need a wagon.'

Her own superstitions running riot in that lonely, ghostly place, Diamond tried to comfort Perfy. She finally admitted, in reply to Perfy's insistent questioning, that Jack had been attacked by a crocodile, and then had to cope, as expected, with Perfy's screams that echoed and racketed through the still of the night. She listened as Perfy raged at her father's death, blaming Ben Buchanan for bringing them there, claiming that it was deliberate, that he was trying to kill them all, that he would not come back, ever. They would both die here too, left in this frightful wilderness to be attacked by those same crocodiles or other wild animals! While she knew this wasn't true, that Ben had risked his life to save Jack, wading into the creek that he knew was infested with crocodiles, Diamond shivered in fright. She wondered if she'd have rushed into the muddy water so fast if she had known what was in there. And it was Ben who had pushed her aside. That crocodile, still fighting, could easily have turned on her.

The night was sheer terror. Diamond kept the rifle handy while she built up the camp fire with wood Ben had cut for them before he left. She stole nervous glances at the canvas-clad figure, well away from them, that she had also been instructed to defend in case dingoes came foraging. Neither of the women made any attempt to sleep. Diamond encouraged Perfy to pray, unable to recall the tales and legends she'd so easily been able to tell her in the safety of the Middleton house in Brisbane, and she prayed too. She prayed for someone to come by; tribal people, miners, outlaws, she didn't care. Anyone! To rescue them from their ghastly isolation, and protect them from the evil spirits that she was sure were roaming angrily around.

Long before they came into sight, she heard the sound of galloping horses and wept with relief, realising that, as the hours crawled by, she too had begun to worry that Ben might not return. Three men from Merri Creek Station were with him. They paid their respects to Perfy, tall strangers muttering condolences by the light of the camp fire, and standing back respectfully to wait for the morning and the arrival of the wagon. The buggy, she heard, had been sent by the wife of the station owner, who guessed, correctly, that Mr Middleton's daughter would be in no state to ride on to Caravale.

Riders came out to meet them, to confer with Ben, and to race ahead to Caravale. By the time they travelled round to the back of the house, past various outbuildings and into a large courtyard, men with lanterns were out to meet them and there was a general air of alarm. Voices shouted instructions as the horses, spooked by the confusion, reared in their traces. Hands grabbed them as Perfy and Diamond were helped down.

Diamond saw a crowd of blacks standing fearfully apart, watching this strange event, and then she was ushered towards the house. A red-haired woman, dressed in black, was standing at the top of the steps in the lamplight and Diamond experienced a physical shock as if she had run smack into a stone wall. The woman had an air of fierce authority, and although she stood stiffly back to allow them to pass, Diamond had the impression that she saw this calamity as an affront. Her name, Diamond heard, was Mrs Buchanan.

'Ever since Darcy died, we've had nothing but trouble,' Cornelia raged. 'Why can't you just bury that body in the morning and get it over with?'

Ben made sure the sitting-room door was closed. 'Because everything has to be above board. The doctor's on his way, he can issue the death certificate. As soon as that's done I can send a message to the police in Bowen to advise Mrs Middleton. It'll be a bad shock for her.'

'Pity about her! God moves in mysterious ways. He's punishing them for trying to steal our property, to which they have no right under the sun. Have you got those men bunked down?'

196

'Yes. How's Miss Middleton?' He didn't think it wise to refer to her as Perfy in his mother's presence.

'The girl was close to hysteria. We dosed her with laudanum and put her to bed. No stamina, those town girls, that's the trouble. I don't know what Darcy saw in her, a wishy-washy sort, I'd say.'

Ben stood at the window. He was very tired, and not a little shocked himself. 'Don't underestimate her, Mother. She's in a bad way at the minute and that's understandable, but I've been able to observe her over the last few weeks and she's rather self-willed. A determined sort of person.'

'Well, of course, that's how she snared Darcy.'

'It's not just that. She's thoroughly spoiled. Her parents think the world of her, hence that name, Perfection. Whatever she wants, she gets. She's used to having her own way.'

'We'll see about that.' Cornelia said. 'I'm going to write to the widow myself, offering our condolences.'

'That's a good idea. You can explain to her what happened. I don't want any of them blaming me.'

Mae knocked at the door and peered in. 'The young lady's asleep now, Mrs Buchanan. Where do I put the maid?'

'The black girl? Send her down to the camp, of course.'

Mae sucked in her breath nervously. 'I did, but she won't go.'

'What are you talking about? She won't go!'

'She says she won't sleep down in the blacks' camp. She says she don't belong there.'

'Where the hell does she think she belongs? Would she like my room? I don't know what the world's coming to with gins thinking they can give orders. Kick her out. She can sleep in a tree if she likes.'

'Hang on,' Ben said. 'We don't want to antagonise Miss Middleton. That gin, Diamond, is obviously used to better treatment. She's clean and they dress her well. Isn't there a bunk in the old creamery, Mae?'

'Yes.'

'Then give her a lantern and put her in there.'

Mae ducked away.

'Damn cheek!' Cornelia said. 'Did she expect to sleep in the house?'

'I don't know,' Ben replied. 'And I don't care. The boys tell me two more stockmen took off for the goldfields while I was away.'

'Ungrateful wretches,' Cornelia said. 'What do they know about gold digging?'

'What do any of them know?' Ben muttered. 'You write your letter to Mrs Middleton and it can go in with the message to the Bowen police.'

2

The Finns decided to remove themselves to Townsville for easier access to the goldfields. Because the fishing was so good and so lucrative in Bowen, they hadn't moved from the bay, but now they felt it was time to get serious about prospecting. The night before they sailed, they gave themselves a send-off with lashings of food and a supply of ale, schnapps and gin, and invited all their friends in the harbour. It was a rip-roaring party. Lew stumbled back aboard the junk at dawn, managing to stay on his feet just long enough to wave farewell to his departing friends. Then he fell into his bunk to sleep off the after-effects.

At four o'clock that afternoon he emerged, dived into the sea to complete the cure, and climbed back on board, refreshed, to find Hong waiting for him, looking very concerned.

'What's the matter?' Lew asked him, in Chinese, since Hong's English was still hopeless, even though he was very proud of his efforts.

'Big trouble in the town last night, Captain. The white men went berserk, rioting, and chased Chinamen all over the place. Beating them up!' Then Hong grinned. 'But this time the Chinamen were ready. They waited up by the lumber yards, and when the white devils came chasing, honourable Chinese gave them some of their own medicine. Very good fight. They cut some of them with elegance.'

'Oh Jesus!' Lew groaned. 'You tell the crew to stay here. They're not to go into the town for any reason. It's not our fight. We keep right out of it. You hear me?'

Lew dressed and went into town looking forward to a good feed. He'd become accustomed to the way colonials ate, steaks as big as boots, even for breakfast, loaded with three eggs, gravy and slabs of bread. They were big meat eaters and liked potatoes instead of rice. They ate few green vegetables, and when they did, they were boiled tasteless. He'd noticed that quite a few Chinese had begun to grow vegetables on small plots outside the town. They'd have no trouble selling their produce, and it occurred to him that these small farmers might stay here. They were a stoical race, well able to ignore racial slights and bright enough to see they could live well here as market gardeners with any amount of space and no irrigation problems.

The pubs were churning with angry miners growling about the Chinks who'd attacked their mates, vicious sly 'yellers' who'd used the most cowardly of weapons, daggers, on blokes who were just out having a good time. Lew heard that the Chinks were responsible for all the villainy perpetrated in the town, that they were purveyors of all manner of vice and that no white woman was safe from them. Lew tired of the company of boring braggarts and went to see Mrs Middleton. It was difficult to gauge from all the boozy rantings just how serious the trouble had been, and with Jack Middleton away, his wife could be nervous, alone in that house.

Alone? Halfway up the path, too late to turn back, Lew heard the piano. Herbert Watlington was there! Bloody Herbert, turning himself into a permanent fixture!

'Lew! How nice of you to call,' Alice said. 'Do come in. Have you had supper? Yes? Well, never mind, you must join us for coffee. Doesn't Herbert play well? You know Mrs Tolley, don't you? Yes, of course. Now, just sit down here . . .'

'I was worried,' he said. 'There was trouble in the town last night.'

'Yes, I believe it was dreadful,' Mrs Tolley said. 'But they stayed up the other end of town this time. They say those Chinamen are such vile creatures.'

Herbert turned from the piano. 'My dear Mrs Tolley, don't say that in front of Lew. He's part Chinese.'

'I am not,' Lew growled, feeling disloyal, knowing that Herbert's remark was a calculated irritant.

'He doesn't look Chinese,' Mrs Tolley said, crimping her tight curls and rearranging her wide purple skirts.

'I speak the language,' Lew replied, further annoyed that he was explaining; he hated having to explain himself.

'My, you young gentlemen are clever,' the woman replied. 'I declare, Alice, your Perfy is fortunate to have two fine beaux like this.'

'Don't be so silly,' Alice snapped, embarrassed by the woman's tactlessness. 'Could you play some more of those waltzes, Herbert?'

Lew liked Alice. She had the drawn, strained face of a woman who had been worked hard in her day, a face that would never go to fat. The blue eyes had faded but still retained the glow of former loveliness. Perfy had those eyes, but hers were in the ascendant, large blue eyes, arresting in their wonderful colour.

He felt a lurch of heartache. He missed her! He was still cross with her for insisting on that ridiculous pilgrimage to Caravale, because that's all it was. A visit to the shrine of the dead fiancé. And Jack had humoured her. There was no other explanation. Maybe he felt beholden to the late Darcy Buchanan for the generous bequest to his daughter. Damn Darcy Buchanan! Why hadn't he died quietly and gone on about his business without complicating Perfy's life. Lew had deliberately avoided meeting Darcy's brother, Ben. He couldn't help feeling a mite of sympathy for the fellow. To have strangers claiming half your estate must be a huge pain in the arse. It wouldn't do for a more civilised country like China. That sort of legacy would be considered outrageous, illegal. And to force on with it as Perfy was doing could cause murder and mayhem in the families.

Jesus! He was suddenly startled. Would Perfy be safe there? He'd heard it said, right here in Bowen, that the squatters – which seemed to be a catch-all term that included any sheepmen or cattlemen who owned huge tracts of land – that the squatters were a law unto themselves, powerful men who lived separate lives from the rest of the populace. But then Jack was with her.

Lew listened to the piano. He had to hand it to Herbert, he really did play well even if he was a strutting snot. Lew had met his share of Herberts, swanning around the Far East, keeping clear of Orientals, looking for that quick quid in the opium trade, or better still a wealthy English bride in lands where English gentlemen were in short supply. He didn't regard Herbert as competition, just a nuisance. When it suited him, he'd scare Herbert off very smartly, but right now it wouldn't be sensible to offend Alice by thumping her favourite piano player.

The bank manager, Tolley, arrived, and some other people. Lew felt obliged to play the gentleman. After all, when he married Perfy, they'd have a home and they'd entertain like this, English style, he supposed. His wife would expect it. The prospect did not excite him, but they'd have people their own age, people they liked and whose company they enjoyed.

After ten o'clock, when he was preparing to leave, there was a loud hammering at the back door.

'I'll go,' Tolley said. 'You stay put, Alice. You never know, these days.'

The room was silent, expectant, until he came back. 'It's for you,' he said to Lew. 'A Chinaman wants you.'

It was Hong. Hong in tears! Hong soaking wet, wringing his hands, bowing, apologising.

'What the hell's the matter?' Lew demanded.

'Oh, Captain. Greatest misfortune. What misery I bring you, forgive me, sir. We tried but there were too many.'

'What happened?'

Hong's weeping was almost out of control, so Lew shook him. 'Answer me! What's wrong?'

'The junk. Our *Perfection*, Captain. They burned it! The white devils came and threw torches, inflammable rags, all burning on to the ship. Too many, Captain. Too many. They burned our ship!'

Lew couldn't believe what he was hearing. 'They burned it? The junk? How much damage?'

'Too much, Captain, all burned up. Finish. Burned to the waterline, the beautiful *Perfection*.' He was weeping again.

Lew was stiff with rage. He couldn't bring himself to go back into the household among all those parlour people who would never understand.

Hong's clothes were scorched and he had severe burns on his arms, but Lew still couldn't believe, he had to see for himself. 'Let's go,' he said, running now, away from the house and down towards the quay.

Hong was embarrassed that the honourable captain should so lower himself as to apologise, and suffered the ministerings of the English doctor with such a woeful expression, Lew almost laughed. Except that the junk had burned to the waterline. The miners had made a well-organised attack on the most spectacular Chinese vessel in the harbour and although the crew had fought hard to control the fires, in the end they had no choice but to leap overboard.

'Are all your crew safe?' the doctor asked.

'Yes,' Lew said, still appalled that he'd ignored Hong's injuries in his mad dash to the ship. The poor fellow had shocking burns to his arms, chest and neck and was now swathed in bandages like a mummy.

'He should be in hospital,' the doctor said, 'but I'm afraid that's no go.'

Lew nodded. He knew they'd never admit a Chinaman. 'I'll take him down to his own people, they'll look after him. What about the others?' His crew were huddled together by the jetty, looking as miserable as wet cats on a raft.

'Minor burns, that's all. I'm sorry about your ship. I often looked at it in the bay, I thought it was rather noble.'

'Not any more,' Lew said. 'It's finished. I'll have to beach it on the far side of the bay.'

'Then what?'

'I'll find berths for the crew on other ships. That won't be hard. Lots of sailors are jumping ship in these ports and making for the goldfields, so most ships heading north need men.'

'What about yourself?'

'I might as well go out to the Cape diggings and find the owner, break the news to him.' It was easier to refer to Chin Ying than the more complicated issue of Lord Cheong. The ship was well-insured so Cheong wouldn't lose. Ying would have to take passage on another ship to get his men and the gold back to China, but Lew was out on a limb. He'd been paid half his salary, and now he'd have to forgo the rest because he'd failed. The bastards! The local sergeant of police, one Ron Donnelly, had been called to survey the smouldering hulk, but he didn't rate Lew's chances of finding the arsonists.

'Even if you do,' he warned, 'they'll have iron-clad alibis, you can bet your life. I'm real sorry, Captain, but as long as this gold rush lasts, we're whistlin' in the wind trying to keep law and order, just me and me deputy. We don't know these miners and half the names are dodgy anyway.'

'Just the same, could you give me a notarised statement of what happened here. The owner will need it for insurance.'

'Surely will. No trouble.' The sun was coming up in a long rim of fire far out to sea, seeming to dance in tiny flames along the horizon. 'Gonna be another hot one today, Captain,' Donnelly commented. 'We're starting to look for rain, and they'll be begging for water out on the diggings by this.'

Lew was surprised. 'Why is that? Aren't they working along a river?'

'Not all of them. A lot of the tributaries are gold-bearing too, but they run dry. They can't pan for alluvial gold without plenty of water so they stockpile and wait for rain.' He laughed, an infectious rumbling laugh. 'And then, Captain, they're gonna wonder what struck them. When it rains in this neck of the woods, it bloody rains. I never seen the like. Did I hear you say you was going out there?'

'Yes.'

'Then take a tip from me. Jump a ship to Townsville and ride out from there. It's an easier trail. Once all these mugs wake up to that, we'll have Bowen to ourselves again. The local shops and pubs will suffer but I'll live to retire.' He marched away, whistling, and Lew stared moodily at the ruins of the junk.

'Bloody bastards!' he said again. He had a few pounds in his pocket and the clothes he was wearing. That was it. He could work his way to Townsville but then he'd have to buy a horse and supplies to get out to the Cape. Jesus! Broke! He'd have to find some money somewhere. There were always Chinese money-lenders but they charged a heap of interest and hung on like leeches.

By the end of the day he had the crew sorted out, his account of the fate of the junk and a copy of the police report mailed to Macao, and he'd checked in at the Customs House. He arranged to have the junk shifted, ate at the Grand View Hotel and listened around to the local talk, but was unable to get a lead on who might have been responsible for firing the ship. He walked aimlessly up the main street, Herbert Street, and then he remembered Herbert Watlington. He was always boasting about how much money he was making in the land-selling business. Herbert could lend him some cash. Having to ask Herbert would be a fine come-down, but at this point Lew couldn't afford to be particular.

He found him in his office trying to convince an elderly Chinese that he should purchase an allotment rather than struggle along with his tiny plot, and that was a stroke of luck.

Lew spoke to the client in Chinese.

'What did you say?' Herbert asked him.

'I told him not to buy anything until I checked this deal for him first.'

'You've got a bloody cheek!'

'It's business, Herbie. I need a hundred pounds.' Lew wondered how much English the Chinaman understood. Probably a lot more than he let on. No matter, he would not expect Lew to exert his influence without a price.

'Well, don't look at me,' Herbert retorted. 'I heard they burned your junk. One would think your crew would have been properly trained to defend the boat.'

'With guns? Here in Bowen?'

'Of course.'

'And if they'd shot a white man, no matter what he did, they'd be hanged.'

'They might still have saved your boat.'

'Stow it, Herbert. The bloody thing is sunk, so that's that. Now what about our friend here?'

'I'm not giving you a hundred quid, so you might as well push along.'

Lew conversed again with the Chinese, and then he turned back to Herbert. 'You're a bloody fool. This fellow is interested in settling here. He can afford to buy several properties, not just that little farm. He has many sons. But he isn't going to buy one square inch, mate, not without my say-so.'

'Ten pounds,' Herbert said.

'Give me ten and lend me ninety, or I'll tell him you're the biggest crook in town and you'll never sight another Chinaman again.'

'Why do you need that much?'

'Because I'm leaving town.'

'Ordinarily that wouldn't be bad news, but how do I get my money back?'

'I'll see to it. You have my word.'

'Not much to go on,' Herbert shrugged. 'But talk to the Chink for me.'

The patient Chinaman stood impassively as they talked. 'Your sons can expect great good fortune if they buy land here,' Lew told him. 'A much wiser and long-lasting investment than gold-chasing. Also your produce will cause your family to be appreciated by white people and therefore remove you from the attentions of the criminal element here.'

'What you say is no doubt true,' the old man replied. 'Our homeland is ravished by famine and bandits. This is indeed a land of milk and honey. I will settle them here and then return to China to die.'

Lew turned to Herbert. 'This gentleman is prepared to buy.'

'Good. Tell him I'll show him the land myself. Tomorrow.'

Lew translated, and the Chinaman bowed, agreeing. As he shuffled away, he bowed again to Lew. 'Thank you, sir, for your advice.' His face did not show any expression when he added, 'A loan of one hundred pounds to a gentleman such as yourself could be arranged if you so wish.'

Lew grinned. 'I'll keep you in mind,' he replied.

He walked Herbert over to the bank, still arguing with him about the amount of the loan. Finally Herbert agreed to draw fifty pounds for him, but when they reached the bank, there seemed to be some sort of hitch.

Mr Tolley himself came out of his cubicle. 'Herbert, you can't draw cash on that account. It's been closed.'

'What do you mean, closed? It can't be closed! It's the account for my business.'

'That's right, the one you share with Miss Molloy.'

'Which holds nigh on a thousand pounds in it now, of which I own half.'

'You'll have to talk to Miss Molloy about that, Herbert. She drew out all the cash yesterday. And she also sold the real estate business.'

'She did what!' Herbert was stunned. 'I'll see about this.'

'You'll have to find her first. She sold her establishment too and left Bowen yesterday.' Tolley looked at Lew and shook his head. 'When the whorehouses start closing down, Captain, one could say the golden days are over. Very sad for Bowen. We had hopes of being the capital city of North Queensland.'

Herbert grabbed hold of Tolley. 'You let her do this! You should be horse-whipped! She's stolen every penny I had, the bitch. The bloody old hag.'

It took both Tolley and Lew to drag Herbert, kicking and spluttering, out of the bank. As the door slammed behind them, Lew doubled up laughing. 'Welcome to the club, Herbie, old mate,' he said. 'Let's go find your Chinese client, we both need him now.'

'What am I going to do?' Herbert cried.

'I've no idea,' Lew replied. 'There's a ship sailing tomorrow and I'll be on it, Townsville bound.'

'I have to leave here,' Herbert muttered. 'I've got gambling debts and I haven't paid the hotel this month. Dear heaven, just when everything was going so nicely.' He stopped and looked at Lew. 'A ship sailing tomorrow, you say? I'm coming too.'

'Not with me, you're not.'

'If I wish to sail on a certain ship, you can't stop me,' Herbert said haughtily, but Lew was still rocking with laughter.

'You never told us you had such a ritzy partner, Herbert old chap. Glory Molloy, no less! The rose of Tralee! They say she charges you coming and charges you going! And she's skinned you and skipped! I wonder who she's sold your business to?'

'I don't know. But listen, Cavour. You make certain you tell those Chinks that the new owner's a crook.'

'Sure. I'll do that for a friend. And won't the Middletons be thrilled to hear all about your noble associate Glory Molloy.'

'You wouldn't!'

'I might.'

'You're no gentleman, Cavour.'

'That's true.'

He got his loan from Mr Fung Wu, but Herbert had to hand over his new gold fob watch. Together they went to bid farewell to Alice Middleton.

'I was so sorry to hear about your lovely ship, Lew,' she said. 'Such villains, it's terrible when innocent people have to suffer for the actions of those ruffians. Mr Chin will be devastated.'

'Yes, I think he will,' Lew said. 'He left most of his goods, his books, trunks of clothes and beautiful porcelain on board, all ruined.'

'And you're leaving?'

'Only for a while. I'll see what Ying has to say and then I'll be back. By that time Jack and Perfy should be home again.'

'I hope so.' She smiled fondly. 'I think Perfy's all talk. That visit is quite an adventure for her, she's never been any further than here, but once she has a look around I think she'll be glad to come home.'

Lew felt a chill. What did he have to offer Perfy now? She was a woman of means and he had nothing. Maybe when he came back he should head for Sydney Town which they said was the biggest port in the south Pacific now. He might get a ship there. And pigs might fly! He knew he had more chance with the Chinese. He understood how they operated and, besides, the lords, bankers and merchants were immensely wealthy. These people, in this country, only saw the lackeys; they had no idea of the fabulous wealth, the luxury, taken for granted by high-born Chinese. Since Perfy had left, he'd begun to see Bowen more clearly. It would take a century, maybe more, for this land to become civilised to the degree enjoyed by many Chinese, and yet the colonials despised 'Chinks'. Years back he'd fantasised about having a home high on the hill overlooking Hong Kong harbour after he retired from the sea; to Lew that would be the most wonderful place to live, always in sight of the sea, and now the nostalgia for Hong Kong was returning. He should have explained that to Perfy. He hated the country. He couldn't bear to live away from the sea. There were sea people and land people; that was accepted in China, as important as birth dates and ancestral lineage and good omens. Was Perfy a land person? If so, their relationship was doomed.

Herbert was spinning a fine tale to Alice about why he was leaving Bowen. Townsville was booming, a man in commerce had to keep an eye on the market, and real estate in new towns was a profitable business.

'Will you go it alone or take a partner there, Herbert?' Lew asked, smiling maliciously, and Herbert squirmed.

'One doesn't need partners,' he replied loftily.

'You can say that again,' Lew laughed.

He didn't mention his change of heart, that he wanted to make his home in Hong Kong. Even the idea of visiting England had faded. He missed the sophistication, the humour, and the challenge of the complicated Chinese society.

PART SEVEN

1

Caravale Station was quiet. A stillness had settled on the afternoon, broken only by the buzz of blowflies encouraged by the somnolent heat to investigate open windows.

Diamond flicked at them impatiently and stuck a rag in the hole in the wire netting to keep them out. Her little stone bunkhouse, once a creamery, was cool, but it felt like a prison cell. There were so many rules and regulations for blacks on the cattle station, she hardly knew what she was allowed to do, so she ended up sitting in this room, waiting for instructions that never came.

Mrs Buchanan took her nap from two to four in the afternoons and demanded absolute silence around her house. Diamond was sure she'd shoot the crows for disturbing the peace if she had half a chance, but this afternoon even the crows were busy elsewhere. Diamond felt she should be sitting in there with Perfy, but that was also forbidden.

'You don't have to worry about Miss Middleton,' Mae had said. 'I'm quite capable of nursing her. I'll look after her. I'm sorry, Diamond, but once the housegirls have finished their chores, Mrs B. wants them out of the place. They don't come back up until teatime. She doesn't like anyone roaming around the house when she's resting.'

'I wouldn't roam around. I'd just sit there, see if there's anything Miss Perfy needs.'

'No,' Mae said sternly. 'In fact, Mrs B. has said there's no reason for you to come into the house at all. We've got plenty of staff, there's really nothing for you to do.'

'Yes, there is. I could mind Miss Perfy. Look after her clothes.'

'Listen here, miss,' Mae said. 'You can't come into the house and that's that. Personally I don't mind, you seem a sensible girl and you know what you're doing, but it's just not worth my job. If that woman says jump, I jump. It was a godsend for me when I got this job. A woman my age . . . I've got nowhere else to go. So I'm the housekeeper, I do what she says and I mind my own business. Now you do the same. Make the best of it. Go for walks, do what you like. Nobody cares. Just stop making a fuss, it won't do you no good.'

Perfy was worried about her mother, and was anxious to return to Bowen but Ben had assured her that her mother had been informed of the accident, as gently as possible, through Mr and Mrs Tolley. Poor Mrs Middleton, Diamond thought, she'd be shattered. Just like Mrs Beckman. But at least she had Perfy and no money worries.

They'd buried Jack Middleton at Caravale and Dr Palfreyman had conducted the service. Perfy was, naturally, still stunned and still terribly upset, but she'd stood bravely throughout the ordeal, wearing her best day-dress, which Diamond had pressed and put out for her, a dark blue taffeta with a fitted bodice and a wide, full skirt. Mae had found a black veil for Perfy to wear on her head and she'd looked so lovely through that misty shade, her long golden hair resting loosely on her shoulders.

It was a lonely little graveyard on a rise overlooking the river, guarded by two strong beech trees and surrounded by a white picket fence. Diamond noticed that Edward Buchanan was buried there too; obviously Ben's father. There were several other graves – one, curiously, marked only with a cross and no inscription. She was relieved that Perfy hadn't noticed the new marble tombstone over to the left of the gate, a small monument to Darcy who had been buried in Brisbane. After the funeral, though, Perfy had collapsed and Diamond had been allowed to take her to her room to rest.

Dr Palfreyman was very kind. And conscientious. His home was in Charters Towers, he told Perfy, but he wasn't there too often. He did the rounds of the stations and everyone in the district knew where he was by what he called 'bush telegraph'.

'She doesn't look too good,' Diamond heard him saying to Mrs Buchanan.

'Of course she doesn't,' the woman had replied. 'What would you expect? These things take time.'

'I'll be back in a few days, to see how she's getting on. Keep her here. I know she's concerned about her mother, but she's not well enough to travel.'

'There's no better place than Caravale for Miss Middleton to recuperate,' Mrs Buchanan said proudly.

The doctor had simply murmured, 'Quite.'

Diamond disagreed. There was a constant air of tension about this house. It eased a little when the stockmen were around. Early in the mornings, the rattle of activity dispelled her fears, the men shouting and joking as they lined up for breakfast and then saddling up to ride out for the day's work, and she looked forward to hearing them galloping home at night, as if she and Perfy might be safer in the presence of all these strangers.

Perfy's condition did not improve, and when Palfreyman returned he announced she was suffering from a fever, possibly yellow fever. Whatever it was, Perfy was very sick and was plagued by terrible headaches. She was losing weight too, and now, just when Perfy really needed her, Diamond was banned from the house.

'We'll see about that,' she said angrily and left her room to run swiftly, barefoot, across the dusty yards. She cut through the orchard to the house and tiptoed along the verandah to Perfy's room. The french windows were open, net curtains hanging listlessly in the doorway. Perfy was very still, lying on the bed covered only with a sheet.

'I'm hot,' she said to Diamond, her voice so weak it seemed an effort for her to talk.

Diamond felt her forehead. 'Yes, you are. And it's a very hot day too.' She doused a cloth in water from the jug on the washstand and bathed Perfy's face. Then she noticed a bottle of white vinegar on the table. She knew white people put vinegar into water as a cooling agent when bathing feverish patients, so she tipped half the bottle into the basin with water and set to work to wash Perfy down from head to foot. Mrs Beckman had done that, she remembered, when she'd been sick with a temperature. As she towelled her dry, Perfy seemed more comfortable.

'Leave the cloth over my eyes please, Diamond,' she said. 'I've got a splitting headache. Poor Mother,' she murmured, 'there on her own. Do you think she knows about Daddy yet?'

'She's not on her own, Miss Perfy. She has her friends and neighbours. They'll look after her. Mrs Tolley'll take care of her, and don't forget Herbert's there and Captain Lew.'

'If I hadn't insisted on coming out here, Daddy would still be alive,' Perfy wept.

'No, no. Your father wanted to come. You mustn't forget that. It's nothing to do with you, just God's will.'

She was echoing the things white women said, although she couldn't see what God had to do with it. Evil spirits more like it, she thought, and there were plenty around here.

When Perfy drifted off to a sounder sleep, Diamond slipped out on to the verandah, jumping in fright as someone grabbed her arm. Mrs Buchanan!

'What are you doing up here, you black bitch?' She raised her hand to slap Diamond, as Diamond had seen her slapping the housegirls, all of whom were Aborigine, but Diamond pulled away and stood her ground. She was taller than Mrs Buchanan.

'Don't you lay a hand on me!' she hissed, afraid of waking Perfy. 'Don't you dare!'

Mrs Buchanan jerked away, unprepared for this reaction, but she soon recovered. 'Get off this verandah, and get away from my house. I don't know what sort of a gin you are but you're not going to lord it here. Stay away or I'll have you thrown off the station.'

'I am Miss Middleton's maid,' Diamond said, remembering that Perfy owned half this place. 'She will expect me to care for her.'

Rather than prolong the argument, she began to walk towards the steps, but Mrs Buchanan came after her. 'You'll do as you're told,' she sneered, 'or I'll have you both thrown off. Her too! How would you like that? This is a private home, not a hospital.'

Diamond ran. What sort of a woman was this? Surely she wouldn't do that to Perfy, she was too ill.

Diamond hurried back to her room and sat inside, trembling like a little frightened creature in its burrow. What had she done? Had her behaviour placed Perfy in trouble? It was hard to know what to do out here among these strange people. Maybe she should apologise and then they might let her look after Perfy. Not likely though. It would be better to go down to the people's camp and seek advice.

So far she'd only managed to have short conversations with the Aborigine staff, maids, gardeners, dairy workers and a few others, even though she took her meals with them, squatting in a long humpy. She hadn't minded that, it was a chance to meet these people, but the meals they were served horrified her. Large pots were brought out containing leftovers which could contain anything: soup, bones, gravy, scraps of meat, custards, anything, all slopped in together. Stale bread and damper appeared too, on trays, but there was no protection from the flies, though this didn't seem to worry any of them. Their own leftovers were carted down the track to their camp. Diamond discovered that rations of flour, tea and sugar were given to the families in the camp but these house concoctions were considered delicacies.

Fortunately, in the evenings Mae allowed Diamond to take some decent food for herself down to her own room, and that had become her only meal of the day. In the humpy she took only crusts of bread, which pleased her companions.

They were Ilba people and spoke yet another strange language and, once again, had never heard of the Irukandji. They could all speak enough English to get by; at least the servants could, she didn't know about the others. The men didn't talk to Diamond at all, obviously not knowing what to make of her. The girls were shy at first, intrigued by her clothes and her command of English, but they overcame that and she found them less cautious of her, or maybe not as jealous as the Brisbane Aborigines. Just the same, they wouldn't answer questions, not about Caravale, not about the Buchanans. They preferred to talk about their own affairs, babies, husbands, animals, tucker. And they laughed and giggled, shoving boisterously at each other, happy enough, it seemed, and not about to encourage this new woman to rock the boat.

Diamond waited until she heard the kitchen girls coming up the track. They always chattered like a flock of mynah birds until they reached the house; once inside, they were not allowed to talk.

'Mary,' she called to the older of the three. Everywhere she went she found Aborigine girls were given much the same names. The other two were Daisy and Poppy. Male children fared much worse, with silly, foolish names like Jumbo, Tinker, Rags.

'What you want, missus?' Mary yelled and Diamond sighed. She couldn't stop them calling her missus.

'Would it be all right if I went for a walk down to the camp?'

Mary shrugged.

'Maybe I can say hello to your mum?' Diamond suggested.

Mary giggled. 'Whitefeller talk too hard for my mum.'

Poppy came forward proudly. 'My mum talk real good.'

'That's great! What's her name?'

'Jannali. You gibbit her present?'

'Of course?'

'What present?'

Diamond grinned. 'A surprise. You'll find out later.' She went inside and found a pretty red scarf. Jannali would like it, she hoped. It was better to know someone in the camp than just to wander in uninvited, like a stickybeak.

She followed the trail for almost a mile through dry, hard scrub, her feet burning on the powdery ground, but it was November now, well into the heat, and shoes and stockings would be worse. Finally she came upon a group of children splashing around at the edge of the river. She slid down to paddle, cooling her feet. 'Where can I find Jannali?' she asked.

Two little boys skidded to her aid, escorting her like proud custodians with military elan past groups of tribal people who were resting in the sparse shade or pottering about charred fire sites. Diamond wondered where these boys would have seen troopers.

Some women were sitting flat-legged by a humpy, expertly weaving dilly bags from pandanus leaves, nimble fingers flying as they watched her approach. A naked baby crawled bravely away from her mother to investigate another yard of the world, dogs yipped, a pet joey hopped fearfully to safety and Diamond's escorts leapt in among the bare-breasted women like a pair of jumping-jacks. 'Jannali!' They pointed, then flung their arms round the neck of a middle-aged woman, who grinned at Diamond. 'You new housegirl?'

'Sort of. I'm only visiting.'

'Ah! Visiting!' Apparently that explained the question that had them all interested.

'Can I sit down?' Diamond asked, and the woman shrugged, so she sat cross-legged and handed over the scarf.

Jannali was delighted with it. Everyone examined it with sighs of admiration and Jannali tied it round her neck. 'Good, huh?' she asked the others and they grinned their approval.

'What you want?' she asked Diamond, a trace of suspicion in her voice.

'Nothing,' she said. 'That's a present for Poppy's mother.'

Jannali smiled. 'Good girl, Poppy. What name you?'

'Diamond.'

Jannali spat a lump of chewed tobacco in disgust. 'That whitefeller name. What your blackfeller name?'

'Kagari.'

'Ah, pretty.'

Other women closed in, curious to meet the stranger, presenting their babies for her to hold and talking amiably in their own language, expecting her to understand. They smashed big round nuts between rocks and handed her the delicious kernels. The white people called them simply Queensland nuts.

'This Ilba country?' Diamond said.

'All over Ilba country,' Jannali said, waving her arms about.

'Do you like living on the station?'

Jannali shrugged. 'Go walkabout sometime.'

'Why do you come back?'

'This our place. Allasame sit-down place. Sacred for dying.' Diamond knew it was important for her people to die in familiar places so that their spirits could find their homes in the Dreaming, and she felt a nervous twitch about her own salvation.

'Get hungry,' Jannali added. 'White men all over, killem niggers. No more hunting neither. Safe here.'

Diamond thought it best to edge up towards finding out about Mrs Buchanan. 'You remember Darcy?'

'Aaah!' the women wailed in unison, tears in their eyes.

'White feller killem too,' Jannali sighed.

'Mr Ben the boss now.'

Jannali grinned quickly. She leaned over and pinched Diamond on the breast. 'You look out. Mr Ben like nice nigger girl allasame you.'

Diamond was startled, and embarrassed. She'd only seen Ben a few times since the funeral and he'd hardly noticed her. He was a very attractive man and she found herself thinking about him a lot, but what was this woman saying? Had he made love to one of these girls? Or more?

The women were giggling madly now. 'You likem Ben?' Jannali poked her, teasing. 'He give you bloody good time, you see.'

To end this, Diamond changed the subject. 'Mrs Buchanan? The missus?'

Abruptly the laughter stopped. They looked from one to the other, all recognising the name.

'I think,' Diamond said carefully, 'she is not a good woman.'

They nodded soberly.

'She doesn't like me.'

They rolled their eyes. 'Better you run away. You go hide with your people,' Jannali said.

'I don't know where they are,' Diamond told them and they stared, mystified, shaking their heads at this bewildering information.

On the other side of the river a kangaroo was grazing. Trying out her own language, Diamond pointed to it and said 'Gangarru', and they smiled patiently, thinking she was speaking English. She realised then how close the Irukandji word was to the English word, and suddenly that seemed important. Where had the white men heard that Irukandji word? 'What do you call him?' she asked.

'Him bundarra.'

Nothing like it, she thought. Absolutely nothing like gangarru.

Jannali stretched and stood up. She was wearing only the scarf, and a lap-lap strung under her belly. Her dark skin glistened with grease. She walked further along the river bank and Diamond followed. 'What totem you?'

'Kookaburra,' Diamond replied and Jannali approved.

'Him big king fisherman. Lissen me. You go up whitefeller burying place.' She shuddered, obviously afraid of the graveyard. 'No feller hurt you there.'

'What do I do there?'

'Up there you lissen, that allatime lissen.'

The advice didn't sound too helpful but Diamond promised to go.

From round the bend of the river she could hear a rushing noise; it sounded like the sea. Everything reminded her of the sea. 'What's that?' she asked.

'Big water falling,' Jannali told her. 'No go there. Blackfeller no go there.'

'Why? Is it a sacred place?'

'No. Good place. Too good for niggers, missus say. Only for whitefellers swimmings and pickernicking. You know that word?' she asked proudly. 'Pickernicking.'

'Indeed I do,' Diamond said. 'You understand English very well.'

'Yes,' Jannali winked. 'Missus bloody bitch. Whip black people. You stay away from bloody bitch.'

'Wouldn't Mr Ben stop the beatings?'

She shrugged as if the question were too silly to answer.

Coming back to the homestead area was like entering a village. The small dairy herd trundled ahead of Diamond to the cow bales, placidly expecting their servants to do their duty and relieve them of a few pints of milk. It was easy to see this wasn't dairy country. These cows carried scraggy udders, not like the bloated milk-rich beasts on the coast. No one seemed to care much about the tame creatures; the masters of this land were the hefty, hard-eyed beef cattle that roamed the prairie and every so often could be heard bellowing complaints from the maze of cattleyards on the far side of this miniature township.

Stockmen eyed her curiously as she walked past the horse paddocks, and two men, saddles hitched on their shoulders, fell into step beside her. 'What's your name, girlie?'

'Diamond,' she replied pleasantly.

'You're a bit flash for a gin, aren't you?' one of them asked, shoving his hat back on his head, red lips grinning through a dark beard.

'Thank you,' Diamond replied, determined not to take offence.

'Where'd you learn to talk proper?' he asked. 'And dress up so fancy?'

'In Brisbane,' she said simply and decided to deflect the conversation. 'Have you been riding out there all day?'

'Since bloody sun-up,' the man replied in a knee-jerk reaction to her sudden question.

'Is it hard work?'

'Hard work? I dunno. I s'pose it's what yer used to. It's all right.'

The younger man poked his head forward to look at her. 'We been roundin' up strays. Some o' them jokers can get tricky, ride yer insides out trying to catch the bastards. They hurtle into the scrub and just as likely pull up dead on you. Break yer bloody neck if youse don't watch what yer doin'.'

'Bullshit!' His companion spat a chaw of tobacco.

'All bloody well for you, Paddy! Your horse can turn on a thruppeny bit. My bloody nag's hardly broke. I turn me back on him, he's likely to head for the mulga hisself.'

Diamond was pleased. They seemed to have forgotten her.

'Well, save your bloody pay and get yourself a decent mount. Tom Mansfield's got some for sale over on his patch. And you'd better make it bloody fast. I reckon we'll be musterin' soon, the rains'll be early this year.'

'Who says so?'

'I bloody say so. I can feel it in me bones. November now, two bob says they'll start in December.'

'You're on! Bloody December! February more like it.'

'Two bob,' Paddy said firmly.

They were approaching the barns. 'Excuse me,' Diamond said. 'I've got a horse. Do you think it would be all right if I went for a ride tomorrow. To have a look at the countryside.'

'Why not?' The young one laughed but Paddy looked at her thoughtfully.

'I wouldn't risk it,' he said quietly.

'I won't get lost,' she argued but he shook his head.

'That's not the point. It'd be a bad move.' The subject was closed. 'What tribe are you anyway?' he asked.

'Irukandji,' she said hopefully.

'Go on. I've travelled a fair share of this country but I never heard of them.'

They turned off into the barn without bothering to make the usual 'See you later', but Diamond felt reassured. At least they'd talked to her.

She passed the blacksmith who was busy now, the ringing double-clang of the hammer and anvil almost drowning the whistles of the cowboys lounging outside his forge, and went on up to the kitchen.

'Where have you been?' Mae said. 'Miss Middleton's been asking for you.'

'But I'm not allowed inside,' Diamond told her.

'I know, but the coast's clear. Mrs B. went out in her gig and she's not back yet.'

'Where'd she go?' Diamond asked, hoping she'd fallen out of the gig and broken her neck.

'She traipses around keeping an eye on things. She'll be back any minute, so get on in there.'

Perfy seemed better, although her skin retained its yellowy colour and she was still weak. 'I feel terrible,' she said. 'Stupid. I feel stupid making such a nuisance of myself.'

'They don't mind,' Diamond murmured.

'I know,' Perfy replied, 'and Mrs Buchanan has been so kind.'

Diamond's eyes widened. Kind? Mrs Buchanan?

'She reads to me,' Perfy continued. 'And brings me soup, and scones and tea, I can't eat much yet. But are you all right, Diamond? Mrs Buchanan said it's best for you to have a little holiday here because the black maids would get jealous if you took over any of their jobs.'

'I'm fine,' Diamond said.

'Ben brought me in those orchids,' Perfy said, pointing to an array of pink and purple flowers still clinging to a branch. 'But I get embarrassed when he comes in, with my face so yellow. I look like a pumpkin.'

'No, you don't, the yellow's fading. It was just the sickness, and your eyes are clearer now. You'll be up in no time and we can go home.'

'Oh yes, that's what I wanted to tell you. I had a letter from Mother. She's broken-hearted about Daddy but she insists I stay here until I'm really well. The neighbours at home are being very good to her but she worries about me now. Poor Mother. Mrs Buchanan has replied for me, to let her know I won't be travelling until I'm as fit as a fiddle.'

Diamond nodded numbly. She wished she could leave. She had never felt so useless in her life. And she hated sitting in that empty, stone prison-room that had once been a storage for dumpy old cheeses. She could still feel their clammy presence.

That night after supper she walked across the moonlit fields to the graveyard and wandered along the picket fence looking in at the white gleaming headstones, trees rustling softly nearby. Jack Middleton was resting peacefully now, his ordeal over, and she felt comforted in his presence. Further along she stood and stared at the unmarked cross, wondering who was buried there.

She must have stood there for quite a while because suddenly she was cold. A chill night wind had blown up, whistling over the crest of the hill. She turned to leave but a voice in the wind, or in her head, she couldn't tell, seemed to be chattering, excitedly, urgently, and she looked again at that white wooden cross. The voice was soundless and yet it was shouting, a non-voice, neither male nor female. It was screaming at her in a rage, telling her something too frightening to listen to. She clapped her hands over her ears, but the voice persisted, hissing terrible threats that she couldn't decipher, a story of something terrible, crying for revenge, an evil voice.

Diamond fled. She ran and ran, down the hillside, climbing fences, running swiftly for the safety of her room where the voices faded and then were shut out. Whatever it was up there that Jannali knew about, Diamond was not ready to confront it, no matter what it had to say. And yet she slept peacefully that night, waking early in the morning to the lovely bell calls of bush birds.

Sunday. The worst day of the week. No work today so the men were amusing themselves, throwing horseshoes outside the bunkhouse, playing cards in the shade, swaggering across the white-hot yards between the various outbuildings, hats tipped low against the glare. Only the three black girls ran giggling back and forth from the kitchen, for water, for milk, for fresh vegetables from the garden, under Mae's watchful eyes as she cooked Sunday dinner for 'the family': Mrs Buchanan and Ben. And possibly their guest. For Diamond, there were eyes everywhere, watching her, with nothing better to do. She hated emerging on Sundays, feeling like a pariah, not needed or wanted by anyone. Only hunger drove her up to the back door where Mae handed her a tray covered with a net, so that she could take her Sunday dinner wherever she liked.

Except for the flies, the humpy was deserted so Diamond continued back to the creamery and sat on the step to eat her roast dinner and pudding with custard. She would have liked a cup of tea but that meant another march up to the house and she decided against the idea. And so she sat staring out at the orchard and the row of beehives that nestled nearby.

The heat was intense, up around the hundred mark easily, she guessed, and she thought enviously of the Ilba people who'd be cooling off in the river, but she didn't dare join them. Stripping off in front of the black men would be no different from stalking naked among the whites, not for her. Then she decided to go for a walk to those falls. So what if they were out of bounds to blacks? She didn't care. She'd say she didn't know. Someone was sure to see her heading off in that direction but she really was past caring. She had to do something.

The track was overgrown, not much used lately and fast losing its fight with the creeping scrub. And then the thought lodged that the Buchanans, or rather Ben, wouldn't have done much entertaining this year what with the death of his only brother, and Perfy owning half this property – curious he didn't seem to resent her – and then another tragedy, Jack Middleton. Ben must think someone had put an evil eye on him. The track was wide with traces of skittering gigs and wagon wheels and Diamond pictured young ladies in white dresses and floppy hats riding this way, clutching picnic baskets, and gentlemen in their shirt sleeves and cream flannels, laughing, teasing, romancing their girls, their lady-loves.

Red-tailed wasps zipped around her as she pushed on, this blackfeller, she grinned to herself, with the pulpy feet of a white girl. She had to shuffle to rid her feet of the fine sharp bindi-eye spikes that lurked in the dry grass, and she scratched and itched all the way against the onslaught of tiny sandflies that were raising stinging lumps on her ankles. In future, she decided, she would wear shoes out here. And stockings. It was an affectation on her part not to wear them, trying to keep a foot in both worlds. She laughed at her own pun. Silly. Silly! She'd been bitten mercilessly by mosquitoes at the Ilba camp because she couldn't bring herself to apply their dirty rancid fat to exposed skin.

What would Missus think of all this? 'Silly girl,' she'd say. 'Mein Gott! Home you should go.' But where was home? Diamond knew she couldn't return to Mrs Middleton without Perfy. It would be unthinkable.

And poor Mrs Beckman.

Diamond had written to her of her new address in Bowen and Missus had replied from the cold fogs of Hamburg, pouring her heart into a long letter. She still missed her darling Otto. She despaired of ever seeing the sun again, and in her old age she complained she'd been relegated to the back room of her son's home with no status. Helga, the daughter-in-law, hated her. Lloyds of London had paid up for the loss of the *White Rose*, but her son was handling her financial affairs now. The proceeds from the sale of the Brisbane house had been enough to pay her fare home to Germany and for the transport of the fine furniture made by Otto's own hands, but now the rest had to go for her board and keep in another woman's home.

The noise of the falls was louder now and Diamond hurried on, sprinting the last few yards to a rocky outcrop. Then she stood back in wonder. Beautiful! Absolutely beautiful!

She was standing level with the stream that dropped like an endless silver ribbon over the edge of a cliff, maybe only thirty feet high but enough to lend magic to the water, cascading over ribbed granite and smooth boulders to a green pool below. Moss crept up the cliff face under ridges and brave greenery lit with orchids hid in crevices, safe from the spilling flow.

Diamond slid down the banks, finding man-made stepping stones carefully placed to ease the descent among tall trees hugged by huge staghorns, some of them six feet across. She marvelled at this enchanted glade and then stood, staring at the crystal pool, deepened by erosion, that allowed the delight of fresh bubbling water to overflow and continue on its path down the gully. For a minute fear grasped as she searched around for the yellow eyes of crocodiles, but she knew in her heart that this was no place for the monsters. This was a heaven place and she was filled with love for her mother earth and all her beauties. Fish leapt in triumph, birds whistled and carolled; downstream she saw a furry platypus slipping swiftly through the shallows. As she watched him, duckbill nudging mud and twigs, she realised he was clambering up the banks to rebuild his cave-like nest well above the waterline, and she remembered what Paddy had said. That the rains would be early this year.

But it was hot standing there, the afternoon sun pounding on the rocks and steaming the misty foliage. Diamond took off her turban and wiped her face, and then she looked guiltily around. Not a soul within miles of this place. She stripped off her clothes and dived from the heat of the day into the tingling cool of the magnificent, wide, deep, swimming hole. She trod water to balance under the falls, her long hair now free to stream with the flow, slapping mischievously around her face, her breasts taut, invigorated, and her body, free at last of the whitefeller wrappings, lithe as a sea-snake, diving, cavorting, in love with the world.

He saw her go. He saw her stroll from the creamery and make for the orchard and he thought she was headed for the blacks' camp again. He'd heard she'd been down there. He walked up to the verandah to get a better view and picked out her bright blue turban bobbing off in the other direction. She climbed the fence on the other side and disappeared down the track that was a complete dead-end. It only led to the falls. And then he laughed. She'd have the cheek to go there too. She was some nigger, that one!

He remembered the immediate and fierce assistance she'd given him with Jack Middleton and felt a twinge of remorse that he'd never bothered to thank her, but it was awkward. Ben had never seen her likes. Neither had anyone else on the station. All the men, black and white, were right on to her, and with good reason. She was a classy piece of work if ever there was one, the tall sleek body, the head as aloof as it was inviting. The stockmen called her 'Black Velvet', but Ben had put the word out: 'Hands off!' No fooling with that one. She was no flighty little gin willing to lie down in the hayshed if you tickled her tummy; more likely to stick a knife in them, he'd warned. He'd seen that knife, strapped to her leg. It had come out fast after he'd shot the croc and plunged into its belly as easily as if she'd been slicing butter. Not that the men need take that into account. The boss had said 'hands off' and Ben's word was law. Up to a point. Paddy had told him he'd warned Diamond about riding out on the range alone, and he was right. If one of these horny bastards grabbed her miles from the homestead she wouldn't get back to tell the tale. As if he didn't have enough trouble. Ma was buttering up Perfy with a view to talking some sense into her about the station, when she was well enough. And she'd collected some orchids and made him take them in to her.

'Agreed,' she'd said, 'she's a good-looking gal. Darcy knew his onions after all. Good English stock even if the old man was a convict.' Cornelia had played the part of the shocked mistress of Caravale when they'd brought in Jack's body but in fact she saw it as a stroke of luck. There were times when Ben hated his mother. Her utter lack of compassion infuriated him, even though he knew her logic was spot on. Now they only had to deal with Perfy.

Perfy. Miss Middleton. When he met her again in Bowen, Ben had been so overcome with remorse for Darcy that it had been an awful strain trying to talk to the Middletons. Only Perfy had kept the conversation going. Jack Middleton had looked at him sometimes with an expression of such hatred that Ben had been confused.

Jack had been fatherly, interested in everything, seemingly a pleasant chap enjoying the safari to Caravale. Born and bred in the bush, Ben could sit around a camp fire relaxing, but always wary, always alert for danger – snakes, blacks, hobos. 'Allasame watchem' as the blacks called it. It was at those times, in a quiet check around him, that Ben had seen the hatred. He'd been very much afraid of the Englishman, and he'd kept his rifle handy. A shot in the back and Ben, like Darcy, would be out of the picture. Who then would get Caravale? He remembered he'd never bothered to write a will, not like Darcy. But what the hell? If he bought it, then Ma could have the place and she and Perfy could fight it out. What a double! The thought caused him a choke of laughter.

He liked Perfy now, he really did. And that gave him more reason for remorse. She was so direct, devoid of any of the chat and banter of the local girls, not given to the blushes and fluttering of city girls.

'Righto, Ben, what do we do now?' she'd asked when they'd dismounted at the first campsite. And he'd enjoyed her company. She hadn't complained about the ride, though he knew her bum was sore after days in the saddle. She soon stopped pretending it wasn't and wobbled around rubbing her behind as if that were quite natural in the company of her dad and Darcy's brother.

He hoped they could resolve this problem of the station. It would be easier when he could talk to her on her own, without Ma hanging about the sick room.

On impulse, he swung down from the verandah and made for the stables. He'd ride out to the falls track and see for himself where Diamond had got to. She was a city black, just as likely to stand on a snake or . . . Christ! That's all he'd need! First the father and then the maid! Perfy would never believe they were accidents! He was sweating in his starched Sunday shirt as he grabbed his saddle and bridle from the barn and whistled up his horse.

Just then his manager Tom Mansfield rode in. 'Just as well I caught you,' he said, not bothering to ask where Ben might be going. When the boss was saddling up, he didn't have to give an explanation.

Damn! Of all people. 'What brings you this way on a Sunday?' Ben asked.

'There's an officer with three of those bloody black troopers a couple of miles back heading for the homestead.'

Ben nodded. Some bright bastard had formed a military troop of black volunteers to keep tribal blacks in order, and they were more trouble than they were worth. Renegade blacks from distant tribes, armed with rifles and dressed up in ugly uniforms, were more vicious than any white troopers, added to which, their fanatical white officers let them have their heads in 'cleaning up' a district, ambushing and murdering groups of Aborigines who might, or might not, be guilty of criminal acts. Darcy and several other cattlemen had lodged a petition with the Governor to have this disgraceful army corps disbanded but no action had been taken.

'Piss them off,' Ben said to Tom. 'Don't give them any rations. I don't care if they bloody starve.'

'It's not that easy,' Tom said quietly. 'They've got a dozen prisoners with them.'

'What sort of prisoners?' Ben asked, his voice urgent with worry now.

'Blacks.'

'Oh shit!'

'You've never seen such a mob. They're wild blacks. Christ knows what tribe they dragged them from. The poor bastards are shackled hand and foot. I reckon they've bashed hell out of them, and starved them too. If the Caravale blacks spot them, we'll have a riot on our hands.'

That was true. There were more than a hundred Ilbas living in mobs along the river. They were quiet enough these days but very easily upset. The occasional whippings for thievery or trouble-making didn't seem to bother them but black troopers were hated.

'The prisoners look like a collection of wild men from Borneo, long hair, long beards matted with mud, and a couple of young lads with them, only kids,' Tom said. 'What can we do?'

'You halt the column out there and the Ilbas'll be on to them. It's a wonder they haven't heard already.'

'What then?'

Ben stood uncertainly and then he made a decision. 'Round up the men, arm them, and bring the blacksmith.'

Tom grinned. 'We set the prisoners loose?'

'What choice have we got?'

'Right,' Tom said.

As he rode out with his men, Ben glanced towards the falls track and felt a sense of loss. He realised he'd been kidding himself, making excuses. He wanted to see Diamond, to talk to her, to touch her, to feel that velvety skin, to make love to her.

They galloped fast across country and descended on the column, rifles loaded and aimed at the white officer. The pitiful blacks cowered to the ground.

'What's the meaning of this?' the officer shouted.

'Drop your arms,' Ben said. 'We've had enough of you bastards.' His men growled their agreement. They too knew that trouble with Caravale blacks could take weeks, maybe months, to settle.

'You too,' Ben yelled at the black troopers who quickly dropped their firearms.

'I'll do no such thing,' the officer shouted but Tom Mansfield rode calmly up to him and took his pistol and rifle.

'Give them water,' Ben said, jerking his head towards the prisoners. They drank greedily from the waterbags offered them, and then the blacksmith went to work.

Once freed, the skinny, timid prisoners stood fearfully, wondering at their fate. 'You can go,' Ben called to them, but they stared at him, bewildered.

The Caravale men were laughing, shouting at them to go, to bolt while they could! Within minutes the prisoners were racing for the bush.

'I'll report you for this!' the officer shouted.

'Do what you bloody like,' Ben replied.

'You can't take our weapons!'

'We just did,' Tom told him. 'We'll mind them for you for a few days to give those poor buggers a head start.'

'They're criminals,' he argued. 'I was taking them in to be formally charged.'

'They can't even speak bloody English,' Tom said. 'You're riding with bloody criminals. Now you get them shit-soldiers off this property.'

'You heard him,' Ben said. 'You keep going east and don't look back.' He turned to the black troopers, mean-looking characters with dark cruel eyes. 'You fellers never come near here again, you hear me? Or we'll hang you.'

'Yes, boss, we go.'

A few shots over their heads sent their horses rearing and they took off without any argument, heading east. 'You better catch up with your mates, if you can,' Ben told the officer. 'And on second thoughts, don't come back for your weapons. I'll send them in to Bowen. You can pick them up at the police station.' He wheeled his horse round and headed back for the homestead. 'Give the lads a drink, Tom,' he said. 'I'll see you later.'

Diamond was drifting and dreaming, looking up at the burning blue sky. It was time to go. Reluctantly she floated over to a wattle tree that hung lazily, like a luxurious curtain, brushing the surface of the water, and climbed out of the stream. She retrieved her clothes, her body drying in the heat as she dressed, and sat down to fluff her hair.

'So this is where you get to?'

She jumped up to find Ben looking down at her. Embarrassed. Wondering how long he'd been standing there. A blue-tongued lizard scuttled soundlessly across a nearby rock.

'I just had a swim,' she said nervously. 'It's so hot.'

'Good day for a swim,' he remarked, moving down to the water's edge.

'It's beautiful,' she said. She thought he might jump in, clothes and all, the way he was studying the pool, but he turned back to her.

'I never did thank you for helping me with Jack,' he said.

'That's all right.'

'It was a terrible thing for you to see.'

'Yes.' Her long hair was dripping on to her shirt but she felt immobilised.

'First time I've seen you without the scarf,' he commented. 'I didn't realise your hair was so long.' He reached out and touched her hair and then let his fingers slip down her cheek, stroking her face as if it were silk. 'You're different, Diamond,' he said. 'Different from anyone I've ever met.'

She nodded. Struck dumb. Afraid to speak and break the spell. She wanted to reach out and touch him but she didn't dare. Both hands were stroking her neck now, around and under her hair, and when he put his mouth on hers she was ready for him with all the loving in her soul. He drew her back under the wattle and down on to the mossy ground, undoing her shirt, kissing her gently, lovingly, removing her clothes so slowly that she knew he was waiting for her to stop him but she couldn't. She arched her back as her skirt slid down . . .

'You're so cool,' he said. 'Your body is so cool, we should both go for a swim.' But then he was kissing her again, taking off his clothes to lie with her. He looked into her eyes and smiled. 'Later?'

'Yes,' she said, her arms round him. 'Later.'

And when they did swim together they were like children, freed from cares, duck-diving into the mirrored depths, teasing, laughing, spluttering under the rushing falls, then resting, braced against smooth rocks in the shoulder-deep water, allowing the river to flow on past them.

'I have to go,' he said suddenly. 'I can't meet you down here again. What if I come to your room tomorrow night?'

She nodded, watching him go, watching him dress, marvelling at his strong body and his brown back and the whiteness of his buttocks. She loved this man.

'Don't stay too long,' he warned and was gone.

As soon as she heard him riding away, she climbed from the water once more, wishing she could just lie in their place again under the tree and dream of him. The Ilba spirits were kind to her this day, they had accepted her.

Time passed too quickly after that. Perfy was recovering and Diamond was dreading the day they'd have to leave, praying he'd want her to stay. Most nights he came to her, making love to her in the little room that was their haven, a blessed place, transformed by his presence. On the nights that he stayed out on the range, working too far away to come back to the homestead, she ached for him, sitting on the step under the great canopy of stars, picturing him by the camp fires, stretched out, sleeping under these same stars, wondering if he was thinking of her.

2

Before he left Bowen with Herbert, Lew had written to Ying explaining about the junk. He knew the Chinaman would never send his gold in to Bowen in the hands of white men. If Ying didn't come himself, the competent Yuang brothers would be the carriers and they'd guard it with their lives. They'd soon find out through the Chinese community what had become of the junk if his message didn't get to Ying. And Mr Fung Wu, his new backer, promised to keep an eye out for them. It was all Lew could do. He could be no further help to Ying in Bowen; he just hoped to catch up with him on the goldfields.

In contrast to Bowen, Townsville was an ugly place clinging to the base of a single angry-looking peak known as Castle Hill. The waterfront was tangled with mangrove swamps and yet the dust-dry main street of hastily erected shanties and pubs looked as if it hadn't seen rain for a hundred years. The few trees left standing bore a wilted, defeated air as if waiting for someone to put them out of their misery. A large green island was visible from the port; Magnetic Island, he was told, named by Captain Cook, and it seemed to have no relation to the dry landfall.

'I don't like the look of this place,' was Herbert's first comment. 'I thought it would be pretty and tropical like Bowen.'

Lew was unsympathetic. 'You wanted to come here.' The abrupt change in landscape interested him. The surrounding terrain was much flatter, apart from that great hill, and the air was drier. He could see already that it would be an easier trail out to the goldfields.

'Do you realise we're now a thousand miles from Brisbane?' Herbert complained.

'What's that got to do with the price of fish?'

'My dear fellow, I never counted on getting stranded this far from civilisation. What can I do here?'

'Sell land again,' Lew laughed. He glanced down the ramshackle street. 'I can't see any land or house agent signs.'

'There aren't any bloody houses, and you couldn't give this land away.'

The other passengers on the coastal steamer were all miners or would-be miners. They'd surged from the overcrowded ship to disappear among their fellow prospectors.

Lew and Herbert made for the nearest pub, crowded with diggers and the usual camp followers of gaudy raucous prostitutes.

'Not a piano in sight,' Lew grinned as they bought a bottle of beer each and pushed out through the swing doors to sit on the rough edge of the raw timber verandah.

Herbert ignored him. 'I don't fancy sleeping in any of these ratholes,' he said. 'I'd rather sleep on the beach.'

'And get eaten alive by mosquitoes. That's not a beach, it's a swamp.'

'Oh Jesus.'

A tall thin man with a shock of white hair and white furry sideburns stopped in front of them. 'Excuse me, sirs. I'm looking for Captain Cavour.'

Lew eyed the black serge waistcoat over the checkered shirt and put him down as a clerk of some sort. 'I'm Cavour,' he said.

'Oh, thank God I found you,' the man said, taking out wire-rimmed glasses to get a better look at Lew. 'I'm Weller. From the Customs office. We've got a problem here and I was told you could help.'

'How.'

'There's a lugger in the harbour and the captain's taken sick. I mean he took sick. He had a heart attack this morning and went and died. So she's got no captain. She's stuck here.'

'Bad luck,' Lew said.

'I believe you just disembarked from the *Lady Belle*?'

'That's true.'

'Yes.' Weller adjusted his glasses and wiped his sweating face with a handkerchief. 'The captain of the *Lady Belle* informed us that you were in town. We want to offer you the job as master of the lugger. She's a good ship, the *Pacific Star*, bound for Brisbane. Owned by Captain Towns.'

'Who's he?'

'Oh sir, a famous man. Military title, you understand. This port was named after him.'

'You don't say,' Lew commented bleakly.

'Captain Cavour, if you'd take this ship to Brisbane, I can assure you Captain Towns would be most grateful and you will be well recompensed. I mean to say, sir, you could call your own terms at this stage.'

'He'll take it,' Herbert said, brightening up. 'Consider it done.'

'I'll think about it,' Lew replied. He didn't like to be sidetracked. His main interest was to see how Ying was faring. It was still a source of amusement to him to imagine how the Chinese gentleman was coping in these mad surrounds, and besides, even though he was loath to admit the fact, Lew himself was tempted to have a shot at digging up gold. There was so much talk about it, there were so many success stories, a man couldn't help leaning a little that way.

'In the morning,' the Customs man said. 'You can inspect in the morning if you like. We'll have the papers ready.'

'Where's she from?' Lew asked.

'The Solomons, sir. A fine seagoing vessel.'

'Crew in shape?'

'Indeed, sir. Everything's in order. Just no captain. Can I expect you in the morning? Mr Weller. Just ask for me, Mr Weller. Our office is only a shed yet but we'll see better times. This will be an important port one day.'

'I'm sure it will,' Herbert said enthusiastically.

'See you tomorrow,' Lew said, finishing the bottle of beer. The Solomons. He hadn't been that far out in the Pacific. It'd be a good new run, especially taking in these colonial ports. He could have a look at Tahiti, and New Zealand, and learn about traders that sailed the Pacific Islands. One day he hoped to have his own ship trading out of these ports. Buy his own ship.

And then reality trod on his dreams. With what? It would take a long time on a master's pay to earn that sort of money. In the meantime there was Perfy. His dreams of her were fading too. A lost cause. Why pine after a girl whose face was firmly turned to the west while he looked to the east, to the sea? What was Perfy doing now? Lording it over her estates like a diminutive dowager? Counting bloody cows? Drinking sherry with fellow squatters and their wives, living her own fantasy in the society of the local elite?

'A word, Captain Cavour,' a voice said from behind him and Lew twisted round to stare at a high-booted gent lounging against the wall behind him. A squatter type in the flesh. He'd learned in Bowen to pick them. Well-spoken, British-sounding, well-fed, tanned, not grimy-white like the scurrying diggers. He had a heavy revolver hanging from a low-slung cartridge belt.

'Do they tag everyone that comes into this place?' Lew growled.

'They could, for all I know,' the fellow answered. 'I just happened to over-hear your conversation.'

'And what's it got to do with you?'

'Not a thing. The names's Jardine. On my way home to Somerset, Cape York. We've got a cattle station up there.'

'At Somerset?' Lew queried. He'd called into that steamy port on the voyage south. 'How'd you get enough cattle up there?'

'Trekked them,' Jardine said cheerfully. 'The brother and I. But I wouldn't recommend the route. We were lucky to get through with our scalps, let alone the herd. It took us nearly a year from Rockhampton to the Top End.'

Lew was impressed. He'd heard about the exploits of these intrepid frontiersmen but never expected to meet one of them. He stood up and shook hands with Jardine. 'Pleased to make your acquaintance,' he said. 'And I stand corrected for my discourtesy.'

'Truly a land of wonders to make him apologise,' Herbert added, introducing himself, but Jardine laughed.

'A man's business is his own here, we don't ask too many questions. But in the case of the *Pacific Star*, Captain, beware. She's a blackbirder.'

'What's that?' Lew asked.

'A nice name for a slaver.'

'Jesus!' Lew said. 'That's illegal.'

'They get round it,' Jardine continued. 'They kidnap men and boys from the Solomons, shove their marks on contracts and bring them here to work on the south Queensland sugarcane and cotton plantations. After that it depends on which planter becomes their master. Some of the Kanakas, that's what they're called, are treated moderately well, but the majority end up as slaves. That's why they're in such a hurry to get the *Pacific Star* out of this port. The hold's crammed with the poor buggers.'

'I wouldn't touch a ship like that with a forty-foot pole,' Lew said.

'Very wise of you,' Jardine said, but Herbert was disappointed.

'You transported coolies,' he snapped at Lew. 'Why not this lot?'

'Coolies are with their own people,' Lew said angrily. 'They understand their situation.'

'Do they?' Jardine asked. 'A ship went down off Somerset recently. Overcrowded to the hilt with coolies. They didn't have a hope in hell, they all drowned.'

'Then that's the fault of the ship's master,' Lew flared.

'It's still not the British way,' Herbert said primly. 'But I don't know why they bother bringing in natives from the Solomons when they could employ the blacks here.'

Jardine looked at the pair of them, bemused. 'You gentlemen must both be new here.' He turned to Herbert. 'Could the Americans get the Red Indians to work for them? Not on your bloody life! Our Aborigines are the same. They'd rather cut our throats, and can you blame them? They're fine warriors.' He nodded towards the pub. 'Come, I'll buy you a drink.'

Meeting Jardine was fortunate. He found them bunks in a half-finished boarding house. The outside wall of their room had not been completed and the gap was hung with canvas, but the heat was so intense neither Lew nor Herbert complained. In the morning he introduced them to a horse dealer.

'I'll need a good mount and a packhorse,' Lew said.

'No, we'll need three horses,' Herbert added. 'I'm coming with you.'

'Since when?' Lew was annoyed. He didn't want Herbert trailing along. 'I thought you hated the diggings!'

'I do, but I can't stay here. Besides, I might get lucky this time.'

Acting on advice from Jardine, they bought supplies, equipment and weapons, and bade him farewell.

'Look me up in Somerset any time you're up that way,' he said.

'I'll do that,' Lew replied.

'Not me,' Herbert said. 'I'm not going any further north in the tropics than here. I still say it's no place for an Englishman.'

Their trek out to the Cape across a ragged landscape of dry trees and high grey anthills like jagged teeth sticking up from the patchy wilted grass was a saga in itself. They joined a column of hopeful miners, and despite the burning, relentless heat everyone was in high spirits. The riders passed hundreds of men on foot, families with their wagons, bullock teams dragging supplies, couples in flimsy gigs, and a horse-drawn lorry bearing painted ladies shaded by parasols, out too to earn their fortunes.

Returning travellers passed them by without a glance, neither admitting their ill luck nor advertising their joy. Troopers patrolled the Ross River crossing, where the water was low, warning of crocodiles and waiting to meet the heavily armed gold escorts on the last leg into Townsville, for this was a favourite ambush spot.

The two Englishmen were welcomed at camp fires along the trail. Lew enjoyed the general air of camaraderie, the boisterous optimism reminiscent of a ship's company headed for home port. Everyone shared food and swapped yarns; they smoked as they waited for the billies to boil and sang rollicking songs. The tunes were familiar to Lew, they sounded like songs British sailors sang, but the lyrics were new, they had a sting to them, like the defiant Irish ballads. They warmed him, they raised the blood, like marching songs, and he realised he was hearing the first stirrings of a nationalistic pride in this wild, mad place at the bottom of the world.

'They're a good lot of blokes,' he said to Herbert, who sniffed.

'They might be now, but wait until the fight's on for gold. I saw a man kicked to death outside one of their filthy taverns at the Cape. And no one turned a hair.'

'What for?'

'I didn't wait around to find out.'

There was no time for names in this passing parade, only 'handles'. Lew was easily tabbed as Captain, Herbert became 'the Kipper', which didn't impress him; there was Lofty, and Tich; and the Banker, the Chemist, the Farmer, all named for their previous occupations or appearance.

Men who travelled alone were pitied. Not to have a mate in the world to join you on this expedition was considered worse than bankruptcy. Quite a few of the diggers had come from other goldfields and Lew discovered that a man on his own had little chance, he had to have a friend, even a woman, to help him work and guard his claim. He wondered if Herbert had found that out the hard way and was now using him.

'All we have to do is get a miner's licence,' Herbert said, 'and stake a claim. If a man leaves his claim for more than twenty-four hours, it's open go.'

'I'm looking for Ying,' Lew said. 'I didn't say I'd go prospecting.'

'You will,' Herbert laughed. 'You've got the bug. How did you get to be a captain anyway? You're not a naval type.'

'I signed on with Meridian and Company, Canton. I would never have got promotion in your navy. But I was keen and I speak several Chinese dialects so I was also a translator. That put me in touch with officers who gave me a push along. The merchant service is better pickings for a sailor.'

'Nobody ever gave me a push along,' Herbert grumbled, taking one of Lew's cheroots.

'Stiff luck,' Lew said unsympathetically. 'I'll give you some advice though. Don't play cards out here. I watched you playing on the ship and you're a bloody cheat. You pull those stunts at the diggings and I won't turn a hair if they kick your head in on the street.'

In the event, Herbert was useful at the Cape, though Lew would never admit it. He couldn't believe the confusion, the clatter, the determined activity of the place. Tiny shanty centres had sprung up in the bush and the goldfields fanned out all around them, ranging along the river banks, creeks, gullies and gorges. Prospectors chased reefs like hares, miles into rough scrub, the earth upended, turned over, piled in heaps, dug into trenches, as if a ploughman had gone berserk there as far as the eye could see. And everywhere there were bent backs, pans jangling, tents flapping, men shouting and straining, horses dragging sleds of crushings, vendors. Chinamen dodged about, pigtails flying under their wide peaked hats; coolies sweated with winches; women, skirts tucked high, lumped baskets. Toil, everywhere sweating, panting toil. The stench of human excrement rode high in the heat and flies blackened the air.

'Jesus,' Lew said to Herbert. 'I can't stay here.'

'You don't have to,' Herbert said. 'We can go out a bit.'

'Where?'

'Word has it there's gold for twenty miles around, so don't go soft on me.'

'I have to find Ying first,' Lew said stubbornly.

They dismounted and led their horses up and down the man-made inclines, bare of any foliage like a moonscape, save for a few bedraggled trees, and at each turn Lew watched for Chinese and spoke to them. Eventually he was directed to a claim, down Shamrock Gully, registered as Golden Sun.

He found several of Ying's coolies working feverishly at the river's edge, and they greeted him like a long-lost relative. Soon he was ringed by bony men, all talking at once.

'Mr Chin is not here at present. Mr Chin has gone to Charters Towers. But Mr Chin has three claims working exceedingly well for him.'

'When will he be back?'

'The master does not tell us his intentions.'

No. Of course not. Lew dispatched one of the coolies to Charters Towers with a letter, repeating his bad news about the junk and letting Ying know he was at the Cape diggings and would await his return.

231

They staked a claim downstream at Bracken Creek, registering it as the Waterloo at Herbert's insistence, and began panning right away. Ying's coolies had recommended the spot since the creek was still flowing and they showed Lew how to work the claim, explaining how to identify payable gold and how the claims followed the elusive reefs of gold-bearing rock. Soon it became necessary to build a pulley and cages to remove the disgorged material up the banks. The cradling and panning went on, and little by little Herbert and Lew's supply of alluvial gold began to grow and the search became more intense. They were on the job at dawn, clothes, hair and skin stained with yellow clay, and Lew was having the time of his life.

He had expected to find gold, to leap about in joy and depart, rich, but this process was a slow tease, a worse addiction, he feared, than liquor or gambling. But he didn't care. They were earning money in this circus atmosphere and no way could they leave until the gold ran out. As the leather pouches of gold filled, Herbert was ecstatic and demanded they stake another claim further down Bracken Creek. Lew saw the sense of it. While they hadn't struck plugs of gold as others had done, they were earning an average of fifteen pounds a day which was, in their straitened circumstances, a fortune.

They pitched their tent beside a German covered wagon owned by a farmer from New South Wales, Jim Bourke. He was accompanied by his wife Marjorie and daughter Marie. The two women, dressed in men's shirts and moleskins and cotton sun bonnets, worked hard, seemingly unconcerned by the rough life, and panned as well as Bourke himself. Since they were neighbours, Jim Bourke suggested they share their rations, which the women cooked, so each night Lew and Herbert dined with the family on stews and damper, and cake covered with treacle.

As night fell the whole area was dotted with lanterns like a continuation of the lower stars. Their camp was quiet, well away from the louts and rowdies who frequented the shanties along the main river. There was little socialising; working from dawn to dusk at this all-too-temporary employment, they were glad to make for their bunks after supper to ease their aching bodies and sleep.

Then one day Chin Ying came to visit. He wore a dark shirt and padded, pyjama-like trousers and he had discarded his elegant embroidered caps for a wide cabbage-tree hat.

Lew stared. 'I hardly recognised you without your feathers,' he said, helping Ying down from a fine bay horse.

Ying looked up at him. 'Captain, I am presently resembling a commoner but you look like a coolie.'

'Sorry about the mud,' Lew said, 'but water's short here, I have to go up to the main river to clean up.' He noticed one of the Yuang brothers, on horseback, stationed at the bend in the track. 'Lord have mercy! Don't tell me your servants ride now.'

'It is essential,' Ying said.

'Come up to the tent and I'll make you some tea.'

'I brought tea, the potion they sell here is undrinkable. And I also brought some decent wine.'

'Well done! And I'm glad to see you, damned if I'm not.'

Lew made the tea and they sat at the makeshift table in his tent. 'I'm sorry about the junk, Ying.'

'Don't let it concern you, it belonged to Lord Cheong, not me. Serves him right.'

Lew was amazed. 'What's this? Do I detect a note of bitterness against your famous lord and master? The one who could do no wrong?'

'It is not a matter for amusement. He sent two men to follow me in case I cheated him.'

Lew shrugged. 'That doesn't surprise me. From what I heard of that joker, he'd have Buddha followed.'

'Ah, but you don't understand. He has been holding my family in desperate disgrace to make certain I send back the gold. So why would there be any need to pursue me? I am an honourable man.'

'A dishonourable man sees only himself in others.'

Ying nodded. 'I fear there is truth in that. Now, Captain, listen carefully. I cannot stay long. Cheong's two men came in useful. I sent them back to China with plenty of gold. I was ignorant when I left my home. They had me convinced I should return with treasure chests full but I now understand the true value of gold and Cheong has already been well paid.'

'Your men have been doing well?'

'Exceedingly well. With my knowledge of metallurgy and geology I chose correctly the diggings.'

'Fifty coolies would have helped. I wish I had them.'

'You will,' Ying said mysteriously. 'My greatest concern has been my mother and my wife, but a friend brought me news. News that Cheong has kept from me. My dear mother was unable to accept her disgrace and so she took her own life. My wife, who blamed me for her fate, has chosen to go into concubinage. That leaves only my brothers. I have sent a message to them to escape from Cheong's mansions quickly, so that he has no further hold on me.'

'That's sensible.'

'I have just sent Cheong's last payment to him, with a letter informing him that my obligations are now fulfilled. He's a greedy man, the gold will make him happy. He'll forget about me.'

'You hope.'

'That's why I can't go back to China just yet.'

'Where will you go?'

'Ha! Now, this is important. I have many friends here, even among the white men, and I hear a lot of things, so I want you to keep in touch. If you leave here, come to my house in Charters Towers.'

'So you didn't send all the gold home?'

Ying grinned. His moustache had grown into two long strings, stiffened with beeswax, that reached down below his chin, and he had shaved his forehead back three inches from the hairline in the fashion of the Chinese upper classes.

'Well?' Lew persisted.

'I am master now,' Ying stated. 'And a gentleman. Cheong had to pay for the destruction of my family.'

'Quite so,' Lew said, smothering a laugh. 'I hope you exacted an honourable settlement.'

'Indeed, yes. I am a rich man, according to my family standards, but I intend to be much richer. For this matter, you should not be grubbing here. I heard the loss of the junk caused you to have to seek a loan from Mr Fung Wu.'

It didn't surprise him that Ying knew about his loan, there were so many Chinese around and the Chinese were the most prodigious gossips, both men and women.

'It has been paid,' Ying went on. 'So forget about that. Now I met a fine gentleman called Mr Mulligan—'

Lew laughed. 'Come on now, Ying. Don't let yourself get sweet-talked by an Irishman, they'd sell you the Wondrous Wall.'

'Not this one. The accents are difficult for me to define but I believe he is a colonial. This honourable gentleman is what they call a bushman, an explorer. He travels far into the wilds. He tells me he loves to travel where only black men have trod, to put his steps into unexplored land. You understand?'

Lew nodded politely. Ying had changed but he was still young enough to be caught up in sudden enthusiasms.

'Mr Mulligan informs me,' Ying whispered, 'that he is convinced that great treasures in gold are still to be found in this state. He says there is more gold here than ever they found in Ballarat.'

Lew had heard of Ballarat in Victoria. The miners never stopped talking about it, about gold nuggets, the biggest the world had ever seen, some weighing two hundred pounds. It was hard to tell whether or not this was an exaggeration, but the riches of Ballarat were not exaggerated. 'And where do we find these fabulous reefs?' he asked.

'Do you know a place called Georgetown?'

'No,' Lew replied and Ying tut-tutted his ignorance.

'How can you expect to succeed, Lew, if you do not learn all you can?'

'Maybe I'm just not a studious type like you,' Lew replied, joking.

'Do not apologise. We have complementary talents,' Ying told him solemnly. 'Georgetown is the most northerly outpost of civilisation, a result of a gold rush a year or so back. It is several hundred miles north of Charters Towers. But hear me, Mr Mulligan and some bushman friends went north to explore and watch for gold. On their return they will have to come through Georgetown.'

Lew lit a cheroot. 'You forgot to say *if* they get back. And who says they'll find gold?'

'I say,' Ying replied imperiously. 'There are some things beyond our normal senses, of which you as a Chinese-bred man well know. I saw it. I read this in his eyes and I am preparing an expedition. At this very minute I have a man waiting in Georgetown. When Mr Mulligan returns, my servant will ride fast back to me in Charters Towers and we will act.'

'How?'

'My first expedition to the Cape was fraught with problems which I will not bother to relate. This time my expedition to Mr Mulligan's gold will be a paragon of exceptional organisation. And,' he was whispering again, even though they were speaking Chinese, 'we will be among the first. It's the first-comers who reap the harvest.'

That was true. The first miners on the Cape had done well; the followers, apart from the occasional stroke of luck, had to keep ploughing away.

'And when will this happen?' Lew asked.

'Be patient, my friend. You can potter around here until you hear from me. When the time comes, I will shut down all my claims here immediately and withdraw the coolies, and we will proceed with all haste.'

'Whatever you say. If I get sick of it here I'll ride up to Charters Towers. And thank you for paying Mr Fung.' Lew knew it would be bad form to offer to recompense his friend. The debt was paid. That was over.

He led Ying's horse up the track and greeted one of the Yuang brothers (he could never tell them apart), who was decked out like a Mongolian warrior in a wrap-around jacket, a sword and a rifle. Lew had noticed that Ying, too, had a shiny Colt lodged in a holster under his jacket, and he was relieved that they were aware of the dangers. In this tenacious struggle for every inch of ground, clashes were inevitable and the racial antagonism was heightened. The Chinese had to be constantly on guard.

'By the way,' Ying said as he leapt on to his horse with the new and astonishing vigour that had replaced his former languid demeanour. 'In Charters Towers one meets many estimable landlords and their cowhands from the great ranches.'

'I suppose you would.'

'Yes. And I hear that your young lady with the beautiful name is presently residing at the Caravale ranch of which she is—'

'I know all about that,' Lew interrupted. So they were still out there. Still playing out this farce of becoming squatters.

Ying's almond eyes narrowed at the rebuff. 'Ah so. Then you would also know that Miss Perfection is betrothed to the station Lord, Mr Ben Buchanan.'

Lew felt a rush of heat to his face. He managed to nod an affirmative and wave Ying off with apparent unconcern, but he was devastated. His first thought was to ride out to Caravale himself, but what would that achieve?

He'd only make a fool of himself, the discarded suitor still trying to claim the lady in the face of impossible odds. After all, Ben Buchanan held the trump card, he was 'dear' Darcy's brother, the next best thing. Had Perfy seen her first love again in the face of his brother?

Maybe he had misjudged Perfy's ambitions. He had been attracted to her in the first place because she was warm, unaffected, a girl with natural charm, and she had not misled him about Caravale. She had made no bones about her determination to see and probably hold her share of the cattle station, but he hadn't counted on her marrying her partner. This betrothal would make her richer still. Is that what the Middletons were all about? Cold, hard ambition?

Lew felt disappointed in Jack Middleton. But then Jack would be looking out for his daughter's interests and what chance would a seafarer like Lew Cavour have against the Buchanans?

Herbert had come up from the stream. 'What did the Chinkee want?' he asked.

'Nothing,' Lew said savagely. 'And if you call him the Chinkee again, I'll flatten you.'

3

Mrs Buchanan was so kind to her, Perfy wished there was something she could do in return, but Cornelia, as she had told Perfy to call her, had laughed at her. 'My dear, think nothing of it. You've had a bad time and it's our way out here to look out for one another. Country people, you'll find, are far more helpful and hospitable than city people. The main thing is that you're feeling better.'

And she was, at last. When she was able to get up, they'd taken her each day to sit on the verandah which was cooler than her room. Mae had brought her meals out there and Cornelia had seen to it that she had books to read. It had been a wonderful place to convalesce.

As her strength returned she walked around the verandah, able to see the stockmen coming and going, and hear all the activity of the busy station, which fascinated her. Cornelia often sat with her, explaining the various operations required for running a cattle property and pointing out, from the homestead vantage point, the direction of the boundaries.

Each evening when Ben came home they'd sit outside with her, enjoying pre-dinner drinks, and chat amiably about the day's events. They had dinner served on the verandah too, by candlelight which Perfy adored. She was impressed that Ben and Cornelia changed for dinner and wished her father could have lived to see this dignified and pleasant life style.

She took walks in the garden with Cornelia and sometimes sat out there under the trees, to rest. From there she could admire the big sandstone house with its red cedar shingles that had been designed by Darcy's father. But looking at the house, she realised that it would soon be time to leave. She couldn't inflict herself on Cornelia for ever. Darcy had been right in planning to build his own home. This house was definitely Cornelia's. But now . . . Perfy sighed. With her father gone, there was no future for her out here. She missed him so much. They had planned to make the decision about the station together; now she would have to do it on her own.

To make a start, Perfy tried to begin discussions with Cornelia. 'I suppose we ought to talk about the station, about what I should do.'

'Goodness me, girl, you're not well enough to be worrying about it yet. Besides, you've hardly seen an inch of the place. Would you like to come with me in my gig tomorrow? Have a look around?'

'I'd love to.'

Days went by, they took forays out along the river and as far as the boundary road, always accompanied by a stockman on horseback. Perfy was surprised by the emptiness of the land. She'd imagined there would be herds of cattle everywhere but the station was so big they seemed to be scattered to the winds.

Ben laughed when she told him this. 'You'll see them soon enough, we're mustering again now, before the wet.'

Perfy was beginning to enjoy herself. Diamond, who had disliked Caravale at first, had settled down, making the most of her country holiday, so that was one less worry. Cornelia took Perfy on the morning inspections to watch the lubras at work in the dairy and the buttery, checking to see that the salted meats had been turned in the brine, visiting the stables and the barns. Cornelia never missed a corner of this well-run establishment. After that they had morning tea, served in the finest bone china, with delicious cakes and scones. The outings still tired Perfy, but she wouldn't admit it, she wanted to see as much as she could before she left. But the issue of the ownership of the station still had to be faced.

It was Ben's birthday, 4 December. They dined inside at the long polished table, set formally for the occasion, and Cornelia served French champagne.

'We're not always as quiet as this. We usually invite quite a few of the neighbours to celebrate special events,' Cornelia explained, 'and they stay a few days. But since you are in mourning, Perfy, I don't think it would be appropriate, and Ben doesn't mind.'

'Oh, I'm so sorry,' Perfy said, wondering if this was possibly a gentle hint that it was time for her to move on.

'Don't worry about it,' Ben said. 'We're always busy at this time of the year anyway.'

'While you're both here then, we'd better see what we're going to do about the station,' she tried.

'What do you suggest?' Ben asked, smiling at her as if they were discussing sharing a box of chocolates.

'I think it would be best if I sell my share, really. I like Caravale but I would need my own home.'

'You're right there, my dear,' Cornelia said. 'No matter how well we get along, experience has shown me that a house cannot have two mistresses. I'm relieved you understand that. But to sell your share to someone else would make it difficult for us. The next buyer might not be as understanding as you are.'

'I realise that,' Perfy said, 'so I think we have only two choices. As I see it, I could sell to you, or we could split the property in half to make certain you keep your homestead, and I'll sell the other half.'

'Mother,' Ben said quietly. 'Perfy's right, I think it would be best if we buy her out.'

Cornelia was livid. They were in the study on the far side of the house with the doors tightly closed. 'Did you hear that stupid girl?' she hissed. 'Cut the station in half! I'll kill her first.'

'Settle down,' Ben said. 'I've put in our bid, we'll have to buy her out.'

'With what? We can't raise that much cash without a mortgage.'

'No mortgage,' Ben said flatly.

'Well, what are we going to do?' Cornelia's voice was shrill in a whispering hysteria. 'This has to be settled before she leaves here.'

'We could give her a deposit to shut her up and stall on the rest.'

'And how long do you think it would take Jauncy to wake up to that? He'd have that ass Tolley foreclose pretty smart and we'd have to borrow money. You have to talk to that girl, and now's the time. She's not as well as she thinks she is, it takes months to get over yellow fever.'

'What do I talk to her about, for Christ's sake?'

Cornelia stood at the window, her arms folded. 'You'll have to marry her.'

'Oh Christ, don't start that again.'

'Shut up! Don't raise your voice! That's the only answer. While she's here being petted and pampered, she thinks station life is heavenly. Marrying Darcy would have pushed her into society, that's what she's really after.'

Ben slumped into an armchair. 'I don't want to marry her.'

'You will marry her!' Cornelia fumed. 'Use your brains for once. She's all starry-eyed about living in the country, you'll never have a better chance. If she's good enough for Darcy, she's good enough for you.'

'You seem to forget, Mother, that it was Darcy who got us into this mess.'

Cornelia confronted him. 'No. I blame you. If you hadn't gone off socialising you'd have been able to keep an eye on your brother and see he didn't get into that tangle.'

She was surprised that Ben didn't argue. And pleased. She had him now, he would do as he was told. He didn't have any choice. At a later stage, if he baulked again, she'd explain to him that he wouldn't have to stay married to Perfy, he could always divorce her, but as her husband he would own her share and therefore all of Caravale once more.

'I'll pretend I'm not well tomorrow so you can take her out in the gig. Mae can pack a picnic lunch for you.'

'I haven't the time,' he complained.

'You'll make the time,' she insisted. 'Make the bloody time.'

Early the next morning Cornelia sent the gardeners down to clear the track to the falls for the gig and had Mae prepare an elaborate picnic basket of cold chicken and ham and warm bread rolls, cheese and potato puffs, corn scones, iced orange cake and a selection of fresh fruit. She also saw that some bottles of fine white wine were included.

'I had planned a luncheon surprise for you, my dear,' she told Perfy, 'but I'm feeling a bit off so I've asked Ben to stand in for me.'

'You shouldn't have,' Perfy said. 'I don't mind.'

'No, I'd arranged a picnic and you might as well still go. Ben works too hard, a day off will do him good. He can take you.'

'You're sure he won't mind?'

'Indeed, no. He adores picnics. We have lots of them when visitors come, and they all love to go down to the falls.'

'The falls?'

'Oh yes, Caravale isn't all dust and spinifex. The falls area is quite a scenic attraction.'

And it was. Perfy thought how lucky they were to have such a lovely cool spot on their own property with the beautiful sparkling waterfalls rushing down in three separate streams to the rock pool below.

'When the rains come they turn into one big waterfall,' Ben explained. 'It can be quite spectacular.'

'I think it's spectacular now,' Perfy said. She took off her shoes and stockings and sat on a rock to dangle her feet in the cold water. 'Look,' she called to Ben, 'there are fish jumping in the pool.'

He was excellent company, insisting on setting up the picnic himself, and before they ate he sat down on the rocks beside her with the wine and two glasses.

'It's delicious,' Perfy laughed. 'I feel quite decadent drinking wine out here with nature.'

'Then let's be decadent,' he told her. 'I'm glad Mother couldn't make it. This is my favourite place and I haven't been here for ages. Darcy and I used to swim here a lot when we were kids.'

Perfy was quiet, watching the fish dart in the deep clear water.

'I hope I didn't upset you mentioning Darcy,' Ben said.

'No, not really,' she replied. 'Especially not here. It's such a happy place with the noise of the falls and the birds and the cicadas singing, it's so alive.'

'Then I'm glad we came. You're too beautiful to be mourning. I'm sorry I didn't get to talk to you in Brisbane, Perfy, I really am, but I was entirely carried away by the excitement of being offered a seat in Parliament. I mean, it was a sensational thing to happen, so unexpected.'

'I suppose it would be,' Perfy said. She had heard him remark that she was beautiful but he'd kept on speaking as if that were a most natural comment to make. He really was very sweet. But then, being Darcy's brother, why wouldn't he be? 'When do you have to go to the Parliament?' she asked him.

'That dream didn't last long,' he said sadly. 'The idea was for Darcy to run the station so I could go into politics, but I can't leave Caravale now.'

'I'm so sorry,' Perfy said.

'Don't be. It wasn't real, it wasn't meant to be. And once I got back here I realised how much I love this place. I don't think I'd have been happy away from Caravale.'

That's how she was thinking of Darcy these days. As if he were not real. That it was never meant to be.

Ben seemed to read her thoughts. 'Some things are just not meant to be,' he continued. 'But I believe Darcy wanted you to come to Caravale just the same. Caravale is real. We're real.' Before she could think on that, he helped her up. 'Come, mademoiselle, your luncheon awaits.'

He had set out the picnic, the food covered by a muslin cloth, under a big willow tree. 'This is the best spot,' he said, 'but watch out for bull ants, they nip like bees.'

It was a lazy, delightful afternoon, and surely the best meal Perfy had enjoyed for ages. They both ate heartily and Ben retrieved the second bottle of wine from the creek where it had been cooling. They talked happily, drowsily, about Brisbane, about Caravale, and they laughed about the mad things they used to do when they were kids. Perfy was comfortable with him.

'I'm sorry about your dad,' he said eventually. 'I owe you these apologies. But I want you to know I did all I could.'

'I know,' Perfy said to comfort him because he was genuinely upset. 'I'm the one who should apologise. I was hysterical. Diamond explained it all to me when I calmed down.'

'Oh. I see,' he said quietly but he still seemed depressed. 'To be truthful,' he said, changing the subject, 'I'm dreading the day you leave here.'

'You are?' She felt deliciously floaty, with the wine and Ben's closeness.

He nodded. 'When you go, there's just me and Ma. She hates me to call her Ma. You can't know how wonderful it has been to come home at night to find you waiting there. You look so fresh and pretty, and you're always so cheerful. The nights I had to stay out on the range I missed you. I'm going to miss you when you leave.'

'It's kind of you to say so,' she murmured. She was flattered, and charmed by his candour. He was such an agreeable man, not argumentative, and not as demanding as Lew. She realised Ben had so much in common with her, apart from the station. And anyway, where was Lew? Mother had written that his junk had been destroyed and he'd left town.

'We might as well finish off this wine and make tracks,' Ben was saying.

He harnessed the horse back in the gig and she helped him repack the basket. Her hat had slipped down the bank while they were sitting under the tree. He went down to retrieve it and tied it under her chin. 'You look so lovely today,' he said, 'back to your old self.'

'Thanks. I was beginning to panic I'd have a yellow face for ever.'

'Never.'

The horse was frisky so he took her arm to help her on to the first steel step of the gig. 'Did you enjoy your day?'

'I loved it, Ben. It was just perfect.'

He grinned. 'So are you. Does it surprise you that the other Buchanan is in love with you too?'

She stopped as she was about to step up. 'Yes. I suppose it does.'

He shrugged. 'Oh well. I thought I might as well tell you even though I know I don't stand a chance. I love you, Perfy. And God, I'm going to miss you.'

Perfy looked up at him, at the smooth brown face and his soft sad eyes, and she felt a surge of emotion for him, a need for this man who really cared for her.

He secured the reins and looped an arm round her shoulders. 'You belong here,' he told her. 'At Caravale. With me.'

'I know,' she whispered, feeling so safe with him, and he kissed her with a passion she'd never experienced before. She knew he was bruising her lips, marking her neck, but she didn't care; his strong hands moved restlessly over her breasts, caressing her through her soft cotton dress in a quite shocking way, but she loved it. His hands slid down her back, pressing her into him as he kissed and kissed her. She had never wanted a man as much as this man, and it was an effort to push him away.

'We'd better go,' she said, straightening her dress.

'Yes,' he laughed, and gave her a final peck on the cheek.

As the gig skittered along the bush track he put an arm round her. 'Tell me you love me, Perfy.'

She nestled close to him. 'I think I do, Ben. And I'm sure Darcy would approve.'

At four o'clock in the afternoon a dull rumble of thunder came from the west and the blue of the distant sky paled into a whiteness tinged with grey. There were no discernible clouds, the colour simply drained from the sky and was replaced by a darkening wash of grey. The thunder rumbled again, closer this time, as the grey deepened to black and began to spread like ink. A crack of forked lightning split the dark sky with a brilliant flash and a deafening bang, and a beech tree up by the cemetery seemed to throw up its arms in shock before it crashed to the ground, dry leaves ablaze.

Horses screamed and reared in the home paddock as the thunder and lightning flashed and banged over the land, competing, in frightening intensity, in the game of terror. Diamond watched, enjoying the display, unaware that in this tinder-box land a dry storm, unassuaged by rain, could trigger savage bushfires, could send fireballs racing through the bush or even through houses.

When the storm abated, leaving a grey sultry sky, the housegirls came running up from the camp. 'Him plenty big bangs, huh?' Poppy called to her. 'Big corroboree soon,' she added gleefully. 'Rainman comen.'

Diamond knew these storms were the forerunners of the rainy season, but they could go on for months, tantalising with their promise of rain, holding back their bounty from the thirsty rivers and creeks. They talked about rain all the time on the station, for the winters out here were even drier than in Brisbane. Diamond had begun to wonder when they would be going home. She knew Perfy had written to her mother that she would be home well before Christmas, but if the rains came and were heavy, the rivers would be flooded. Impassable, she'd been told. Not that Diamond minded, she didn't care if Perfy never went home, she couldn't bear to leave Ben.

The Ilba people knew about Ben, knew that she and Ben were lovers. Diamond didn't have to ask how they knew, everything talked. When she went down to the camps they grinned, approving, silent teasing in their eyes. They loved secrets. While she was with them, Diamond was proud of their love, but around the homestead she was perpetually on edge. She didn't want to cause trouble for Ben. If his mother found out, there'd be an awful row and there was no knowing the outcome. Better to avoid thinking about it altogether.

They took her for granted around the homestead now and she was able to come and go in the kitchen as much as she liked as long as she kept out of Mrs Buchanan's way. The humpy where the house staff ate had finally become too much for her. Diamond had cleaned it up and with Mae's permission had installed makeshift plank benches and tables of upturned tea chests. She had persuaded Mae to give her netting which she draped on the sides to keep the flies out, and weighted to the ground with stones. At least it was habitable now.

The low clouds had made the night hot and steamy and when Ben slipped out to her room she was waiting for him on the step. 'It's too hot inside,' he said. 'Come with me.' He took a blanket and led her quietly into the orchard and they made love together under the stars. He stayed far later than usual, almost to dawn, and their love-making was so intense Diamond couldn't believe that life on this earth could be so wonderful, to have the man that she loved so dearly there with her, by his choice, night after night. But her dream was coming to an end.

'Is something troubling you, Ben?' she asked.

'No,' he mumbled and then he changed his mind. 'Yes, there is. I don't know how to tell you this, Diamond, but you'll have to leave here.'

It had to come, of course. When Perfy left, what excuse would she have to stay on? But she had to try. 'I don't want to go. There's no life for me away from you.'

'I thought you said you wanted to find your people, the Irukandjis.'

'That was before I met you,' she smiled. 'Couldn't you find me a job here? I don't mind what I do.'

'No, that's not possible.'

They were both silent for a while. Diamond saw the sheen of a small possum as he moved stealthily above them. 'When are we leaving?' she asked.

'Diamond, you don't understand. You just can't stay here any longer, you have to go. There's no future for us. We might as well break it off now.'

A hand of fright clutched at her. Now. He had said 'now'. Was this the end of their love? It couldn't be. Ben had never said he loved her, she admitted to herself, but he did, he must!

'You won't be coming here to me any more?' she asked, almost stuttering.

'Some of the men are going into Charters Towers in the morning. I want you to go with them and they'll put you on a coach for Townsville. Then you can go by ship to Bowen, back to Mrs Middleton. I'll pay your fares. Since they introduced the coaches, it's much easier for women to travel that way than overlanding to Bowen.'

'What are you talking about?' she flared. 'I don't care if it is easier. Why must I go? What about Miss Perfy?'

He sighed. 'She doesn't need you here, Diamond. You know that. Besides, Mother is taking her for a few days to visit Merri Creek Station. It's their annual race meeting.'

'And I can't go?'

'That's not possible, you'd have the same trouble there as here. There's no accommodation for . . .' he hesitated, '. . . maids.'

'You mean blacks?'

'All right, blacks! They wouldn't understand.'

'Are you going?'

'Yes, I always go.'

'Then go,' she said. 'I'll wait here. I work for Miss Perfy and when she tells me to leave, I'll leave.'

'You'll go tomorrow,' he said, standing over her as he tucked his shirt into his pants.

'No,' she said.

He stared down at her, shrugged, and walked off without another word. In her fantasies she had pictured the possibility of their parting, of their fond farewells, the bitter-sweet loving. Of Ben, at the last minute, refusing to allow their love to end. But never this cold rejection. Never.

The next morning, with her emotions in shreds, Diamond helped Perfy to pack for the visit to Merri Creek. She listened to her excited talk about the three-day festivities. 'They're having horse races, and a dance, and buck-jumping events, and they've even got a croquet lawn. People come from all around, it will be such fun. I'm so sorry you can't come with me, Diamond, but you know what these people are like. And you're all right here, aren't you?'

So. It wasn't Perfy's idea for her to leave. 'Yes,' she said. 'I'm quite all right.' She had seen four men ride out that morning with swags on their saddles, and she guessed they were to have been her escort, but she'd ignored them.

Ben would get over this, she told herself. A few days away would do him good. He'd miss her. When he came back he might have a change of heart and at least let her stay until Perfy left. But when that happened, she knew now, she would have to leave Caravale. Unless, and there was always hope, Ben missed her so much in the next few days he would need her to stay.

They were away four days, not three. Diamond swam every afternoon at the falls, she borrowed books from Mae, who was more affable now with Mrs Buchanan away, and she picked mangoes from the big old trees to take up to Mae who was making jam and pickles.

'We had the most wonderful time!' Perfy said. 'I've never had so much fun! The people were all so gay, laughing all the time and playing jokes on each other. There wasn't just one dance, there was a dance every night, and singing! We stayed up all one night and everyone had breakfast still in their formal clothes out in the garden, on the lawns.'

'I'm glad you enjoyed yourself,' Diamond said. And she meant it; Perfy had suffered enough, she deserved some fun at last. 'The break agreed with you,' Diamond told her. 'You look so well now.'

'Not surprising,' Perfy whispered. 'I've kept the best news until last. Ben and I are engaged. We announced our engagement on the Saturday night. That's why we stayed an extra night, they insisted on giving us a special luncheon party . . .'

Diamond wasn't listening. Perfy's excited description of the people and the place was just a buzz in her ears, growing louder and more excruciating by the minute, until she could stand it no longer. She grabbed some dresses for the laundry and fled.

There was no explanation from Ben. The other black women looked sorrowfully at her as they passed. For three days she stayed in her room as much as possible, too devastated to make any effort. Each afternoon, as if on cue, storms rolled out their exhibitions of light and sound but no rain came. There was so much tension in the air Diamond felt ready to snap.

Thinking she was ailing, Mae brought her down a jug of barley water. 'It's this damned weather,' she said. 'Everyone's out of sorts. The men are working against time now to get the calves branded and bring in market cattle, and we've had to send for more supplies just in case these storms aren't dummy runs.'

Jannali came to visit her and stood awkwardly in the doorway, sweat slipping down her lolling breasts. 'This night big corroboree,' she said. 'Plenty tucker and dancings. You like to come?'

'Thank you, Jannali, but I don't think so.'

The woman peered into the dim room. 'You bin cryin' longa time now. No good. Better you go 'way, Kagari. You hear?'

'Yes,' Diamond said dully.

'No good hang about,' Jannali insisted. 'Whitefeller, he don't marry gins.'

Diamond looked at her. 'But they make love to them.'

Jannali rapped impatiently on the door as if to command Diamond's attention. 'No love. Allatime grab gins. No use cryin'.'

At dusk the corroboree began and Diamond could hear the carrying thrum of the didgeridoos but she couldn't bring herself to go down and watch. She felt humiliated, desperately hurt, and furious, and her tears developed into a storm of rage until it was no longer possible for her to remain, cringing, in isolation.

She washed and dressed carefully, putting on her best blouse and skirt, shoes and stockings. She bound her hair up in a bright floral scarf and then made for the kitchen. Once inside, she halted at the long passage into the house. Whenever she'd been to Perfy's room, she'd gone along the outside verandah. Now she realised that she was just as intimidated as the rest of the blacks, unable to pluck up the nerve to go any further, uninvited. That made her even more angry.

As she stood there, determined not to retreat but unsure of her next move, Mrs Buchanan appeared in the hall. 'Who's there?' she called, looking down into the dimness of the deserted kitchen.

'It's me, Diamond.'

'What do you want?'

'I'd like to see Mr Ben.' Diamond seethed inside. Why should she call him *Mr* Ben? Her lover!

'He's not home. He's at the outstation. What do you want him for?'

'It doesn't matter.' She was about to turn away, cowed by this woman, when that very fact caused her to stop. 'Could I see Miss Perfy, please?'

'She's busy, you can see her in the morning.'

Busy? The lights were still on in the parlour and the front hall. Perfy would only be busy sewing, or reading or chatting to Mrs Buchanan, her prospective mother-in-law. 'I want to see her now,' Diamond said firmly.

'Go away!' Mrs Buchanan ordered and turned to go.

Diamond followed her. 'Don't speak to me like that. I wish to see Miss Perfy.'

'You'll see no one!' Mrs Buchanan flared. 'Now get out of my house.'

Perfy appeared at the parlour door. 'Is there anything wrong? Oh, it's you, Diamond. I thought you'd be at the corroboree.'

'I want to talk to you,' Diamond said.

'Dearie me,' Mrs Buchanan sighed. 'I'm sorry, Perfy. I told her to come back in the morning.'

'That's not necessary. What is it, Diamond?'

'Privately,' Diamond said stubbornly.

Perfy nodded, unconcerned as she followed Diamond out through the kitchen to the lamp-lit porch at the back. 'What's the matter? You sound upset.'

To her horror, Diamond burst into tears. Maybe it was just as well Ben wasn't home. She'd probably have cried with him too.

'Come on,' Perfy said. 'It can't be that bad. Are you getting tired of it out here? This weather can be depressing.'

'It's not that. I have to tell you something.' She stopped. Perfy looked so relaxed now, so happy. And innocent. Could she strike such a blow at the girl who had befriended her? She wished Jack Middleton were still alive. What would he have done? That question firmed her resolve. Jack Middleton would have hit the roof! He'd have given his daughter the truth, and confronted Ben Buchanan, just as she was trying to do.

'What's wrong, Diamond? You can tell me,' Perfy urged gently.

Diamond took a deep breath. 'I'm sorry, Miss Perfy, I really am. But Ben is my lover. He has been for a good while.' The last few words came out in a whisper.

Perfy stared at her. She went to speak but she seemed to be winded, her voice was a gasp. But then she took control of herself. 'Diamond, don't say things like that. It's a wicked lie, and it's very cruel of you.'

'It's not a lie. You can't marry him, you must not. He's been sleeping with me all this time.'

Perfy clapped her hands over her ears. 'I don't believe you! I don't know what's got into you since you've been out here, but I won't let you say things like that about Ben.'

Spots of rain started to fall in large splotches on the steps. Diamond studied them as she stood mutely before Perfy. What else was there to say now?

'You'll have to leave here, Diamond. Ben would be furious if he heard this.'

'Oh, I'm going. He's already told me to go. He wanted me out of here so that . . .' Before she could complete the sentence Mrs Buchanan burst outside in a fury. Obviously she'd been eavesdropping.

'I told you that gin was trouble, Perfy, but you wouldn't listen to me,' she cried. 'As for you,' she turned to Diamond, 'you get away from here with your filthy talk! Lubras are all the same, they get on heat and covet the white men, imagining all sorts of dirty things! Come inside, Perfy, this minute.'

'You're disgusting,' Diamond yelled at her, feeling better now that she had someone to vent her anger on. 'Perfy's too good for this family and the sooner she wakes up to the fact the better. She's been living in a Dreamtime here, not me.'

Perfy, white-faced and shocked, was being pushed inside by Mrs Buchanan, but Diamond took her arm. 'No, maybe I have been too. I'm sorry.'

She went down the steps feeling the cleansing rain thudding around her and by the time she got to the creamery it was pouring down, lovely dark comforting rain, hiding her from the misery outside.

In the morning, Perfy was at her door, her hair streaming, her clothes drenched.

'Come in out of the rain,' Diamond said, but Perfy refused.

'No, thank you. I just want to ask you one question. And don't lie to me. I beg you not to lie to me, Diamond. Is it true?'

'Yes.'

Perfy nodded. 'Yes, I thought it would have to be. Well, I'm leaving here today. You can come or stay, please yourself. I don't want to see him again, and I'll never forgive either of you.'

'Why me? Don't you think I have feelings too?'

'I'm not interested in your feelings. If you'd given me some hint of what was going on I wouldn't be in this awful situation.'

'Really?' Diamond said acidly. 'And what if I had told you? You wouldn't have approved.'

'No, of course not, but I could have told you he'd ditch you anyway!' Her words stung but Diamond did not flinch.

'Do you want me to help you pack?' she asked Perfy wearily.

'No, thank you, I'll do it myself. I'm going up to tell Mrs Buchanan we're leaving. What do you want to do?'

'I'll come with you. We can go to Charters Towers and out to the coast from there.'

'I know that,' Perfy said angrily. 'We'll go to Charters Towers but after that you're on your own. You can please yourself where you go.'

Diamond shrugged. Perfy's reaction was not unexpected. Their mutual anger with Ben Buchanan was no basis for overcoming the rift between them. Besides, she still loved Ben. She wondered if Perfy did too.

Cornelia sat in her room at the writing desk, tapping her fingers, deep in thought. Thank God Ben was working with Tom in the western range. With any luck, she'd have this problem sorted out before he came home.

That black bitch! A hoity-toity wretch, it wouldn't have been hard for her to seduce a healthy man like Ben. Perfy just didn't understand these things, so they'd have to deny it all the way. It was only the gin's word against Ben's. Cornelia blamed herself for not spotting their affair. He must have been very careful this time. She wondered if Diamond was pregnant. But no, she couldn't be or that would have taken priority in her bleatings.

Cornelia stared out at the rain. It might be just a summer storm, but welcome. They needed the water, the bores were running dry and Ben had been forced to move cattle so that they had access to the few creeks and billabongs that were still holding. Sometimes, though, these early rains petered out and the big wet of February and March never came about. That spelled trouble. She forced herself back to her more immediate problems. First she had to get rid of the trouble-making gin. She'd have the men take her quietly out to the boundary road and send her on her way. It wouldn't be the first time they'd had to ban renegade blacks.

There was a knock at her door and Cornelia wheeled round. What now? It was only five o'clock in the morning. 'Come in,' she called.

Perfy stood there, looking like a drowned rat.

'My dear,' Cornelia cried. 'What have you been doing? Look at you, you're soaked to the skin.' She jumped up and handed Perfy a large towel. 'For heaven's sake, dry yourself. Just as well it's hot,' she said felicitously, 'or you'd have caught your death of cold.'

Perfy took the towel and draped it over her shoulders. 'Cornelia, I've come to thank you for your hospitality, and for looking after me, but I wish to leave Caravale today. I'm glad I didn't wake you, I'd like to get an early start.'

'For heaven's sake, my dear. You can't just go off like that. We'll have breakfast together and sort this out.'

'No. I've made up my mind. I'll be leaving as soon as possible. I'd appreciate it if you'd arrange for me to be escorted into Charters Towers.'

'But Perfy, what about all your clothes?'

'My trunk came out ahead of me by bullock train, you can send it back to Bowen the same way.'

Cornelia smiled. 'Perfy, dear, I didn't mean that. I meant that one doesn't just ride out like that. One has to prepare for the road. But, goodness, surely you aren't leaving because of what your maid had to say?'

'As a matter of fact, I am,' Perfy said. 'Right away.'

Cornelia took her arm and sat her in a chair, aware that the girl's damp clothes would ruin the brocade. 'Now listen to me. You don't understand the blacks. They're very strange people. They're always getting crushes on white men.' She laughed. 'Surely you don't believe Diamond's ramblings?'

'Yes, I do. And I'm terribly sorry, Cornelia, that you are being burdened with this but I daresay you've had to face worse problems over the years.'

She was so determined, so matter of fact, that Cornelia was surprised. She'd thought of Perfy as a namby-pamby, rather hysterical type since they brought her into Caravale, but now she was seeing the girl's mettle. They'd done too good a job of curing her of the fever; a few draughts of the poppy ash might have kept her quieter. At one stage, Cornelia had in fact considered that, but had decided it wasn't necessary. What a fool she'd been, underestimating this girl. And what a bloody fool Ben was! She'd give him hell when she got her hands on him.

'I can't see any problem,' she said. 'The least you can do is wait until Ben comes home and give him a chance to speak for himself.'

'I'd rather not.'

'Don't you think you're being unfair? I'm his mother. I know my sons. Neither Ben nor Darcy have ever gone near the gins.'

'Except for Diamond,' Perfy said flatly. 'She's different. I can understand that he found her attractive.'

'Rubbish! She's not attractive, they're a different breed.'

They argued on but Perfy was so determined that Cornelia appeared to give way. 'Very well. I'll see what I can do. But you must remember, Perfy, I'm not the boss here. Ben is. The men have work to do. And these fellows are rough. I can't send you off with just anyone.'

'I want to go today.'

'Your mother would never forgive me if I sent you out into the bush without proper gentlemen to look after you. God knows what would happen to you, I fear to think about it. Now you just rest today, and I'll see what I can do.'

The morning stretched into an afternoon of patchy steamy weather. Diamond received no word from Perfy, so she went up to see her.

'Mrs Buchanan is arranging for us to go to Charters Towers,' Perfy told her.

'When?'

'As soon as she can,' Perfy said stiffly.

'Miss Perfy, I don't want to upset you any more, but I don't think she'll let you go. It's me she wants to get rid of.'

'You can't blame her for that! But I can leave any time I like.'

Diamond stood, silently, miserably, not wanting to argue but certain she was right. And Perfy, who had been sitting in a cane chair trying to read, or rather pretending to read, finally put her book down. 'All right,' she said. 'I'll go and find out.' Cornelia hadn't appeared for lunch and Mae had simply said Mrs B. was having a rest day. Her inactivity had worried Perfy, but since Mrs Buchanan often issued instructions through Mae, it was possible she had made some effort.

'Are you there, Mrs Buchanan?'

'Yes, dear, come in.'

'I hope I'm not disturbing you but I was wondering . . .'

Cornelia was propped up on her bed in a pink cotton dressing-gown, leaning against a mound of pillows, with a damp flannel over her eyes. 'I know, you're still wondering about going to Charters Towers,' she breathed without removing the flannel. 'But really. All this fuss about nothing. I'll be up soon and we'll have tea. I've told Mae we need something light today, and then we'll play German whist. That will cheer us up.'

'You don't seem to understand. I would like to leave Caravale.'

Cornelia sighed. 'That's now. In a few days you'll have forgotten about that girl's sordid lies. Run along, dear. I can't let you do something you may regret for the rest of your life.'

Despite Cornelia's solicitous tone, Perfy heard a hard edge to her reply, the voice of the mistress of Caravale who was accustomed to obedience, and it annoyed her.

When she returned to her room, Diamond had gone. Perfy was relieved, she was in no mood to explain things to Diamond, so she went looking for Mae.

'How far is it from here to Charters Towers?' she asked.

Mae looked up in surprise. 'Charters? Oh now, let me see. The men do it in a couple of days. Are you thinking of going shopping? They say it's quite a busy town now.'

'Yes.'

'Oh well, if you ladies are going, it's easier to make for the Twin Hills homestead, then ride on to Ironbark Station and the next day, well, it's only about twenty miles further. Mrs B. hasn't been up that way for ages. I'm glad to see her getting out and about again now. She's hardly moved from Caravale since Darcy passed on.' Mae stopped abruptly. 'I'm sorry, I didn't mean to remind you . . .'

'That's all right, Mae. Don't mention Charters Towers to Mrs Buchanan yet, I'll see how she feels about it first.'

'Righto. She'd probably want to go in the wagon anyway, that's much slower.'

Perfy felt trapped. She went back to her room, desperately trying to figure out how to get away from Caravale. She had no doubt now that any instructions she gave to the stablehands or the stockmen would be countermanded by Mrs Buchanan, and she couldn't leave without their help. The thought of having the same argument with Ben appalled her as much as having to accept him as an escort if he did agree to take her to Charters Towers. She hated him. And she wished she could stop thinking about him, thinking of how everyone had admired him at Merri Creek Station, his confidence, his excellent manners. 'A gentleman, like his father,' one woman had said.

A sob rose and fell within her like a small wave, but she would not cry. Compared to the finality of the deaths of the two men she had truly loved, this was no crying matter. She was desperately hurt and there was a temptation to wonder why misfortune had sought her out but she pushed this aside as self-pity.

And Lew Cavour. Contrarily, she was angry with him too. What had he done to meet her halfway? Nothing. He disliked socialising, he only owned one decent shirt and he couldn't dance a step. He was so intense, refusing even to discuss her suggestions, her ideas about Caravale. At least Ben had been more fun. She'd tell Lew that.

On second thoughts, maybe not. A fleeting vision of Ben with Diamond caused her to blush. Mother had not heard from Lew since he left Bowen, so maybe he wouldn't know about the engagement. He need never know. God, how she hated Ben Buchanan! She'd never forgive him, and she'd make him sorry he'd humiliated her like this. Contemplating revenge, Perfy found, was comforting.

She stood up and brushed her hair, tying it back with a ribbon. 'They think you're a fool,' she said to the mirror.

Mae knocked on her door. 'Tea's ready. Will you be joining Mrs Buchanan?'

'Yes, Mae,' she replied. 'I won't be long.' She couldn't hide in her room. And whether she liked it or not, Cornelia would have to face the fact that the engagement was off.

Jannali had come looking for Diamond. 'Quick, you come longa me. You hide.'

'Why?'

'Whitefellers looking for you bad.'

They stole down through the orchard and Diamond saw two horses tethered near the creamery. 'I don't understand.'

'Two fellers inside. Sit down. Grab you, girl. Missus tell them fellers take you big walkabout, you troublemaker.'

Diamond stared. 'Are they inside? In my room? What are they doing in there?'

'They got ropes, waitin' for you.'

'This is stupid,' Diamond said. 'Even if they did catch me, what could they do? Take me to the boundary road? I'd walk back, and then they'd be in trouble.'

Jannali's eyes grew wide. 'No! Them fellers take you into the bush, hold you down, they give you plenty pokes first, you bet. You fight? You get a good beltin'.'

Diamond shivered. 'They wouldn't dare!'

But Jannali shrugged. 'Missus doan care. She tell them fellers get rid of rubbish nigger. Jumbo hear them laughin'.'

'But Mr Ben,' Diamond insisted. 'If they touch me he'd be furious.' As she spoke she saw Jannali shaking her head, and she realised what she was saying. No matter how Ben reacted at this point, it wasn't relevant. The danger was real, and imminent. 'I'll go up to the house,' she decided. 'To Miss Perfy.'

'More better you hide,' Jannali told her. 'Missus say you liar, and then fellers grab you.'

'But I can't hide for ever.'

'You wait for sun-up. Mine brother Pitaja, he take you far off, safe.'

Diamond was confused. She had met Pitaja, he was a big surly fellow, a tribal man who despised the whites and refused to be enlisted as a station hand. He had two wives and several children and lived at the camp under sufferance, his own. She had heard Mae talking about him, a borderline case, not entirely trusted to 'behave'. Although she didn't dare say so, Diamond was a little afraid of him. He seemed to regard her as some sort of traitor.

'Pitaja good feller,' Jannali said. 'He say he mind you plenty good from white bastards. If you want he take you to the big whitefeller camp.'

'Where? Charters Towers?'

'That place. Pitaja best guide,' Jannali said proudly.

For the minute Diamond let that suggestion go. 'Can I hide at your camp?' she asked but Jannali told her that was not possible.

'Missus punish allasame Ilba people something cruel. Whitefellers look for you there first go, bring guns, frighten people. You comen alonga me.'

Dusk was settling in a steamy lavender haze as the two women moved steadily up the hill to the graveyard. Diamond remembered that one of the beech trees had been struck by lightning. She had meant to go up and see the result, but had forgotten about it. Now the huge trunk and the shattered branches provided her with a refuge, a small camouflaged shelter. Jannali crept in beside her, crunching among the burned crumbling timbers. 'You stay now?'

'Yes,' Diamond said. She kissed Jannali. 'You're so kind to me, thank you.'

'You good girl,' Jannali said. 'Clebber girl.' She gave a deep sigh, grasping for the words. 'All black people cryin' these times. Doan forget your people.'

Diamond put her arms round the gentle woman and wept.

The moon was struggling up from a bank of bloated clouds, causing the nearby tombstones to stand out in relief against their shadowy surrounds, their shapes distorted, and Diamond tried not to look in that direction. They seemed larger now, and threatening. Chills of fear crept over her, forcing her to keep changing position in case someone, some thing, pounced on her from behind. She reminded herself she was hungry, to take her mind off this silent place, wishing Jannali had stayed with her, and stared down the hill towards the homestead, wondering if those men were searching for her.

Overhead, an owl hooted, and she jumped at the sudden noise, her heart beating so fast she could hardly breathe. Determined not to let anything else rattle her, she settled back, her head on the soft trunk and tried to sleep, but she kept opening her eyes to check that she was still safe. What if those men came looking for her up here? She should stay on guard.

In front of her the white picket fence had a mesmerising effect, giving the illusion of movement, like running stick figures, and she thought she could hear those voices again. Afraid, and against her will, she found she was listening for them, to make sure, and then they were there again, muttering and mumbling, a volley of voices that seemed to be talking among themselves, complaining and calling names. She heard a man's voice. 'Clem,' it said. And again, louder this time. 'Clem.'

Diamond didn't know what it meant, but the voice was so close to her she could feel breath on her cheek. 'Clem,' he said again. And then he screamed. 'Clem!' It was so loud she leapt up, terrified. Whatever happened down at the homestead, it couldn't be as bad as this. She had no right to be with these spirits, they were sending her away. Softly, fearfully, she edged out from among the spread branches and made her way along the fence.

A white figure seemed to leap out at her and she almost screamed in fright but she saw it was only a bush of white flowers, the big white angels' trumpets, hanging bell-like from their greenery. She stopped and stared at them, realising the voices had stopped too. Everything was quiet, as if waiting expectantly for her next move . . .

Diamond contemplated that bush, those brazen white flowers, and she thought of Mrs Buchanan, who had hated her from the start, who was determined to keep Perfy there; and who had set those men on her. She was an evil woman, and standing here now Diamond felt the spirits were in accord. She pushed aside the flowers and broke off some leaves, long flat leaves, like green and shiny knives, that lurked behind the false sweetness of their splendid blooms.

Searching around the rocky ground she found some flat stones and ground the leaves into a fine mulch, hardly a teaspoonful, but that was plenty. She transferred it into a corner of her scarf, knotting it in place.

Lamps were still burning in the front of the house as Diamond glided through the garden and slipped round to the kitchen. Mrs Buchanan's night tray was in its usual place. Mae had set out her cocoa in the large china mug with the milk and sugar already stirred into it. All the mistress had to do was take the mug to the stove and fill it with hot water from the large black kettle kept warm over the dying fire. Diamond took several pinches of the sap mulch and stirred them into the cocoa, wiping the spoon clean on her scarf. Moving soundlessly in the darkness, she washed her hands in water from the iron slop bucket and dried them on her skirt, shoving the contaminated scarf deep into a skirt pocket. Then she went to the verandah outside Perfy's room and settled down against the wall behind a large cushioned settee.

Perfy was still awake; Diamond could hear her moving restlessly. The lamplight made a pretty pattern through the lace curtains, filtering on to the polished verandah floor. As she studied the delicate tracery, Diamond drew her knees up under her chin and dozed.

* * *

Cornelia was dreaming. She could see a beautiful castle in the distance, it was silver, gleaming in the sun, with tall spires of gold, each flying brilliant pennants, all colours of the rainbow, and she hurried towards it. From the towers, voices called to her, glorious voices, singing in sweet harmony, and as she ran the drawbridge was lowered, beckoning to her. But the faster she ran, the further away the castle seemed to be and the spires began to stretch and heighten as if they were made of rubber and some cruel hand was pulling them oafishly out of shape. Suddenly she'd made it; she ran across the drawbridge, that endless drawbridge, her feet burning on white-hot iron, but she didn't care, she had to reach the castle. Too late she realised that the gateway was a huge slathering mouth, foul-smelling, gawping, with teeth like shark's teeth closing on her. She screamed, but there was no sound as she ran past, her body wracked with pain, calling to those people to help her. They came towards her, hands outstretched, and she threw herself forward. A man grabbed her, his hands like claws, and she saw it was Clem Bunn.

'Get away from me!' she screamed, terrified by this apparition and ran to another, but it was Clem again, and another, always Clem, or people in masks, pretending to be Clem. She had to find him and kill him. He was doing this to her. If she could kill him, the others would go away, the copy-cats. They were all grabbing her with their cats' claws, scraping and scratching at her face, tearing her hair, raking her flimsy clothes to shreds, their eyeless faces yellow with slime. Cornelia ran from room to room, searching for Clem, down long halls, searching for her rifle, but the castle was as dark as a tomb, the walls seeping blackness. Slivers of light tantalised from under closed doors and she made for them, shouting and hammering for him to come out. 'You fiend!' she screamed. 'I know you're in there. I won't let you take away my castle!' It was Clem who had done this, he'd hidden the beautiful silver castle. If she could get rid of him she'd find it again . . .

Perfy's clothes were packed. She sat on the edge of the bed idly turning over the pages of old newspapers. It had been useless trying to talk to Cornelia about leaving, she had simply refused to discuss the subject.

'We'll all go to Bowen at Christmas. Won't your mother be pleased? Most station people go to the coast during the summer, it's too wet to do much out here. So we can have the wedding there. Your mother must be missing you, dear. It's only a few weeks away now. It's all very exciting. What are the shops like in Bowen now?'

The woman was impossible. Perfy supposed it was understandable that she wouldn't believe such a thing of her son. About Diamond. Perfy didn't like to dwell on that. And no doubt Ben would deny it too. It would be awful arguing with both of them, and damned embarrassing. Where was Diamond anyway? Cornelia had predicted that she would run off rather than face Ben with her lies, and that worried Perfy. Mae had said she wasn't in her room, and the housekeeper had seemed very nervous. What had she heard? Had Cornelia told her about Diamond's charges? What if Diamond had lied? Surely not. But doubt was budding.

Noise burst on the quiet household like a stampede. Someone was yelling, shouting, banging on walls, screaming abuse. Perfy sat taut, scared. She wanted to open the door and look out but she was too frightened. The noise was deafening, echoing in the house. She glanced at the open french windows as an escape route, thinking one of the blacks had gone berserk and had broken into the homestead. She could hear glass smashing . . . The curtains parted and Diamond stepped into the room.

'Oh my God!' Perfy said. 'You gave me the fright of my life. What's happening?'

'Shush!' Diamond said, pushing her out of the way. 'Be quiet.' But before Diamond could reply the door burst open and Cornelia was there! Cornelia! In a flannel nightie that was ripped to shreds, her hair, that neat, faded red hair, was hanging wildly around her head like a scarecrow's and her face looked weirdly misshapen. 'Where is he?' she shouted in her madness.

'He's not here,' Diamond said quietly.

Cornelia tried to push past but the tall black girl held her back. 'He's not here,' she said. 'Go away.'

'Yes he is, you liar!' Cornelia fought Diamond to get past her. She pointed at Perfy who was cowering on the other side of the bed. 'That's him! That's Clem. Kill him! We have to kill him. Quick!' She went to dodge round Diamond, punching the lamp from the dressing table. As it fell, the flame hit the dry lace. Perfy jumped across the bed, plunging a pillow across the curtains to prevent a fire, and Diamond fought to push Cornelia out of the room.

Diamond called to Perfy, 'Get out.'

'Get your hands off me!' Cornelia shrieked. 'You're not Clem.' She saw Perfy run out to the verandah. 'Get the bastard. I have to stop him!'

In her mania she had a grip on Diamond's hair, and she clenched and shook her head so violently Diamond was sure her hair would come away by the fistful. With her other hand Cornelia was clawing at Diamond's face, drawing blood. 'It's a mask!' she screamed. 'A filthy black mask!' Diamond hurled herself at Cornelia, dislodging the clutching hands with such force that Cornelia fell back into the passageway and crashed to the floor, Diamond stumbling after her.

The shock seemed to change Cornelia's mood. She clutched at Diamond. 'He's my husband,' she whimpered, hands pleading now. 'We have to find him. Don't you see?' she cried, the voice rising to hysteria again. 'It's Clem.'

'I know,' Diamond said. 'It's Clem. Your husband.'

'Will you help me find him?' Cornelia whispered. 'They mustn't know.' She was giggling insanely. 'They mustn't know.'

Diamond thought she could smell the tree again, up there by the grave-yard, the smoky residue of that lightning strike, but smoke curled around her as she broke loose from Cornelia. The hall at the front of the house, where she had never been permitted to enter, was a blaze of light, a shower of spitting, sparkling orange.

Mae rushed past her, then Paddy the foreman and other men, and soon there were yells that the homestead was on fire right through from the main bedroom to the hall, to the parlour and down to this wing. In her rampage Cornelia had smashed lamps and left them to burn. They lifted her up, ignoring her screams of abuse, and carried her outside. The blacks came racing from the camps to help the station people fight the blaze. They ran a bucket brigade from the tanks and Diamond heard a man say: 'Why doesn't it bloody well rain now when we need it?'

The moon rode high, blessing the clouds with haloes as Caravale home-stead burned, a huge bonfire that could be seen for miles around.

Diamond felt nothing. She just stood and stared as the flames roared. Timbers splintered and crashed, and men leapt to safety to escape the burning, tumbling rafters. Wet sacks were hauled forward and the fire-fighters worked to contain the blaze. They couldn't save the house but the precious outbuildings had to be protected, fortunately not a difficult task since the night was clammy and still, there was no wind to carry sparks and fan them into new fires.

Piccaninnies danced excitedly around, dashing about trying to help, throwing handfuls of sand at the burning perimeters. Diamond gathered the children and ushered them out of harm's way, cautioning them to stay clear. She was amazed at how fast the fire had devoured the house and as the smoke began to rise from the hissing embers she realised Pitaja was standing beside her. He looked down at her, his black bearded face copper-red from the glow of the ruins. 'Now you go home,' he said.

Diamond shrugged with the same answer she gave herself, 'I don't know where home is.'

'You know.' He tapped his head. 'In here, you know.'

'Will you take me to town?' she asked him but he shook his head and pointed at Perfy who was standing dejectedly with Mae.

'No need. She take you now. The white miss.'

4

Perfy boarded the coach in Charters Towers, bound for Townsville in the company of four other passengers, and as she did so her depression eased. She was looking forward to this journey, quite an adventure to be travelling alone, and such a relief to be alone, free from questions and the consideration and curiosity of acquaintances. Riders from Twin Hills Station, alerted by the glow of the fire in the distance, had come galloping over to assist in the emergency but they were too late. They strode around in their high-heeled boots, guns slung low on their hips because they'd feared that Caravale had been attacked by bushrangers or blacks, but all they could do was to commiserate with Paddy and wait for Ben and Tom Mansfield to arrive.

When the two men rode in, all eyes were on Ben. He remained on his horse, staring at the ruins in disbelief, too stunned to talk. He circled the remains of his home in tight-lipped silence before reining in beside Paddy.

'What happened?' he demanded.

'The lamps, boss. Caught fire,' Paddy replied evasively.

'Where's my mother?' He peered over the despondent crowd.

Equally evasive, Mae spoke up. 'She's resting, Mr Ben, in the cookhouse.'

He nodded and looked over to Perfy. 'You all right?'

'Yes, thanks, no one was hurt.'

Arrangements were made for Perfy and Diamond to be taken to Twin Hills Station. 'You go,' Mae said to her. 'I'll stay and look after Mrs B. I gave her a dose of laudanum that'll keep her quiet.'

'But Mae, what on earth got into her?' Perfy asked.

'I don't know. Some sort of a turn.' She glanced around to make sure no one was listening. 'Looked suspiciously like the DTs to me. She's inclined to give the gin a real belt at times. She'll be all right, so don't be worrying. I'll explain to Mr Ben when I can get him on the quiet. But Miss Middleton, I'm sorry about your clothes. All your lovely things burned . . .'

'That's nothing compared to this catastrophe,' Perfy replied.

'No, I suppose not. They'll fit you out at Twin Hills. The Chesters are a big family, they've got a couple of daughters your age.'

'The Chesters? Is that where they live? I met them at the Merri Creek house party.'

'That's good,' Mae said, but Perfy wasn't so sure. They'd be talking about her engagement to Ben.

When their horses were saddled and Ben came to see them off, he took Perfy aside. 'Are you sure you don't want to take the buggy?'

'No, I'd rather ride.'

'Well, just stay at Twin Hills until I get this sorted out and I'll come over.'

'I won't be staying there,' she said. 'I'm going on home.'

'Yes, you might as well, but I'll come with you. I'll have to rebuild the house as soon as possible so I'll need to go into Bowen to order building material and line up some builders.'

Perfy knew it wasn't the best time to be breaking this news to him but it couldn't be helped. 'Ben, I've decided the marriage would be a mistake. I can't marry you. We're not engaged any more.'

He took her hands. 'Don't be silly. Don't let this rattle you. I'll rebuild in no time. You're just upset.'

'No, I'm not,' she said firmly. 'I made up my mind days ago. I just don't want to get married.'

'But why? This is ridiculous.'

He was entitled to an answer but she couldn't bring herself to give the reason.

'Ask your mother,' she said and turned to go, but he stopped her.

'What about my mother? What has she said?'

'Oh nothing.' Perfy twisted uncomfortably. 'Just talk to her. She'll explain it. I can't.' She pulled away from him. 'Now let me go.'

A group had gathered so he could hardly hold her back. He had no choice but to assist her on to her horse. 'I'll see you in Bowen then. We'll talk it out there.'

'I don't think so,' Perfy replied. 'Goodbye, Ben. I'm dreadfully sorry about the house.'

And she was. He deserved some sympathy. He'd lost his house and his bride. She gritted her teeth. He'd also lost his mistress!

The other passengers on the coach were Gus and Mary Hallam and their teenage sons, station people from way out on the Gilbert River, en route to Sydney for the summer, taking their first coach ride.

'My first too,' Perfy told them, pleased to be in the company of complete strangers. As the coach trundled out of the town and down the hill, gathering speed on the flat, she felt a cold sense of detachment listening to the horses galloping along, taking her away from all the worries that had beset her lately. They had been escorted on from one station to the next and then into Charters Towers by friends of the Buchanans who were immensely kind. Once in the town, she had parted with Diamond.

'Here's twenty pounds,' she said. 'That will tide you over until you get a job.'

Diamond had thanked her and turned away without another word. Heads turned as she walked down the street, and Perfy felt a twinge of envy. She knew it wasn't just that Diamond was a neatly dressed black girl, an unusual sight in the west. Diamond's movements were fluid, she walked with the lithe strength of a cat, and she was just as self-assured. Despite her colour, despite her modest clothes, she gave the impression of being someone of importance, a quality that Perfy had admired. Until now.

Perfy wondered where she would go, what she would do, but then she angrily dismissed those thoughts. Diamond and Ben, and their sordid affair, it was disgusting. And that crazy woman, Mrs Buchanan! Perfy was convinced now that Cornelia was mad. And the men thought so too. As they were grappling with Cornelia, dragging her out of the house, she'd heard one of them remark: 'She's as mad as a cut snake.' Whatever that meant, Perfy considered it sounded apt. They were all mad. She didn't want to see any of them again.

Perfy rested her head on the hard padded leather and closed her eyes. She was going home. She was finished with Caravale. She would sell her equity in the station, but not to the Buchanans, to anyone but them. They'd never get their hands on the rest of their station now. It was appalling to think that Ben might have been marrying her just to unite the station, but it was a possibility, an awful degrading possibility that loomed as a final insult. Not that it mattered any more, she had escaped from them and she'd try not to think about them.

The coach rattled and bumped along the road, traces jingling, whips cracking over the heavy crunch of iron-clad wheels. The steady rhythm of the horses' hooves aroused a sense of deliverance, as if they were transporting her away from the confusion of the last few months, to scatter the ashes of the past.

The passengers had been advised that when they reached the big river, they would have to be ferried across to another coach, on the other side, which would whisk them on their way to Townsville. Then Perfy could board a ship, on her own, and sail to Bowen. It would be exciting. She needed excitement, things to do, activity. That was why Caravale had appealed to her. Caravale. The last resting place of her dear father. She swallowed, fighting back tears again.

She had to look ahead now. At least her father died knowing his wife and daughter were well-placed financially. To them, Perfy was wealthy, but she knew, having seen the female guests at Government House with their magnificent gowns and jewellery, that even with the sale of her equity in Caravale, she would simply have a sizeable bank balance. Not wealth in their terms.

And what then? Marry and retreat to a life of suburban gentility in Bowen, with a band concert a big occasion? She wondered idly what it would be like to be really rich, with country homes and seaside homes. To be able to entertain with balls and parties and grand outings. To meet all sorts of exciting, interesting people.

Despite the bumpy ride, Perfy dozed.

Twenty pounds. Diamond sighed. Mrs Beckman had left her ten pounds, with love. Perfy had given her twenty pounds as a duty, and with contempt. Now she was truly alone in the world. Alone in the busiest town she had ever seen. She had heard people say that more than two thousand new arrivals had swarmed into Charters Towers in the last two months. She could well believe it, the few streets were jammed with traffic. There had been more gold strikes all around this centre, with the result that the morning resembled a Saturday night in Brisbane. But basically it was just another country town with a wide main street, several stores, and a large number of pubs. The latter was a good sign. She should be able to find a job in one of them.

She was wrong. She knocked on the kitchen doors of several hotels before it was plain to her that none of them would give a black girl a job, so she changed her plan and began to search for a room. Each place she approached was packed, as she dismally expected, but twice she was told they wouldn't take a nigger anyway. At midday, standing uncertainly in the street, she saw a sign advertising 'Pie & Tea or Coffee, 1/6', so she marched into the little cafe.

The woman behind the counter stared at her. 'What do you want?'

'A pie and a cup of tea, please.'

'You got any money?'

'Of course I have.'

The woman hesitated. 'Well, all right then, but you don't eat in here. Go round the back.'

Diamond nodded dully and made her way to the back of the shop where she sat among a pile of packing cases to eat her lunch. The yard backed on to the rear of a store and she saw two men unloading produce from a wagon. She walked down to them. 'Excuse me, could you tell me where I might find accommodation?'

A grey-haired man in a sweaty flannel shirt laughed. 'There's a boongs' camp down by the river, Mary.'

Diamond glared at him. 'Don't you understand English? I said I'm looking for accommodation.'

He hooked a bag of flour on to his shoulder and stood up, winking at his partner. 'Ah! Is that what you was sayin'? Well now, let me see . . .'

'A boarding house,' Diamond prompted.

'Why don't you try the Chink's place in Turpin Lane?'

'Is that a boarding house?'

'In a manner of speaking.'

'Thank you,' she said, 'I will. Which way is it?'

'Turn left at the next corner, and left again,' he said pointing further down the main street.

She found it easily enough, a two-storeyed building with the front verandahs completely enclosed by coloured glass windows, causing the customer to seek entry down the lane. A large plump woman was sweeping the carpeted lobby, raising more dust than she was removing.

'Can I get a room here?' Diamond asked.

The woman sent another cloud of dust towards the entrance. 'Ask the boss.'

'Where do I find him?'

'First door past the parlour. And mind your manners. Knock first.'

'Enter,' a voice called when she knocked. She opened the door to find herself confronted by a tall, ornate Chinese screen. Disconcerted, she peered round a panel to see someone sitting at a long desk silhouetted in the glare of an open barred window. She blinked at the bright light.

'Come in,' the gentleman said and Diamond advanced nervously, feeling the soft carpet under her feet.

'I was looking for a room.'

'Ah yes, a room,' he replied vaguely. He seemed to be studying her. The desk had two unlit brass lanterns at each end, with dark blue shades, and in front of him were several books and ledgers. 'You do not remember me, Diamond?' he said, startling her.

'I'm sorry . . .' she began and then she saw him more clearly, his polished face, the long drooping moustache. 'Good Lord! You're Mr Chin!'

He stood and bowed. 'In person. It is a relief to know one is not so easily forgotten. Please sit down.'

He sent for tea and they talked. Mr Chin seemed to have all the time in the world and since Diamond had nowhere else to go, she was content to chat. He wanted to know, of course, why she was no longer working for Miss Middleton and Diamond told him only that Perfy did not require her services any more.

'She is to marry the station gentleman?' he asked.

'She was. She changed her mind and went home to Bowen.'

Fortunately, Perfy's affairs didn't seem to concern him. He was more interested in Diamond, who she was, where she came from, how she had acquired an education. It was pleasant talking to this quiet man. She found herself telling him all about the Irukandjis and her search for her people, and he nodded, understanding, when she spoke of her present problems. She had to find a room and a job, but the latter could be hard for a black girl.

'An income is essential,' he murmured.

'Don't I know it,' she said miserably. 'But even if I get a job, it will only mean my keep. They won't pay blacks.'

262

This was the first time Diamond had ever spoken of the unfairness of her situation, of the discriminatory rules that had irked her for years, and here was a man willing to discuss the subject as an intellectual discourse rather than just hear her complaints.

He ordered more tea.

'As I see it, you cannot earn money as a servant and there are few opportunities available to you otherwise,' he said.

Put as plainly as that, Diamond knew her future was grim. 'None,' she said dismally.

'Do you want some money?' he inquired, but she shook her head.

'Thank you, Mr Chin, but I couldn't repay you.'

'Ah, but you could. Here, with me, you can make a great deal of money.'

Diamond remembered the sniggers of the men who had directed her here. She stared at Mr Chin. 'This isn't a boarding house?'

He smiled at her as if she were a favourite child. 'No, miss, this is where a few beautiful young ladies make excellent money.'

Diamond gasped, hesitating, and then she burst out laughing. 'Oh my God, what an idiot I am.'

He sipped his tea. 'I do not believe you are an idiot. You are a sensible girl who has also the good fortune to be blessed with lovely features and a fine form. You should consider making the best of those blessings.' He placed his manicured hands on the table. 'The decision is for you to make. If you wish to stay here I will see that you are cared for and protected. This is is a discreet house, I do not permit rabble.'

As he talked in his quiet sing-song voice, Diamond felt bemused. They were discussing prostitution as if she were being interviewed for normal employment. But what other employment could she get? And what other employer would bother even conversing with a black gin? She liked Mr Chin. She felt safe with him. She would be safe here.

'You can come back,' he was saying. 'You don't have to make up your mind this minute.'

'I've made up my mind,' Diamond said, greatly daring. 'I'll stay. For a while anyway, if that is all right?'

'Of course.' He rang a bell and a young Chinese woman came shuffling in, bowing. 'This is Fan Su. She will take you to the bath-house and attend to your grooming.' He gave his instructions in Chinese. 'She will also find you some more feminine attire and show you to your room.' He smiled. 'See, you have your own room. Is that not what you came for?'

Diamond knew he was trying to alleviate the nervousness that had suddenly gripped her. What had she let herself in for? Sex for money? What would Mrs Beckman say? And who would these men be? She shuddered and had a sudden urge to run. But where?'

'You need shelter,' he commented, 'and your only true shelter will be

263

money, Diamond. Here you will earn money, and I will show you how to invest and make more.'

'Thank you,' she muttered. It all seemed unreal.

'I will appoint you the special lady of my house,' he continued. 'You will be very special. And with a name like Diamond,' he smiled, handing her over to Fan Su, 'a veritable treasure.'

5

Edmund Gaunt was feeling better. Traipsing the countryside with Billy Kemp had worn him out. He couldn't cope with Billy's non-stop charge at life. Every day, to Billy, was the day before the 'big strike', the strikes that never came. They'd panned gold at Gympie, no fear about that, but Billy had blown it. 'What's the use of a few quid?' he said. 'You have to enjoy life, Eddy. Ten quid, fifty quid – that's small fry. We're after the big stuff. One lucky strike and we'll go home millionaires. Don't say it can't be done, mate, we've seen it happening with our own eyes.'

Billy could talk, he'd give him that, and his palaver had got them many a free feed when they were down and out, but it hadn't helped them spot too much bloody gold. Then he'd heard about the Cape River. 'We're off, old son! They can keep this dung-heap. Fair winds to the north! The firm of Kemp and Gaunt is sailing for warmer waters!'

Except they didn't sail. They hoofed it, carrying their swags.

'Only a couple of hundred miles,' Billy had said.

And the rest. Boots worn to their uppers. Cadging rides on wagons, marching along in the burning heat and freezing at night on that overland trail. Latching on to gangs of diggers and taking their whack of stolen cattle or sheep that were butchered right there on the road, dodging bullets from the guns of snarling squatters. Bastards, them blokes. As if they'd miss a steer or two.

Eddy was exhausted by the time they got to the Cape River, and skinny as a rake, but give him his due, Billy was a good mate. He scavenged, found grub, looked after him, and while Eddy rested in a ti-tree hut, Billy raised the cash somehow to register a claim and they set to work again. He called their patch Taipan Gully, mad name, Eddy thought, until Billy explained that it would keep out thieves. Taipans were the worst, the deadliest snakes around, and Billy spread the word that the gully was full of them. It worked, no one came near them.

And so it was the same thing all over again, gold found, gold spent. Easy come, easy go, always searching for the big nuggets or the greatest prize, a new reef. Then they'd discovered Charters Towers. Right from the word go they'd loved the place, not like stinking little Gympie or the mud traps they'd come through on the trek north. Charters was a little rip-roarer. It thumped with life like the great stampers that pounded away, crushing ore, twenty-four hours a day. And it had grown so fast! Every time they came to town they couldn't believe their eyes. More pubs, more whorehouses, more stores, more mills. There were concert halls, gambling houses galore, banks, eating houses, and the sale yards sported the finest horses they'd ever seen.

Surrounded now by goldfields, Charters had burst on the world like a great charge of dynamite and the world had come to its doors, rushing to pay homage to the richest town since Solomon's days. And everyone called this town 'The World'. A marvellous place, but a bloody trap. They always went back to the diggings broke.

Eddy sighed. No point in whining. They had a good time and there were always other days. Until he got the camp fever. Sick as a dog.

Billy didn't trust the quacks that hung up their shingles at the goldfields and charged like wounded bulls, he'd put Eddy on a bullocky's wagon and taken him into Charters to a real doctor, and there he'd had to stay for months, too weak to work, with Billy footing the bills. It wasn't only the fever though, the doc had diagnosed consumption. Bloody bad luck, that's what it was. He'd felt bad being such a drag on Billy, hanging around the town all day, sitting in the sun like a knot on a log, never well enough to go back to the diggings. So he'd found himself light work here and there, swabbing out bars, working around stables, any old thing for a few shillings. He'd called at the Chink's whorehouse, looking for odd jobs, and chanced on the Chinaman himself. His name was Mr Chin.

'I've got a job for you,' the Chinkie had said, 'and I'll pay you well as long as you keep your mouth shut.'

'Not a word, sir,' Eddy had said eagerly. 'You can count on me.'

So here he was, in Georgetown, with the cushiest job of all time. Doing nothing, just sitting listening, and getting paid five shillings a day and a bonus when he got back. The Chinkie had even given him a good horse and supplies to go to Georgetown which was just a rat-trap joint on the way to the Gilbert River diggings, way out west.

There was a catch to it, of course. Mr Chin had introduced him to the nastiest pair of Orientals, his servants, that Eddy had ever seen. A real pair of cutthroats. 'If you let me down,' Chin had said, 'they'll find you and you won't live to steal another horse.'

'You can trust me, sir,' Eddy had insisted. 'I'm an honest man.' And that was true. He hadn't even told Billy where he was going, just left a message that he'd be back shortly.

Shortly? He'd been hanging about Georgetown for nearly two months. One of the Oriental servants had turned up to check on him and give him some more cash but otherwise they'd let him be. His mission was to watch for the return to Georgetown of a party of men led by a Mr Mulligan, to find out if Mulligan had located any new goldfields and report back quickly to Mr Chin.

Here in Georgetown, everyone seemed to know Mulligan, so all he had to do was sit and wait. It occurred to Eddy that Mulligan might not come back at all, but that was the Chink's problem. As long as they were paying him, he'd stay. The enforced rest and regular tucker was agreeing with him and he was enjoying his role as a spy. Bloody smart, those Chinks.

He was dozing on the steps of the Red Dog tavern when he heard the yells that Mulligan was back. He couldn't believe his ears. The Chink had bet on a sure thing! Now he had to find out what Mulligan had to say. What if it was no dice? What if Mulligan had struck out? Who cared? His job was to report back, and he would. Time to be making tracks anyway, Billy would be getting worried.

Eddy ran out on to the road, joining the men who had rushed to meet this fellow Mulligan. One glance told him these three bearded bushmen had been out in the real wilderness. Their torn buckskin pants had lasted the distance but their boots and jerkins were made of kangaroo skins. Eddie shuddered. They were real frontiersmen, Mulligan and his two mates, armed with rifles and pistols and heavy-duty knives, with cartridge belts slung across their chests. They rode three abreast down the street acknowledging the cheers of the men marching behind them like children on the heels of the pied piper.

'What news, Mulligan?' they called but the bushmen gave no indication and continued on until they dismounted at the Gold Commissioner's office and went inside.

Silence descended on the crowd. They stood there like stone figures. A tornado could have struck, Eddy mused, and none of them would have moved a muscle. There was more suspense in the air than in the verdict of a hanging judge.

The warden came out, his face deadpan, and took an age to tack a hand-written notice to the wall.

Eddy leapt forward and caught a glimpse of the carefully penned report before he was shoved aside in the crush.

Voices from the rear yelled: 'What does it say?' and then a great cheer rang out.

'You little beauty, Mulligan!'

'Gold's what it bloody says!'

'Where? Where?'

'Payable gold on the Palmer River, it says!'

'Where's the Palmer?'

'Christ knows!'

The Irishman himself came out. The silence was instantaneous. No one could afford to miss a word Mulligan had to say. He stood at the top of the wooden steps, a thumb tucked in the bandolier, dark eyes peering from his bushy face as if assessing their worth. 'Now, a word or two, lads, before you go runnin' mad.' He held up a lump of gold the size of his hand. 'I found this in the Palmer River and me and my mates have staked a claim but there's plenty more. The warden has officially proclaimed the Palmer a goldfield.'

'Where's the bloody Palmer?' a voice shouted amid the cheers, but Mulligan's reply was drowned as hats flew in the air and the audience whooped and jigged. One man executed a heel-toe right there in the dust and another took hold of Eddy and danced him around.

'Hold your horses,' Mulligan grinned. 'You'd better hear the rest. The Palmer is about three hundred miles north-east of here, and you listen good, mates. It's no place for the fainthearted. It's rough going. The locals there, our Aborigine friends, would rather shove a spear in you than shake hands.'

'Ah, bugger them!'

'So you say now,' Mulligan warned. 'And another thing, don't try that route without plenty of supplies or you'll perish. This is the last outpost inland. From here you have to cross four big rivers, the Lynd, the Tate, the Walsh and the Mitchell, which means there's no getting back in the wet. You'll be stranded there and, without supplies, you'll starve.'

The crowd was shuffling impatiently now, no one was interested in his warnings. Some even began pushing past him to inspect the maps in the warden's office, so Mulligan raised his voice to a shout. 'I'll be getting up a decent expedition. I'm prepared to take a hundred miners with me. I expect some of you will want to bring your families but I'd advise against it. I'll need a rest and then I'll fit out the expedition with horses, at least a hundred bullocks, and wagonloads of supplies . . .' His voice trailed off as he watched men break away from the crowd. The race for the Palmer had already begun. Mulligan shook his head. 'And God help you all,' he added.

Eddy moved closer to listen as Mulligan turned to the warden. 'The Palmer, it's a river of gold like nothing you ever saw, but only the brave, the desperate and the ignorant will take it on, and that's a frightenin' mix.'

But the warden, too, was caught up in the enthusiasm. 'Is it really that good?'

Mulligan sighed. 'I tried to tone it down a bit, for their sakes, warn them to wait for a fully equipped expedition. But yes, this isn't just a strike. When the truth gets out, there'll be madness in the land. I tell you now, the Palmer is all gold. We brought back what we could carry. It's a river of glittering, gleaming gold waiting to be picked up.'

Within the hour Eddy was on his horse, heading south on the two-hundred-mile ride back to Charters Towers with his news.

It had been a battle to get the few rations he needed. The local store was selling out fast to men determined to make for the Palmer right now. Tents were disappearing, packhorses were being loaded and some riders were already galloping out of the town. He was the only one heading south.

As he rode fast down the track, Eddy savoured the news. He had promised to keep his mouth shut, but surely he could tell Billy. This was the big one, the one he and Billy had waited for. But would Billy heed Mulligan's warnings? Not bloody likely. The storekeeper had told him it would take a couple of months for Mulligan to round up the equipment and stock he needed in a lonely hole like Georgetown. Even Eddy thought a delay like that would be disastrous; the gold could be all gone by the time they arrived. And then he remembered what Mulligan had said. The brave, the ignorant and the desperate!

Well, he wasn't brave, and when it came to the real bush he was ignorant. And desperate? To tell the truth, he wasn't that desperate to find gold that he'd take on wild blacks or risk starving to death hundreds of miles from the nearest store, cut off from civilisation by those rivers. Maybe he wouldn't tell Billy after all. Say nothing.

But the Chink wasn't taking any chances. He thanked Eddy for a job well done, paid him fifty quid, a fortune, and then locked him in a barred cellar.

'You are not in any danger,' Mr Chin said. 'You will be well cared for. But it is essential to my operation that you stay incommunicado until such time as news of the Palmer strike reaches this town. I need the time. You understand?'

No, he didn't bloody understand, and he said so. He thought the Chink was bloody ungrateful. Hadn't he done his bit? And shown him on the map exactly where the Palmer River was located? He, Eddy Gaunt, was educated; he could read charts damned good, Captain Beckman himself had taught him.

But Mr Chin ignored him and Eddy was a prisoner in a whorehouse! He had promised not to tell anyone but that didn't cut any ice either. And to top off this indignity, one of the brothers Yuang, those evil-looking offsiders, held a dagger at his throat and warned him if he made a sound in that cellar he'd have to slit it open. Jesus! Thanks for nothing.

A black Abo whore brought his meals and he offered to pay her a fiver if she let him out but she shook her head. To begin with she'd been cold, not interested in his plight, and then she began to listen to him, head cocked to one side like a bloody bird.

'You have to help me,' he said. 'Get me out of here. What are you staring at?'

She sat on the cellar steps in the gloom. 'Your voice,' she said. 'I've heard your voice before. Where do you come from?'

With nothing else to do he told her about his days at sea, about the shipwreck . . .

'The *White Rose*,' she said. 'Captain Beckman.'

'That's right. How'd you know?'

She was so excited, she grabbed his shirt and shook him. 'Were you on board when they picked up a black girl?'

'What black girl?' he whined. 'Leave me alone.'

269

'A black girl,' she insisted. 'Mrs Beckman was on board too.'

'Oh yeah. That was years ago. She never sailed with us again. Jesus, she was crook. So was I, that first trip. Got over it though. Had to. Us sailors—'

'Do you remember a native girl? She was only young. They rescued her from the sea somewhere.'

He scratched his head. 'I dunno, the blokes sneaked gins on to the ship sometimes. Bloody hell to pay when they got caught! But wait on now, there was this kid. I remember her now. Jeez . . .' He was about to say how could he have forgotten her? Stark bollicky naked with pointy little tits, but even to a whore he couldn't bring himself to mention that. 'Yeah, you're right. We picked up a black kid. And I'll tell you somethin' else, now I come to think of it. I was the one spotted her.'

'Where?'

'In the sea she was, half-drowned. Right out to sea.'

The whore didn't believe him. 'How could she have been in the sea? She couldn't have fallen off a ship. You're lying! They must have kidnapped her from some village.'

'Who bloody cares now?' He drank the tea she'd brought him. 'This tea's as weak as piss. Next time make it stronger.'

'I care,' she said meanly, 'and you'll answer my questions or I'll bring Yuang Pan down to do the asking.'

'Christ,' he moaned. 'You're all bonkers in this place. I told you, she was in the sea. That's it.'

'Then why didn't they put her ashore?'

'You'd have to be jokin'. No one would go back there, the bloody Abos speared two of our crew.' He was putting it together now. 'That's right, it was the same time. Two of our shipmates murdered there, and they was only lookin' for water, poor bastards.'

'Where was this place, Eddy?' Her voice was silky, she was different now, more respectful. 'Do you remember where it was?'

' 'Course I remember. We never went near there again, no bloody fear!'

'Where, Eddy? Tell me.'

'In the Whitsunday Passage. Gave us the creeps every time we sailed past there.'

'Does it have a name, this place?'

'Sure, everyone knows it. Endeavour River. It's at the mouth of the Endeavour River.'

'The Endeavour River,' she repeated. 'And is that in the north?'

'Yes.'

'Is it far from Townsville?'

Eddy was fed up with all this. 'What am I? A walking bloody question box? It's nowhere near Townsville. Are you going to get me out of here? I'll give you a tenner.'

She stood up. 'I'll just do what you did. I'll bring your meals.'

He stared at the locked door. What was that supposed to mean? Stupid boong. She was probably trying to up the price. Next time he'd have to offer her more. If only he could get a message to Billy. And he'd bloody tell Billy about the Palmer, too. That'd serve the Chink right for double-crossing him.

Chin Ying was busy, very busy. He'd sent Yuang Pan to tell Lew Cavour to come in to Charters Towers right away, and to collect all the coolies. There was no time to waste, Yuang Pan could take the coolies straight through to Townsville. Ying had studied the charts and had decided the fastest way to the Palmer River was by ship. The goldfields were only about a hundred miles from the coast as against a difficult and dangerous overland trek of more than five hundred miles. Yuang Fu could stay behind to sell his two houses and his many leases at the goldfields here, then he could follow them to the coast. A Chinese friend was already waiting to purchase the brothel and Yuang would have no trouble selling the mining sites.

The brothel had served its purpose. Racial conflict was still a serious problem and successful Chinese prospectors were singled out for attacks. Greed and envy engendered not only spite but vicious retaliation. Two of his coolies had been murdered by claim jumpers, and another two had been robbed of their gold before Yuang Pan had been able to make the collection. It had been necessary to make an example of these men, so the Yuang brothers had hunted them down and disposed of them. And Ying knew he had to take measures to protect his own safety, for the diggers targeted the Chinese bosses, believing that if they removed the head of the dragon, the body of coolies would be helpless. This was not so, of course; other Chinamen simply took over. Nevertheless, men like Chin Ying couldn't travel anywhere without bodyguards.

As his wealth had increased, Ying had decided to establish a high-class brothel to distract attention. He charged outrageously for his ladies, but his clients didn't mind. They boasted that they were permitted to enter the most expensive whorehouse in The World. They approved of the Chinaman making money running a brothel; he was no longer, they thought, in competition with them. The Chinaman's occupation was acceptable, he was providing a service for the gentlemen. Ying smiled. Not only was he receiving a steady supply of gold from the diggings, the miners were falling over themselves to bring their gold to his door in return for the pleasures of his eight lovely ladies.

Besides, living in the brothel was far more pleasant than the flea-ridden tents on that vile goldfield. He felt ill at the thought of the disgusting living conditions out there. The Palmer River would be different. A clean environment for the first men at the fields. By the time the main body of miners figured out how to get there, Ying expected to have swept in with his coolies, collected as much gold as they could carry and leave the place to be fouled by those who came later. A magnificent plan.

Nor would he be coming back to Charters Towers. He was wealthy enough now to retire and the Palmer gold would be the cream on his very rich cake.

Ying finished sorting through the drawers in his desk and turned his attention to his two safes, irritated by a knocking on his door. When he didn't reply, Diamond came in. 'I'm so sorry, Mr Chin, but I must talk to you, it's important.'

Ying sighed. 'Not now.' He liked Diamond, she had intelligence, but she could be difficult, not as pliable as his other women. She had blossomed here, groomed and tutored by Fan Su, and she was in great demand by the white men who professed to loathe gins.

She looked around her, surprised. 'You're packing?'

'Yes.'

'Where are you going?'

He pursed his lips, it was not her place to be questioning him. 'What do you want, Diamond?'

'I came to tell you I have to leave.'

'Very well.' The brothel no longer interested him. 'I will be paying everyone out this evening.'

'Thank you.' She noticed some maps on his desk. 'Do you mind if I look at your maps? I think I've found out where my people are.'

As she stepped forward he snatched the maps away. 'Excuse me, these maps are private.' Ying had marked the Palmer River on one of them.

'I just want to look at the coastline,' she said. 'Surely that won't hurt?'

'Come back later, I'm busy now.'

Diamond stood very still. 'Mr Chin, this is terribly important. I need your help. If you won't let me see them, please look on the maps and see if you can show me where the Endeavour River is. That's all I want to know.'

He was startled. 'Why?'

'Because that's where the Irukandji people live.'

'Really?' He sat at his desk. Ying knew exactly where the Endeavour River was. The landing place for their route to the Palmer River. He searched for an unmarked map and pretended to study it. 'Ah, here we are.'

Diamond ran round the desk and stared at the map. She looked very beautiful these days, her hair free of that cheap turban she used to wear and now trimmed by Fan Su into neat curls round her face. The long hair at the back was wound with ribbon into a thick coil on the crown of her head. Very elegant.

'That's it,' she cried, throwing her arms round him.

'Please!' he said, extricating himself.

'I'm sorry, Mr Chin. But I'm so excited. That's where I'm going.'

'It is wild country,' he told her, 'mostly unexplored. And what if you do find them? Are you able to speak their language?'

'I can remember some words, and the rest will come, I'm certain it will.'

Ying nodded. He agreed. And if she was right and this landing place really was the home of the Irukandji people, what an asset it would be to have one of their own along. One who could speak the language, obtain guides. 'I am travelling to Townsville tomorrow,' he murmured. 'If you wish to accompany me you may do so.'

Fan Su unlocked the door and admitted Lew Cavour, who looked around the lobby at the gentlemen seated comfortably on plush armchairs and sofas, accepting drinks and cigars served by a pretty Chinese girl.

'You like champagne, sir?' she asked. 'Or whisky maybe?'

'No, thank you,' Lew replied, resisting an impulse to laugh. 'Mr Chin is expecting me.' He'd had no idea that Ying lived in a brothel, or owned one, more like it. He'd heard about this place, the exclusive no-name brothel, simply referred to as the Chink's. So Chin Ying was the Chink! Good God, what next?

He opened the door into Ying's quarters, wondering why the screen was there. Privacy, or the old superstition that the evil ones travel in a straight line, therefore the screen protects? Both, he supposed.

'Ah, Lew. Very good. I hoped you would not delay.' Ying seemed unconcerned about the premises. 'I have the best news.'

'You own this place? Why didn't you tell me?'

'Why should I? It is of no importance. Simply a means for me to live in a clean place without disturbance from thugs.'

'And pick up extra cash at the same time,' Lew laughed. 'I hear this place is pricey.'

'Of course,' Ying fluttered a hand, dismissing the subject. 'Do you require a drink? I have the very best of Scotland whisky.'

'Lead me to it. After the foul brews we get at the diggings, my taste buds have taken a hiding.' He looked around. 'You're packed, ready to leave! This is urgent.'

Ying poured the drinks himself, which also amused Lew. What had happened to the Chinese gentleman who clapped for his servants to attend to his every need?

'I have been waiting for you with much eagerness,' Ying said. 'Come now and view these maps. As I expected, Mr Mulligan did find gold, a river of gold, but no one down here knows about it yet.'

Lew was fascinated as Ying explained his news and the whereabouts of the Palmer River. He could feel the tingle of gold fever again; it had begun to wane on the hard slog of the Cape diggings. This new field sounded too good to be true.

'Will you come with me?' Ying asked.

'You bet I will,' Lew replied.

'What did you do with your claim at the Cape?'

'I gave it to my partner, Herbert Watlington.'

'You gave it to him? That is not good business.'

'No. He's not a bad chap really, quite funny when you get to know him, but distinctly unhappy with hard work.'

'Who isn't?' Ying commented.

'All very well for you, but I figure if the gold's there, we might as well go after it. Anyway, he's happy to be rid of me. He can potter along in his own time and there's a family next to us who can give him a hand.'

'Did you make much gold?'

'I've got a bank of about a thousand pounds. It was worth my time.'

By the look on Ying's face, he didn't seem to think so, but he was too polite to remark on it. He turned back to the maps. 'As soon as we get to Townsville, we'll charter or buy a decent boat – I hear there are plenty in that port – and go north. We have to take horses and enough provisions for all.'

That reminded Lew. 'What about your coolies?'

'They are already on their way to Townsville.'

Lew whistled. 'Good work. Do you really believe it's a river of gold?'

'If Mr Mulligan says it is, we can believe him.' He pulled on a brocade bell-rope. 'I have ordered a decent meal for you. Fan Su has been waiting to serve.'

Shortly there was a tap on the door and Fan Su came in with a tray of dishes, followed by another girl carrying two steaming bowls. Lew stared. Diamond!

'Good evening, Mr Cavour,' she said calmly, and left the room with Fan Su.

Lew exploded. 'What the hell is she doing here? And don't tell me she's your cook. Not dressed like that.' Diamond had looked sensational in a flowered peach-satin kimono buttoned with cord loops down one side, without the wide sash favoured by Chinese women, and her hair was dressed with tiny flowers. The whole effect was sleek, very sensuous.

'Diamond works here by choice,' Ying remarked, offended by Lew's outburst. 'Since when do you disapprove of prostitution?'

'I don't disapprove, but Diamond has no place here.'

'Ah! So where is her place? Where else might a black girl earn money?'

'Oh Christ. I don't know. But she shouldn't be here.'

'Your Anglo-Saxon values are mysterious. The gentlemen who come here accept whores as long as they are someone else's daughters. Regular customers insist they would kill their daughters if they became whores.'

Lew helped himself to another whisky. 'Spare me your philosophising. I'm taking her out of here.'

'You are so kind. I presume you would return her to her former occupa-

274

tion as an unpaid servant? Don't be so naive. She would not consider such a proposal now. However, fate has pre-empted you. Diamond wishes to accompany us to the north where she hopes to find her tribal family.'

Lew scowled. 'What bloody rot! We're not taking her up there.'

'Then I suggest you do your arguing with her, not with me.'

'Why isn't she still with Perfy out at that station?'

'I understand the separation was by mutual agreement. And Miss Perfection is no longer at the ranch, she has gone home to Bowen.' He looked slyly at Lew as if considering whether or not to let him have further information. 'I hope you don't have ideas now of returning to Bowen?'

'Why should I? She's engaged to Ben Buchanan. Probably married by now.'

'The marriage has been cancelled.'

'What?' Lew was amazed. Delighted. 'Why?'

'This I don't know. It is intriguing but Diamond will not discuss the matter. I sense their mutual agreement to part was not on the best of terms. She has nothing to say regarding her former mistress.'

Lew was silent. This changed things. If he had any sense he'd head back to Bowen right away. It sounded as if Perfy's dream of the ideal country life had fizzed. Good. He laughed. 'That's the best news I've ever heard. I wonder what happened? Not that it matters, she's free again. I'm going to marry her, I kept telling her that. Maybe she'll listen now.'

'You can't go to Bowen yet,' Ying said sternly. 'There's no time. I'm depending on you.'

'I know,' Lew said, but he was hesitating. What if the Palmer gold was just a dream? He would have to invest in the journey north. Should he gamble his savings now? And they'd be away for months. Would he lose Perfy again? But the description of the river of gold sent his blood racing. He had to go north, it would be madness to turn his back on the opportunity of a lifetime. 'Don't worry,' he told Ying. 'I'll stick with you.'

6

Where the hell was Eddy? Billy Kemp was getting fed up with hanging about. The blokes in town seemed to think he'd probably picked up a job as a bullocky's offsider, carting supplies from depot to depot. Bloody bullockies were making a fortune these days, even on the Cape, charging twenty-five shillings a dray-load to cart washdirt to the nearest creek. It was getting to the stage a man couldn't afford to turn round. Their claim had run dry and Billy had sold it to a new chum for fifty quid, which wasn't bad going since it wasn't worth a green bean. There were scores of reefs cropping up all over the place now but they'd been pounced on fast and the miners were going deeper, chasing the lode. That took money for equipment. Sinking shafts and dynamiting heavy rock faces was tough going.

He wandered up to a corrugated iron shed that served as a tavern and general store and bought himself a pint of ale. It had been raining on and off the last month, which amazed Billy. This country looked as if it'd never seen rain, but it had turned the diggings into a bloody quagmire. He swore he had a foot of topsoil caked on his boots.

'Hey, Billy,' the innkeeper called. 'Where's your mate Eddy?'

'Buggered if I know,' Billy said angrily.

'There's a letter here for him, looks as if it's been to China and back.'

'Ah cripes. Give it to me.'

The innkeeper found the letter, a battered envelope, watermarked, with the ink well-smeared. It was from Eddy's old man, someone had written it for him. It was months old, containing the usual nothings, hoping Eddy was all right, the weather, telling him he ought to go back to sea. And so on. But then Billy read some interesting news. The girl next door. Perfection Middleton – Billy grinned at the name, remembering the pretty girl he'd kissed goodbye – she'd come into money. And she owned a station out that way called Caravale. The Middletons were real posh now, he read.

He sat on the muddy steps and contemplated this. Caravale. It wasn't all that far from here. A hundred miles or so to the east. They ought to pay her a visit. A neighbourly visit. Where the hell was Eddy when he needed him? He was the bloody neighbour. Ah well, why not? She might be good for a stake.

It took him a couple of days to get there and someone directed him towards the station headquarters, but only the outbuildings remained, the homestead had been burned down. He was making for the stables when a typical squatter-type barred his way. 'Where do you think you're going?'

'To water the horse, mate. She's dry as a bone. And who are you?'

'Buchanan. I'm the boss here. You looking for a job?'

'Not particularly. I've come to see a friend of mine.'

'Who would that be?'

'Miss Middleton. She owns this place, don't she?'

'She has equity in the station, but she's not here. She has returned to Bowen.'

'Ah, bad luck. I was looking forward to seeing her. We're old friends, neighbours we were, in Brisbane. You've had a bit of bad luck here yourself by the looks of things.'

'Yes,' Buchanan said gloomily. 'We're short-handed too. You sure you don't want a job?'

'No, mate. I'm not much of a hand with cattle, couldn't rope a post if it chased me.'

'I need carpenters too. We're building a temporary house until I can get plans drawn up for a new homestead.'

'Carpentering? I've done a bit in my day. Pay and keep?'

'Yes,' Buchanan said. 'There's room in the bunkhouse. You can start tomorrow.'

Billy grinned. 'Right you are, mate.' He might as well rest up here for a while. He'd send a message in to Eddy's digs in Charters Towers to tell the bloody fool to get his arse on out here to Caravale. By then Perfy Middleton might be back. No wonder she wasn't here, with no damn house to live in.

They'd just about finished building the four-roomed cottage to house Buchanan, his housekeeper and his bloody old war-horse of a mother, who nagged and argued over every plank and nail, when Eddy tottered in. The useless bastard. He'd got lost, of course, ridden about fifty miles in the wrong direction through empty scrub, run out of tucker and water, until some blacks found him riding round in bloody circles.

'You're bloody mad, that's what you are,' Billy railed at him. 'And where have you been?'

Eddy guzzled the soup greedily and held out his plate for more. 'You think you're smart, Billy Kemp,' Eddy snarled, 'but I tell you what, I know somethin' you don't know. I know somethin' all your mates here would give their eye-teeth to know.'

'Is that right?' Billy laughed. 'Give us a hint. You found out what colour britches Kerry Kate wears.' Kerry Kate was the most notorious madame in Charters Towers, a gun-toting harridan, so rough and tough some claimed she was a man dressed up as a woman.

'Very funny.'

'Well what?' Billy urged. 'Don't keep me in suspenders.'

'Not here,' Eddy said, looking down the long crowded table at all the station hands and cowboys. 'I'll tell you later.'

'No one's listening,' Billy said. And they weren't, the hungry men were too intent on getting their share of the beef stew and mash. Cook's hotchpotch of mashed potatoes, carrots, parsnips, onions, and any other vegetables that he could get his hands on was a hot favourite with all the men.

'Later,' Eddy muttered mysteriously.

But when Eddy finally told him the long, tedious story of the job the Chink had given him, Billy was dozing before he came to the point. It was a hot February night without a breath of a wind so, like most of the others, they'd dragged their straw mattresses out of the bunkhouse to sleep outside where it was a mite cooler.

'You're not listening,' Eddy complained.

'I am. You went to this joint called Georgetown and you got paid for sitting on your bum. And then you came home and they locked you up in a whorehouse. I should be so lucky.'

'I wasn't near the whores. They just brought me the munger. Then one day this evil-looking Chink let me out and told me to keep me mouth shut or else he'd cut me throat.'

'You want me to believe this cruddy story?'

'You better.' Eddy nudged him. 'I'm comin' to the good part. I reckon they let me out because they didn't care then. The boss Chink had gone, and taken the black whore with him—'

'Jesus! This beats all.'

Eddy ignored him. 'Just the same, I wasn't taking no chances. I went back to me digs, got your message and high-tailed it out of Charters Towers to put distance between me and the cutthroat Chink. And here I am, and I never told a soul.'

'Bully for you.'

'Don't you want to know what I wasn't allowed to tell anyone?'

'Go to sleep, Eddy.'

'They found a river of gold, Billy. A bloody river lined with gold! Running over with gold!'

Billy's eyes were open. He didn't believe a bloody word of it but he was listening. He reached out and lit one of the boss's cheroots that he'd lifted from the storehouse. 'Yeah. And I suppose you know where this gold river is. They told you, did they?'

'Jeez! I told him, the Chink! And he took off like lightning.'

Somewhere in this rigmarole Billy heard fact, if only because Eddy wasn't capable of inventing it. 'What's the name of the river?'

'The Palmer,' Eddy whispered. 'You remember where Bart Swallow and the other bloke were killed by the blacks?'

Billy shuddered. He'd never forget it. 'That's not the Palmer, that's the mouth of the Endeavour River. And you needn't think I'm going there again, gold or no gold.'

'We don't have to,' Eddy said, relieved that Billy was at last taking notice. 'The Palmer River is about the same latitude, a hundred miles inland. We could overland.' Eddy recounted Mulligan's warnings about supplies, and about the rivers, and the blacks.

Billy nodded. 'That'd be right too, we'd need plenty of rations, and arms, packhorses . . . It'd take dough. Let me think about it. They can't keep this quiet for long.'

Money! Even if they joined Mulligan's expedition, they'd have to pay their share. Better to be independent. He thought about Ben Buchanan. He was the only person he knew who could put up the cash. It hadn't taken Billy long to hear all the station gossip. Perfy didn't have equity in this place, as Buchanan had said, she owned half. She and the boss had been going to get hitched, which would have placed the ownership of the station on an even keel again, but Ben had been humping a black gin and Perfy found out, and shot through. Fair enough, the men had laughed, the trick was not to get caught. And then the house burned down, something to do with the old battleaxe, Mrs Buchanan. But the upshot was, and this interested Billy, the boss had to find the cash to buy Perfy out since she'd gone off in a huff.

Buchanan needed cash. In a hurry. Why not tell him about the Palmer? Get in first. The boss was a first-rate bushman, worth his own weight in gold on a trek like this one. And Billy had a plan, a humdinger, one that would leave all the others on the trail for dead.

At sun-up Billy was waiting for Ben outside the shower sheds. 'Can I have a word with you, boss?'

Ben mopped his face and slung a towel over his shoulder. 'What's up?'

'Nothing's up. I've got a proposition for you.'

'What sort of a proposition?'

'To get straight to the point,' Billy said, seeing impatience on the boss's face, 'I know where there's gold and plenty of it.'

'Why don't you go and get it then?' Ben laughed.

'Because it's in the bush and I wouldn't make it on me own. Just give me a few minutes. Let me explain.' Before Ben could get away, Billy was explaining the situation, keeping the story short and to the point: Mulligan found gold. Eddy Gaunt was in Georgetown and got the lowdown, and rode straight back here to tell his mate. 'We're going up there, boss, but to do it right I reckon we'd need four to six blokes, a proper troop.'

'Yes,' Ben said, 'I guess you would.' He questioned Billy for a while. 'I'll think about it,' he finally agreed. 'I have to look at a map. I lost all of mine in the fire, but Tom Mansfield's got a few over there.'

Billy came crowing back to Eddy. 'I've got him! He'll be in it, you watch!'

'Yeah. Just as long as he doesn't go racing off on his own and leave us flat, now that he knows.'

'He won't do that. It's a secret, dummy! He knows we have to keep this quiet. And anyway,' he added with a grin, 'if he tries to run out on Billy Kemp, I'll spread the word around the station. There wouldn't be a man left working here.'

The builder, Joe Flynn, who hailed from Sydney, was pleased to have an extra hand. He put Eddy to work nailing down the floorboards. 'And keep it even,' he said, 'or the Missus will have your hide.'

Billy laughed. He'd been put on the job of building the tank stand outside, away from her interference. The low platform was being built from fine cedar, a shocking waste of good timber, but in their haste to please the old woman the station hands had felled and pit-sawn more timber than they needed, enough to build a couple of cottages. But it wasn't his problem. Billy worked happily, knowing this was his lucky day. And sure enough, when the boss came in that afternoon they began to make plans.

'There are some big rivers up that way,' Ben said. 'They're going to slow us down. The horses can swim but it'd be rough on the packhorses and we couldn't afford to lose our supplies.'

'Not if we take a boat,' Billy said. 'What's the difference between pulling a boat on a trolley and driving a wagon? Lighter, I'd say. Some of those German wagons I've seen on the trails weigh a ton.'

Ben stared. 'A boat?'

'I read about it,' Billy said loftily. 'Those real explorers that headed out into the mulga, they carted boats, and they didn't have any bloody idea what was ahead of them.'

Ben nodded. 'They did too, now I come to think of it. But where would we get a boat?'

'We'll build one in no time, mate. You just get the rest of the show on the road. And what about some walking beef?'

'That's no problem. I'll round up about fifty head to keep us covered against losses.'

Ben was well aware this was a risky operation, but he had no doubt the story of the Palmer River gold was true and he was determined to get his share this time. A big gold strike would solve all his problems.

'I'm going away for a while,' he told his mother, who was now residing angrily in the creamery vacated by Diamond. 'We can't do much once the wet sets in.'

'If it does,' she grumbled. 'You can't call these showers a wet season. You mark my words, we'll get no real rains this year and then we'll be in trouble.'

'That's why I'm going. There's been a new gold strike in the north and I'm not about to miss out this time.'

She shook her head. 'Gold digging? Are you mad? Your place is here. You caused all this trouble, and you're not going to leave me here on my own.'

'I've told you, Mother, you can go and live in Brisbane for a while if you want to.'

'Oh yes, you'd like that, wouldn't you? Get me off the property and keep me off.'

'You could take Mae with you for company, and while you're there shop for furniture for the new house.'

'What new house? I don't believe you have any intentions of building a decent house. And I refuse to live in that wooden thing those men are building. It's no more than a shepherd's cottage.'

'Then stay here in the creamery.'

He was fed up with her, with Caravale, with everything. In one respect this prospecting venture was an excuse to escape. Ever since Darcy had died there'd been nothing but trouble and he felt anxiously that he was still being punished. Billy Kemp had no idea what that far north country was like, he was like a big kid off to the fair. Ben knew better, he'd heard enough to know it was savage country and it would take all their strength and resourcefulness to get there. Closer to the equator, the wet season couldn't fail; it'd be a nightmare for travellers and it had probably already begun. Not that he cared, he almost welcomed the punishment they'd certainly have to endure, to absolve himself, once and for all, from his awful guilt.

'If you hadn't been messing around with that nigger,' Cornelia screamed as he strode away, 'we wouldn't be in this trouble.'

Ben ignored her. He had steadfastly refused to admit that he had made love to Diamond, not because it mattered any more, but to maintain his authority by keeping her in doubt. After all, she had burned the house down. The woman was incredible; she had no conscience about that at all, it was simply an accident, she claimed, it could have happened to anyone. She even had the cheek to say it was fortuitous, it provided a ready excuse for the departure of his fiancée, and she kept telling visitors the engagement was still on. What a bloody mess! He had considered going after Perfy but he'd seen the contempt in her eyes and he knew it was useless. She hated him now, almost as much as he hated Diamond. Christ! It had never occurred to him that Diamond would admit to their affair!

Admit? 'Boast,' Cornelia had said. 'She brazenly threw it in Perfy's face.' No wonder she'd quit.

Rumour had it that Diamond was whoring in a Charters Towers brothel. That didn't surprise him, she was just trash like the rest of them after all. But it annoyed hell out of him to think of her in a local brothel handing it out to the riff-raff, making a fool of him. And as for Perfy, in a way the broken engagement was a relief. He'd never been in love with her and she'd been so damned pigheaded she hadn't given him a chance to explain. She was the loser, he told himself. She'd thrown away the chance to become mistress of Caravale which was what she'd wanted all along. Married to Darcy or to him, what had she cared as long as she could grab for the high life? Well, she'd be in trouble trying to sell to anyone else, even in his absence. Cornelia would see to that. And she'd only get rock-bottom price out of the Buchanans. When he came back with the gold he'd pay Perfy off for a pittance and get rid of her once and for all. She had been the cause of their troubles right from the first day she'd met Darcy.

His thoughts turned back to the gold. He was convinced they were on to a sure thing and the prospect excited him. The gold was for Caravale. The station was more important than any of these women, Cornelia included. He'd had enough of her too. Despite her tales, it was evident that she'd burned the house down during a drunken binge. He'd see to it she didn't get another chance. When he returned he'd send her to live in Brisbane and she could burn down the whole city for all he cared.

He told the station staff that he was going on a little prospecting jaunt out to the Gilbert River, to avoid mentioning the Palmer, and the men were amused.

'You'll be sorry,' they laughed as the small expedition saddled up. 'It's a bugger of a place. If the mossies don't get you, the snakes will.'

'I hate snakes,' Billy Kemp growled, hitching the horses to the boat trailer.

Ben took no notice. Snakes would be the least of their problems. They were headed into the heart of the Cape York Peninsula! Even now Kemp and his mate Eddy had no idea of the dangers ahead. It was equatorial country, everything that moved would be a threat.

Ben had ridden into the hills and found old Tinbin, an ancient tribal Aborigine he and Darcy had known since they were kids. He must be ninety years old now if he was a day. Tinbin was known far and wide as an elder of the Mian people, neighbours of the Ilbas who inhabited Caravale and its surrounds; a former chieftain, it was said, and known to be a wise man with great powers. To the boys he'd simply been an ugly old black-feller with a white beard who always had a supply of edible berries and nuts, but Ben remembered that his name, translated, meant 'wind coming from the north'. Tinbin might be able to give him information about his destination.

And he was there, in the same place, squatting outside his cave by a long-dead fire, the wild grey hair matted with burrs but his rheumy old eyes alert and curious. He lifted a scrawny claw to welcome Ben. 'Long time no comen see Tinbin, you Ben.'

'Yes, long time,' Ben said. He unwrapped a checkered cloth to present a cooked chicken, a loaf of damper and some biscuits.

Tinbin chortled, breaking off a chicken leg. 'Boys comen, boys jus'' mates. Man comen want something. What you want, mister Ben?'

Ben laughed. 'You old villain, you don't miss much, do you? I need your help.'

Tinbin motioned to him to eat some of the chicken he was breaking apart, so Ben took a wing and sucked the meat from it. 'I'm going north for a while,' he said, knowing the old hermit would not accept small talk. 'Into strange country.'

Tinbin's gnarled face broke into a toothless grin. 'You seek the gold rocks, you cross big rivers with your canoe. Tinbin know all these things.'

'You bloody old fake, the people told you that,' Ben smiled. Tinbin never moved from this spot; other Aborigines brought him food and told him everything that was happening.

Unconcerned, Tinbin nodded. 'Everything talks.'

'I'm not going to the Gilbert River. I'm headed north, far north,' Ben told him, and Tinbin nodded.

'Yes. The big rivers.'

Ben realised he had fooled the white men but not the blacks. They seemed to have an extra sense of understanding that he'd never been able to plumb. 'That's right,' he admitted. 'But I need to know about the people up there. Your people. What tribes?' It was important to know who they were, what they were. Friendly or unfriendly.

'Better you stay home,' Tinbin warned.

'No. I have to go. What tribe lives the other side of the Mian country?'

Tinbin answered that easily. 'Them fellers Kutjali.'

'Good people?'

Tinbin considered this, and then replied, 'You doan touch nothin'. You doan killem one even possum, doan take their honey, they leave you live.'

'I'll only be passing through,' Ben said. 'I won't touch their food. I'll have my own.' He drew a mud map of the region. 'What people next?'

'Them Jangga. Medicine men. Magic people.'

Ben had heard of the Jangga people, shy, hermit types, very ancient, much respected by the blacks. From what he could make out, they were the philosophers of the black civilisation, the scholars. They wouldn't bother him. 'After them?'

'Here Banjin,' Tinbin pointed. 'Here Kalkadoon.'

'Oh shit!' Ben said.

Tinbin grinned comfortably, taking a piece of bread and wrapping up the rest. 'Tinbin tell you, better you stay home. Big tribes.'

Ben thought about that. Tinbin didn't mind silences. Tinbin was silence. He had all the time in the world to contemplate sound or no sound. And as he sat there, Ben felt he was learning again, like he and Darcy used to do. They would sit flanking Tinbin, cross-legged, squatting on the rocks, playing at being blackfellers, saying nothing, looking out over the valley, hearing everything, even the scratch and chuckles of birds. The

283

screech and chatter became silence because of their constancy. Earnest little boys wanting to belong to Tinbin's world of mystery.

'What if I ride fast through their country?' Ben asked knowing the question was pointless. A herd of bullocks couldn't move fast, and if he left them behind, they'd starve. Even the sailor Kemp knew that. 'A totem,' he said to Tinbin. 'What do they fear?'

The old man burst into cackling, choking laughter. He punched Ben in the shoulder. 'Whitefeller guns,' he screeched. 'Best totem.'

Ben laughed too. He was getting as bad as the Aborigines, looking for magic answers. Old Tinbin had more sense. Of course, well-armed they were well-protected.

'Righto,' he said. 'Now look here. Not much further to go. This river whitefeller call Walsh. Next river whitefeller call Mitchell. What tribes live between those two rivers?'

Tinbin fanned himself with a twine of leaves. 'Many long years allasame Tinbin walkabout that country, allasame safe, big strong magic. Rainbow serpent totem.' He winked, a wink that seemed to close half of his face. 'Carry good presents. Tinbin givemup pretties, shells, them givemup tomahawks, knives.'

Ben understood. The blacks had trade routes all over this country, like the Marco Polo trade routes he'd learned about from his tutor. 'Will I take them presents?' he asked, by which he meant anything but weapons.

Tinbin spat. 'No good presents. Kukabera bad fellers now.' He lunged at Ben, imitating a tomahawk blow and Blue, Ben's dog, sprang up, snarling.

As he pacified the dog, Ben became increasingly worried. 'How many damned tribes are up that way?'

'Kunjin blackfellers,' Tinbin continued. 'All nicey, nicey. Send gins in to lovey up newfeller camps. Then sssh!' He put a finger to his lips and grinned meanly. Whispering, he explained a sneak night attack by this tribe.

'Aren't any of them friendly?'

'Nebber. Tinbin know. All killem any feller. Merkin here,' he pointed right on the Palmer area and Ben edged forward. He might be able to steer clear of some of the others, but he'd have to confront this mob.

'Maybe I give those men good bullocks,' he offered. 'I'll make them a big feast.'

Tinbin scowled at him. 'Maybe you get good sense. Stay home. Him Merkin you see, wear umurri feathers.' He pointed at the trees where Major Mitchell cockatoos were harassing butcher-birds.

'They wear white cockatoo feathers?' Ben said.

Tinbin nodded. 'Them warriors chop heads.'

Ben sat back appalled. 'Christ! Headhunters!' He had heard that New Guinea natives were headhunters but not Australian.

Tinbin shrugged. 'All good warriors, mind their land. You keep out, Ben.' He took Ben's hand in both of his. 'Bad men up there, worse than Kunjin even.' Tinbin's grip tightened; his scraggy hands were surprisingly strong. 'Giant fellers. No feller talk of them, bring evil spirits. Taboo.'

'I have to go,' Ben said, realising now he would have to enlist more men to his team. He'd find some miners in Georgetown. He stood up. 'Don't you worry, I'll come back.'

Tinbin looked at him sternly. 'You come back!' he ordered. 'Or Dar-say lost.' That was always his pronunciation of Darcy's name. 'Dar-say spirit come home soon. Wait for Ben. Say cryin' finish now. All better.'

'What do you mean?' Ben asked apprehensively but old Tinbin closed his eyes and began to chant. Darcy and Ben had always laughed at Tinbin's 'mess of mumblings', as they called it, used by the old man to get rid of people when he was sick of talking to them. Now he hoped Tinbin was putting in a good word to his spirits for him. For all of us, he amended silently.

PART EIGHT

1

There were eight in the party when they left Georgetown, well behind the first mad rush but ahead of Mulligan who was still assembling his expedition with methodical care, irritating some of the miners who had invested in his operation. Ben had made a point of introducing himself to Mulligan to find out as much as he could about the northern terrain, and the man himself had given Ben the nod. 'You're well organised,' he'd said, 'but keep in mind you're responsible for your men. Stick together, stay with your herd or you'll put your drovers at risk. It's slower, but safer.' And then he laughed. 'That's what I keep telling my impatient gents. The hare and the tortoise. The word's out now, the telegraphs are buzzing with news of the Palmer gold but I say there's no hurry. Take your time, son, we'll get there at the tail end of the wet season and have a good six months before we have to make a run for it.'

Ben understood. He'd seen the Burdekin in flood, miles wide. All those northern rivers would be the same, they hurled down walls of water from the tropic wet. The Buchanans had friends in the wild Gulf country whose cattle stations were cut off from civilisation for months, not weeks, once the rains came. He planned to be well away from the Palmer by September at the latest, sooner if possible. Their supplies would be lucky to last that long. He shuddered. A man might survive for months stranded between those rivers, as long as the ammo held out, eating native animals, but he wouldn't like to try it. Especially not with some of the blokes in his party, who knew nothing about the bush.

His drover Jack Kennedy had been at Caravale for years. He was a good hand. Ben had waited until they arrived at Georgetown to tell Jack they were going up to the Palmer, not west to the Gilbert River diggings, and Jack had chosen to remain on the job. Then Ben had enlisted four other men, two former shearers from New South Wales and a couple of miners from the Cape River, all of them eager to go and grateful for the opportunity to travel in company. They seemed a reliable lot of fellows, all wildly enthusiastic about the Palmer gold. Only Billy Kemp's mate Eddy worried him. Ben wasn't sure the little bloke had the stamina for a trek like this, but Kemp assured him he could make it.

Their slow progress brought on the inevitable arguments as the miners demanded to be permitted to ride ahead and let the small herd follow, but

Ben was adamant. 'Anyone who leaves is on his own. Don't come crying back to me for help.'

They followed a stock route, knowing it would eventually lead them to an outback station. They crossed several rivers without too much difficulty until they came to the Lynd which was in full flood. Impossible to cross. The station owner, John Galbraith, and his two sturdy sons visited their camp, relieved that they had their own supplies. 'It's a nasty problem,' he told Ben. 'We couldn't see men starve but we can't go on feeding the diggers. If they've run out of rations at this point we tell them to turn back.'

'What about the blacks?' Ben asked. 'We haven't seen too many around.'

'Most of them go walkabout at flood time,' Galbraith replied. 'But from now on in, watch your backs. There's a territorial war going on here at the minute between the Banjin and the Kalkadoons, so that's keeping them busy. But they're a murderous lot up here. Our homestead's been attacked so many times I've lost count. We keep on, they keep on, someone's going to have to give sooner or later.' He showed them the easiest place to cross, further downstream. 'In a couple of weeks the Lynd will settle down,' Galbraith said cheerfully. 'Don't attempt to cross before then. She's still a fury, but you've missed the worst of it.'

'A couple of weeks!' Billy Kemp growled. 'We can't sit here all that time. We'll cut east, get round it.'

'Not worth the climb into the ranges,' Galbraith told him.

Even then, the crossing was difficult. They lost two bullocks in the swirling waters and Jack was washed from his horse but, being a strong swimmer, went with the current and clambered ashore further down.

By nightfall they'd made it to the far banks, exhausted, but the next day they were all eager to be on their way. It was great country, Ben observed, the gums were huge and the undergrowth minimal. No wonder these cattlemen hung on here, no shortage of feed. For two days they pushed on until Jack warned Ben they were being tailed by blacks. To placate them, they killed a bullock and left the carcass on the trail, but the following night, even though they kept guard, spears flew all around them. It was such a silent, sudden attack that by the time they grabbed their rifles to return the fire their attackers had gone. Ben shouted so the two shearers who were on guard, relieved to hear them answer.

'I am sorry, boss,' the shearer Jim Forbes yelled. 'We didn't see a thing. Didn't hear a bloody sound. Christ! Is anyone hurt?'

'I don't think so,' Ben said as the other men emerged but Eddy Gaunt, shaking with fright, grabbed his arm.

'Fred's hurt, boss.' Fred was a miner. 'He's still in his tent. A spear went right through it.'

They lit a lantern and plunged into the tent. 'He's not hurt,' Billy said. 'He's a goner.' The heavy spear had ploughed through the canvas and into Fred's back, hurling him to the ground. Billy was right. The miner was dead.

In the daylight they discovered that nine of their bullocks had been wantonly slaughtered.

'Ungrateful bastards,' Billy commented coolly. 'We won't give 'em no more.'

'It's no joking matter,' Ben snapped. The other miner, Daniel Carmody, and Eddy Gaunt were already talking about turning back, but they only had a hundred miles or so to go. He couldn't allow them to turn back now.

Within days they were joined by other prospectors, some with families, glad to fall back now and travel in the relative safety of numbers. They too had been attacked by wild blacks and suffered casualties. They introduced disorder to Ben's trek. It infuriated him that he was no longer in command, that he was forced to travel with more than forty trigger-happy strangers who were constantly firing into the scrub and spooking his cattle. The trek had become desperate. Where there should have been accord, in a common purpose, the element of 'every man for himself' prevailed, spurred on by the all-consuming competition for gold. As they straggled through the endless scrub, wading through waist-high grass, their troubles increased. There were fights over rations, arguments about directions, thefts of equipment, accidents and serious incidents. Several men suffered snake bites from which they recovered, but one woman died and was buried in a lonely grave.

The humid weather gave way to stark heat and even Ben was shocked at the ferocity of the sun. The high-standing white-trunked trees offered no respite. There was an awful sameness about the land now, and with a sinking heart Ben realised that this uneven landscape, dotted with low hills, was to be their lot all the way to Palmer. The boat, and two wagons that had joined them, had become a handicap. In places the ancient soil had withered to dust, great drifts of dust feet deep, worse than quicksand, in which the wheels kept getting bogged. But they couldn't leave the boat, they had the Mitchell to cross before they reached the Palmer. And instead of pushing straight through the bush, they had to wind round the hills and detour away from the huge trees that barred their way, taking a day to cover five or six miles.

His drover, Jack Kennedy, whistled to Ben. 'We're going to have to make a change, boss.'

'What now?' Ben asked angrily.

'This bloody heat. She's a killer, mate. We'll have to pull up for a few hours in the middle of the day or we'll all drop in our tracks.'

Ben groaned, though he'd been beginning to think the same thing himself. The horses were drooping and the men on foot had been staggering along or begging rides on the already over-loaded wagons. 'Yes,' he said finally. 'I've never been so hot in my life. It must be well over a hundred degrees.'

'And the rest,' Jack said. He'd brought along his thermometer, his proudest possession. 'Get a load of this.'

Ben stared. It was 112 degrees.

'And it'll get worse,' Jack told him. 'We're heading north, so it won't get better. If this keeps up, my thermometer's going to go bust. We've got to carry more water or we'll dehydrate.'

The decision to rest during the heat of the day caused a split in the ranks.

'I vote we dump the boat and the wagons and get moving,' a man called and the majority agreed with him, including one of the wagoners. He unhitched his horses and packed what he could on the spare horse.

'Maybe he's right,' Billy Kemp said to Ben. 'The cattle are slow enough. I never knew the boat'd be so much trouble.'

'No, we'll keep it,' Ben said.

'But listen. These blokes crossed the rivers without boats. They rafted over.'

'Yes. But you heard what they said – men were drowned. They've forgotten them already. And what about their supplies? They lost a heap of supplies, we haven't lost an ounce.'

Prospectors travelling on foot trudged off over the hills leaving Ben and his small party to their fate. Now he only had his drover, Billy Kemp and Eddy Gaunt, and another wagoner, a sturdy Scot who was travelling with his wife.

The Scot, Jock McFeat, grinned at Ben. 'No point in waste, laddie.' He climbed down and began to strip the abandoned wagon. He handed some bedding to his wife. 'I still say the wagon's the safest place for Mrs McFeat if we're attacked, so we'll stay with you.'

They wound on slowly for days. The next attack came from a new quarter. As Ben led his band through a gap in the hills, two masked riders bailed him up. The spokesman had a rifle trained on him. 'Drop your arms. And tell your mates to do likewise.'

Eddy Gaunt, who'd been riding behind Ben, unbuckled his rifle quickly and dropped it to the ground. Ben followed suit, removing his rifle and pistol. 'What do you want?'

'The blokes are getting bloody hungry up ahead,' the bushranger told him. Ben recognised the voice, it belonged to one of his former companions but he couldn't place the name. 'You can stay here with your wheels, we're taking the cattle.' He jerked his head at the McFeats. 'Climb down, you two, or I'll drill the boss here.' The other bushranger lounged lazily behind him, rifle across his knees, and Ben and Eddy had no choice but to dismount. Ben was more worried about their lives than the cattle.

They could easily track the rustlers if they were allowed to keep their horses. If they were allowed to live . . .

Suddenly a shot rang out. In an instantaneous reaction the gun pointed at Ben jerked skywards and fired. The bushranger screamed, a red patch gushed across his face and he hurtled backwards from his horse. The other bushranger stared, shocked, backed his horse a few paces, then wheeled and galloped away.

Stunned, Ben looked around him. Jack Kennedy, he knew, was trailing the cattle, way back. Then Billy Kemp rode down the hill. 'Just as well I was keeping a lookout,' he laughed. 'I reckoned they might come back for a feed.' He walked over and nudged the body with his boot. 'Yeah. He's dead.'

'I could have been killed!' Ben cried, still stunned. 'He had his finger on the trigger, you bloody fool.'

'That's a chance I had to take,' Billy told him. 'But I reckon they'd have shot you anyway.'

'You could have circled round behind them.'

The Scot took Billy's part.'There might not have been time, laddie. We owe Billy a debt. That was a good shot, couldna done better meself.'

'A lucky shot,' Ben growled.

They toiled on, resting during the scorching midday heat and keeping watch at night, but they saw no further sign of the other prospectors, all apparently swallowed up in this vast, empty landscape.

Days were wasted as they searched the banks of the Mitchell River to find a place to ford with the wagon. Ben's men cursed McFeat's wagon now, but although the Scot was a stubborn, difficult man, he had a determination that Ben envied, nothing would deter him. Ben didn't even mind that McFeat had taken charge of the trek. His own strength was failing and he had trouble sleeping. When he did sleep, nightmares beset him and he awoke disoriented at first, and then desperately depressed.

When they reached the far bank Ben suggested they take a few more days to rest but he was howled down. The Palmer was ahead of them. The fabulous Palmer! Only Agnes McFeat agreed with him. 'We should rest, Jock. Ben and Eddy can't take much more of this.'

Ben was mortified at being lumped in with Eddy Gaunt who curled up in the wagon at every opportunity, claiming every ailment from sunstroke to yellow fever. It was hard to tell whether the man was sick or not, and in the end nobody cared because he wasn't much use anyway.

'I'm fine,' Ben told him. 'If you want to keep going, that's all right with me.'

When they struck on again he and Jack Kennedy rode ahead to explore the land, searching out kinder routes. When they came back to camp several hours later they found Billy at his post as lookout, grinning happily at new developments. 'The Scotties have got visitors,' he laughed. 'Looks like the blacks on this side of the river are friendly for a bloody change. About time too.'

Jock and Agnes McFeat, and Eddy Gaunt, were entertaining a group of giggling black gins and their children, handing them slices of damper, allowing them to dip their fingers in tins of treacle and smiling encouragingly at the naked wild women.

'Look,' Agnes called. 'They're guid, sweet people. You lads come quiet now. Dinna frighten them.'

Kennedy obeyed. He climbed down slowly from his horse, smiling at the newcomers, hitching the bridle to a tree branch. The women bobbed and fluttered like nervous quail but they stayed.

Ben remained on his horse searching for a reason for his disquiet. Why would these blacks be any different from the rest if they hadn't met white men before? What white men? Why would one tribe be friendly? They hadn't set eyes on any blacks since they left the Mitchell but all along the trail they'd seen those fires in the hills. What was it old Tinbin had told him? He pushed his hat back and ran his hands into the knots of his matted hair, wondering what he must look like these days with his hair and beard grown wild. Agnes had offered to cut their hair but it was protection against sunburn to keep their skin covered. It amazed him how this auburn-haired woman, in her forties, with her freckled, fair skin, managed to ward off blisters with just a bonnet. For that matter it amazed him how she managed always to look so neat, how she survived at all. She could drive the wagon as well as her husband and camp-fire cooking never bothered her. Nothing seemed to bother her, not even the hordes of sticky flies or the murky creek water they often had to rely on for billy tea.

'Murky,' he repeated to himself. Murky. Why had that word stuck? Ah yes. Merkin tribe. And the Kunjin tribe! Tinbin had warned him against the cruel tribe that sent in their gins to lull travellers into a false sense of security! God Almighty! What if this was a trap?

He fired his rifle and charged down beside the wagon, scattering the blacks. 'Out!' he yelled at them. 'Get them out!' His horse reared, the women screamed and grabbed the children, running for cover.

Agnes ran forward to him. 'Stop this, Ben! Have you gone mad?'

As best he could, Ben explained his actions but they all disapproved, even Kennedy who felt that they should take every opportunity to make friends with the blacks, and not provoke them.

'You've placed us in jeopardy,' Jock accused. 'Never let it happen again.'

Ben felt he had been relegated to the status of stockman and so he dropped back with Kennedy to drive their dwindling herd.

Only a day's march further on they came across what seemed to be a deserted camp. The tents were still in place, but the camp fires were cold and the billy still hung despondently on its bracket.

'This place stinks,' Billy said as they rode in and Ben nodded. He knew the smell of rotting carcasses.

They found the bodies of six prospectors strewn in the scrub, scalped, macabre evidence of a tribal attack.

'If you hadn't chased those gins,' Billy said, 'we might have struck up a deal with the blacks.'

'The gins were decoys,' Ben argued. 'They were bloody decoys!'

No proof though. He was sick of the lot of them. And he was sick. His head ached all the time, and he sweated too much. He drank as much water as he could to replace the moisture his body was losing but he knew it wasn't enough. In this territory the water was becoming scarce.

Eddy was in the wagon all the time now, and Agnes confronted Ben. 'What did you bring that fellow for? He's coughing. Spitting blood. He's a consumptive, he needs a doctor.'

So do I, Ben thought. A brain doctor, for taking on this insane trek. What if we do find gold? How the hell will we get back? He had lost weight; he'd notched his belt and his pants sagged on his hips. He thought of Caravale. It seemed like a million miles away. And Perfy. He should have followed her to Bowen and talked this over with her. Man to man or whatever the equivalent. Put his cards on the table. Apologised. A truce. Beg her to give him time to buy back Darcy's share of Caravale. In Darcy's name. Out of respect for Darcy. That would have got to her. And Diamond? He rode dully alongside the herd, horses now accustomed to the rigours of the trail picking their way like the cattle through the never-ending wall of timbered scrub. It looked dense from a distance but was bewilderingly sparse at close quarters. Not an optical illusion, just the vastness of it, hot blue skies, tired high foliage and white skeleton trunks jutting from scrappy yellowed grass, a never-changing, terrifying scene no matter what direction you faced. It would be so bloody easy to get lost. He patted his compass for comfort.

Diamond. A whore. Why not? What else was she fit for? But the thought of other men handling her, using her, sickened him.

Jack Kennedy was as tough as old boot leather. He rode each day as if it were a new day. Checking his treasured thermometer, clucking at the heat, worrying about the cattle, about water, about their feed. The herd was leading now, crashing relentlessly through the scrub, their leaders smelling for water in the mornings, deliberately slowing at dusk like recalcitrant children, bellowing their complaints.

It was dusk now and Jack whistled to Ben. 'Lights ahead,' he murmured. 'Camp fires.'

They halted the herd, squinting at the last orange lamps of sunset because in the distance they could see the pinpricks of camp fires. Exhausted, Ben sighed. If it was blacks, they'd have to detour again.

He followed Jack to the crest of a hill and looked into the darkness of this twilight-free land. Behind them the bellows of the cattle seemed the only sound in the universe.

'Too many,' Jack warned as more and more camp fires twinkled into life in the low country. 'We'll have to take another look in the morning.'

'Wonder where all those other bastards got to?' Jack asked. 'We haven't seen hide nor hair of them.'

'We know where six of them are,' Ben said. They'd recognised the belongings of some of their former colleagues back at that deserted camp but the faces had been maggot-ridden and no one had felt inclined to investigate further. They'd just buried the bodies.

As they turned to ride back to meet the wagon and their much-travelled boat they heard a strange sound.

'What was that?' Ben asked.

Jack stopped. The night was still, the toneless mutterings of the cattle carried, but there was something else, a thin sound. They listened again. The temperature, Ben thought bleakly, had dropped to only about ninety degrees, yet the stars looked crisp up there in that cold black sky. He wished he could join them, leave this awful earth and join them, and he wondered if Darcy were up there somewhere, feeling sorry for him. Sorry that he'd punched him, decades ago it seemed, back there in that Brisbane hotel, just because he'd made some stupid remark about Perfy. What the hell did it matter now?

Jack Kennedy was laughing. He slapped Ben on the shoulder. 'Don't you hear it? It's music! Listen, music! Oh Holy Mary and blessed be her name! It's a bloody squeeze box! We're there, boss! It's the Palmer!'

Suddenly I'm boss again, Ben thought, unable to grasp the significance of the thin reedy sound, but for Jack, there was no time to waste. He went charging recklessly down the hill, shouting the news. 'The Palmer!' his voiced echoed. 'It's the Palmer, lads, we've made it!'

In the morning Ben tried to match their enthusiasm, but he was reeling. He marched along beside his horse, hanging on to the saddle for support. Only his dog, Blue, nudging close, felt his pain, whimpering as Ben stumbled, yapping at cattle that came too close. The others were surging along like crafts on an ingoing tide. Jock McFeat rode beside his wagon with Agnes 'giddyapping' at her tired horses. Eddy sat astride the boat, copying her enthusiasm as if the terrain had changed, which it had not; they still had to trudge in and out of the coppled cruel scrub, but everyone was in high spirits.

Some riders rode out to meet them. Twenty strong, hard-faced men behind the beards. They bade them a fine good-day, shaking hands with Jock and Billy, raising their hats to Agnes McFeat.

'And this is the Palmer?' she asked breathlessly.

'Have you found gold?' Billy shouted.

'More than you'll ever need in a lifetime,' Ben heard one man reply as he came forward, and he felt a pinch of joy. As soon as he was well he'd celebrate.

The welcoming contingent produced a bottle of whisky and even Agnes took a slug. 'And why not?' she exulted. 'This is a great day.'

'Have Mulligan's mob arrived yet?' Ben asked them.

'Mulligan!' the spokesman laughed. 'He'll wait till they put down a railroad track. Now lads, who owns them cattle?'

'I do.' Ben straightened up and faced them, womdering whether his general malaise was the cause of a sudden nervous twist in his stomach.

'Pleased to meet you, mate.' The stranger swung down from his horse, hand extended. 'Dibble's the name. Jim Dibble.'

Ben shook hands with him. 'Buchanan,' he replied warily.

'I've got to hand it to you, mate,' Dibble said. 'That's some trek with cattle. You're the first to bring cattle to the Palmer and we're bloody grateful to you.' He turned back to his companions.'Eh, mates?'

They responded with impatient cheers.

'So let's talk business,' Dibble continued. 'How much do you want for them?'

'They're not for sale,' Ben said flatly.

'Twenty pounds a head,' Dibble offered. 'In gold.'

'No deal,' Ben told him. 'I'll give you a few head to keep you going, but we plan to stay the winter out.'

'You don't need all of them.'

'All of them?' Jack Kennedy interjected. 'We've only got a few dozen left.'

Dibble ignored him. 'Thirty quid,' he said to Ben.

'I'm sorry,' Ben told them. 'No sale. If you wanted beef you should have brought your own.'

'I don't think you understand, Mr Buchanan,' Dibble said quietly. 'There ain't no butcher shops here, and we need the beef. Now, like I told you, we're willing to pay, so you can sell the easy way or the hard way. The bidding's now thirty quid a head, so you've made a good profit. You can keep four. Round 'em up, lads.'

'Six!' Billy Kemp shouted.

Dibble laughed. 'Righto, you can keep six. And Jesus, will you look here. They've got a damned boat! You want to sell the boat?'

'No!' Billy yelled. 'That's my bloody boat!'

Ben didn't care about the boat, but he was furious at losing the cattle. He watched helplessly as Billy demanded payment on the spot for the cattle and Jock carefully weighed the gold when the buyers lined up. 'Eight hundred quid you've made, laddie,' he said cheerfully. 'Not a bad return.'

'Tell me about it when you're eating worm-ridden kangaroos,' Ben snapped.

They followed the track to the main diggers' camp, a cleared patch on a ridge overlooking a river that seemed no different from any of the others they'd crossed. At each river and creek they'd fossicked around hoping to find gold, wondering why the Palmer should be so blessed. Down below they could see figures panning all along the banks. Everybody's friend, Billy Kemp was racing about shaking hands with strangers asking how much gold they'd found, but the men were unwilling to talk. They grinned, stroked their beards and walked away.

'It's best to camp up here,' Dibble told Ben affably.

'Is this place worth the trek?' Ben asked.

'There's not a man here won't go home rich, if he can get home,' Dibble replied. 'We camp up here for safety. Don't stay down on your digs at night.'

'Blacks?' Ben asked.

'Not just the blacks. Gold hasn't got a brand on it, remember that. Three men have been murdered already, coming back through the bush, and their gold's missing. The Abos don't take gold. We found one old fossicker with a spear in him, and that just about caused a riot until they noticed the blackfeller spear had been jammed in to cover up a bullet hole. So everyone's keeping mum about the day's work.' He laughed. 'But when a man's just filled his pouch with gold, no power on earth can keep that smile off his face.'

'But if they've found gold, why don't they leave? Get out while the going's good?'

Dibble stared at him. 'You're a real new chum! Would you be satisfied with the trotters when you can have the whole hog? Mulligan was right. The Palmer's paved with gold, and there's not a man alive will stop until he comes to the end of the street.'

'I will,' Ben told him. 'I need a stake and when I get it, I'm out.'

'The poker player's catch-cry,' Dibble replied. 'It's not the winning, Buchanan, it's the game that gets you in.'

Ben walked to the rim of the ridge and looked along the Palmer River. Jock McFeat joined him. 'God save us, laddie,' he said peering at the roll of hills beyond. 'Is there no end to this country?'

Accustomed to distance, Ben's keen eyes searched the river banks, taking stock of the place. The ridge was only about fifteen feet above the river. Across from him a red, damp water-mark in a worn cliff hung like a mezzanine floor another fifteen feet higher than his present position. In the wet, the camp would be wiped out.

He took in the staggered trees dropping down to the tangled banks where roots writhed from the deep, like bloodless limbs, and black-waisted mangroves glistened their heavy green. Snake haunts, he noted, python territory. Fish plopped in the fair-flowing river, and a body of stiff reeds had managed to take up residence in a shallower patch, marching well out to midstream. A good spot to locate mud crabs, lobbies and yabbies, tasty crustaceans. Slowly, as he surveyed the opposite banks, he took in a bold yellow wattle among the skinny gums and, nestling behind it, the unmistakeable holly-like waxy leaves of the native nut tree. Ben turned to point it out to Jock. These nuts were not only nutritious, they were tasty. But Jock had returned to his wagon. Ben shrugged and continued his surveillance.

On the near side there were sandy banks and wide reaches of riverstone rocks interspersed with jutting ledges of scrub, now marked out in claims with poles and ropes, like rows of market stalls. Each makeshift fence was hung with small flags and the litter of domesticity, shirts, pans, waterbags, boots, odds and ends that clashed with the lonely, yellow-tinged sway of the river and its surrounds.

Ben was relieved, he had feared that this might be desolate canyon country, but it was no different from the contrary riverlands that he knew so well. Except that the trees were taller, older, and the bush was denser, visibility poorer.

As he stared over at the far banks, not yet occupied by prospectors, he felt a sensation of movement, as if there'd been a small quake and the forest of trees had moved imperceptibly. He chose one tree and kept his gaze on it, refusing to allow his focus to drift, and then he saw them. Tall black bodies standing motionless, skin mottled with the grey of the tree trunks. It was impossible to tell how many were there, but he felt the hair rise on the back of his neck and he knew these men were not just the 'nuisance' blacks that padded into white men's camps out of curiosity, or for tucker. They were warriors; they didn't need to be fed, their own land fed them abundantly.

He decided to say nothing about them. There was no point. What would the prospectors do? Start firing wildly into the bush and give the blacks a reason to attack? No matter what Dibble said, Ben decided then that as soon as he had found a decent share of gold, he would be off. This place was too bloody dangerous. He prayed that the Palmer gold held out until he had his chance.

As he rejoined the others, he wondered about these fools, starving in the bush. Now that he had observed the land, he realised it was possible to survive here without the beef; the river could feed them. But it could not prevent scurvy. They were so anxious to get their hands on his beef, no one had asked him about greens. 'Well, fellers,' he said to himself as he looked around at the men marching up from their day's work, 'that's your problem.' Ben knew where to find bush spinach and the non-poisonous berries, and the green seeds he and Darcy had called 'plum puddings', and the pods that tasted like green peas. And he knew where to look for fat witchety grubs, rich, nutritious and nutty tasting. But that sort of foraging took time, and he had no intention of supplying a camp this size. He grinned now, thinking of the money he'd made on the cattle. He wouldn't stay at the Palmer long enough to watch this lot disintegrate.

The journey over and his hopes high, Ben slept well that night but Billy Kemp was up at dawn, too excited to allow anyone to rest. They left Eddy with Mrs McFeat and bumped and dragged the boat downhill to launch it in the stream.

Billy and Jock rowed while Ben appeared to rest behind them, but he kept a constant watch on the far banks. The shrill screech of insects gave warning of yet another scorching hot day. Ben trailed a hand in the clear water, disappointed to find it tepid, uninviting. They travelled downstream, well away from the marked claims, and rounded a bend.

'It all looks the same,' Billy said. 'Turn back, Jock. We're wasting time.'

'Keep going,' Ben instructed. 'I want to see what's ahead.'

'Who cares?' Billy argued. 'What are we? Bloody explorers?'

'Don't hurt to know,' Jock said. 'Keep an eye out for a break in the banks, a mon told me once the wee gullies and creeks make bonny storehouses.'

'What for? Leeches?' Billy snapped.

Ben jerked up. 'He's right! They'd trap heavier rocks.' He shifted his attention to water level. 'And listen, you blokes, watch out for crocs.'

As one, the two oars lifted from the water and both men turned on Ben. 'Crocodiles?' Billy yelped, while Jock's face turned a nasty shade of grey. 'Nobody said nothin' about crocodiles.'

'Maybe not,' Ben told them, 'but I can't see any reason why they wouldn't be in this river, so keep your eyes skinned, they move fast.'

'Oh Jesus,' Billy said.

Jock grabbed his arm. 'Steady, lad, veer left here.'

'What for?' Billy wasn't taking any chances now.

'Not reptiles,' Jock laughed. 'See the current moving away from the main stream there.' He directed Billy to row towards a breakaway creek, its mouth almost hidden by overhanging branches. 'We'll see what the wash has left behind.'

They shoved the branches aside and clouds of mosquitoes lifted to attack from ti-trees. Batting away the insects, they manoeuvred into the creek and beached the boat, climbing out to explore the snagged shores. The deadly bush loomed high overhead as each man stepped gingerly from the boat, peering around, poking over riverstone rocks polished from their long journeys, tramping along the dried-out sides of the creek that resembled a cobblestoned street.

Ben was amazed that he saw it first. That it should happen at all. He saw the glint in the shallows and tapped it idly with a stout stick. Small fish glistened and flipped away, distracting him for a minute. Then he bent to pick it up, only a small, yellow misshapen piece, but heavy, as big as his thumb. He stared at it, wanting to call to the others, but afraid of making a fool of himself. He peered at the cobbled river bed again, the water rippling gently over that section, only about a foot deep. He saw the glittering yellow again. He moved stealthily now, as if it might flash away from him like the fish, and reverently collected another piece of gold, hard, rock-solid gold, brave enough, strong enough to have out-lasted the world around it, to have refused to succumb to eroding waters, tumbling along to settle in this creek bed, blinking in the sun.

'Here!' he croaked, almost rendered speechless, to the backs of the other two, but further down Billy pounced.

'Jesus bloody Christ!' he shouted. 'Oh God Almighty, come and see!' He leapt high in triumph, holding up a nugget, and then threw himself in the water, laughing hysterically. 'It's gold! We've found it! It's all over the bloody place! We're rich!'

His voice echoed and echoed until Jock ran to quieten him. 'Do you want the rest to hear?'

'They can't hear us,' Billy laughed. 'They're miles away. We've done it, Jock, you cranky old Scotchman, we're bloody rich.'

When the elation died down, caution entered. 'If they'd take the cattle, the gold's not safe either,' Jock said. 'We'll stake our claims right along here and mark off more claims on the main river to throw them off the scent. We'll have to be damn careful, lads. Until the law arrives and there's a proper gold commissioner, we'll never get out of here alive.'

'He's right,' Ben said. 'We'll bury what we find today and go back as if nothing's happened. And we ought to camouflage the entrance to this creek properly.'

'Let's give it a name,' Billy said. 'I vote we call it Scotchman's Creek. Jock saw it first.'

Ben grinned. It was rare for Billy to be so magnanimous, but now he could afford the gesture. What a day! Ben felt marvellous. His troubles were over, it had all been worth it after all. How much gold was in this creek? Not knowing the extent of their finds was agony. He wanted to remain there now, to guard their precious creek, to prospect for as long as necessary, right now. Never in his life had he experienced such frenzied excitement. Dismissing the dangers, he and Billy would have continued their search until the sun set if Jock hadn't insisted they come away. 'We tread carefully now, lads.'

They took it in turns to stand guard and patrol the creek while the others worked, digging, panning, sluicing, moving further inland along the narrow erratic waterway, too shallow for the boat, and every day their gold stocks grew. By this time Ben had no idea what his gold was worth; there were no scales to weigh alluvial finds. He copied the others and filled tins with gold, jam tins, tobacco tins, anything they could find. Every now and then there was a screech of joy as another nugget was discovered. So far,

Jock had found the biggest, which they estimated weighed a good ten ounces. At night they stared upriver wondering where the main reefs were, planning to go upstream when Scotchman's Creek was cleaned out.

But the heat now was intolerable. Jack Kennedy announced that the temperature by noon was hitting 114 degrees and no one disagreed; the hard sun burned through the sparse, high foliage, and all around them the land was becoming tinder dry.

'It's no use,' Jock said finally. 'This place is like an oven. I won't work any longer past noon, and young Eddy there is near dropping dead.'

Only Billy and Ben were determined to keep working. 'It's hot no matter where you go,' Ben told them.

'No, it's cooler on the ridge. We can get some proper shade under the wagon.'

'He's right,' Jack said. 'I'll take them to the camp and come back for you two later.'

Ben doused himself in the sluggish water. 'See you get us out of here before dusk or we'll get eaten alive by insects.'

'Righto.' Jack packed up his gear. 'We'll see you two later.'

But they were never to see Jack Kennedy alive again.

The blacks attacked the camp on the ridge, not at night, as expected, but at two in the afternoon when the main body of prospectors were down at the river and the remainder in the camp were dozing, exhausted, in the tents or under trees. They moved swiftly, silently, into the clearing, spears thudding, tomahawks smashing. Others ran with blazing branches, firing the tents and the wagon, and as the screams of their victims rent the air, more than fifty warriors clubbed their way out and sped into the cover of the bush. They ran for miles upstream to where their canoes were hidden and crossed the river to safety, white cockatoo feathers bristling triumphantly over grey-striped faces. The Merkin had begun to fight.

There hadn't been time cleanly to cut away the hair of white men for trophies. Besides, their value had dwindled since they had found that the hair was only remarkable for its lack of virility. Several scalps had been brought in from isolated encounters and were no longer a novelty, but young Garangupurr wore his booty round his neck, hanging from a cord. After he had felled her with one blow, it had taken only a second to slice the roll of white woman's hair from the back of her head, and now, unravelled, it hung in gleaming fair strands for all the world to see. A genuine curiosity.

They heard bursts of gunfire in the distance but it didn't concern them. It could be anything, trigger-happy miners took pot shots at all sorts of things, at one another if there were fights. But as the sun turned a fiery orange and began to drop into the hills, Billy became worried.

'He'll be here,' Ben said, 'Jack's reliable. You know that.'

302

They rubbed mud on their faces and arms to protect themselves from the millions of sandflies and mosquitoes that took over from sticky flies at dusk, and waited at the river bank. But there was no sign of the boat.

'Bastards,' Billy said. 'I bet some bastard's pinched my boat.'

'We can't stay here,' Ben said eventually. 'We'll have to walk.' They followed the river in the pitch blackness of the night, stumbling and cursing down gullies and through bracken, scrambling for footholds on the slippery banks, feeling their way over fallen trees. Hours later, their clothes torn, limbs scratched and bleeding, they came upon the hushed and sullen camp.

The massacre shocked Ben. Nine people killed, including Jack Kennedy and Mrs McFeat, and young Eddy Gaunt. Ben was surprised at the depth of Billy Kemp's grief. He never knew what to make of Billy; definitely not a man to be trusted, yet at times he could be incredibly loyal, to the point of viciousness. Ben knew he wasn't too popular in this company, known derisively as 'the squatter', but when a bruiser had attacked him, claiming he had stolen his tobacco, Billy had clouted the man with a stirrup iron without a second's hesitation. Later Billy had calmly produced the missing tobacco and smoked it.

'Poor bloody Eddy,' he wept. 'He never had a fair go. And did you hear what Jock said? He said Eddy could have run away, but he ran back to the wagon to help Mrs McFeat. Jock saw him pick her up, try to pick her up, but he got a spear in his back, then they clubbed him. But Jesus! What a time to pick to play the bloody hero! Jock saw it!' Billy lifted his tear-stained face to Ben. 'And wouldn't you bloody know? Jock said she was already dead.'

Ben was worried about Jock. He was one of the first to be hit. As he walked round the wagon a spear had thudded into his stomach, causing a frightful wound. He was hurled to the ground, unable to move, and an Aborigine running past struck him another blow, shattering his right leg. After the raid, Jock and several others were found to be still alive and a makeshift hospital was set up for them. Most would recover but Jock's injuries were serious. A former apothecary performed surgery on the victims, warning of infection; Jock already had a tropical ulcer on his leg and his condition was precarious.

The miners buried their dead and returned to their labours but Ben and Billy stayed with Jock, trying to keep him cool as the fever set in.

'I've had enough,' Billy said. 'No amount of brass is worth this. I vote we take the gold and bolt.'

'We can't leave Jock,' Ben whispered, beckoning Billy away from their patient.

'He won't be needing his share,' Billy said. 'He's headed for the banks and braes. We'll bury him next to his missus and do a moonlight flit so we don't get followed.'

'Jesus, Billy, you talk as if he's already dead.'

'He might as well be with the hole in his gut and all the rest. He's in shockin' pain. We'd be doing him a favour to put a bullet in him.'

Ben was appalled. 'How can you talk like that?'

'I seen you putting your cattle out of their misery but you won't do it for a mate.'

'Shut up, you bastard,' Ben raged at him. 'That's a barbaric suggestion. He's a human being, not an animal.'

'Righto, you sit and listen to him scream. I can't.'

Ben didn't see Billy for a few days. He kept a lone vigil with Jock, building a ti-tree humpy to shelter him and dressing his wounds with boiled water, sickened to see the infection spreading. He allowed maggots to feed on the leg ulcer to eat away the rotting flesh, but the smell was frightful. Jock was in agony, terrible agony, but he gritted his teeth and hung on, rarely making a sound, and Ben's admiration for the stoic Scot grew. At times he felt ashamed that he was regarding his efforts as a battle with Billy; he wanted to prove him wrong, and it surprised him that these days he never thought of his other existence, back there in Caravale. It was as if the Palmer had taken over his life; that reality was this miserable place, as close to hell as any man needed to come, with everything in nature pitted against his frail resources. Even the dingoes howling at night unnerved him now, when back home he'd taken them for granted.

Sometimes Jock prayed, his lips moving with the cadence of the familiar words, and Ben prayed too as he plodded up and down, to and from the river across the muddy banks closest to his camp. He knew that the muddied site, tramped to slippery slush by the daily traffic, was best avoided. Even a small cut exposed to this overheated breeding ground could become infected. But he dragged up bucketsful of water which he strained through mosquito netting and then boiled, making broth of scrub turkeys in his determination to fight the devils that were grasping for Jock.

One afternoon as he dragged off his perpetually saturated boots he saw a black festering hole in his foot, amazed that he hadn't felt a thing. The mushy tropical ulcer was well-established. Without delay he heated a knife and cut deep into it, screaming with the pain he was inflicting on himself, aware now of Jock's real suffering. No person observing pain can estimate the level, he told himself, they only think they can. He was angry at himself and, madly, at an old dentist who years ago had jerked out one of his teeth, saying, 'Sit still, lad, it's not hurting.' That night, in a mood of hysteria, he dreamed of murdering the dentist with hot knives.

Billy Kemp appeared. 'How's he doing?'

'He's in a bad way,' Ben said, staring down at Jock's sweating grey face and the rough bandages of torn shirts that he'd begged and bought from around the camps, since the McFeat wagon had gone up in flames.

Billy nodded. 'Is there anything I can do?'

'No.'

'Righto then.' Billy was his old self again. 'Did you hear the news?'

304

'What news?'

'Upriver's swarming with diggers. Hundreds of them, they say, turned up practically overnight.'

Ben had trouble digesting this. His headaches had returned. 'Where did they come from?'

'Aha! That's the good part. They came from the coast. It's only about a hundred miles over the hills to the sea from here. I always swore I'd never go near that bloody Endeavour River again, but now I can't get there fast enough! Thanks to the diggers, there's a marked track now. We can march right out of here.'

'As soon as Jock's better.'

'No. The lads are getting up a gold escort to take this new trail. They say there's a port being patched up at the Endeavour Harbour, called Cooktown, so that's for me. We're leaving tomorrow. You can have the boat.'

He wondered hazily why Billy insisted it was his boat since Ben had financed the expedition, but it didn't matter now. He was tired, he wished Billy would go away. Let him leave! As soon as he and Jock were better, they'd start prospecting again. It would be safer now with the population on the Palmer growing. Listening to the other diggers, he'd learned how to estimate the value of gold and he almost had enough to pay cash for Caravale. The Palmer was a big river, there was plenty more gold yet. His hands tingled at the thought. Men were turning over bigger nuggets now, some he'd seen weighed up to sixty ounces. If he picked up a couple of those . . . Ben sucked in his breath with excitement. Billy was foolish, no staying power, that was his trouble; he'd always be a tramp, footloose. But not Ben Buchanan, no sir. He'd go home a rich man, employ foremen under Tom Mansfield and resume the career he really wanted, in politics.

He took his rifle and stood guard over his patient and the pouches of gold hidden under Jock's bunk, gold that had been dredged from the river by the late Jack Kennedy, by Jock and by Ben himself.

In total, a fortune.

The arrival of Mulligan's party caused a stir in the daily routine of the Palmer workforce but Ben hardly noticed, he was too busy to care. He attended to his duties with jealous intensity, refusing assistance, unaware that his constancy was sapping his strength, reducing his grip on reality as the weeks passed.

Leaving the dog on guard he often crept away into the bush prospecting, not for gold but for precious greens, stockpiling rotting berries and wild grapes under a mound of leaves in the corner of the humpy. The pain of ulcers spreading on his leg caused him to smile grimly; like self-flagellation they served their purpose in assuaging his guilt, because sometimes he saw Darcy lying on that bunk, and at other times it was Jack Middleton whose wounds he was treating. As his confusion increased, Ben was convinced that he could, and would, save them all.

He kept his lantern burning all night to watch for nocturnal visitors, crushing spiders, evicting flicking lizards, banning pretty-eyed gekkoes who only came to stare, and pouncing on the occasional snake with shouts of triumph.

One by one his cattle disappeared, and then his horses were gone, and in his muddled state, 'the hermit', as he was now known, approved. 'They need exercise,' he explained to Jock, not realising that he had forgotten to water them. The men who commandeered his horses claimed ownership in the name of pity for the hobbled animals, for few would normally dare steal a horse.

The men he knew drifted away and newcomers with their own frantic dreams had no time for the shabby, bearded hermit and his gaunt-eyed patient, or for the vicious blue heeler that bared his teeth at the approach of strangers. They avoided his camp, and Ben Buchanan was lost. Forgotten. Other men had gone mad with the heat, with fever or starvation on the trail, what was yet another one? Supplies had again become a serious problem. Riders had discovered the emaciated bodies of men who had starved to death trying to reach the coast, bags laden with gold still bound to the corpses.

2

Herbert returned to Bowen. He had a bankroll now, enough to pay his debts and take it easy for a while until he considered his next move. Paying long-overdue bills wasn't really his line, he would have preferred to forget them, but men in this neck of the woods had long memories and could be quite savage, he'd noticed, about 'welshers', as they called them. They cheated, fought, stole among themselves but even the much vaunted 'best mate' could be in serious trouble if he welshed on a gambling debt. And Bowen seemed like home to Herbert now after six months in the bush. He had nowhere else to go.

He took a decent room at the Palace Hotel, delighted to be welcomed back by O'Keefe, the publican, like a long lost friend. 'It's mighty good to see you again, Herbie. You've been prospecting, I hear. How did you go?'

'Extremely well, thank you.'

'I hear they're still digging up gold at Charters Towers by the cartload.'

'That's true, miners are darting all over the place, but there's still a lot of luck involved. First in makes the killing, after that it's damned hard slog.' He looked at his calloused hands and laughed. 'My old man would never believe this.'

' 'Tis a crying shame to bust up them piano-playing hands, Herbie. You ought to look after them. No one plays my piano any more. Bowen's changed. Gone quiet now, boyo.'

'It certainly has. Quite astonishing. I have to look up a few gentleman, pay what I owe, clean the slate so to speak.' He inquired the whereabouts of three of his former card-playing colleagues and O'Keefe grinned. 'Patsy the dealer won't need your cash now, he lost in a shootout with Digger Grimes. And Digger took off to parts unknown in a hurry. As for your other mate, he went down to the bright lights, made for Sydney. So I reckon you might as well write him off too.'

What a pleasant homecoming, Herbert thought, feeling virtuous with an extra six hundred pounds secure in his pocket. There was only the Chinaman to pay now. He took his swag and dumped it in his room. First thing to do was to invest in some decent clothes.

When Lew left him the claim at the Cape, Marie Bourke had come to help him and he'd found her engaging company. She'd bossed him around almost as much as Lew had, but her teasing, light-hearted manner appealed to him. She had always been cheerful, no matter how disappointing the day, no matter how hard they worked; and that figure of hers, strong, lean, but with full firm breasts, had been disconcerting. If her father hadn't been so watchful, Herbert might have been able to romance her. In fact, now he wished he'd at least tried. He missed her.

Lew had sent a rider out to him with a letter in which he informed Herbert that there'd been a new gold strike in the north, and if he wanted to join him on a northern expedition, to make fast for Townsville. And he had warned Herbert not to mention this news to anyone.

A few days later he'd sat up late drinking whisky with Jim Bourke. 'You heard from Lew?'

'Yes.'

'What's he up to?' Bourke asked.

'He's going north on some mad scheme. Invited me to join him, but I wouldn't consider it. God, it's bad enough here, any further north would be asking for trouble.'

'What sort of mad scheme?'

'I'm not supposed to say, so keep it to yourself. A new gold strike, of course. He's got the fever worse than I ever had it.'

'I heard a rumble about that,' Bourke said. 'Did he mention where?'

'No, only that they'd be leaving from Townsville.'

Bourke looked perplexed. 'Townsville? Why Townsville?'

Herbert smiled. 'My dear fellow. One simply has to put two and two together. If Lew is leaving from Townsville instead of going directly from Charters Towers, then our captain is making north by sea.'

'Is that right?' Bourke murmured. 'Those coolies have gone too, Chin's coolies. They've disappeared from around here.'

'Oh yes, he and Chin are partners. Have been from the start.'

'Have another drink, Herbie.' Bourke poured a stiff drink into Herbert's tin mug. 'You know, these claims of ours are about done.'

'Yes. What say we stake new claims nearer to Charters Towers?'

Bourke chewed his thumb. 'Be smarter to catch up with Lew. Fresh fields. And to go by ship! What an opportunity! Do you reckon he'd take us too?'

'Us? I'm not going, no damned fear. Count me out.'

'The Bourkes then. I don't believe Lew would turn us down. Now let me see. We'll pack up here first thing in the morning and go hell for leather for Townsville.'

'You're crazy, Jim. We'd do just as well here. We'll open up new leases, stay where we know what we're doing.'

'Panning for leftovers, you mean. This is the real thing. If Lew and the Chinaman have pulled out their teams, then there's something big on, and a man would be crazy to hang about here. We're for Townsville, lad, pray to God we're not too late. You should have told me earlier, we've wasted days.'

'I wasn't supposed to tell you at all.'

Damn! Why the hell had he opened his mouth? It was the whisky talking.

They'd ridden into Townsville and, sure enough, there was Lew and his Chinks loading a schooner chartered for the voyage – to where? Lew wouldn't say at first. but then the news broke about the Palmer gold.

Lew agreed to take Jim Bourke but wasn't happy about taking the women until Marie persuaded him. 'It's not as if we're not accustomed to diggings, Lew. Mother and I have been at the Cape River for a year.'

'Where my husband goes, I go,' Marjorie said firmly.

Jim Bourke pleaded with him. 'If you don't take us, we'll find another ship, Lew, but we'd rather travel with your mob.'

'Are you coming or not?' Lew had asked Herbert, who'd wavered at seeing them all depart, leaving him stranded. He didn't want to go back to the Cape on his own.

'No,' he said stubbornly. 'It's a fool's run. I won't let you talk me into it.'

'Who's trying to talk you into it? You can please yourself.'

'I am. I've decided to return to Bowen.' That was a spur-of-the-minute decision which he knew would irritate Lew. He'd been intrigued to find Diamond was on board and no explanation given, but he now knew that Perfy was back in Bowen, after the engagement debacle. He couldn't wait to find Perfy. 'I'll give her your regards,' he'd said to Lew in farewell.

In the bar, O'Keefe and the local policeman were able to give him the full and horrifying story of Jack Middleton's death, since Diamond would only say he'd been killed by a crocodile.

'She doesn't like talking about it,' Lew had told him. 'Apparently she was there at the time. But I sent our condolences to Mrs Middleton and Perfy right away. A terrible business, and a damned shame. He was a fine man.'

That news caused Herbert to approach their house with trepidation, dressed formally in a new tropical suit of cream duck, a striped shirt and starched collar. He found the women resigned now to the loss, although his sudden appearance and his compassion caused a few tears. Alice seemed to be making the best of her widowhood. 'We miss him terribly,' she said, 'but he's gone to God and no use us sitting around feeling sorry for ourselves. I've taken a job, voluntary of course. I work at the hospital, looking after the patients. The poor doctor is run off his feet. For such a healthy-looking place, there's a lot of sickness here, fevers, and accidents keep us busy. Perfy comes in occasionally.'

Herbert thought he heard a note of criticism in the inflection on 'occasionally', as if Alice expected her daughter to do more.

'We had a letter from Lew,' Perfy said, 'but we couldn't reply, he didn't leave an address.'

'He's gone to the Palmer River, chasing gold again. Utterly mad, I told

309

him. He wanted me to go with him again but this time I bowed out. The place, as far as I can make out, is far beyond civilisation. A person can take just so much rough living. I positively wallowed in my clean bath at the Palace, and to sit down to table with linen and cutlery again is sheer joy.'

'You did find gold out there, Herbert?' Alice asked.

'Indeed. This time I was far more successful. Came home with quite a tidy stake. I thought I might purchase a business here.'

'What sort of a business?'

Herbert had no idea. It had just seemed the thing to say. 'One would have to investigate,' he replied.

'The gentleman who bought your agency didn't last long,' Alice told him. 'He closed down after a few weeks. Obviously he didn't have your experience.'

Or Glory Molloy to back him up, Herbert smiled to himself. He recalled selling one block of land to three different buyers, in three days, thanks to Glory's glib tongue. 'O'Keefe tells me business is quiet in that line now,' he said.

As they chatted on, Perfy was quiet. He was itching to learn more about that broken engagement of hers. What an obvious ploy on Buchanan's part! He was glad Perfy had woken up in time. He hadn't forgotten Buchanan's threat, via Tolley the bank manager, not to attempt to sell her share of Caravale to anyone. Damned cheek of him. 'Do you still have shares in that station?' he asked Perfy.

'It's on the market,' she said.

'Sad memories for Perfy now,' Alice explained. 'Jack's buried there.'

More to it than that, Herbert thought. His curiosity was teasing him, he had to get Perfy on her own. 'Mrs Middleton, would you mind if I invited Perfy to dine with me this evening, at the Palace?' he asked, 'I deserve an evening out.'

'Not at all, Herbert,' she replied. 'You should go, Perfy, it won't do, your sitting around here all the time.'

'Very well,' Perfy shrugged.

Herbert bridled. 'I wouldn't want to put you to any trouble.'

She smiled. 'I'm sorry, Herbert. That was rude of me. I'd love to have dinner with you.'

He ordered a slap-up dinner, not to impress Perfy but for his own satisfaction. He was celebrating; this time the money in the bank was unencumbered, he was his own man and it felt wonderful. No matter that it could be a temporary situation since he was more of a spender than an earner, something would turn up. This afternoon he had written to his parents to tell them that he had come to rest at Bowen after discovering gold at the Cape River. Every time he thought about it, he was convulsed with laughter. The family would be turning cartwheels wondering how much gold he

310

had 'discovered'. The word was excellent, truthful and yet ambiguous, calculated to pierce the pompous Watlington bubble, for despite their genteel airs they were a mean lot, dead careful with their pennies. To hear that Herbert, of all people, had found gold would hurt. Yes, hurt, that was the best part. He had deliberately not enlarged on the story but had assured them he was in robust health. Oh happy days!

'Forgive me if I intrude on your private affairs, Perfy, but what have you been up to? I heard you were engaged to Buchanan, brother number two. They must hold a fascination for you.'

Perfy stared. 'Who told you?'

He had his own reasons for not mentioning Diamond yet. 'Lew heard. The squatters come into Charters Tower, you see . . .'

'Lew knows about it? Oh God! Does he know that I called it off?'

'Oh yes. But why? And what possessed you to consider taking on the brother?'

'I don't know. I was devastated when Daddy . . . died, and Ben was so kind to me. He and his mother, Cornelia. I was ill for weeks and then it all seemed so natural.'

'It didn't occur to you that he could have had an ulterior motive? Like getting his hands on your share of Caravale.'

'Not at the time, but it does now,' she said angrily. 'He'll never get it now. And I'd rather not talk about that. I'm so pleased to see you, Herbert, I really am. I'm so bored here and dreadfully lonely. If it weren't for Mother, I'd go back to Brisbane where at least I know people my own age. But Mother loves Bowen and she loves the house. I feel an awful guilt that if I hadn't been determined to see Caravale, Daddy would be still alive.'

He took her hand. 'Now stop that, Perfy. I was here, remember? Your father was keen to see the station himself, to him it was important, he said as much to me. In fact he told me in no uncertain terms that he wouldn't allow you to be pushed aside by Buchanan.'

'Yes, I think he wanted to get a proper estimate of the station. Poor Daddy, he tried to help.'

'Cheer up, old girl.' He ordered champagne. 'I think this is the national drink up here, so we might as well enjoy it too. You're looking lovelier than ever, so here's to your good health.' Some other time he'd have to try for that story of Caravale. Buchanan must have been clumsy. To get the girl almost to the altar and then put his foot in it, seemed to Herbert too stupid for words. He wondered how Perfy came to wake up in time. 'Tell me then, why are you bored here? I mean, dear girl, you're well off, you have a lovely home, a delightful mother. Or are you still pining for Buchanan? Ben Buchanan.'

That startled her. 'Of course not. I hate him. I'll never forgive him. I wish you hadn't mentioned him. No, I'm just restless. I've nothing to do.

And don't tell me to put in more days at the hospital, that depresses me even more. I don't know what's wrong with me.'

He laughed. 'I do. You haven't got a beau.'

'Don't be ridiculous.'

'I'm not being ridiculous, it's a normal feeling, even for nice young ladies. I'll have to see that you're entertained again.'

She nodded, uncertainly, not very enthusiastically, he noticed.

'And how is Lew?' she asked. At last. He had expected that inquiry.

'He's fine. Busy with his expedition.'

'He must think I'm the most awful fool. Getting involved with Ben Buchanan. What did he say about that?'

'Nothing much.'

'What's nothing much?'

'Well, to be honest, he didn't sound all that impressed.'

She looked up at the accordion player who was delivering the most excruciating tunes for the benefit of the diners. 'Are my affairs out there in the country such common knowledge?'

'Oh no, not really. We knew of course that you were going out to Caravale, but it appears that Mr Chin who was residing in Charters Towers, and who by the way has amassed a considerable fortune and is bankrolling the Palmer expe—'

'Herbert, forget about Mr Chin, what were you telling me?'

'Oh yes. Chin heard you were engaged to Buchanan through the squattocracy since he's moving in moneyed circles. But it was Diamond who told Lew that you had broken off the engagement and returned to Bowen.'

Her reaction was even better than he had expected. Her face flushed red and her hand shook as she replaced the glass carefully on the table. 'Diamond? Where did you see Diamond?'

'On the schooner. Didn't I tell you? She's gone to the Palmer with Lew.'

In the quiet of her room that night Perfy wept. Rage? Self-pity? What did it matter. Any excuse would do rather than admit that she had lost Lew Cavour by her own stupidity. Knowing her father had died, he could have made the short voyage back to Bowen to see her. But he hadn't bothered. And why would he? From his point of view, she had preferred Ben Buchanan to him, pushed aside his feelings. If only she could explain to him how it was out there at Caravale, how unreal it had all been, isolated from the rest of the world. If only she could apologise to him and ask him to try to understand. She wept again, praying that Diamond would never tell him why the engagement had been broken; it would still place Lew as second best. The truth . . . If Diamond hadn't broken the spell she'd been under, she would have married Ben. 'Oh my God,' she wept. 'How could I have been so stupid?'

The rest of the evening with Herbert had been an awful strain, she'd had to pretend to be unconcerned, unable to cry off with a headache because he'd gone to so much trouble to see that they had a pleasant evening. And then the O'Keefes had joined them, bearing a splendid sponge cake layered with whipped cream and covered with Herbert's favourite passion-fruit icing.

And why was Diamond with Lew? How dare she! Perfy's thoughts rambled angrily around the pair of them as the night encouraged her imagination to run riot, refusing her the solace of sleep. Was Lew her lover now? Why not? First Ben and now Lew. She flung out of bed and lit the lamp. What she ought to do was go up there herself. Other women had. Herbert had said his friends the Bourkes were sailing on Lew's ship, the mother and daughter. Miss Bourke. He had sounded quite fond of that Miss Bourke, describing her as about twenty years old and very attractive. No shortage of women for Lew, even in a place like that.

Perfy determined she would go to the Palmer too, find Lew and explain to him. Tell him she was selling Caravale, that he had been right all along, she should never have gone out there in the first place.

But as the cool coral pink of dawn began to spread across the sky, she steadied, regaining control of her emotions. She couldn't go rushing to the Palmer, that would be yet another stupid decision and she'd made enough lately. Herbert was right, she was bored with no romance in her life and that was a silly attitude. And as the day grew, Perfy listened to the cheerful busy birds singing outside her window and smiled. It was time she took stock of herself instead of blaming other people for her misery; time to grow up, time to live her own life and stop chasing rainbows. If Lew really cared for her, he'd come back, and if not, then it was over.

She realised that, immersed in her own brooding, she hadn't been much support for her mother. She'd never mentioned Diamond's affair with Ben, just that she'd had a row with him. Alice had listened quietly, gently to her story and simply told her to put it all behind her. When Perfy thought of how much her mother must have suffered being transported as a convict in degrading circumstances, she felt ashamed of her paltry complaints.

Samuel Tolley studied the letter from Cornelia Buchanan. The Buchanans were his bank's best customers now. He'd lost a lot of the station accounts to branches in Charters Towers and Townsville so he was prepared to bend over backwards to please Mrs Buchanan. But how? That silly Perfy Middleton had made a right mess of things and there was a real fight on now for control of Caravale. He didn't want to end up on the wrong end of the stick, so he was prepared to back the formidable Cornelia against Perfy.

For weeks now he'd been mulling over the problem. Perfy was willing to sell but not to the Buchanans. They must have had a mighty row out there, what with the broken engagement. Other rumours were filtering back too. Some were saying now that Jack Middleton's death was no accident, and there were other, murkier tales about Ben Buchanan and some black gin, but that sort of stuff was always flying about. They were even saying that the fire at the homestead had been deliberately lit. All very interesting, he'd love to get the full story but Perfy wasn't talking, and Alice, he'd gathered from his wife, was just glad to see her daughter home. She'd never been in favour of keeping Caravale.

He'd spoken to Alice, the saner of the pair, about letting the Buchanans have first option, and she was amenable, not one to hold grudges, but Perfy was adamant. No go.

He felt sorry for Cornelia. Ben had gone off to the Gilbert River diggings leaving her to worry about the station. Most unfair of him. But at least he gave her power of attorney to pay the wages and the bills, in case of accident. She'd insisted on that apparently, anything could happen on the goldfields, and he'd agreed. It wasn't the first time of course. Cornelia had held power of attorney when both lads had gone down to Brisbane that tragic summer. But now Cornelia wasn't letting the grass grow. Originally she and Ben, with their old-fashioned fear of mortgages, had refused his offer of a loan to buy out the Middletons, even though he'd tried to explain to them that the cattle business would boom with the gold rush. Tolley was cautious of loans, but not to cattlemen these days; they were rolled-gold safe, many of them now buying up land they'd been leasing for years.

Cornelia was now ready to take out a substantial loan, and his bank would benefit from the interest but that damn Perfy wouldn't sell to her! Damned stubborn girl! He'd had a few inquiries from squatters interested in splitting the huge property but Cornelia would have none of that. She'd threatened to shoot surveyors for trespassing on Buchanan property. And now neighbouring graziers were ganging up with the Buchanans. They felt sorry for Cornelia, losing her son, then half of her property, and seeing Ben desert the station in a desperate effort to find gold. They were displeased with the situation and had made Tolley and other businessmen in Bowen aware that they expected the problem to be resolved. Those cattlemen, they could ruin Bowen. Turn it into a ghost town. Tolley shuddered. It wasn't only the bank; he'd invested in property here, right in the main street. If the cattlemen, their staff and families blackballed the town, everyone would suffer, from the port to the saleyards.

All because of one silly, stubborn girl.

Well then. He'd told her. Purchase of the house and their living expenses had used up the Middleton cash resources. He'd allowed Perfy credit, with Caravale as collateral, but there'd be no more. Time to pay up. The girl was a villain to argue, though. She'd pointed out, correctly he admitted, that she was entitled to annual income from the station profits, which were now due. All very well. But Cornelia had an answer to that. She said the station books were Ben's domain and no such assessment could be made until he returned. The only way Perfy could collect in the meantime was by taking legal action.

Her Brisbane solicitor, Jauncy, had retired and his partner, Bascombe, had no interest in these squabbles. He'd simply advised her to sell, placing twelve thousand pounds as a fair figure, with the annual dividend to be paid at a later date when the books were available. But what would Brisbane lawyers know? Even without the house, Caravale was worth a great deal more than twenty-four thousand, what with stock and improvements. If the Buchanans could buy back at the figure Bascombe set, which Perfy had accepted, they'd be doing well, but the price itself was a danger. A bargain was on the market. A bargain that could endanger the lifeblood of the town.

How dare she take on Cornelia Buchanan anyway? Tolley was proud of Cornelia, defending her rights, her land, against upstarts like this. If Jack Middleton had been alive, he'd have put a stop to the nonsense, he'd have seen the wider picture. Money was money. The bank manager sighed. There was only Herbert now, Perfy's rather dim-witted friend. Quite the ladies' man was Mr Watlington. He could be the one, given enough incentive, to sweet-talk Perfy into a new arrangement.

Herbert wasn't given to premonitions but he headed for the bank with a sense of foreboding. What did Tolley want of him this time? He wasn't in debt, yet. Really, to be wakened so early and summoned to Tolley's office was irksome, to say the least. The man seemed to think he owned Bowen and all who sailed in her. Let him wait. Herbert had dressed carefully and taken a leisurely breakfast before emerging into the hard heat of the morning. The relentless blue skies of this place were beginning to get on his nerves. He yearned for a real winter, for low-slung clouds and bracing winds and roaring fires, to see and to feel the seasons change, to be able to recognise and welcome springtime. There was no spring here, or if it did exist he hadn't observed any signs.

He walked down the main street trying to locate the source of his gloom. Maybe it had to do with that Caravale place again. What was it Alice Middleton had said to him? 'I think we're being sent to Coventry, Herbert.'

Women get funny ideas at times, but this one was a lulu. 'My dear Alice,' he'd laughed. 'What an extraordinary idea. I doubt anyone here has even heard of Coventry.'

'I have. Did you know they don't need us at the hospital any more?'

'That's no cause for complaint. You've done your bit.'

But Alice shook her head. 'No one calls on us any more, and we're not invited anywhere.'

Herbert watched as she set the table for afternoon tea. 'I do believe I heard my widowed aunt remarking on this very subject,' he told her cheerfully. 'When the husband dies and the mourners depart, the widow finds herself excluded because of the foolish insistence of hostesses in having the exact gender match at their tables. She was very cranky about it, claimed she was looked upon as half a being.' He grinned. My Aunt Edith's wrath was something to behold.'

'And how did it end up?'

'I don't know. I left England about that time. But the same syndrome possibly applies here. You and Perfy are attractive ladies. The poor dreary Bowen hostesses are probably bolting their doors for fear of losing their husbands to your charms.'

Alice laughed. 'You're very kind, Herbert, but I think it's worse than that. I know I shouldn't care about these things but I do. It was lovely to have friends around. Now you're the only person who calls.'

'It will pass. Village people get bees in their bonnets, you know that.'

Perfy came in, obviously having overheard the conversation. 'You two are English, I'm not,' she said angrily. 'I don't know about villages, you must tell me about them.'

Herbert was surprised at the bitterness in her voice. He stood as she took her place at the table, and looked to Alice for a cue, but she began pouring the tea, refusing to meet his eyes.

'Mother and I went to the church fete on Sunday,' Perfy snapped, 'and they cut us dead. No one spoke to us, no one sat with us in the refreshment tent and no one asked us to join them. We were invisible. Did she tell you that?'

'Well, no . . .' Herbert began.

'So what were you saying about hostesses?' Perfy asked him.

Alice intervened. 'That's enough! I'm sorry I mentioned this to you, Herbert. We're probably imagining things. Ghosts in the attic.'

'Not that it matters,' Perfy said. 'I don't care about these people. They're not worth worrying about. We have enough worries. Did you tell Herbert we're broke, Mother?'

Herbert touched his lips neatly with his napkin. 'How could you possibly be broke?' he asked eventually.

'We don't have any cash. The bank won't advance any more on Caravale. What money we had was spent on buying this house and on our living expenses over the last year or so, since we've had no actual income. The Brisbane lawyer is demanding his fees, and not a store in town will give us credit. So, here we are and we don't have a bloody bean!'

'Perfy! Your language,' Alice admonished but Perfy brushed her aside.

'This is what Daddy would have called a "rill pickle", wouldn't you agree, Herbert?'

He nodded, wishing now that he hadn't exaggerated his gold finds. A gentleman should offer to assist but his bank balance now measured around the low hundreds. He had even considered returning to the desperate slog of the goldfields.

'Would a hundred pounds be of any assistance?' he heard himself asking.

'It would be very much appreciated,' Perfy replied, 'and you know I will repay you.'

Their predicament, he was sure, had something to do with the vexed question of that station. A bunch of squatters and their women had come riding into town a few days ago and were staying at the Bellevue Hotel. Among them, he'd been told, was the famous Mrs Cornelia Buchanan. He wondered if Perfy knew she was in town but decided to avoid the subject.

Now, was Tolley preparing to warn him, once again, not to assist Perfy to sell? Delivering another threat from Ben Buchanan? Damned annoying. The cheek of them all. If he could locate a purchaser he'd carry him to Perfy's house on his back. Maybe the two women were not imagining the sudden chilly reception they were receiving. These cattle kings, as they were proudly known, were powerful people, it was feasible that they were leaning on the whole town, like many a squire back home. And that would account for the bank hauling in Perfy's credit. 'Good God!' he said to himself, irritated that he hadn't given the matter more thought before this.

He made no apology for arriving more than an hour later than the time mentioned by Tolley's lackey and was interested to note that Tolley seemed unconcerned. Instead he had coffee brought in and offered Herbert a fine Cuban cheroot.

'No, thank you,' Herbert said. 'Now what's the problem? I have quite a lot to do today.'

'Of course,' Tolley beamed. 'I'll get straight to the point. I need your help, Herbert. A business arrangement you understand, in which your co-operation will be amply rewarded.'

'What sort of a business arrangement?'

'Well, now . . .' Tolley lit his cheroot. 'Did you know Mrs Buchanan is in town? Mrs Cornelia Buchanan?'

'I heard.'

'Good. Now the gist of the matter is this. Cornelia wants to buy Perfy out, but Perfy refuses to sell to her.'

Herbert grinned. 'I gather the Buchanans are no longer in Perfy's good books.'

'Which is ridiculous. This is a very serious matter.' He lowered his voice. 'The squatters, friends of the Buchanans, don't like her attitude.'

'They don't?' Herbert smiled. 'How sad. Tell me, Samuel, what's the difference between a squatter and a grazier?'

'It's the same thing,' Tolley said testily. 'I have explained to Perfy that

317

this town cannot afford to lose the goodwill of the squatters, and do you know what she said to me?'

'I can't imagine.'

'She said we shouldn't allow ourselves to be bossed around by the likes of the Buchanans. She has no conception of the trouble she is causing. However, there is an answer to this stalemate, I'm pleased to say, and no one's feathers will be ruffled.'

'Oh yes. And what might this master stroke be?'

'We want you to buy her share. She'd sell to you.'

Herbert stared at him and then laughed. 'What with? I don't think she's taking stones this week.'

'The money can be arranged. I'll see to that.'

'You mean that in your goodness you'll give me the money to buy half a cattle station?'

'Loan,' Tolley corrected.

'That's a hefty loan, old chap. Which fairy godmother prompted this act of providence?'

Tolley coughed delicately. 'It's quite simple, Herbert. I will arrange for you to buy Perfy out. We have our own Lands Office here in Bowen now, so the title can be transferred without delay. Then you in turn sell to the Buchanans. You will of course receive a bonus, a suitable bonus.'

Herbert raised an eyebrow. The sneaky old trout! 'One does not regard profit on a legal sale as a bonus, sir. How much profit could one expect to make on the resale?'

'Two hundred pounds,' Tolley responded eagerly.

'Not a great deal for such an accommodating arrangement,' Herbert murmured.

'Two fifty,' Tolley offered.

'Three,' Herbert said.

'Very well, three hundred. I have the contract already made out, from Miss Middleton to you. Now you sign here, and I'll have Perfy sign and the problem is resolved.' He handed Herbert the pen and watched as he signed. 'You won't regret this, Herbert, believe me.'

'I'm sure I won't,' Herbert said. 'But it would be better if I approach Perfy myself, otherwise she'll be wondering why I hadn't mentioned my interest to her before this.'

Tolley hesitated. 'I suppose you're right.'

'Of course I'm right, the girl's not stupid. You couldn't just walk in and spring this on her. Now write me out the cheque for payment and the contract and I'll buy your property for you, don't worry.'

Samuel was delighted.

Perfy thumped her hand on the contract sitting on the kitchen table. 'What sort of an idiot do you take me for, Herbert Watlington? How much is

Cornelia Buchanan paying you to act the dummy, to sell to her tomorrow?'

'Three hundred pounds,' he laughed. 'Money for jam. You save face. The town is rescued from the ire of the squatters and so forth.'

'For God's sake, Perfy, sign the thing,' her mother said. 'I'm fed up with the worry of it. We need the money, this is no time to be uppity.'

'No. I will not. The result is the same. I'm sorry, Herbert, I hope you understand.'

He nodded amiably. 'I never thought for a moment you'd fall for it, but just leave it on the table for a few days, and we'll see what happens. Don't burn your bridges.'

'Yes, you have to think about this, Perfy,' Alice said. 'Just think about it.'

As Herbert trotted back to tell Tolley he'd have to wait for her decision he was looking forward to giving Samuel another headache. How dare he try to involve Herbert Watlington in double-crossing his friends? And on behalf of a fellow who had once threatened him. Herbert didn't like to be threatened. He smiled. He would not deceive Perfy and Alice under any circumstances, but if he got his hands on Caravale, Tolley and his pals might find a different opponent from two defenceless ladies. 'Jolly old Tolley,' he laughed. 'You need a lesson in manners. One does not send friends to Coventry.'

He tipped his hat to some acquaintances as he passed by. 'And further, Mr Tolley sir,' he said to himself, 'one becomes extremely bored at being underestimated. Especially by jumped-up bank tellers.'

Cornelia was not enjoying her stay in Bowen, even though the Bellevue Hotel was well-managed and the rooms that she and her station friends had taken had splendid views of the sea. Until the matter of Caravale was settled, nothing else was of any consequence. The Chesters from Twin Hills Station were great ones for organising parties and picnics, and Aggie Lamond from Merri Creek seemed hell-bent on upstaging them with lavish dinner dances. None of them appreciated what Cornelia had gone through and their efforts to cheer her up simply reflected their selfish determination to have a good time, despite her worries. Jim Chester had told her Samuel Tolley would sort out the problem if he knew what was good for him, and she hoped he was right. But when? They had been in town a week now and still nothing had happened. All Tolley could tell her was that negotiations were under way.

How under way? How long did it take to sign a contract? Had somebody tipped the girl off? No, she supposed not. Tolley had said the dummy buyer was reliable. A young Englishman, he'd said, a fellow who was short of cash and unemployed. Those types would do anything for money, that was obvious, since he'd pushed Tolley into promising a three hundred pound pay-off, another aggravation for Cornelia. She'd instructed Tolley not to go any higher than two hundred. That could be looked into later. Once the Englishman prised Perfy's share from her and sold the station back to the Buchanans, she'd give him two hundred pounds, take it or leave it. It was still a huge amount to pay someone for simply acting as a go-between; the fellow could buy two houses here for a hundred pounds. The amount he was demanding was nothing short of extortion.

Cornelia had waited in her room all morning, expecting to hear from Tolley, but not a word, and she was tired of waiting for these muddlers. She'd go to see Perfy herself. She was fed up with these men pussy-footing around; she knew how to handle Miss Middleton.

Perfy answered the door herself, and positively spluttered: 'Why! Mrs Buchanan!'

'Yes, dear. And how are you? I hope you don't mind me arriving unannounced but a person could hardly come to Bowen without calling on you.' She stepped forward deliberately and Perfy had no choice but to stand back.

'Won't you come in?'

'Thank you, dear. What a charming house this is. Nice high ceilings. I do envy you the sea breezes. I've been positively run off my feet since we came to the coast, so many social engagements.' Still talking she preceded Perfy into the front sitting room. 'It is such a gay round here in Bowen what with luncheons and soirées and all sorts of lively entertainments. I've been keeping an eye out for you. I felt certain a young lady like you would be on the invitation lists.' She felt the firm cushions on the sofa and sat down. 'What fine furnishings you have. Excellent workmanship. Where did you buy them?'

'They were in the house,' Perfy mumbled, and then with a physical effort she pulled herself together. 'Mrs Buchanan, what can I do for you?'

'Goodness me, Perfy. What a welcome. Do sit down, you're a bundle of nerves. I declare you were much better out at the station.'

Alice Middleton appeared in the doorway and Perfy seemed relieved. 'Mother, this is Mrs Buchanan.'

'Call me Cornelia,' she said sweetly. 'How nice to meet you at last, Mrs Middleton. I've heard so much about you.'

Perfy's mother responded stiffly and seated herself on the edge of an occasional chair, making it plain she didn't expect to be there too long. She looked to Perfy but Cornelia spoke first.

'We've all had such dreadful misfortunes the last year or so, you losing your husband, Mrs Middleton, and me, already a widow, losing my darling son, I felt I should come and pay my respects.' She sighed. 'But it's no use dwelling on the past. And I specially wanted Perfy to know I bear her no grudge for breaking off her engagement to Ben so suddenly.' She turned up her gloved hands in an expression of reluctant resignation. 'These things happen in the best regulated circles.'

'Yes,' Alice replied, her voice, Cornelia noted, as bleak as that hard-jawed face of hers.

She turned to Perfy. 'Now, dear, we really must talk about the station. You rushed off before we could have a proper discussion. Not that I blame you, with the house gone. It was one of the renegade blacks, you know. I was quite hysterical, Mrs Middleton, seeing my lovely house burning down around me. Wild blacks are always a danger, it's not the first homestead they've burned down. You are safer back here in Bowen, Perfy. We westerners have learned to cope with these dangers.'

Neither of them replied and Cornelia found their stony silence insulting. She'd love a drink. They could at least offer her a sherry but what could one expect from this pair of peasants?

'I believe you are ready to sell your share of Caravale, Perfy, and I do think that is for the best. Darcy would approve. My poor Darcy, I still miss him so.' She dipped a lace handkerchief in the tears welling in her eyes and straightened her elegant black hat. She could see herself in the wall mirror opposite and thought it looked very fetching. It was a sweeping velour swathed in black satin and georgette, the only relief a stunning gold brooch with a circlet of gleaming black pearls.

'Do you still have the contract Mr Tolley delivered to you on my behalf?' she asked.

'Oh yes,' Perfy said coldly. 'There are contracts everywhere.'

'I wouldn't know about that, dear,' Cornelia replied, careful not to admit she had any knowledge of the Englishman's proposed purchase, her fall-back position. 'I am referring to the only contract you should consider wherein you return the property to the Buchanans.'

'To Ben Buchanan, as I recall,' Perfy added.

'That is correct. Now, if you would kindly sign and let me have it, I shall see that you are paid in full this very day. The cheque is substantial.' She smiled brightly. 'A great deal of money. You and your mother will be well provided for.'

This should have pleased the mother, but still she did not react. She was regarding Cornelia with the cold stare of a turkey guarding its nest. What was it about this woman that was vaguely familiar? Cornelia wondered. Maybe it was just her attitude. She'd had several housekeepers before Mae, and most of them had displayed the same stubborn antagonism towards their betters. Mrs Middleton's grey wiry hair was pulled back in an unbecoming bun, and her weathered skin had obviously never seen a dab of cream so necessary for ladies in this country. No wonder she looked uncomfortable confronted by a woman of style. 'Those are superb drapes on the bay windows,' she commented. 'The brown velvet really sets off the cream curtains between. Did you make them yourself?'

'No,' Alice replied.

'Mrs Buchanan,' Perfy said. 'You know quite well that I will not sell to Ben.'

'Am I to understand you expect to be paid more?' Cornelia's tone was deliberately accusing. 'You won't get any more, you know.'

'It's not the money, it's his behaviour. I won't sell to him. You people thought you could dupe me, now you can face the consequences. You think you can ride roughshod over everyone but let me tell you how wrong you are.'

'I don't believe we are wrong at all,' Cornelia said angrily, resisting the temptation to take off her gloves. 'Since you persist in this attitude, you are the one who will suffer. I happen to know you have no other money, and that the townspeople resent the trouble you are causing.' Her voice was becoming harsher but she didn't care, a few home truths would push them into signing with the dummy if not with the Buchanans. 'Everyone knows you hardly knew my son Darcy. My boys mixed with the highest circles of Queensland society, with the Governor's set. People are wondering how come Darcy got mixed up with a housemaid?' She saw Perfy flinch and her face redden, and satisfied she was now giving the girl no less than she deserved, Cornelia pushed on. 'Our friends are asking, with good reason, what you did to coerce my son into signing over his inheritance to you?' She jabbed her finger in the air. 'Did you seduce Darcy? I'm inclined to think that you're not the soppy little virgin you pretend to be, since I've heard you had yet another man here in Bowen, a sea captain no less.'

'How dare you!' Perfy cried but, strangely, her mother said nothing.

Encouraged by her silence, Cornelia began to believe she was on the right track. 'And what about Ben? I suppose you seduced him too. That would have been easy enough under our roof. I find you quite contemptible. That business about your black maid. Nobody believed a word she said, but you did. And why? I'll tell you why. It was because you were sleeping with Ben yourself, and storming out of Caravale was nothing more than jealous rage.'

Perfy jumped up, her face white with shock. 'Get out of my house,' she cried. 'You are the most awful woman—'

'No. Wait!' Alice said. She was smiling. Laughing in fact. She went to the mantelpiece and picked up her glasses, and as they both stared at her, she put them on and turned to study Cornelia. Then she began to laugh again, a rich, merry laugh. 'What a performance,' she said to Cornelia. 'It must have taken years of practice, Nellie.'

'I beg your pardon,' Cornelia replied loftily.

'Ah, don't come the high and mighty with me, Nellie,' Alice said. 'I've been sitting here trying to work out where I've seen you before and it's finally come to me. You're Nellie Crabtree. Fine lady indeed!' She walked over to Perfy. 'She's no bloody lady, she comes from Bethnal Green, same as me. About the worst slum in the whole of London, the like of which

322

you'll never see, Perfy. Nellie here was a dip, a pickpocket, among other things.'

'I don't have to listen to this,' Cornelia said, grabbing her handbag. 'I've never heard such lies.'

'Oh yes you do! You had your say, now it's my turn. You and your boy friend Clem Bunn were a right nasty pair of wretches. I should know, Clem Bunn was my cousin. You married him. Or you thought you did. He was already married to Hetty Cornish but when she took sick with the consumption she was no use to him any more. That's why he partnered up with you. He used to boast you had hands of velvet. When he got caught, he sent for you to bail him out, but you'd nicked off with his stash.' Alice grinned. 'You bolted with his money and left him to rot. I never heard what became of Clem after that.'

Amazed, Perfy looked at Cornelia. 'He's buried at Caravale, isn't he? In that unmarked grave. I bet it's him.'

Cornelia staggered to the door. She had to get out of here! She'd already forgotten the reason for her visit in the shock of Alice's disclosure. Clem Bunn had been married all the time! She remembered that skinny, sickly Hetty Cornish. His wife! God, no! And she'd shot him when there'd been no need. She hadn't been married to him at all, she was legally married to Teddy!

She rushed out of the front door and across the verandah. Clem Bunn had lied himself into a shotgun blast. The killing that had cost her Caravale!

A man was coming in the gate but she shoved him aside and blundered into the street. Head down, she ran wildly, stopping suddenly outside a tavern to pay a lad to go in and buy her a bottle of gin. She stuffed the bottle in her large handbag and hurried down to the Bellevue Hotel, ignoring greetings from people in the lobby. Behind the locked door of her bedroom she wrenched the bottle open and poured herself a stiff drink. Clem Bunn had come back to haunt her again, his evil presence was everywhere. She knew now it was Clem Bunn who had burned down her house, the ghost of Clem Bunn. But he wouldn't beat her. When she got back to Caravale she'd have that grave destroyed. She poured another drink, her hands shaking.

'Who on earth was that?' Herbert asked. 'She went out the gate like the hobs of hell were after her.'

'They were,' Alice laughed. 'It was Cornelia Buchanan.'

'Oh. I presume you ladies are still arguing about Caravale.'

'Yes,' Perfy said, still trying to digest all that she'd heard.

'No, we're not,' Alice announced. 'I want no more of it. I'm glad you're here, Herbert. Perfy is ready to sign your contract.'

'I am not,' Perfy said.

'Yes, you are,' her mother said. 'Cornelia's just had her come-uppance and enough is enough. Herbert has been very kind to us, the least you can do is sell to him and allow him to make a small profit.' Perfy's face was set but Alice continued, 'You've never said what caused the rift between you and Ben Buchanan but I'm beginning to get the drift now. So you either sell that damned place or go out there and live. I've got to get on with my life. If there's no money I'll get a job, it's no skin off my nose to start again.'

Perfy relented. 'I'm so sorry, Mother. I didn't realise this was upsetting you so much.'

'We've paid dearly for that inheritance of yours, Perfy, and I'm not blaming you at all, not for any of these events, but it has brought us bad luck, so you end it now. Get rid of the place.'

Herbert stood by as Perfy signed the contract. 'Mother's right. I feel better now it's over. Do you still have the cheque?'

'Right here,' Herbert said, taking out his wallet. 'If I were you I'd bank it before they change their minds.' He handed Perfy the cheque for twelve thousand pounds. 'Very nice, what?'

'Marvellous,' Alice said. 'God, what a relief.'

Samuel Tolley was delighted. He went to tell Cornelia the glad news, that their plan had worked, but she was indisposed, so he trotted down to the Palace where he found Herbert idly playing the piano for the lounge customers who were enjoying the treat. 'I hope O'Keefe's paying you for this entertainment,' he said, being more amenable to Herbert now.

'Wouldn't dream of charging,' Herbert smiled. 'Have a snifter of brandy. It's excellent.'

'Not just now, I have to get back. I just came to congratulate you on effecting that sale. I knew you could do it.'

'No trouble at all, my dear chap. What happens now?'

Tolley pulled over a chair and sat close so that Herbert could hear him. 'I was holding the title deeds as collateral. They now go to the Lands Office to be transferred into your name. You go over there in a couple of days – I've insisted on all speed with these papers – pick up the deeds and bring them to me so that I can organise your sale to the Buchanans.'

'And pay me three hundred pounds,' Herbert reminded him.

'Of course. On the dot.' Tolley rose, feeling so pleased with Herbert he almost changed his mind about having that drink, but it was near to closing time at the bank. He patted Herbert on the shoulder. 'That's a nice tune you're playing. What is it?'

Herbert continued with the Chopin Valse. 'It's a little thing I wrote myself. I'm glad you like it, Samuel.'

It was time to go home. He missed London, and the proximity of the European cities which had always entranced him. This country was too rough, and devoid of culture. He hated goodbyes. He promised himself he would write to Perfy and her mother and wish them well once he was on his way.

Since Tolley had first spoken to him about the sale of Caravale, Herbert had been checking the shipping movements and found that the trader *Goodwill*, bound for Calcutta via Batavia, was due, giving him enough time to complete his last Australian commercial transaction.

As *Goodwill* sailed out of Bowen harbour and nosed into the Whitsundays, heading north, Herbert asked the first officer to be sure to point out the Endeavour River and the new village of Cooktown.

'We're not stopping there, sir,' the officer warned. 'No bloody fear. That's the new gold port, the outlet for the Palmer gold. They say that river's running with gold. If we stop there half the crew'd jump ship.'

'I didn't particularly want to go ashore there,' Herbert said, 'just wave farewell. A gesture, so to speak. I have friends there.' He smiled benignly. 'I hope you stock a good cellar. I'm accustomed to the best.'

'Indeed we do, sir. Captain Baar runs a fine ship. He's a Dutchman, you know.'

'Dutch, eh? That's interesting. I look forward to his company. They say Amsterdam's an amusing city these days.'

'If you've got the money, sir.'

Herbert nodded wistfully. 'I suppose so, that's always the problem.' No point in alerting the crew to the gold he had hidden behind a panel in his locked cabin.

The officer went back to his duties and Herbert leaned on the rails, smiling at the green landmass that had served him so well. A pity he wouldn't be able to see Tolley's face when he found out that his 'dummy' had collected the title deeds to Caravale and had sold Perfy's former share the same day. That old Chinaman Fung Wu, the money-lender, knew a bargain when he saw it, but they'd still haggled for days over the price. And when Herbert had produced the title deeds, he'd sent one of his lackeys to check their legitimacy.

'Fair enough,' Herbert had said affably in answer to Fung Wu's apology for his lack of courtesy. 'I don't mind, just tell him not to waste time.' *Goodwill*, this fine ship, was sailing that very day.

Finally they'd agreed on the price of twenty thousand pounds, paid in gold, since the Chinese did not trust the banks.

Herbert had watched with rising excitement as Chinese servants weighed out the gold on small brass scales, making strange entries on their scrolls. Then, to oblige Herbert, they had carefully placed the nuggets in a small leather bag. The contract had been signed by both parties, Fung Wu even signing his name in English, in a clear hand. He called in two white men passing by to witness the signatures, and Herbert appreciated his caution. The witnesses signed happily, pleased to be asked, and were even more pleased when Fung Wu handed round small cups of an exquisite liqueur to seal the deal and celebrate the occasion.

When they left, Fung Wu bowed to Herbert. 'I must delay you no longer. If you miss that ship you could be in serious trouble and I wish no complications.'

'What ship?' Herbert asked innocently.

'Mr Watlington,' Fung Wu replied with gentle patience, 'it is my business to know your business. Do not be alarmed. Two of my men will follow you to the ship to see that you get there safely with your gold. And I have arranged with the captain to sail as soon as you board.'

He padded from the house he had built near the moongate and Herbert followed. 'I wouldn't recommend that you return, Mr Watlington,' he said. And Herbert had a sudden lurch of conscience. He quite liked this smart old fellow.

'I hope I haven't caused you complications.'

'No need to concern yourself on my behalf. If you gentlemen involve yourselves in strange proceedings, that is your affair. My actions are entirely legal. It is a great day for my family to become partners in such a prestigious enterprise. I have investigated this station. I doubt there are that many cattle in the whole of China.'

And of course he'd been right. As soon as Herbert boarded, the ship's crew sprang into action and *Goodwill* was on her way.

PART NINE

1

They were not the first by any means. As the schooner nudged carefully into the mouth of the Endeavour River, Lew admired the competence of the skipper. He had a whaleboat leading, making soundings. It was a tricky exercise, but Lew admitted he couldn't have done better himself.

The south bank of the Endeavour was already coated in tents and strange makeshift humpies. Some of the ships moored in the estuary were Chinese. That was understandable, he figured. After all, edging down the coastline the Chinese would have inquired at any sign of settlement, and this was the first after Somerset. They were lucky to have hit the jackpot so quickly.

Inland, green mountains loomed in the oppressive heat and Lew shuddered. He felt his insides spinning with that excitement again at the thought of the Palmer River, just over the range. It was a fine irony that he had brought Chin Ying and his entourage right past this site on their original gold expedition.

Everyone had travelled well on the short voyage. The coolies squatted together on the deck, tough, skinny men, chattering happily as they watched a chosen few attend to the horses, a much envied task. Their constant cheerfulness impressed Lew now. He'd taken them for granted in China, but in a different environment, their stoicism, their acceptance of their lot in life, was admirable and, he realised, not a little sad. No wonder Perfy had been upset at her first encounter with men whom she regarded as being treated like beasts of burden. Then again, he began to argue with himself, she didn't understand the mass of humanity in China. The coolie considered himself fortunate to have work; few rose above that level and the alternative was starvation.

The Aborigines of this land would never become coolies, the concept was outside the cognisance of the Europeans here, and the local natives resented the whites so much they'd hardly be likely to co-opreate. Some of them were still fighting the invaders, giving the whites hell in an ongoing series of guerrilla wars across the frontiers. It was surprising that the rest of the world seemed unaware, still, of the battles raging in the Australian outback. He wondered what the blacks were like here. Friendly, he hoped. This time there were no defined trails to follow, they'd have to make their own way out to the Palmer and make an effort to befriend the natives if they encountered any.

He looked at Diamond as she stood right at the prow of the ship, studying the shoreline. Maybe her people were here. Ying seemed to think so, but Diamond herself wasn't so sure now. Because of the sameness of this coast, it would be difficult to recognise any point from the memories of childhood. She'd had little to say about Perfy except that they had decided to part, but he was certain there was more to it. Surely Perfy wouldn't have just dumped her like that! Then again, Ying insisted prostitution had been Diamond's choice. 'Everyone needs money,' he had said, 'even black girls. Why should a beauty like that accept the humility of being an unpaid servant? She is exotic, exciting. In China she would not be a diamond but a superb black pearl, she could become a highly respected concubine.'

Lew looked over to where Chin Ying was, as usual, holding court. This time the Bourke family were the recipients of his philosophising, hanging on his every word. The man should have been a teacher, Lew thought, he enjoyed 'discoursing', as he called it, with strangers. Lew was still annoyed that the Bourke women had insisted on joining them. They had no place here, but he supposed very soon Cooktown would be another goldrush town and there'd be plenty of women to keep them company.

He watched some porpoises skimming playfully alongside the ship and moved aft to get a better view of them, placing himself, incidentally, within earshot of the other passengers, realising they were talking about Diamond.

'She frightens me, that girl,' Mrs Bourke said. 'You wouldn't want to cross her.'

'That's silly,' her daughter Marie objected. 'I think she's very nice, and ever so polite.'

'Oh yes,' her mother replied. 'She's that but there's something about her that makes me fearful. Something evil . . .'

Chin Ying raised his hands. 'No, no! Not evil. What you see is a different ethic. She does not have your Christian sentiments, her reaction to events is more basic.'

'That's what I mean,' Mrs Bourke hurried to agree. 'She's a heathen.'

With his back to them, Lew grinned. She walked right into that one. He listened as Chin Ying sighed. 'I do not have the Christian ethic, either. Would you regard me as a heathen too?'

Embarrassed now by her tactless comment, Mrs Bourke mumbled her confused apologies and Lew left them to it.

'Well, Diamond,' he said as he joined her at the prow. 'Is this your home town?'

Her dark eyes were dancing with excitement. 'I think so. I really think it is. I can't tell from the beach, they all look the same, but there should be a big waterfall just a little way inland. And if I'm right, this river, you be careful, keep away from the river.'

'What do you mean?' They had a whaleboat and he and Ying proposed to explore the Endeavour River first, as the fastest way to work out a route if the prospectors who'd already landed hadn't made any headway. He guessed that at this stage finding a way inland would be a matter of trial and error.

'Crocodiles,' she said. 'If this is the place, the banks of that river is alive with them.' She shivered. 'After what happened to poor Mr Middleton, I never want to see another one as long as I live.'

'Well,' he said, 'we'll soon find out.'

Cooktown had sprung up practically overnight, thanks to telegraphed news of the Palmer gold. The steamer *Leichhardt* had landed almost a hundred diggers days ahead of Ying and Lew's arrival and now, as their expedition was disembarking, the armed schooner HMS *Pearl* sailed into the estuary. The government had acted quickly; by this time Queensland authorities were experienced in the management of goldrushes. The Gold Commissioner, Howard St George, was already in charge, backed up by a squad of mounted police, but despite the presence of the law, there was near panic in the town. They had discovered that the natives were far from friendly. Unseen attackers had already murdered diggers who had made the mistake of wandering too far from their camp.

By nightfall hundreds of native fires could be seen in the hills, a clear challenge to the intruders.

As Ying's coolies sprang into action, setting up their tents, Lew called a meeting of their group and announced that under no circumstances would he take the women any further, and that included Diamond. The dangers, he told them, were far worse than he had imagined.

'They can't stay here on their own,' Bourke said.

'So you stay with them, Jim. It's your problem, not mine.'

The government surveyor who was to lead the first party to blaze a trail from Cooktown to the Palmer also refused to take the Bourke women, so the Bourke family were temporarily stranded in Cooktown.

Lew watched the first expedition set out, content to follow their trail when all their supplies and equipment were unloaded and sorted out. MacMillan, the surveyor, rode into the bush with other horsemen and a large number of diggers on foot, and Lew noted they were all heavily armed with Snider rifles and Colt revolvers and each man carried heavy swags and tools. No wagons this time, the going would be rough. It worried him that they did not have enough firearms to distribute among the coolies, and now it was too late to purchase any more.

Ying was unconcerned. 'We will protect them, and my servants will see that they all have knives. It's the supplies that worry me. I wonder now do we have enough?'

'It's only a hundred and sixty miles,' Lew said. 'We can do it in a week. Storekeepers, publicans and the rest follow goldrushes. We'll be able to come back here for supplies. More ships have come in today, the estuary's beginning to look like a busy port.' He was to recall that optimism when they were struggling on the terrible march to the Palmer. A week indeed!

'And what about Diamond?' Ying asked. 'I'm glad we can't take the other women, but we must take Diamond, she is important.'

'Not on your life. She stays too.'

'I have to come with you,' Diamond said. 'You can't stop me now, Lew.'

'Don't talk rot, Diamond. You don't know where you are. You can't move out of here to explore the countryside and see if you recognise the place any more than we can, without guards, and we haven't time to be fooling around.'

'If I could just find some of the people—'

'For God's sake, take a look around you, Diamond. This isn't Townsville or Charters Towers. There's not an Aborigine in sight, and that means the only ones we'll find will be standing at the other end of a spear. It's too late for you, Diamond, even if these are your people. Best you wave to them from here and get ready to go back home.'

That night Diamond sat by the camp fire of huge ironbark logs, preferring to be alone with her thoughts. She was frightened, terribly frightened, not only for herself but for all the people in the hills. She had heard the talk of these brutish men as they polished their guns and packed up ammunition, laughing about notching up the killings ahead of them. Boasting. 'No black bastard'll get in my way! Let the buggers learn what guns are about and they won't be too handy with their spears!'

She hated them, all of them, Lew Cavour too. Mr Chin was wiser than any of them, he was ready to try, through Diamond, to parley, to talk to the people, to come to some arrangement wherein they might be permitted to pass through the territory without harming anyone. It could be done, Diamond was sure it could. But Lew had no faith in her. She had complained to Mr Chin, but he would hear no criticism of Lew. 'He only thinks of your safety. I was naive. I thought we would find black people here, as in the other towns, so that we could inquire of your tribe. But you see now, in this matter we have no point of reference, no means of communication with the tribal natives here. It is sad but I believe he is correct. You stay with the Bourkes until we learn more about who owns this land.'

Diamond smiled. 'Who owns this land,' he had said, and she loved him for it. It was the first time any non-Aboriginal person had spoken the truth as it was. Some tribe owned this land, maybe the Irukandji, maybe some other tribe, and Mr Chin had afforded them that respect. This was their land, he understood this, not like the rest. Mr Chin simply wanted to take the gold they didn't need and leave them in peace. The rest of the bloodthirsty lot were despicable. Not for them the possibility of mercy, there would be none; they were prepared to slaughter their way to the Palmer.

As the moon rose, the white tents glistened against the dark backdrop of the ranges, incongruous in this hot, humid night on the edge of the forest.

The camp was quiet now, the men were tired. They worked hard all day chopping and sawing, felling trees, hauling cargo ashore; white men exhausted by this heat. She listened to the sounds of the forest, the squeaks of small animals, the occasional shrieks of angry disturbed birds, and the songs of the frogs. Some drunken diggers staggered by and Diamond sat very still, her hand on her knife, but they didn't notice her.

In the far distance she could hear the surf crashing on the great reef, but strangely it seemed closer, and different; the surf had a long roar about it as if sea devils were hurling it at rocks; it was a perpetual rushing sound, this hurrying of water. She twisted her head to listen. It was water, no longer competing with the sounds of the day. Why hadn't she thought to listen the last few nights, for everything talks. This was the waterfall, the big falls that rushed down from the two sister-rocks. It was. She stood up and held out her arms towards the sound, the familiar sound of the Irukandji falls.

Quietly she crept into the tent Mr Chin had ordered for her. Even here she had no place, not with the men of course, and never with the white women, but now she was glad. She picked up her canvas bag, emptied the clothes out and took it down to the supply tent where she almost ran into Yuang Fu who challenged her with his rifle.

'It's only me,' she called, jumping back in fright. He looked so ferocious, like an Oriental prize-fighter. 'I need food,' she said, relieved that he lowered the rifle, but he still barred her way. 'I want you to tell Mr Chin that I have gone to find my people. No need to wake him now. Tell him in the morning. He will understand. Are you listening, Mr Yuang?' she asked of the expressionless face.

'Yes, missee.'

'So can I get some food?'

He stepped aside and lit a lantern which he handed to her. 'What food, missee?'

'God, I don't know,' she said, looking around the big tent piled high with crates and packages, but eventually she emerged with some salted meat, apples and oranges, a loaf of bread and, to fill up her bag, tins of biscuits. At least they had lids. The men opened tins of beans with their knives but she hadn't mastered the art. This lot would do. She felt a little light-headed, as if she were going on a picnic, but she knew the perils ahead.

'Tell Mr Chin I'll be back as soon as I can,' she said as she left, but then she turned. 'If I don't get back, will you thank Mr Chin for his kindness to me?'

'Yes, missee.'

Even as Diamond disappeared into the bush that surrounded the isolated port, Chin Ying was being informed of her departure. He stood outside the tent from where he had been summoned by his servants with

333

remarkable stealth, so that Lew Cavour, in the other bunk, should not hear, and looked up at those warning firelights that now resembled low-hanging stars against the blackness. 'It is her destiny,' he said. 'You did well. We may never know the outcome.'

In the morning Lew was distraught to find Diamond missing. He searched the camp, routing out grumbling sailors and angry diggers who might have abducted her but in the end he had to admit that she must have gone into the bush of her own accord.

'What chance will she have?' he despaired. 'They'll kill her on sight. If I knew which direction she's taken, I'd go after her, but where to look in that bloody jungle?'

'Maybe it's for the best,' Marie Bourke said, trying to console him. She'd always found Lew far more interesting than Herbert, much more attractive.

'It's not for the best,' Lew snapped. 'She could get killed out there!'

It was then that Marie Bourke realised that she'd made a terrible mistake. She should have stuck to Herbert who'd been really keen, but she'd set her sights on Lew Cavour. Her mother had been right. 'It will take a very special woman to rope him in, if it can be done at all. You ought to be satisfied with Herbert. He's a gentleman, not as demanding as Lew.'

She wondered where Herbert was now.

2

A lone hawk floated lazily in the pale morning sky with disarming indifference, drifting in warm air streams, red wings spread as her sharp eyes took in the most minute detail of her territory. Nothing escaped the steady gaze of the hawk, Diamond knew. She climbed through the rainforest towards the falls, stepping carefully through ferns and the moss-shod undergrowth, and she wondered how long it would take for the sharp eyes of the people to become aware of her presence, to spy this unaccountable movement.

Back there, threading her way through the lowland scrub by the light of the moon, she had been nervous, jumping at every sound. But as the dawn filtered through the forest and she had begun her climb, a wonderful sense of exhilaration filled her. She, Kagari, recognised the familiar smells, the sweetness of the air. With practised ease she avoided the drops and gullies hidden some six feet deep under innocent layers of ferns. Many a child, she recalled, had fallen yelling down into those traps to be rescued swiftly from the dark depths that harboured coils of sleek-eyed snakes. They would be a trap too, she thought sadly, for any poor horses urged across them.

Kookaburras hollered back and forth and Kagari exulted with them. She was on her way home at last. It had taken so long, but soon she would find her family, her beloved mother and father, and all the others, and what a welcome it would be. She envisaged welcoming arms, excitement, tears, the joy, their amazement, as she tramped round the lonely boulders that had been cast down long ago in the Dreaming. Every child knew this was the crossroads; one path led down to the monsters of the river, the other to the sea whence she had come.

The grey granite intensity of the huge boulders was intimidating, and she stumbled, panting, trying to clamber across them, surprised at the effort this entailed. She felt her confidence ebbing, being replaced by a nervous chill. What if she came upon strangers? Could she make herself understood? Would they listen to her? In these clothes, they might take her for a white person. What would they know of skin colour? With an acute sense of embarrassment, she removed her skirt and blouse as well as her footwear and hid them among the roots of an old fig tree, marking the trunk with her knife. She ripped the wide lace from the hem of her petticoat and stood up, looking guiltily around her. The sleeveless cotton shift with bloomers tucked up underneath would have to do; she hadn't the courage to undress further. She remembered the time she'd ripped off her clothes to hand to Ben as he frantically tried to help Mr Middleton, leaving her breasts bare, and she blushed. But that had been an emergency.

Ben. Her heart still ached for him. Her body had searched for that same passion with all of those other men at Mr Chin's house, but it had fled. Her actions had been mechanical, and their hurried entries into her body simply relief, like cows needing to be milked. Oddly, they seemed to find more excitement in watching her undress, in gaping at her naked body. They were nothings. All of them just stupid nothings. But Ben, he had made love to her so passionately, surely he'd cared a little for her. He must have.

She ate an apple and set off again, grasping at trees to pull herself higher up the steep slopes, warily now, watching at every step for any sign of movement. She was making for the head of the falls, guided by the continuous rush of the waters. From there she would go on to the caves. Food and shelter, that's all Aborigines needed, she mused, and yet in the white world so much more was essential, especially money. She pushed aside heavy curtain vines, and screamed! A white-painted face was staring at her.

He grabbed her arm roughly and pulled her clear of the vines to pin her against a tree, and then he grasped her shift, bunching it in his large fist and shaking it, shaking her with it as if she were a rag doll.

'Stop,' she yelled, automatically in English, shoving the confused young man away from her. 'Irukandji!' she shouted imperiously, and he blinked, stepping back to stare at her.

'Irukandji,' she shouted again, terrified now. What if he were not? What if he, too, had never heard the word? How could she get away from him?

He licked his lips nervoulsy and nodded. 'Irukandji.' A question, 'Irukandji?'

'Yes, yes, yes,' Kagari shouted, laughing, throwing her arms round him. 'Irukandji. I am Kagari.'

Astonished, he drew back. He was only about sixteen, too young to remember her and not sure how to cope with this unprecedented situation, but he soon recovered and jabbed his spear at her.

Smiling to reassure him, Kagari held her arms wide in an attitude of surrender, which didn't help. He shoved her hard and she fell backwards, and as she fell he grabbed her leg, wrenching it savagely to take her knife. Her shoulder ached from the force of the fall and tears of pain stung her eyes as she moved her knee. 'Damn you,' she muttered in English. 'Now look what you've done.'

He prodded her to get up and watched, nodding, as she lurched forward, hanging on to trees. She realised he had deliberately incapacitated her to prevent her from running away. He was as tall as she was, with a slim hard body, and wore only a rope bag attached to a cord slung from his

336

hips, to protect his genitals. His chest and face were smeared with mud and daubed with large white dots. He didn't seem so ferocious now but she knew she had to be very careful; he was agitated by her presence and his eyes kept searching the bush in case she had company.

She made a huge effort to speak, but her mind would not respond, the language would not come to her. She limped forward, the spear jabbing at her back. The pain in her knee was excruciating, made worse by the uphill journey, and she gritted her teeth every time she had to put her weight on that leg. She stumbled several times but he made no effort to assist her, and her tension turned to terror. What a fool she'd been. She should have waited until someone made contact with the Aborigines. This impatient young scout, or warrior, hadn't actually said what tribe he belonged to, he had simply recognised the name. He might be taking her to more strangers. She had to find her own family, someone who would recognise her.

Her hands were bleeding, sliced by thorny vines and bushes she had unwittingly grasped for leverage, and she stopped for a breather, staring down at them. 'Wogaburra,' she said turning back to him, and then the words came rushing out unhampered now by her conscious pressures. 'Take me to Wogaburra. I am his daughter, Kagari.'

He took it for granted that she spoke his language. 'That man is dead. Keep moving.'

'Oh no,' she groaned. Even though she had allowed for this possibility, it was still a shock. 'My mother, Luka. Do you know Luka?'

'Yes. Luka is not dead.'

'Then take me to Luka.'

He shook his head. 'You lie.'

She straightened up and faced him. 'Then I will see Tajatella,' she instructed boldly, praying he was still alive. 'I am his friend, and he will punish you if you harm me.'

That shook him. He stopped uncertainly and gave a piercing whistle, not unlike one of the many calls of the kurrawong, and then they waited.

Other men, heavily painted, some with small bones through their noses signifying rank, began to filter like wraiths from the forest. They stood and stared at her, then retreated to whisper their comments and decisions, and soon Kagari and her keeper were on their way again.

She was sitting in a cool, dim cave when he appeared at the leafy entrance. They all looked fierce but this one more so, his wiry grey hair waxed into a topknot that seemed to emphasise the hard cruel eyes that glared at her from under a headband. His face and chest bore severe initiation scars highlighted by white and ochre paint, and he wore a meagre loincloth of fur. His wrists and ankles were decorated with thick, frilled, reed bracelets and he carried a tall barbed spear which he pointed at her as he approached.

To show deference, Kagari stood, hoping this was Tajatella because she'd forgotten what the man looked like.

'Who are you?' he asked while the men behind him crowded in to listen.

'Kagari,' she said, 'daughter of Wogaburra.'

His hand shot out and whacked her across the face. 'You dare speak of the dead! You are an evil one.'

Reeling from the blow, her jaw numb, she confronted him. 'Kagari is not dead. I am Kagari, come home.'

There was a hiss of disapproval from the audience that she should contradict the chief, whoever he was.

'I was only a little girl,' she told him, indicating the height with her hand. 'I was lost in the sea and white men took me away. White men came ashore that day long ago.' She looked at him, pleading. The language was hard for her to pronounce now.

'Many white men have come from the sea,' he replied angrily. 'You are an evil spirit sent by them.'

'No, no. See me. Look at me. I am Irukandji, of your people.'

A woman was thrust forward, a plump naked woman with matted hair almost obscuring her face and for a minute Kagari hardly recognised her mother, but then she stretched out her hands, smiling. 'Tell them,' she said. 'I am Kagari, your daughter.'

Terrified, the woman cringed away from her, shaking her head, and the chief nodded, satisfied. He bared his teeth and spat. 'Take this evil thing away.'

Just then the watchers parted to allow yet another tribal man to pass through. 'Tajatella is a great chief but I have the extra power of the ears. I hear her voice and I alone know her voice. She is Kagari come back from the dead. I will prove this. What is my name, woman?'

Kagari sighed with relief. 'You are Meebal, my brother,' she told him, 'whose eyes were poisoned and made blind.'

The others hissed and muttered, some in wonder, some in fear.

'I am not a spirit, Meebal,' she insisted. 'Not a spirit.' She thought it better now to give a slightly coloured version of her reappearance. 'I was captured by the white men when you were only a boy, but I have escaped from them.'

Luka, her mother, crept towards her gingerly, but Tajatella had had enough of this. After all, she was only a woman.

'So be it,' he announced and strode away with his entourage.

3

The screams were the most shocking Lew had ever heard in his life. With everyone else in the camp, he ran down towards the river only to be met by a bolting horse which charged straight at them. Just in case Diamond had been right about the crocodiles, he'd kept his camp well away from the river but other travellers were located at various points around the banks.

Lew heard a gunshot and then a man emerged from the riverside scrub. 'Don't go down there,' he shouted. 'Keep away.'

'What in God's name happened?' Lew asked him.

'It was terrible,' the stranger said. 'These great crocs came from nowhere and grabbed my mate's horse. The poor beast that was screaming but we couldn't save him. They had him in the river in a flash, so my mate shot him to put him out of his agony, poor bugger. Those things are feeding on him in a real bloody frenzy.'

Chin Ying was upset. 'It's a bad omen,' he said.

'No, it's not,' Lew told him firmly. He couldn't allow Chinese superstitions to disrupt their trek. 'We just have to be very careful where we hitch the horses. I had no idea they'd be big enough to grab a horse.'

The next day they began their climb, following the line of blazed trees marked by the first contingent of diggers. In the distance he could hear the distinctive roar of a waterfall and wondered if this could be the one Diamond had talked about. And where was she? In this country waterfalls wouldn't be rare. Maybe she'd followed this same trail, although it was obvious the route was taking them away from the falls.

Lew's assessment of a week's march soon proved to be optimistic. The terrain was rough, with dense rainforest and many creeks to cross at the base of each hill, and the hills became progressively higher, the creeks wider. After four days they'd barely covered sixty miles.

'According to my calculations,' Ying said, 'we are travelling too far north. This is very worrying.'

'They're experienced men,' Lew told him. 'We can't strike out on our own. We have to follow their lead.'

That night, they were attacked. Spears and burning branches were hurled at them from all sides, turning the camp into chaos. Diggers fired their rifles wildly, unable to spot any of their attackers. Within fifteen minutes the battle was over, but it had seemed like an age to Lew. Risking making himself a target, he took a lantern and began checking for casualties. Two diggers at the rear of the camp had been killed and two others injured; a coolie was dead and his comrades were wailing over him, making a terrible racket. He went in search of the Yuang brothers and was surprised to find them in the tent attending to Ying.

'What's going on here?' he asked.

'The master was hit by a spear, sir,' they answered. 'In his arm. A great catastrophe.'

'When did this happen?' He had been right beside Ying, firing from the cover of trees, but he hadn't heard him cry out. 'Let me see.'

The wound in Ying's upper arm was deep and ragged. 'Fortunately,' he explained to Lew, 'the spear was losing momentum as it fell into my arm which was foolish enough to be in its path, so I was able to remove it with a tug, which was most unpleasant.'

'I daresay it was,' Lew remarked. 'You take care that infection doesn't make it any worse. When they finish bandaging you up, will you send the lads down to look after the other casualties?'

From then on their situation deteriorated and Lew wondered if this march to the 'promised land' was doomed. They were constantly harassed by stray spears, by booby traps of vines set across the path to trip men and horses, and branches of stinging bushes strung from trees. They caused vicious rashes that burned like fire. Boulders were hurled at them from the heights, and at one stage even scores of snakes were thrown at them, causing the horses to panic and the coolies to drop their loads and run screaming into the scrub.

All along the track the blacks were waiting for them. One thing perplexed Lew: the route was strewn with goods dumped by diggers – tins of food were scattered in the bush, canvas and equipment, lanterns, even precious bags of salt and flour. They also passed several graves which upset the coolies. What with the snake incident as well, when the Yuang brothers had rounded them up with whips, lashing them into order, Lew felt they were close to mutiny.

Two men came down the track carrying a wounded man on a bush stretcher.

'Go back, mate,' they told Lew. 'It's a death march. Not worth it. You've got to get to the top of the granite range ahead and there's no other way. We were attacked there by hundreds of blacks, bloody hundreds of them, a full-scale fight. We were told no one lived here. Like hell they don't. There's thousands of blacks in this country.'

Lew asked him about the supplies dumped on the track.

'Stragglers. They had to drop them, they couldn't keep up and it was too dangerous to get left behind. And the party got split up,' he said bitterly. 'A lot of blokes on horses took off, they wouldn't wait for us, the bastards. You lost any of your men yet?'

Lew nodded.

Chin Ying also listened to the strangers but he was unruffled by their dire warnings. 'They have to go back,' he told Lew. 'Their friend has a broken leg. They exaggerate the dangers to compensate for their failure.'

'I'm not so sure,' Lew said. 'The evidence is all around us. Men would have to be desperate to throw down their supplies and make a run for it.'

'And stupid. It would be more logical to run back to Cooktown since no supplies are to be had ahead of us. No, I think they were too lazy and too weak to carry their own goods. We do not have this problem.'

'I don't know about that. I feel responsible. I don't want to lead men into danger.'

'Ah, but you are not responsible. The prospectors who have joined us are not your concern and the Chinese are mine. It is only your own skin you have to worry about.'

So they pressed on, past a large and very beautiful lagoon abounding with wild life where they feasted on fish and wild ducks. Then they moved deep into the rainforest again, the last of them, Lew hoped; the other side of the mountains should be more open country.

They had brought only three horses with them, one each for Ying and himself and one packhorse. The riders went ahead to find the blazed trees while the Yuang brothers kept to the main body of men. After returning from a short reconnaissance, Lew found the column had stopped. The diggers were grumbling, wanting to keep going, but Ying had called a halt to investigate the disappearance of two coolies, the last two in the line.

Some of them, Lew had noticed, were beginning to suffer from the strain of their heavy burdens and the torrid heat, their joints swelling painfully. He decided that when they topped the range he would insist they rest for a few days.

He dismounted and set off down the trail on foot with Yuang Fu but they covered more than a mile without seeing any sign of the missing coolies.

'Maybe they've just bolted, made a dash for the coast,' Lew said, but Yuang Fu shook his head.

'They would not have taken their baskets, sir.' He looked about him warily. 'It is very difficult to fight an enemy you cannot see.'

'That's true,' Lew said. No wonder the poor fellow was bewildered. He was an expert in the martial arts, but those talents were no use to him now. Apart from shadowy figures, swift movements among the trees, they'd never set eyes on any tribesmen.

Eventually they gave up and returned to camp.

'We have to find them,' Ying announced. 'The wretches have probably absconded and are hiding in the forest waiting for us to leave. This is a bad example. They must be caught and punished.' He ordered the march to cease and the next morning instructed his two servants to scour the bush for the two men.

Lew saw them return at midday and followed them to where they were conferring with Ying. As he approached, the conversation ceased suddenly.

'They are not to be found,' Ying said. 'They must have gone back down the mountain under cover of darkness.'

'No sign of their baskets either?' Lew said.

'No, sir,' Yuang Fu replied.

Later it struck Lew as odd that the brothers had returned at midday. He had heard Ying telling them to search until dusk, and they never disobeyed his instructions.

The next afternoon, as they made their way along a winding section of track, two more coolies disappeared. The last two again. The remainder bunched up together, crying hysterically, pointing back down the path. But no one had seen or heard a thing; the two porters had disappeared as silently as the others. The last ten diggers still trekking with them packed their swags and left, refusing to listen to Lew's warning that they should stay together. They claimed that being with the Chinese was bad luck.

'Oh Christ!' Lew groaned. 'Now it's their turn to be superstitious.'

Chin Ying didn't seem to care that the diggers had gone forward without them. 'I don't think it matters,' he said. 'Maybe the savages will attack them next and leave us alone. They are very clever, they play us like the cat with the mouse.'

He was right. Slowly but surely the continuing harassment from the blacks was breaking them down mentally as well as physically. They had enough difficulty coping with the natural hardships as it was. Insects fed on them, swarms of bees attacked them, dingoes tormented their horses, the heat exhausted men and beasts; every day there were accidents and minor injuries. Lew had been caught by a stinging bush and his neck and arms burned, and he had sprained an ankle in a ditch. He was limping badly, his boot tightly laced for support; he thanked God for the horse.

The shocks, worries, and endless physical discomfort, coupled with lack of sleep, created tension between Lew and Ying. They seemed to be unable to agree on even the most unimportant details and when Lew announced he would organise a full-scale search for the two coolies, working to a set pattern, Ying flatly refused to permit his men to take part.

'You can't make up your mind about anything,' Lew shouted at him. 'Last time you sent us to search, this time you're not bothering. These are your own people, we have to find them! Christ, Ying, they might have just fallen down somewhere, waiting for us to rescue them.'

'No search,' Ying said firmly. 'We will proceed.'

'Proceed, hell! Give me your men, just for today. We'll beat through the bush together. We could find them that way.'

'No.'

'Then I will tell the coolies that you are a bad boss. That you don't care what happens to them. I will ask them for help.'

'You cannot walk far with that ankle.'

'I can and I will.'

Ying sighed and motioned to the Yuang brothers who had been standing by. 'You may go with the captain to look for our lost brothers.' He turned to Lew. 'My servants can go with you, no one else. But first put plenty of guards round the camp.'

'Oh sure,' Lew said sarcastically. 'I'll see to it you are well guarded before we go.'

All three men were heavily armed as they went back along the track and then began to widen their range, first one side and then the other. It was Yuang Pan who found them. Instead of firing a shot as they had arranged to do, he moved quietly back to Lew and, jerking his head, led him to a small clearing by the mouth of a cave. Yuang Fu joined them. Neither of the brothers said a word as Lew stared in horror.

'You knew!' he screamed at Ying as he burst into the tent. 'You bloody knew! That's what happened to the last two poor bastards, wasn't it? And you sit there on your duff and do nothing.'

'What could I do? Let the others know what happened? Do you want to drive them mad? Drink this whisky. It is very good to settle you. Unless of course you wish to demonstrate your compassion by telling the truth to those miserable coolies who are already frightened out of their wits.'

With shaking hands Lew took the cup and gulped the whisky. 'You could have told me,' he mumbled.

'I did you a favour in not telling you. Yuang Pan has been guarding the rear since that time but he had to come forward to assist some bearers when their baskets split.'

Lew downed more whisky, even more distressed now. If Yuang Pan had been there, he might have saved the poor fellows.

'So that was fortunate,' Ying continued. 'The silent enemy is stalking us and Yuang Pan could have been killed. That would be most inconvenient for me.'

'Oh Christ!' Lew said, refilling the cup. How could he have let himself in for this nightmare? Two leaders with attitudes that were miles apart when it came to life and death, stumbling around in this wilderness, in this steaming green hell. The whisky was spilling, the cup slipping from his hand . . .

'Put him on his bunk,' Lew heard Ying say through a deepening haze, and as he began to crumple he realised that the Chinaman had doctored the whisky.

4

As the days passed, Luka became less shy of her daughter and even allowed Kagari to touch her, to take her hand and speak gently with her of times past, but Luka refused to accept Kagari's explanation of her disappearance. The other women crowded round, agog with curiosity, and Luka boasted to them about her daughter, the magic one, who had returned from the Dreamtime. Was not her father a great magic man?

Kagari now knew she had committed a serious error in mentioning his name. No one spoke the names of the dead. She should have known that, other tribes she had met had the same rule. What a fool! No wonder Tajatella had clouted her.

Ancient people with ancient ways. They fascinated and appalled her, and she wondered if the Aborigines in Brisbane or even at Caravale had any recollection of tribes like this. After all, the whites had been in this country for a hundred years, for generations. But these wild northern tribes had no understanding of European civilisation. They knew only that white men were beginning to land in their territory and they were angry. The women giggled and chatted about this new war, the first for many generations, and it was an exciting time. They mixed the paints, collected special food for the warriors, and relearned the legendary war songs. In this hugely important time of their lives, Kagari's appearance was a three-day wonder. Because she was quiet, squatted in the cave near Luka and Meebal, listened rather than talked, they soon lost interest in her.

Many people lived in the huge, smoke-filled cave, most of them relations or friends or of the same totem as Luka, it was hard to tell. And Luka had another husband now, a very old man whom she shared with two other women. Her main duty was to keep him fed, since he was too old to hunt. At first Kagari thought the smoke of the fires would asphyxiate her, but she forced herself to become accustomed to the putrid air and the stink of burning fur as small animals were tossed on the fire, unskinned. She had searched for this place and she'd found it. She knew now she couldn't stay but the sweetness and the warmth of the people held her just a little longer.

They took immense pride in their strong unclad bodies, the women, like women everywhere, sighing over the sleek young men and girls. Embarrassingly, Luka took pains to point out her daughter's charms. Her cotton underclothes had been taken from her but Kagari had retrieved them and washed them at the spring to the merriment of Luka's friends.

It was all a strange dream and Kagari drifted with it in this timeless land. Luka became more possessive, her love for her daughter returning more each day until her face took on an expression of such joy that Kagari knew her homecoming had been worthwhile. She preened Luka's hair, rubbed the hard body with coconut oil and sat cross-legged with her, scaling fish, pounding roots into homegrown flour, sorting out the day's collection of nuts and berries emptied from dilly bags, smiling at her mother, wanting to please her.

She hated the cave, but the days, wandering the forest far from the war trails, were sheer delight. They were always accompanied by friends, and if they met new people in their wanderings, Kagari was petted and touched like a new baby. There were children everywhere, fat rollicking children, carried in slings or trotting happily with the adults, minded fiercely by the families to protect them from danger and never physically chastised. No matter how naughty or intrusive, no one struck a defenceless child. The hard lessons in life began at puberty. Kagari understood now why she had reacted with such violence when that housekeeper back at Government House had slapped her face. She shrugged. That had been a wrong thing to do, and now she was dead. Kagari thought of telling her mother about this but it was all too complicated. Everything she tried to tell Luka and Meebal about the white man's world was too complicated, impossible. It was easier to be from the Dreaming. But she did sing songs to Meebal, songs Mrs Beckman had taught her, songs the people sang round the piano at Perfy's house in Bowen. And his dear face became transfixed with pleasure, believing he was hearing lovely music from the Dreaming where one day he would go because he had tried, even with his humiliating blindness, to be a worthwhile person in the community.

'I have always been afraid to die,' he told her, 'because it has been so hard for a blind man to earn a place. I am not a warrior nor even a scout, and no woman will have me. I wander with the women. What would the spirits want with such a useless man? But now I hear your singing I know that you, Sister, have spoken for me. Tell me truthfully, do I have a place in the Dreaming?'

With tears in her eyes but with a firm, steady voice, Kagari told him, 'There is a place for you, high in honour, because you have suffered enough with good heart. Listeners are needed, to hear and recognise the wondrous music around us, that seeing people forget. You alone knew my voice. You are greatly beloved.'

Somewhere in there, Kagari knew, was the voice of Mrs Beckman who had often said troubles were sent to try us. Not that it mattered. Meebal embraced her; when the time came he would die in peace.

Luka took her high on the range so that they could look out like kings over the low country. It resembled the ugly tree and anthill splattered land outside Townsville, harsh ground, waist-deep in speargrass.

'Down there,' Luka spat, 'Merkin people. No good, any of them. But they too fight the white men now. Dirty fellers, white men,' she said. 'Leave their shit around. They never cover up.' Then she laughed. 'Easy to track, eh? Just follow the stink.'

Kagari sat with her on a high granite outcrop. 'Luka. Do you know why the white men have come here?'

'Oh yes,' Luka said loftily. 'To take our food. To steal our women. Irukandji women make the best babies in the world. Everyone knows that. But we never let them come up here. You're safe up here.'

'The valley down there. What is that valley?'

'Merkin country,' Luka said, a little exasperated at having to repeat herself. 'They call that their sun river. But it is our river. It is born in our mountains on past the two sisters.'

'Can you take me there?'

'Where?'

Sometimes she knew things. Sometimes certainties were so clear they cried out to her. Kagari wasn't sure whether it was inherent knowledge endowed by these ancient people or simply a logical progression that told her that she was looking out over the headwaters of the river that Lew and Mr Chin sought. She had seen and studied their maps.

'Why do they call it the sun river?'

'I don't know,' her mother replied. 'Their language is very base. Difficult to understand. You don't want to go right to the top, do you?'

'No, just to the river.'

Luka laughed. 'When it swells with our mountain's rains, it descends on the Merkin with a great wall of water, the message of the Irukandji. It tells them to stay clear of us because we are invincible. They have to run far away for safety.'

'Luka. Do you know what gold is?'

'I do not know that word.'

They took an interminable time to reach the river. Luka had to show her daughter the secrets of the land, she would need the knowledge after her mother had gone forth; they had to defer to the calls of kookaburras, their totem, and leave offerings of fat worms and tiny lizards for the parents, because everyone knew kookaburra babies never left the nest until they were almost too fat to fly and the poor mother and father had to work tirelessly to feed their offspring.

Finally they came to the river, climbing down to the gorge which had taken aeons to carve in a seemingly lazy meander through the heights.

'We will sleep here tonight,' Luka said. 'It's a very pretty place. I'm glad we came.'

Kagari had expected a rushing waterfall, but it was just another river, not very deep, sashaying along through the natural course of the twisted hills, bubbling in velvety smoothness over a swathe of rocks and shands.

They drank the crystal cool water and Kagari slipped into a rock pool, remembering Ben. Always Ben. While her mother fished for their supper, Kagari watched for gold, the yellow stones that could make the white world bearable. She knew she would find it. She knew that if the Palmer, down there on the plains, had gold, it had to come from a reef somewhere. No one in the white world ever seemed to talk about anything but gold, every man was an expert. She saw a rough, thick, yellow line above the waterline and swam over to study it.

Clay? No, too hard. Too brittle. It glittered and danced, reflected in the shifting waters. She ran her fingers along the vein, smiling, laughing. She dipped and turned in the pool like a porpoise, flashing about like a silly fish, her naked body on show to the whole glorious world. 'Take a look,' she cried in English, to the blue skies, to the red-scaled cassowary that stuck its head out from the banks above her. Startled by her outburst, the huge bird ducked and clacked its disapproval. She wondered why emus were so plain while birds of the same size like cassowaries were as gaudy as peacocks. She was sure her mother would know the reason, from the Dreamtime, but there was no time for that now.

She took her knife and gouged out lumps of gold.

'What are you doing?' Luka had slipped over to join her.

'Mother, this is gold. I must have it. But I beg you, never tell people about it or it will bring great trouble on everyone.'

Luka smiled. If it pleased her poor childless girl, then this would be their secret. She wondered when Kagari would have to return to the Dreaming. She expected this to happen soon, and was preparing herself for the inevitable. Kagari was greatly loved by the spirits, that was easy to see; they had taken good care of her, nourished her in body and mind. The girl was blessed with intelligence, her sweet eyes reflected the wisdom of her father. Maybe he had sent their daughter back to her to break the mourning bonds that had burdened her heart ever since she lost her little girl. After all this time, the good spirits of the earth had taken pity on her and she was filled with gratitude.

They returned to the caves to find that a terrible tragedy had befallen the people. Women were wailing and screaming, slashing at their breasts with sharp stones, showering themselves with dust that clotted their faces, mingling with their tears. There had been a great battle with the intruders beyond the sacred lagoon. Tajatella had sent a large band of warriors to destroy these men once and for all, but the attack had failed and an appalling number of Irukandji men had been killed. Fathers, brothers, sons, every family had suffered the loss of at least one beloved. Luka fell down in a faint when she heard her brother and her second son, whose names would never be spoken again, were among the fallen. Never in their proud history had a calamity of such proportions been inflicted on the Irukandji people. When one person died, the whole tribe mourned, but how to cope with all of these violent deaths was beyond their comprehension.

Tajatella tried to rally his people. He called a meeting high on the plateau and Kagari followed her weeping family through the forest, her heart breaking for them. Great fires were lit and men stamped and swayed in mournful precision, their faces painted white, signifying death, and in the background the women chanted, pounding muffled sticks on hollow logs, creating an ominous thrum that turned their mourning to rage.

Tajatella looked more fearsome than ever in a high clay head-dress and a necklace of shark's teeth, the skeleton of his glittering black body outlined down to his feet in white paint. He shook his spear fiercely at all points of the earth, threatening revenge, exhorting all his people to join with him in driving the fiends from their land.

After the ceremonies, all the people gathered round the fires for a huge feast to give them strength; hundreds and hundreds of Irukandji people swarmed forward for their share. Kagari waited with the women at the rear, for the men took precedence. The women around her, although still sobbing, were sniffing hungrily at the aroma of the roasting meat, hoping, she guessed, there'd be enough for them. She went along with them although she wasn't hungry, she was too sick at heart for their future. They had no chance against the guns. They'd do better to hide up here and let the diggers go through to the Palmer. After the gold rush they might just go away. But she knew it would be useless to try to explain. They were suffering, and they would fight. It was their way. Nothing could change their traditions.

The women grabbed hungrily at the last of the meat on the hot coals and then retreated to sit down together. The hunters must have been busy, Kagari thought, to bring in such plenty; kangaroos probably. Then she stared, and stumbled back in shock. This wasn't just kangaroo or possum, or even fish. What they were eating with such gusto was unmistakeably human flesh. The smell of the flesh was horrifying. She looked wildly around her, sickened by the terrible scene, and fled, pushing her way through the crowds, running hysterically into the bush, dry retching, weeping. Memories came back to her, hidden knowledge hammering her brain. The Irukandji ate their enemies, didn't they? voices insisted. You knew that. It was the final insult. The fearsome reputation of the invincible tribe.

She tried to push the scene from her mind but couldn't banish the horror. Whimpering, she hid in the soft forest darkness. 'Oh mein Gott!' she cried, unintentionally echoing Mrs Beckman's cry, and nostalgia for the German woman and those happy days with the Captain flooded over her. She wished she could see Mrs Beckman again.

Luka nodded calmly when Kagari told her the next morning that she must leave. 'You go to the winds now,' she smiled. 'The spirits have surely honoured me.' She went into the cave and brought out a heavy dilly bag made of possum skin. 'Here, don't forget your yellow stones. They will prove to the spirits that you were here.'

'Thank you,' Kagari said numbly. Still in shock, she had forgotten the gold. It seemed to weigh a ton now.

She embraced her mother and the sad group watching them but her farewells were interrupted by Meebal. He came running. 'You must leave,' he told her urgently. 'They are saying you are the evil one, that you have brought these calamities upon us from the world of evil spirits. Hurry. They will kill you!'

Kagari hesitated. She knew there was no time to argue but she was afraid for Luka who might be punished instead. 'No,' she said loudly, for all to hear. 'That is not true. I am going to the good spirits, to my father, to get help for the good people of this tribe.' She hoped that invention would protect her mother, cause enough uncertainty to ward off punishment.

Luka folded her arms proudly. 'You hear?' she called. 'My daughter will speak for us.'

'Come away,' Meebal hissed, grabbing Kagari's arm. 'I'll show you the quick way.' As surefooted as any other, the blind man led her down the mountain, hurrying across creeks, pushing aside foliage as if he could see it as easily as she could.

'I have to find the big boulders at the cross paths,' she told him.

'What for?'

'I have clothes there that I must wear.'

'What clothes. Why?'

She shook her head wearily. They'd been travelling all day and she doubted she could explain. 'It's necessary,' she said.

At last they stopped. 'This is my camp,' he told her. 'I live at this place where I can look down on the outside world.'

'Look?' she queried. They were on a craggy ledge with a view along the coast.

'I feel the winds,' he smiled. 'I smell the sea. I smell the camps of the white men now and I hear the bangs which I now recognise as guns. They came, those people, so fast and so many of them, our warriors could not stop them but we are safe up here.'

She hoped they were.

'This is my lookout,' he continued. 'Down there are the boulders that we skipped and tumbled over as children. When you return, come to this place and call for me. Everything talks. I will know you are here.' He patted her cheek. 'You will be back once more while I live. And in years to come you will return for the yellow stones. Their magic will protect you, is this not so?'

'Yes, Meebal, they will indeed be my protection. You have great wisdom and I am so happy to have found you again. I'm proud of my brother.'

5

Chin Ying emerged from his tent and watched black kurrawong birds chase screeching white cockatoos from their trees. He sighed. 'It is the way of the world.'

He stood enjoying the aerial battle as the birds swooped and plunged in death-defying dives until the flock of cockatoos, protesting loudly, were driven off and the kurrawongs soared in triumph against the blue; then Ying forced his attention on the land.

They had rounded the northern edge of the range, turned south-west and dropped down to the plains. Now they had to run the gauntlet of open country to get to the Palmer, with possibly another fifty miles to go and more wild blacks to hinder them. He was sorely tempted to suggest to Lew that they mount their horses and ride for their lives, leaving the Yuang brothers to bring up the coolies, but he knew Lew wouldn't agree. He was still bleating about the two coolies he'd seen hanging from trees by their pigtails with some limbs and buttock flesh cut from their bodies. Poor fellows, he thought; flesh as tough as goat's knees, they wouldn't make much of a meal. He had entered the incidents in his journal, together with his deliberations on aspects of cannibalism. He found the subject fascinating, and wondered how many other gold seekers had ended up as the black gentlemen's dinner.

Last night they'd encountered some riders returning from the Palmer, serious, concerned men who'd temporarily forgone their own prospecting to ride fast back to Cooktown to warn of the shortage of supplies and order ships' captains to advise the authorities in Townsville. Apparently, as expected, the first diggers who had galloped north the minute Mulligan broke his news had found gold, but were reduced to eating their horses and boiling their boots for succour. Chin Ying found this marvellously ironic, gold-rich men starving on the wild empty plains. But it was heartening to know that gold was plentiful.

One thing he had decided. He did not intend to end up as Chinese chops. Once they reached the long and splendid Palmer River, the gods willing, they would not return with their gold on this route. The ship had served them well, delivering them ahead of the main body of prospectors, but the retreat would be overland, far away from cannibal country.

And then it would be time for him to consider his options. He yearned to return to China, his own dear land. Cheong would be a threat no matter where he was based but to stay in this barbarous country would be to invite a lifetime of derision. One possibility appealed to him. He could assume a new Chinese identity.

Contemplation of his future plans had given him many hours of comfort, a buffer against the dread and desolation of this awesome land. The Lord Cheong's threats were as the wings of moths against the perils of the Australian outback which invaded his dreams. He would return to China with a new name and he would be a gentleman in the English fashion. He would not, like Lord Cheong, be encumbered by the necessity to defend his mansions and provide food and shelter for his minions; that was an old-fashioned life style which attracted enmities. This excursion into a British environment had afforded him the opportunity to study European financial institutions via newspapers and discussions with bank personnel. English gentlemen invested their funds and let their money work for them while they resided in private mansions.

Lew came trudging up. 'We're ready to go. Yuang Pan will lead, and his brother will bring up the rear. You and I will patrol beside the coolies, on our horses, to protect them. They're exhausted, poor fellows, but I have explained it will soon be over and each man will be rewarded in gold.'

'As you say,' Ying agreed, irritated at being relegated to the inferior position of horse-guard, but then if this man was to be his partner, his figurehead, in the Hong Kong enterprise he was preparing to found, then let him have his way. He prayed that by the time this ordeal was over, and they were back in civilisation, they would both still have their heads, that no enterprising Aborigines would have claimed them.

Tribesmen started grass fires that turned the forest country into blazing furnaces, forcing them to detour and adding days to the awful trek. It was then that Ying actually saw the enemy for the first time, huge black men, naked bodies glistening in the firelight, with white cockatoo feathers displayed in their hair like bobbing kites. They were so close, only about a hundreds yards away, three of them, that he froze with fright, completely unnerved by their defiant stance. It was as if they were daring him to attack. By the time he screamed to Yuang Pan to fire on them, they'd gone. He could not explain their disappearance.

There was something very strange about those natives; all along he'd felt an unearthly quality about their presence, as if peoples as ancient as this, untouched by other civilisations, had magical powers. He tried to explain this to Lew but he disagreed. 'There's nothing strange about them except that they know the country and we don't. And they're bloody cannibals! That's enough to give anyone the horrors.'

They were a sorry sight when at last they staggered upon the Palmer River. Ying had lost weight and his battered European clothes hanging limply about him were an embarrassment. He was saddle-sore and exhausted but Lew seemed to have reserves of strength commensurate with his size. While Ying's servants brought him fresh water and set up his tent, Lew went off to find out if the Palmer was living up to its reputation.

Wearily Ying turned his attention to a more immediate problem. Four of the coolies had collapsed and had to be carried on makeshift stretchers, slowing them up. They had outlived their usefulness, and now in Lew's absence he discussed them with Yuang Pan. It would be best to put two of them out of their misery with some herbal 'medicine' and let the other pair know they'd go the same way if they didn't get back on their feet smartly. Ying smiled grimly as Yuang Pan went off to attend to them. That was one of Cheong's methods of curing malingerers and it was known to be successful.

Ying lay down in his tent and waited for Lew to return. The moment of truth had arrived. The Palmer would spell the difference between quiet wealth and fabulous riches. While he waited, he drank cup after cup of strong wine to quell the anxiety gnawing at him. If he had miscalculated, the awful journey would have been in vain and he would have to stay in this country, possibly for years, until he recouped his fortunes. He could only return to China safely as a rich man in his own right, hidden behind a wall of financial security, one of Hong Kong's faceless money merchants.

Lew came bounding in to rescue him from depression. He practically knocked the tent down in his excitement. 'We've made it, Ying! You were right! There's gold here, high-grade gold, stacks of it! This river's full of it. The Gold Commissioner said they'll be carrying it out of here by the ton! Can you imagine that? Not by the ounce but by the bloody ton!'

But still Ying was not convinced. 'There are so many miners here already. I had hoped we'd be among the first. What if there isn't any left?'

'Don't panic, there are only a few camps and it's a long river. The gold is here, no question about it. They're picking it up by the bucketful. Picking it up! Do you hear me?'

Ying sat back and smiled. 'Have some wine. I think I am already a little drunk, and I intend to become drunker, for we must celebrate. Tomorrow you shall take me to inspect this wonder. Our river of gold. Ah, the blessings of the gods on that Mr Mullingan.'

'Amen!' Lew grinned, raising his cup. 'To Mr Mulligan.'

Between them they calculated they had the manpower to work twenty leases under various names, four of which would constitute Lew's share of the returns. As each site relinquished its gold, they would relocate to new sections along the river.

'One fellow told me he has swept gold up like peas in the shallows,' Lew exulted. 'It's unbelievable.'

The following day they staked their claims on a lonely stretch of the river and set to work. Lew went at it with gusto and even Ying took a hand this time, paddling over the riverstone rocks, happily panning and picking his way, barefoot, in the warm waters.

He had made his decision. He would arrive in Hong Kong as Mr Wong Sun Lee, gentleman, with papers purchased in the right quarters in Brisbane. Then he would buy himself an appropriate residence and from there he would contact financial advisers to assist him in the establishment of a superior shipping company to be known as Pan Pacific Company. It would have a reliable gentlemen at its head, a gentleman conversant with the ways of both Chinese and British. All that remained now was to persuade Lew Cavour to come back to China, for who better to command this company?

6

By the time Diamond returned to Cooktown, the whole area had changed. The estuary was jammed with ships, cargo was piled up on the shores, and sailors and labourers toiled to drag building material and supplies into the town now under construction. The air rang with the clang of axes and the rasp of cross-cut saws. Horse teams were hauling logs to even out a main street and excited people were hurrying everywhere. She was amazed at the number of horses that had been shipped in so quickly by these enterprising men, but even more surprised to see how many Chinese had disembarked here. They seemed to outnumber the whites. Hundreds of well-dressed men like Mr Chin trotted around and crews of coolies carrying bundles and baskets burrowed through the noisy assemblage.

She found the small government office built of timber slabs and pushed her way inside through the sweating crowds. The room was like an oven, and glancing up she saw why. They'd put a corrugated iron roof on the building; it had become so hot a person could fry a meal on it. They'll never learn, these people, she thought, remembering the leafy roofed gunyahs she'd seen in Irukandji country. But still, she didn't feel out of place among these oddly attired men and women. Her clothes, when she'd recovered them, had been covered in mould and she'd had to scrub it off in a creek, ending up with a badly crumpled outfit. But now she saw she wasn't the only one; there was a smell of mould everywhere.

The government office was really a general information centre and she was able to establish that Lew and Mr Chin had left Cooktown some time back, so she went in search of the Bourke family.

Jim Bourke was building a store, having come to the conclusion that this was the way to prosperity in a new town. He had dispatched his wife back to Townsville by ship to buy all the supplies they could afford.

Marie Bourke was pleased to see her. 'Diamond! What happened to you? We've been so worried. Where have you been?'

'I went exploring in the hills,' she said carefully. Her gold was buried out there, safe from prying eyes.

'It's a wonder you didn't get your head chopped off,' Jim Bourke said. 'They reckon them blacks are fair demons.'

'But your people? Did you find your own people?' Marie asked.

Diamond shook her head. She could be in danger here now if they found out she was one of them. Impossible to predict the reaction. 'No. But I met quite a few of the native people and they were very kind to me. I don't know what the fuss is all about.'

'You're the right bloody colour, that's all,' Bourke growled.

'Can I help you, Mr Bourke?' she asked. 'Looks like you've got plenty to do here.'

'We could do with a hand, but I can't pay you.'

'I don't want any pay. Just somewhere to stay for a while. And I could catch some fish for you . . .'

'Done,' he said enthusiastically.

The gold was no use to her. Yet. Not until men started to return with their gold from the Palmer; if she produced hers now they'd be on to her like a pack of dingoes wanting to know where it came from. And then it would be dangerous, everyone would know she hadn't been out to the goldfields. Her best bet was to wait for Mr Chin to come back; it was too risky for a black girl alone to take passage on a ship returning south. She'd need protection.

Marie Bourke had been minding her carpetbag for her, so she had a change of clothes and her purse containing the money she'd earned at Mr Chin's house. Enough to sustain her for a while.

Jim Bourke roofed his shop with shingle instead of corrugated iron. He stamped dust from shattered anthills into the floor and damped it into a hard firm surface with sprinklings of water. Then he set to work to paint his signs. Everything was in readiness when his wife returned. He proudly showed her the shop and their tiny residence at the back but instead of being pleased with him, Mrs Bourke screamed with rage. 'You stupid man! How did you let that happen?'

She pointed next door to another new building with a long verandah over which hung the simple sign: ROOMS.

'What's the matter with that?' Jim asked innocently and Diamond giggled. Jim knew as well as she did that the women now lolling on the benches outside were prostitutes and that the house was owned by a noisy blonde woman called Glory Molloy.

'You take me for a fool, Jim Bourke. You know what those women are. I demand you get rid of them.'

'How?' he asked. 'I got no way to stop them. Besides, they'll all be customers.'

And so began the feud between Glory Molloy and Mrs Bourke, but Glory stayed and her business flourished, as did the store.

Men came and went, the girls laughed and sang, and Glory sat on her verandah collecting the money. Sometimes Diamond wandered from the shed at the back, where she lived, to sit out with Glory whom she found highly amusing.

355

'What are you doing living out there like a bag of flour?' Glory asked her. 'You could work here and make a quid, a shapely lass like you. The men like coloured gals.'

'I know,' Diamond laughed. 'But no thanks. I don't expect to be here too long. I'm just waiting for someone to travel back with me.'

'Smart girl,' Glory said. 'On them ships the sailors'd see you as fair game, and no pay neither.'

And then one night she heard the voice. The laugh. The same laugh that had been ringing in her ears ever since her childhood. He was a customer, a good customer, Glory said, back from the Palmer with plenty of gold. Diamond listened, steeling herself, controlling her rage, and went out of her way to meet him, stroking the knife on her leg for comfort. She was still afraid of him, and when he spoke to her she trembled, but she had to make sure.

'Billy Kemp's the name,' he grinned. 'Billy Kemp, one of the first winners from the Palmer. Jesus, Glory, she's all right. Don't tell me a luscious wench like this doesn't work for you!' He leaned against the wall, waving a bottle of whisky. 'How much? I can afford her.'

'Have you always been a prospector, Billy?' Diamond asked quietly.

'Cripes, will you listen to her?' He grinned broadly. 'Talks like a lady. No, ma'am,' he bowed, laughing. 'I was a sailor. Gave it away. The bloody ship went down on me, so I said to myself, Billy, that's it. The flaming sharks don't come into your house so you don't go into their sea.'

'Shipwrecked!' Diamond said. 'How lucky you were to escape. What ship was it.'

'The ship? Ah, she was the *White Rose*. Bloody good ship, too. I was an officer, you know, first mate. Cap'n Beckman, rest his soul, treated me like his own brother . . .'

As he rattled on, Diamond studied every inch of the man who had attacked her. He and his mate had nearly drowned her; she would never forget that blind terror. He might have escaped the shipwreck but he would not escape Kagari's revenge.

Glory interrupted him. He needed to be steered back to her girls before he became too interested in Diamond. She slipped an arm through his, squeezing him close to her bosom. 'What an adventurous life you've led, me darlin', but now tell Glory how you got so fast to the Palmer.'

'Brains, Glory my love. Grey matter! I partnered a squatter, an important feller too, believe me, name of Buchanan, and we rigged up a proper expedition. I built us a boat so we wouldn't get held up at the rivers and they all thought I was mad, but I had the last laugh.'

He was turning away with Glory but Diamond leapt up to stop them. 'Who was the squatter, Billy? This man Buchanan? Was he from Caravale?'

'Yeah, that's the one. Ben Buchanan. Do you know him?' He nudged Glory. 'I heard he's got an eye for black gins.'

'Yes, I know him,' Diamond said, her heart pounding. 'Where is he now? Did he come back here with you?'

'No, poor bugger, he's still out there. Too soft, them fellers,' he explained to Glory. 'Had too easy a life living on the fat of the land. The Palmer was too tough for him, he couldn't make the distance.'

'Ah, the poor lad,' Glory said, feigning interest. 'Dead, is he?'

'No. I told you. He's still out there.' He laughed. 'Ben's alive but not kicking, so to speak. Went bonkers, mad as a March hare. He wouldn't come back with me. He's holed up in the bush, not even prospecting any more. Leastways, he's still alive as far as I know. They could have buried him by now. But you know the old saying, you can't help people who won't help themselves. I just gave up on him.'

As Glory led him away, Diamond stared after them. The bold, brash sailor had just saved his own life; news of Ben Buchanan was far more important. Tears stung her eyes as she thought of Ben, with no one to care whether he lived or died. She had to help him. But how? To get out to the Palmer she would have to re-enter Irukandji country and the very thought of that sent a shiver of fear through her. If they caught her it would be certain death, an ugly, terrible death. Meebal had been right to hurry her away, the tribal leaders would show no mercy, especially now, with more and more contingents of diggers marching through their land.

Meebal. He had said she would come back while he lived. Diamond marvelled at his prescience. Meebal would guide her.

'Blind eyes can be useful,' Meebal told her. 'The night and the day are one to me.' He disapproved of her escapade but was intrigued by the challenge. They travelled swiftly by night and moved during the day only when he was certain they had eluded war parties intent on intercepting the lines of intruders crashing through their territory.

Sometimes they crossed the tracks of the diggers and once or twice she saw groups of men struggling with their packs, but Meebal took her across the range with ease, using paths and passes that would have been much easier for the diggers had they known they existed. Within three days he delivered her far to the south of the point where the official trail rounded the range, a much faster route.

'That is Merkin country,' Meebal told her. 'I can go no further. I do not know this land. The Merkin are sly and vicious at the best of times but now they are suffering even more invaders than our great people.'

'Maybe I could catch up with the white men,' she said, nervous about that idea too.

'They journey far to the west, you would still have to cross many miles of open country.' He smiled ruefully. 'By night you would get lost. And there is a smaller river to cross before you reach the one you seek.'

'I'll have to make a run for it,' she said. 'I wish I'd brought a gun.'

'You know how to use those things?' He was amazed.

'Oh yes, they're easy.'

'What wonders you have learned,' he sighed. 'I think perhaps one small person like you could elude the Merkin. They will be busy listening for the noise of the invaders and their beasts, searching for better prey than an Irukandji girl. Their language is similar to ours. If you meet them, tell them you are the daughter of the great chief Tajatella from above, and never turn your back on them. They will be polite, as you must be, but at the first chance, run!'

She prepared to leave.

'The sun is fierce,' Meebal went on, 'drink plenty of water every chance you get and eat only these nuts for strength.'

'Before I go, tell me again, Meebal. Is my mother safe?'

'I spoke the truth. Luka defies your detractors, she spits on them, and she has many family.'

'That's a relief.'

'I will stay in this vicinity,' he said. 'And wait for your return.'

'You are so kind, Meebal. And it is good to know that once more you expect my safe return.'

He shook his head. 'This time I do not know, Kagari. I fear for you but time is of nothing. I will wait until the voices tell me to wait no longer.'

She began her cross-country run unhindered by skirts, wearing only a skin lap-lap strung across her hips, her clothes stuffed in a dilly bag round her neck. Her long legs took up an easy rhythm as she loped towards the sun, thinking of nothing but the necessity to stay calm, to ignore the heat, to keep moving.

Never allowing her concentration to waver, she spotted Merkin women with children far ahead of her, travelling north. She slipped into the cover of sparse trees until they were out of sight, using the time to catch her breath. She immersed herself in the billabongs of drying creeks, the water icy against the heat of her body, and emerged, still wet, to continue. At night she hid in the long grass and slept, too tired to care about snakes. She woke up at the call of the kookaburras and was on her way before dawn.

Eventually she came to the first river. She swam across it and then struck out for the hills ahead that overlooked the Palmer Valley. That night she had no sleep; Merkin camp fires littered the slopes and she squatted, terrified, inside the hollow trunk of a huge old tree. In the morning she crept slowly, anxiously, from shelter to shelter. She had no wish to attempt dialogue with them. She heard them congregating, talking, somewhere in the maze of bush and then shouts that faded as they took off into the distance.

The first sign that she was approaching the Palmer was the neighing of horses, and she realised how little chance the white men had of hiding from the blacks, though the tribesmen would wonder at the strange sound; Aborigines knew nothing of horses. She struggled into her skirt and blouse, tied her hair into a topknot with string and marched towards the corral, looking she supposed like any 'tame' gin in battered white-feller clothes.

No one took any notice of her as she wandered among the tents along the river bank; all the men would assume she belonged to one of the others.

There were hundreds of tents at the diggings and she discovered that this little settlement was called Upper Camp, and was dismayed to find it was one of several. She had imagined the Palmer goldfields as being a single base.

One gentleman at the Land Commissioner's tent knew of Lew Cavour's party which had camped way upriver but no one had heard of Ben Buchanan. 'Could be down at Palmerville,' she was told. 'Overlanders are camped down that way.'

'Where's Palmerville?'

'About thirty miles downstream.'

Loneliness descended on her as the track folded round the curve of the river; ahead lay a landscape of doubts that lashed at her like stinging whips. Was he still alive? How would he receive her? Would he curse and rail at her? Was he even out here at all? Billy Kemp could have lied.

The sun bore down, matted ti-trees barred her way and the vines were as heavy as lead. Voices tumbled and tolled, warning her to abandon this foolish search, to turn back. 'Easy now,' they hissed, teased, cajoled. 'Turn back. Lew Cavour is back there, and Mr Chin. You'll be safe with them. You can rest for days, for weeks if you wish.' And one voice sounded familiar, a hard whine of a voice – Mrs Buchanan. 'Keep away from my son, you black witch!'

It was that voice that spurred her on, defiance replacing fear, granting her added strength.

She stumbled upon the first isolated camp without warning. A genial bearded digger grinned at her. 'Well, look what the cat dragged in! You lost, girlie?'

'I don't think so,' she said. 'I'm making for Palmerville.'

'You look pretty wore out to me. Come and have a drink of tea. It's me smoko time and I don't mind a bit of company.'

The tea was delicious, strong and sweet, and she drank it gratefully.

'I have to go back to Palmerville meself this arvo,' he said. 'If you hang on a while I'll take you with me. Not much of a place, that joint, them as has things charge terrible prices. Never thought I'd see the day when nails was worth their weight in gold.' He sucked on his pipe. 'And what's more, never believed I'd pay up willingly. This old river, she's been kind to me, I can tell you. I'm a Londoner, you know, sold everything I had to get out here and dig for gold. Folks said I was mad, laughed like drains, they did, but they'll laugh on the other side of their faces when I go home. If I go home. Got a fancy for that Brisbane town, I have . . .'

Sitting in the leafy shade of his campsite, leaning against a tree stump, Diamond tried to listen to him but she kept nodding off, dozing.

'Wake up, girlie.' He was shaking her gently. 'You've had a good old sleep there.' He strapped his swag on to his back. 'Time to go. It's a fair march.'

Everyone knew the Hermit, and they pointed the way to his humpy.

'Had a mate with him,' one miner told her. 'Did a good job trying to nurse the poor bugger after the boongs did a job on him, but he was too crook to recover. His mate died but the Hermit, he says nothin', just keeps on minding him until the other blokes woke up. The smell, you know. They had to get in there and take the corpse by force, with the Hermit blathering and screaming at them like they was murderers.'

'He don't like no visitors,' another miner warned her, 'but he's harmless now.' He laughed. 'Since he ran out of ammo, that is. Just stays up there talking to himself and his bloody dog.'

It was the dog she saw first, Ben's cattle dog, Blue. He padded out as she approached, eyeing her, head cocked, ready to attack. She sat down and tried to reach out to him, but the dog backed away, teeth bared, with no sign of recognition. She edged closer, a few inches at a time. She could hear someone inside the brush hut. 'Ben!' she called. 'Ben Buchanan! Call the dog off. Come out here, Ben.'

He hobbled out waving a stick, exciting the dog who began to bark fiercely. Diamond stared at him in shock, unsure that this filthy, wretched human with matted hair and beard almost covering his face was Ben Buchanan.

'What do you want?' he yelled. 'Get away from here, you thieving bastards.' He seemed to think there were others with her.

'It's me, Ben,' she said quietly. 'Diamond. I won't hurt you.'

His eyes searched wildly around and he grinned meanly. 'No one can hurt me. None of you can hurt me. I'll make you jump if you come on my land.' Suddenly, illogically, he turned about and went inside the hut again, talking to someone, as if reporting this incident.

Diamond stood up and walked straight at the dog, pointing to the ground. 'Sit, Blue,' she commanded.

The dog baulked at obeying her command but allowed her to pass, staying close to her heels.

The hut was a rubbish dump of litter, overgrown by unchecked coarse grass, with only a camp stretcher against the one solid wall. Ben squatted by the stretcher conversing with an invisible presence on the cot, rambling incoherently, ignoring Diamond who stood in the entrance, appalled by the scene.

'I'm Diamond,' she told him again. 'I've been sent to work for you.'

He made no objection so she began to clean up, reasoning that if he first became accustomed to her presence, maybe in time he would allow her to attend to him. Everything about the place depressed her, but she'd found him and she would take him home – if he lived that long. He was very ill and horribly thin.

Weeks later Ben Buchanan reappeared. Diamond had bought drugs from a Chinese herbalist to tranquillise him so that she could restore some order into his life and he began to accept her as his servant, allowing her to clean and feed him and later to cut his hair and shave him. Her misery increased when she saw his face, hollow-cheeked and angular, his skin an unhealthy pallor. The drugs had only replaced the crazed look in his eyes with a dull listlessness so she began to reduce the amount of herbs in his tea.

Suddenly he snapped awake and glared at her, recognising her for the first time. 'What are you doing here?' he demanded.

'I'm looking after you, of course,' she said cheerfully. 'You Buchanans need a housekeeper.'

'Buchanans,' he echoed, as if dragging the name from the past, and then he leapt from the bunk and went scrambling underneath. 'You've come for my gold.' He searched frantically and started screaming. 'My gold. You've stolen my gold!' He grabbed his stick and swung at her but Diamond wrenched it from him and shoved him away. He was still very weak. 'Get back to bed,' she ordered in the curt tones of a mother addressing a child.

'My gold,' he wept. 'You've stolen my gold, you bitch.'

She hadn't seen any gold. 'Where did you hide it?'

'Under the bed here,' he sobbed.

If he had had any gold, it was long gone. Anyone could have taken it when he was out fetching water, or even the men who removed his friend's body. She wondered what could have happened to reduce Ben to this state. Illness first, she supposed, and then the fevers that white men couldn't contain in this heat. And the heat was unbearable; there was no breeze at all down in this valley. She had to get Ben out before he succumbed again, as soon as he was well enough to travel. She would be more than happy to get away from the place herself.

Ben worried and fretted all day but that night when she brought him a good meal of fish, he ate it ravenously. 'I'm feeling better now,' he told her. 'Tomorrow we'll start prospecting, you can help me. We'll find more gold. That's what we'll do.' He clutched her arm excitedly. 'I'm going to be rich. Darcy can run the station, he won't need me.'

Dismayed, Diamond realised his mind was still wandering, and she was more than ever determined to remove him from the Palmer as soon as possible. But his leg was a problem. She had cleaned the weeping ulcers each day but they had still eaten large holes in his flesh. In time they'd heal but the holes would remain. Right now, though, he couldn't walk far, he needed his stick to hobble around. The Chinese herbalist had been kind enough to come to the hut and examine the foot. He had given her powdered medication to sprinkle on the sores. 'Velly bad, missee,' he'd announced. 'You catchee just in time. He velly lucky, other men get leg chop-chop.'

'They have to have their legs cut off? Out here?' She was appalled, she hadn't realised the ulcers were so serious.

'Else die,' he said and smiled, bowing, accepting her payment.

She went to see Mr John Perry, the Assistant Gold Commissioner, a tall rangy young man who consented to speak with her in private. She explained about Ben.

'I'm from Charters Towers myself,' he said. 'I've heard of the Buchanans and I'm very sorry to hear about Ben. I had no idea he was the Hermit. But what can I do?'

'I need two horses,' she explained. 'Just to get me as far as the ranges.'

'Two horses! I couldn't get you one horse for love or money. No one would part with a horse.'

'They could have them back. I've got it all worked out. If you could let me borrow two horses, and give me an escort of a couple of troopers just to get us across the plains, then the troopers could bring the horses back.'

'I'm sorry, that's not possible. I'd get shot ordering an escort for just two people. You'll have to wait until the next party leaves with the gold escort.'

'Without horses? That's no good, Ben couldn't walk all that way.'

'He'll have to walk or stay here until he can.'

Diamond sat, knowing he was becoming impatient for her to leave, the interview was over. Then she tried again. 'Mr Perry. What if I can show you a route through to Cooktown, a pass in the mountains that is much further south. A pass that would eliminate the necessity to go north round the range.'

He laughed. 'And where is this pass?'

'On the southern boundary of Irukandji territory. It's much safer than that other route. The Irukandji people prefer to stay in the mountains so you could avoid a lot of trouble. The way your diggers are going now cuts right through their country and they are naturally very angry.'

He sat back on his rickety chair. 'I see,' he smiled. 'And how do you know all this?'

'Because I am Irukandji.'

He came up with a jolt. 'That's not possible!'

362

'You do know the mountain people are Irukandji?'

'Yes,' he said stiffly. 'We have managed to ascertain that from other blacks, and we also know they are cannibals.'

'What does that mean?'

'It means we do not care that they are angry. Vicious tribes like them deserve no mercy. They ought to be exterminated.'

'Really? Then what is your excuse for exterminating the gentler tribes in the south?' Her response annoyed him, the last thing she had meant to do, so she retreated. 'Please, Mr Perry, I can help.' She smiled at him, a warm seductive smile. 'I really am Irukandji, and as you see,' she stretched her neck feeling her breasts growing taut against her blouse, enjoying his discomfort, 'we're not so bad.'

He took out his handkerchief, pretending to wipe the sweat from his neck. 'How do I know you're one of them? How come you speak such good English?'

'Because I was brought up by white people in Brisbane. I was taken from here as a child.'

'I see,' he said again.

Diamond laughed to herself as she stood up. You certainly do, she thought. He couldn't take his eyes from her. If she had to let him make love to her she would, just as long as he agreed to her request. Fortunately, however, this one was too naive to take advantage of the situation.

'It's very good of you to listen to me,' she said softly. 'The Buchanans will be very grateful to you for any help you can give us. And, of course, if you can show the miners a quicker route, they'll probably give you a medal.'

'Where is this pass?'

She was about to tell him but decided against the disclosure; it was now her only bargaining point. 'I can show you,' she said.

Meebal was upset. 'You have brought white men. I heard them coming on their horses.'

'No, my brother. They have brought me safely across Merkin country. They wait down there at the camp for your permission to use the pass that will see them through to the coast, away from our people.'

'Why do they have to come here at all?'

'Meebal, we can't stop them. No one can stop them. It's better this way. I want you to come down and meet them, let them know the Irukandji are good people.'

John Perry was disgusted. 'A madman and a blind man,' he said to the troopers. 'I don't know how I came to let this woman talk me into such a mess. The Commissioner will have my head.'

The troopers grinned. Buchanan, they agreed, was as mad as a meat axe. He'd held them up a dozen times, leaping from his horse and stumbling around on his crook leg, looking for gold. And his gin minded him like a mother hen. 'We've got plenty of gold, Ben,' she'd tell him, over and over. 'It's in Cooktown, waiting for you.' The poor demented fool believed her, too, which showed how mad he was, but every so often he'd forget and she'd have to tell him the tale again, as patient as you like. She was a real looker too, a big girl with splendid tits and a figure as supple as an eel. They had no doubt young Perry'd had her in the cot, the way he looked at her, practically drooling, wanting more. That's what had got him out here acting on her directions.

And now the blind blackfeller! All lit up in feathers and paint to meet the visitors! Diamond explained this was her brother of the Irukandji tribe, which didn't mean a thing to the troopers, they hated this country, the arse-end of the world with a climate like hellfire. They'd volunteered for this duty because it was a chance to get back to Cooktown before the wet season cut the Palmer off altogether, and with luck this painted boong just might know a short-cut.

Surprised and intrigued by the quiet voices of these white men, whom he had expected to be screaming devils, Meebal lost his nervousness, tasted some of their food and was even persuaded to feel the sleek coats of the great beasts called horses. He had never encountered animals of that size before, although in recent times he had heard their thundering hooves. Now he was charmed by the gentle nuzzling of their velvety lips and their puffing, snorting language.

Diamond taught him a few words of English so that he might protect himself in the future from attack, wishing she had done this before, but it was difficult to make him pay attention. Meebal had fallen in love with horses, all he wanted to do was talk about the horses, sit by them, listen to them, hear about them. Diamond laughed, remembering the visitors to Government House in Brisbane who would come out into the grounds to view koalas in the trees, and who begged to be shown kangaroos.

'White men,' Meebal told her, 'are no different from us, after all. But these animals that carry human beings across the land as fast as the wind are the greatest magic. I will weep to have to say farewell to them.'

To Perry's astonishment, the blind man led them surely through a pass and on into the ranges.

'This isn't the way we came,' Diamond said to him.

'No,' he replied. 'This way is easier on the magnificent beasts. I have shown your men a pass, that is enough.'

John Perry and his troopers cheered and clapped Meebal on the back when they emerged from the bush to see the marvellous sapphire-blue Whitsunday seas stretched out before them, one of the most magnificent views in the world. They showered him with presents, the remains of their supplies, coins, neckerchiefs, matches, buttons, for the trail to the

Palmer had now been cut by at least four or five days. But Meebal asked only one gift of them: that he be allowed to sit on a horse for the last few miles before he left them.

Perry himself obliged, delighted with the discovery of the pass, which would surely earn him a promotion. He led the horse, with the ecstatic blind man in the saddle, on their last descent.

'This has been the greatest day of my life,' Meebal called to Diamond, who was riding behind him, leading Ben's horse. 'I will give Luka the other presents. She will be pleased. And she said to tell you if you ever want any more of the yellow stones she will get them for you.'

Forgetting the others could not understand him, Diamond looked about her sharply, then she relaxed. 'Thank my dear mother. One day I might need them. But you must never never tell anyone about them. I dare not even mention the word in this company. Those stones would bring tribes of white men right into your land. They must remain hidden for ever.'

'You are a good woman, my sister,' he said as they parted for the last time, 'greatly blessed by the spirits. Be kind to those white people. No more paybacks.'

With a rush like a vision of banked clouds being pushed by high winds, she saw the face of the housekeeper at Government House and of Cornelia Buchanan, and the cliff of danger that Billy Kemp had approached. She saw the men she had knifed in a Brisbane alleyway, and the many others who had upset her in minor ways and on whom she had taken revenge with secret delight.

'No more paybacks, Kagari,' he repeated. 'You understand?'

'Yes,' she said humbly. 'I will try.'

Consoled by the cool sea breezes and attended by a doctor who recommended rest and quiet for his patient, Ben's distress eased, but he was still timid and nervous of strangers. Diamond took him swimming and he sat on the beach while she collected coconuts washed up on the shores from distant lands, insisting that it was his job to chop them open. The challenge of breaking into them without spilling the milk amused him and for the first time she heard him laugh. They shared the coconut pieces like children with a cache of toffees, squatting in the shade of pandanus trees.

Gradually he began to take an interest in Cooktown and the hordes of excited miners who surged ashore with every new day.

'I wish I could go back with them,' he said. 'It's terrible to be stuck here knowing they're still picking up fortunes at the Palmer.'

'You can't go out there again,' Diamond told him, 'you're not well enough.'

'I know. But to think I had the gold and lost it. I let some bastard steal it from right under my nose.'

'You're not the only one, it happened to so many of the diggers. You mustn't think about it, you're safe now and your health is improving.'

'So it is,' he grinned, reaching for her and pulling her down on to the bed with him. 'Make love to me, Diamond. I swear it's the perfect cure for ailing gentlemen.'

Their time together in the one-roomed cabin on the beach was heaven for Diamond. Freed from the furtiveness of their previous relationship, they now had all the time in the world to make love, to lie together, dozing through the lazy tropical afternoons and enjoying the soft starry nights. Even though he was still subject to moody spells of depression, she was patient with him, remaining cheerful, convinced that this carefree existence would restore him mentally as well as physically. He had lost months of his life; he could recall only fragments of the journey back to Cooktown and very little of his hermit stage.

But as Ben's confidence returned, he became edgy with her. And critical. She knew that his worries about Caravale were a factor once again, so she did not blame him. They couldn't stay in Cooktown for ever, soon they'd have to leave and head south.

He talked to her of Caravale. 'Whether Mother likes it or not,' he said, 'I'll have to raise a loan at the bank and buy back Perfy's share.' It was the first time he had mentioned Perfy, and Diamond was relieved that he could speak of her so casually.

'What if she has already sold it?' she asked.

'She wouldn't dare sell it to anyone else,' he growled. 'And if you hadn't gone boasting to her and Mother about us, I wouldn't be in this mess.'

Diamond ignored that remark. After all, he wasn't really in any mess. She hadn't mentioned her gold. She didn't dare. He would want to know where she found it, and besides causing trouble for her people, she couldn't allow him to become infected with gold fever again. Nothing would stop him going after it, and the Irukandji warriors would kill him. She smiled to herself. When they were well away, when they were back in Bowen, she would give him the gold. He was her love, her man, and she daydreamed of the joy she could bring him. In her mind's eye she saw his surprise and delight. He would not be returning a failure, beaten by the Palmer, they would ride out to Caravale triumphant. It didn't matter if Perfy had been angry enough to sell; they could now afford to buy back her share whatever it cost. Luka, her dear mother, had promised to bring her the yellow stones if she ever needed more. She could arrange to meet her at the falls; it wouldn't even be necessary to go right into Irukandji land again and face the ire of Tajatella.

It was a beautiful dream that began to crumble the very next day.

'Who owns this place anyway?' Ben asked.

'The doctor. He built it when he first arrived but the town grew so quickly he needed a bigger house.'

'Everyone's making money up here except me,' Ben sulked. 'I'm bloody broke.'

'No, you're not,' Diamond said carefully.

'Easy for you to say. The Buchanan name will get me home. The local bank feller was impressed enough to offer me credit for my passage home by ship but apart from that I'm stony broke.'

'You've talked to the bank?' Diamond asked nervously. He had said 'his' passage home. What about her?

'Oh sure. The doctor introduced me. Do you know what I hate most? Those upstarts feel sorry for me, limping around town like a bloody cripple. And they talk to me as if I'm some loony. Poor Ben Buchanan, we'd better send the sorry chap home.'

'No, they don't, Ben. The doctor cares about you, he's been very kind.'

'You don't say.' His voice was heavy with sarcasm. 'They know I'm broke.'

'Only temporarily,' she said, trying to calm him, almost tempted now to tell him about the gold.

'Of course only temporarily. They know where their bread's buttered. The Buchanan name still holds good even in this Godforsaken dump. But they know who's paying the bills, don't they?'

'What bills?' she echoed, her heart sinking.

'Oh, come on, Diamond. I'm not that stupid. We can't live on air. Who has been buying our supplies? Who bought my clothes? Who paid the bloody doctor? I'll bet his services aren't free. And don't tell me your mate Bourke gave you our provisions out of the kindness of his heart. So who's paying?'

'Ben, don't be unkind. I paid but I was glad to.'

'Of course you did. But where did you get the money? A black gin with cash?'

Diamond tried to smile. 'Ben, what does it matter? The main thing is that you're well again.'

'Oh sure. But you haven't said where you got the money.' He grabbed her arm and twisted her to him. 'Where did you get it?'

'I earned it,' she whispered.

'That's right. You thought I didn't know. You earned it as a whore. In Charters Towers. And you seem pretty matey with that harlot Glory Molloy. Did you work for her too?'

'No,' she said. 'I promise you, Ben, I didn't.'

'Why not? A few more customers, what's the difference?'

She turned to him gently and put her arms round him. 'Don't do this, Ben. What does it matter?' She kissed him and began removing his shirt. 'I hated that time, but it's all behind us now. Don't make a mountain of it. You mustn't distress yourself.' As she began to make love to him and

367

he moodily acquiesced, she realised with a rising sense of horror that she was seducing this man as she had recalcitrant and uneasy customers at the brothel. She let her clothes fall to the floor in slow, sensuous movements, parading her long sleek body for him until he relented, but his love-making was cold and rough. He took her as he would a stranger. A whore. 'I love you, my darling,' she whispered, trying to retrieve the tenderness, but it had gone. When he rolled away from her she wept.

'So,' he said. 'It's time I was on my way. I'm sorry I was rude to you last night, Diamond. It was the booze, I suppose, because I am grateful to you for pulling me out of that hell-hole. Christ knows how you did it. For the life of me I can't remember much about it.'

He was in good spirits now. He'd made quite a night of it, plundering her body, she'd felt, while she had searched vainly for the key to his heart, giving and giving in the voluptuous heat, her warm lips roving over him, accepting his punishing drive because she wanted him to need her for ever.

He slapped her bottom. 'Jesus, I'm going to miss you,' he laughed. 'There no one in the world a patch on you in bed.'

She trod carefully. 'You don't have to miss me. Ben, we are perfect together, you know that. I belong with you.'

Ben seemed not to hear her. 'I have to go down to the harbour and get a berth on one of those ships. At least I won't have any trouble getting out of here, they're all going back empty.'

Diamond took a deep breath. It was now or never. 'I don't want to stay here, I want to come with you.'

'Oh Christ, Diamond, don't start that again. We've had a good time. Now it's over. Why can't you understand my position?'

She sat silent, hearing the swish of the sea, wishing she had the courage to walk out there and drown herself but she had another responsibility now. The cycle of earth had told her that a new life was in bud within her, a grandchild for Luka. Wildly, almost hysterically, she reminded herself that Luka must be told, Luka who had felt such pity for her that she was childless so many years after puberty.

'Listen to me,' Ben said. 'Why don't you see things as they are? I couldn't take home a white whore, let alone a black one. Jesus, at least white whores understand this, they'd never make a fuss. You ask Glory Molloy. If I can't get through to you, maybe she can.'

'What should I do then?' she asked him, out of curiosity, out of an hypnotic need to see this man as he really was, once and for all. She knew his reply would wound but she needed the pain now to cauterise, to burn him from her system.

'Why don't you stay here in Cooktown? You'd be better off up here.'

He grinned. 'Honey, with your looks, you'd never starve, and diggers are coming in here rolling in gold.'

'You want me to be a whore again?'

'Oh, quit putting on such a face. What you do is your business. I'm not your keeper.'

'No, you're not,' she spat at him. 'You're just a plain bastard.'

'Temper! Temper!' he laughed. 'You can't even pin that on me.'

'Yes, I can! That grave at your precious Caravale, that unmarked grave. Ask your mother who is buried there.'

'That's old history, it's the bloke who attacked Cornelia.'

'His name was Clem Bunn and he was her husband.'

'Bullshit! Who told you that?'

'She did! So how could she be married to your father? I've been wondering about that ever since.'

He lashed out at her. 'You lying bloody bitch!' but she whirled away from him. When she turned back, her knife was in her hand, a new sharp Bowie knife she'd bought to protect herself, once again, in the crowded streets of Cooktown. As he backed away from her she was in such a rage she wanted to drive the knife into him, but she remembered Meebal's words. 'No more payback.' And she knew that to strike him, even to wound him, would ruin her, would force her out of the white world for ever, with her child.

'Get out of here!' she hissed.

Braver now, he picked up his hat and made for the door. 'Don't you ever threaten me again or I'll knock your block off. It's time you learned your place. I'm going into town to make my arrangements and when I get back, have my dinner ready. Do you hear me?'

She put the knife down. 'Yes.'

'That's better.' He took out a cigar and lit it, prolonging his regained mastery of the woman. 'The trouble with you, Diamond, is that you're just another nigger and you won't face up to it. I meant what I said about Cooktown. You might as well stay here. This is no place for white folks anyway, and you've got nowhere else to go.'

As soon as he left, she packed her few clothes and set off, trudging through the hot sand along the beach to keep clear of him. Strangely, the hurt wasn't so bad this time, the pain wasn't like that first excruciating rejection. Maybe she had known it would happen. But now she had things to do. She would leave her carpetbag with Marie Bourke and slip away into the bush to collect that other one, the strong dilly bag her mother had made for her. No one would look twice at a black woman with a lumpy, plaited bag slung on her shoulders, no one would be interested in the contents. She would buy herself a berth on a decent ship, on one of those big liners now anchored off Cooktown, bringing thousands of gold-seekers. She would be safe on a ship like that, a ship that would take her to Brisbane, because at last she had realised where home was. Home was Brisbane where she had grown up, the place she knew so well. Jannali's brother had been right. He'd tapped his head and told her that she did know where her home was, and she'd known all along. It had just taken a long journey to find her way.

She paddled in the softly shifting shallows, remembering that many years ago, as a little girl, she had fished these shores . . .

7

Bowen! The town was such a green and shining sight, Lew felt no impatience at the slow progress of the ship into the harbour. It was raining, warm misty rain, washing away the dust and polishing foliage like a new-broom housekeeper. What wouldn't they have given for this heavenly downpour over the last few months on that awful trek over parched land from the Palmer down to Charters Towers and east to Townsville? The last section had been the worst, crossing the hard, red-dust country to the coast and finding Townsville tinder-dry, also short of water. A strange quirk of nature, he mused, that these two tropical coastal towns were so different. Townsville praying for rain while Bowen, with its natural springs of fresh water, soaked luxuriously in the first falls of the wet season.

Chin Ying, with an umbrella, joined him on the deck. 'I presume you will dash forth now to see your Miss Middleton?'

'No. I'll get it right this time. Perfy was always impressed by Herbert because he shined up so well in his natty clothes. I'm going into town first to have a decent haircut and get me some fine outfits and the best boots money can buy.'

Ying smiled. 'Is this the seafarer who scoffed at my fondness for gentlemanly attire?'

'Necessity, old chap. I intend to surprise her.'

'And have you given further consideration to my proposition?'

'Yes. I am honoured that you are inviting me to join a company with such marvellous potential and bowled over that you have so much faith in me that you would appoint me your managing director. I really am, Ying. Whatever decision I arrive at, I am still willing to invest with you.'

'Forgive me, but that would not be acceptable. If you do not wish to be appointed executive director, then it would be better for you to go your own way. You can afford to do so. I require a private company with only two directors. I do not need the complication of other investors. Should you decline, I will institute a search for another Chinese-speaking Englishman of good repute to head this company. And one who also understands shipping,' he added. 'In fact, I shall have to seek another with exactly your qualifications.'

Lew shook his head ruefully. 'It's a tremendous opportunity for me, and to tell you the truth, I'm surprised to find I miss China. I miss all the rush and babble, and the complexities of the place.' He laughed. 'I'll even miss you and your devious logic! But I'm going to ask Perfy to marry me. If she accepts, then my answer will depend on her reaction. This time we can't be pulling in opposite directions, our future plans will be the result of mutual agreement. Miss Middleton may not wish to live in Hong Kong.'

Ying shook the water from his umbrella. 'It is difficult for me to believe that my plans hinge on the whims of a woman. The world is full of beautiful women.'

'So it is,' Lew said, 'but I want this one.'

'You still don't understand what I am offering you. Lew Cavour will be Taipan.'

'Taipan!' Lew breathed. The word rocketed in his brain. Taipan! Of course! The head of a foreign investment company in China was Taipan, a great and honoured merchant. Could he possibly refuse? 'I will still have to talk to Perfy,' he said resolutely.

'Well, for heaven's sake! It's Mr Chin,' Alice Middleton cried. 'Please. Come in. Give me your umbrella. Perfy! Come and see who's here! How nice to see you again. What a lovely surprise.'

The ladies ushered him into their sitting room and brought him tea, very strong tea with an unpleasant flavour but he made no comment.

He chatted amiably with them, telling them of the expedition to the Palmer, glossing over the sordid side but giving a glowing account of Lew Cavour's role, pleased to note the enthusiastic reception of that news by the pretty daughter.

'I believe it is an awful place,' she said. 'It must have been very hard on all of you.'

'The heat was the worst,' he replied, 'very trying. At times it was above one hundred and twelve degrees.'

'Lord-amighty!' Alice exclaimed. 'I never heard of such a thing! You were lucky to have survived! And if it is not a rude question, Mr Chin, did you find the gold?'

He was pleased at her forthrightness which enabled him to introduce the subject of their great success without appearing to boast, and they were delighted. He did not add that his coolies, working non-stop, had made him the richest prospector on the Palmer.

He then spoke to them quietly of his intention to return to China and of related matters, not forgetting to mention the glory of the Hong Kong harbour as seen from the mansions on the Peak. 'One of the most magnificent views in the world,' he murmured.

Miss Middleton had matured, she was no longer the jumpy, flighty girl who talked far too much. Her features had firmed, giving those wide blue eyes more depth, and her fair hair was smoothed up into a thick chignon.

Adversity had rewarded her with serenity and Ying approved. Both ladies were gracious enough not to interrupt as he outlined steadily and, he believed, with proper respect for their intelligence the reason for his visit.

When he had completed his discussion with them, Perfy rushed away to dress appropriately to receive the gentleman who she now knew was coming to ask for her hand in marriage.

'And what about you, Mrs Middleton?' he asked. 'Do you think you will like Hong Kong?'

'Not me, Mr Chin. I'll be staying put. This is my home. We had some bad times with the local people for a while but they were frightened. I understood. It's all over now, and I am settled here.'

Chin Ying was astonished. 'But this is not right! You are the matriarch of the family. Mr Cavour has no family at all.'

'They'll soon rectify that,' she smiled. 'I've come to roost here and I'm happy. I can always visit. You'll have to get a move on, though. Since you, too, are starting a new life, I'll be looking forward to hearing all about you – when you are married and when your children arrive. Chinese people are very fond of their families but I've never heard you speak of yours. I think you too have suffered upheavals, like the rest of us.'

Ying felt the sting of tears; the woman was very perceptive. 'It hurts for me to have to turn my back on my ancestors,' he admitted. 'I wrestled with that problem many a long night, but a man must survive. My parent bequeathed me enemies who will not forget. Chin Ying must disappear.'

Alice Middleton sat quietly. She did not commiserate or patronise, she was English-bred, and yet, despite the humiliations she had endured, she displayed the same dignity as the wise old high-ranking Chinese matrons. 'Would you like to see my greenhouse?' she asked. 'It's in the back yard. I've got the most beautiful orchids, there are so many varieties up here. I think you'd appreciate them.'

'I would indeed,' he replied, standing and bowing to her.

Perfy was seated on the cane chair on the verandah with her best Sunday dress arranged prettily around her. It was of the finest white lawn, heavily flounced round the hem, with a band of green velvet at the waist. The bodice was low-cut and neatly pleated to her slim waist but modestly offset by a crisp, handkerchief-pointed cowl of broderie anglaise. She had dropped the chignon at the back of her head to a cluster of tonged curls held in place by slim green velvet ribbons. Attached to her bodice was her only item of jewellery, the jade brooch the Chinaman had given her for good luck.

She tried not to laugh as Lew, in his fine new clothes, came sprinting down the street in the teeming rain, clutching his panama hat which obviously was more important to him now than his black tousled hair which was usually topped by a battered old seaman's cap.

'Oh Jesus!' he said as he stamped up the steps to the shelter of her verandah. 'Bloody new clothes and look at me! Drenched! I'll bet they shrink.'

What an opening, she thought. How romantic! He looked marvellous, sun-tanned as ever, and as masculine as ever. How could she have turned her back on Lew Cavour? She rose to greet him.

'Oh Perfy!' he said, as he flung his arms round her, dampening her dress, not even noticing her carefully planned scene. 'God, I've missed you! And you listen to me, if you've got any more beaux or prospects on the horizons, you get rid of them, do you hear me?' He kissed her, and kissed her again. 'You've no idea how much I've missed you. God, I love you. I've always loved you, you know that . . .'

His intensity allowed her no time for the little speeches she had rehearsed. They were out there on the verandah, in love, with the rain pouring down and his coat shrinking.

'Do you love me, Perfy?' he asked her urgently.

'Of course I do, you silly man,' she said. 'Otherwise why would I be out here making a spectacle of myself for all the neighbours to see?'

'Then I have to talk to you. Seriously. You haven't got company, have you? I mean Herbert's not glued to a chair in there, is he?'

'Herbert?' Perfy burst out laughing. 'Oh Lew! Haven't you heard about Herbert?'

'No, and I'm not interested right now.' He took her arm and walked her inside into the wide hallway. 'I have to talk to you about something. You see, Chin Ying has come up with this idea—'

'You mean Mr Wong Sun Lee?'

He stood back, amazed. 'Who? How did you know that name?'

She laughed. 'He's here. He's out the back discussing the beauty of rare orchids with my mother. Let's join them, darling, I just know I'm going to adore Hong Kong.'

8

The plump German woman hurried aboard the smart new clipper ship *Bremen*, bustling with importance, hastening the porter with over-the-shoulder instructions as she waded through the crowds. All around her, passionate farewells were being enacted as the stay-at-homes lingered to the last minute before departing, turning back like mourners at a graveside for one more heartrending glance. Then as the shouts of the crew heralded sailing time, the hundreds of German emigrants bound for the New World exploded into a battery of excitement, pounding to the rails to wave jauntily to the tearful gazers on the pier.

There was no one to wave farewell to Augusta so she followed the steward to her first-class cabin, gaining his full attention before the rush. He looked at her curiously as she checked her luggage. 'The cabin is satisfactory, madam?'

'Beautiful. Such luxury!'

'There are only four cabins of this standard on the ship,' he replied proudly. 'This will be a long voyage, the comfort will make it easier for you.'

'At my age?' she smiled. 'Don't fret about me, young man. My dear late husband was a great sea captain, much revered in Australia.'

'Ah, so you are making a voyage of discovery, to visit the land he knew?'

'Not at all. I am returning. I have sailed these seas before.'

He was impressed. 'If you need me, just call. I would be pleased to hear advice on this new country because, to tell the truth, I too am interested in emigrating.'

'Then we'll have lots to talk about in the months ahead. I used to get seasick once but I managed to overcome it. I'll rest now. Will you wake me for supper?'

'Certainly, madam.'

When he left, Augusta dropped her cheerful countenance. She sat on the bunk and scowled. Even though the ship was sailing from Hamburg, that spiteful po-faced daughter-in-law of hers had not come down to see her off. Nor had she allowed anyone to bring the two children, which depressed Augusta. Her grandchildren would have enjoyed the opportunity to explore the grandest ship of the German line. But no. Helga, who had for years begrudged her every crust and had relegated her to the back room like so many other widows lacking males or means to protect them, had been very pleased to see the back of her.

'Well then,' Augusta said to the empty cabin. 'That's that.' For what else was there to say?

She grappled with her large handbag, scuffling among handkerchiefs and pills and purses and papers until she retrieved the letter, and opened it, sighing again, as she did every time she read it, her chins trembling with emotion.

The letter was so worn, the folds were small woolly holes, but it didn't matter, she knew it by heart. Reading it again and again gave her such satisfaction, such joy! The letter had come to her rescue just when she was beginning to wonder if life were worth living. Just when she thought it might be easier to walk into the sea until her hat floated. They had taken her money and treated her as less than a chimney sweep, a nuisance foisted on them, and that had been bad enough. But Augusta had never envisaged that her situation could have worsened, that there would only be Helga to contend with, plus her threats to evict the old woman.

She studied the letter solemnly:

House Number 4
Kangaroo Point
Town of Brisbane

Dear Missus

I write to you with sadness to have your last letter telling of the passing of your son from this world, a great sorrow for you. I also feel your unhappiness at being left in the hands of the woman Helga who has no regard for you, and ask you not to despair. Your kindness to me makes for the great love and respect I bear you and will always do so.

Fortune has smiled on me, which is difficult to explain now, taking a lot of time. Your girl is well-off, as they say here. Rich is better, very rich, but that is just between you and me. The gentlemen at the bank tell me that the paper enclosed is a Letter of Credit which entitles you to One Thousand Pounds for your own use.

I am hoping that you will use some of that money to buy purchase of a passenger fare to Brisbane to come home because I have bought the house as seen in this address and would love for you to come to live here with me. The house is very nice with lots of rooms and it looks over the river. You will like it. And you will like my baby son Ben who is a handsome little boy, takes after his father. I need you to help me bring up my son, who like your girl, has a foot in both worlds. Remember the Captain always said you were a good teacher? He was right. Ben would be fortunate to have you as his grandmother. If you would rather stay in Germany then I will see you have your own place and never need again, but I pray you will come to us and we will be a true family again.

I remain,

sincerely,

DIAMOND

POSTWORD

In the battle for the Palmer gold, it is known that at least five hundred prospectors died, Chinese and European, and ten times that number of Aborigines.

Within three years, *thirty* tons of gold passed through Customs at Cooktown from the Palmer River, and more gold was subsequently found in adjacent areas, but no estimate can be made of the huge quantities of gold smuggled out of the region.

The census of 1877 revealed that there were 17,000 Chinese on the Palmer goldfields, which equalled the entire white population of North Queensland at the time.

Cooktown boomed. It was the third seaport in the colony of Queensland with an incredible number of hotels and banks. Wealthy residents built fine homes in the British colonial style and employed Chinese servants, but the town declined after the gold rush. Fire, flood and destructive cyclones took a further toll over the years and when the remaining civilian population was evacuated during the Second World War, Cooktown was in danger of becoming a ghost town.

But now the old town is reviving as a superb tourist attraction at the mouth of the Endeavour River, with unspoiled sandy beaches, lush forests and spectacular falls. It abounds with wildlife, including the inevitable crocodiles, and offshore is the Great Barrier Reef.

Aborigine tribes were mostly decimated or dwindled to hundreds but now their descendants are regaining their appropriate status in the community and are proud to provide visitors with unique information on their ancient traditions.

John Jardine's outpost of Somerset, further north on Cape York, did not survive.